Eight Reasons

by

Stephen B King

Eight Reasons

Cover Art by *Lisa Dawn MacDonald*

The Wild Rose Press, Inc.
PO Box 708
Adams Basin, NY 14410-0708
Visit us at www.thewildrosepress.com

Publishing History
First Edition, 2025
Trade Paperback Print ISBN 978-1-5092-6384-4
Digital ISBN 978-1-5092-6385-1

Published in the United States of America

Dedication

This collection of stories is dedicated to three women in my life. My wife, Jacqui, without whom I would never have been published. Alicia Dean, who asked me to write short stories as a part of her Friday the 13th collaboration. And finally, my very dear friend, mentor, and editor, Melanie Billings. Thank you all, from the bottom of my heart.

Why Eight Reasons?

As I grow older and realize just how precious life is, I try to eat healthily. You know the deal, right? Drink less alcohol, watch the carbs, and lose some weight. And I do—especially with a wife who wants me to outlive her. So now that I'm taking much better care of myself than I did in my younger days, I've noticed that my cravings for fast food have increased significantly. Now I can't have it, I want it more. Sound familiar? My mouth waters just thinking about a greasy hamburger and fries.

Writing is somewhat similar. I've always needed at least 100,000 words to tell the story I want. However, occasionally, I feel the urge to write a short story that gets to the point more quickly. Who was it that said, "Less is more?" The fewer words used, the more impact they carry, theoretically. So sometimes, I feel compelled to write something between 10,000 and 15,000 words— just for fun, my fun.

The issue with short stories is that once they are written, what should an author do with them? I understand that my publisher requires a specific word count to make the effort worthwhile—I get it. The number of magazines accepting short stories has declined over the years, so my tales mostly just linger, waiting for an audience.

My stories, much like my children, mean a great deal to me. Sure, I write for my enjoyment, but what's the point of spending countless hours creating something if no one gets to read it? Over the years, I have found much joy in reading numerous short stories, particularly those penned by my more famous namesake, who, let's be honest, is such an incredible talent that he can make a shopping list sound exciting.

Out of the blue a while ago, my good friend and fellow author Alicia Dean proposed that thirteen writers release thirteen stories of around 13,000 words every Friday the 13th. What a fantastic idea, I thought, and I was deeply moved to be asked to be one of them. Now I had a vehicle for those short stories that wanted to be written, and off I went.

Six of the following stories were offerings for the wonderful Friday the 13th series, and two were not. I will give a short background before each story, explaining why and how each came to be, as I am often asked about my stories' genesis.

Many moons ago, when I created my website (Stephen-b-king.com), I wrote a brief introduction. In it, I shared how much I loved discovering a book that captivated me so fully that I had to stay up late for just one more chapter, even though I needed to get up early for work the next day. I hoped, and still do, that I could craft stories that would evoke the same feelings in my readers. So, here are eight reasons to stay up beyond bedtime. Be warned; some are scary. I advise you to ensure the doors and windows are locked and do not, under any circumstances, read these tales alone by candlelight.

So I hope you, dear ever-patient reader, enjoy my version of fast food as a brief respite from all that healthy reading. As for me, this anthology now has over 100,000 words, so I'm happy, too.

Stephen B King
Perth, Western Australia

Table of Contents:

Glimpse, The Dinner Guest

"We can easily forgive a child who is afraid of the dark.

The real tragedy of life is when men are afraid of the light."

-Plato

Foreword

Some time back, I had an idea to write a trilogy about four people, two married couples, and the impact on their lives when two are thrust together to investigate three serial killers. The two central protagonists are a male detective matched to a female criminal psychologist, and their mutual attraction to each other is, well, electric.

The three books were titled Glimpse, Memoir of a Serial Killer, Glimpse, The Beautiful Deaths, and Glimpse, The Tender Killer.

When the wonderful Geoffrey Boyes, the narrator of the audio versions, completed book three, he pestered me for another installment. Whoever heard of a trilogy of four books, I asked him? He wore me down, and eventually, I wrote Glimpse, The Angel Shot. If you read it, it is dedicated to my dear friend Geoffrey.

Around this time, Alicia Dean invited me to join her band of authors in the amazing Friday the 13th series, and I gladly accepted. While I jumped at the chance, I didn't know what to write that fit her parameters. The Glimpse series dominated my thoughts due to the editing rounds for the book and audio version.

Of all the characters I have created, my absolute favorite is the beautiful, rich criminal psychologist Patricia Holmes. I loved writing for her more than her partner, Rick. In the Deadly Glimpses series, I wanted to write a story in which she and she alone was the show's star.

Mulling this over in my mind one day while driving (I'm often at my most creative then), I had this blinding idea. What if Patricia was invited to a reunion murder mystery dinner with her ex-colleagues from the hospital for the criminally insane? And further, what if there was an uninvited guest who actually was a murderer seeking revenge on the doctors who gave him electrotherapy? What a hoot, I thought, all the while imagining the kind of horror movie stories I loved back before I had a wife who hated that type of entertainment.

And so, dear reader, book 5 of the Deadly Glimpses Trilogy was born. I hope you like it.

Prologue

They will not lock me up again.

I'll die before I let them take me back to that hellhole. Three years, three long years, they stole from me, but now I'm free, and I will kill the bitch who stole my freedom. I don't care what it takes or if I die trying. Being locked up in Graylands was worse than death, and I have nothing left to fear.

The bitch doctor told my bitch wife I was a delusional schizophrenic. Bullshit. They said I was depressed, and then they said I was bipolar. My wife called it a nervous breakdown that followed my so-called accident, rubbish. There was nothing wrong with me; I was okay; I just...heard...voices, scary voices, true. But I would have got better if they just left me alone.

My wife Arlene had me committed. I think she wanted to screw my brother, Henley, and steal my money, so she had them send me to Graylands. "Honey." She always called me that, even though it made me sound like someone else. "Honey, it's just for fourteen days, so they can do some tests and make you well again." I couldn't stop them, and they dragged me out of my home after they injected me with something because I wanted to fight them, kill them if I had to. That's how fourteen days became three years.

I woke up in hell, handcuffed to a bed. The more I tried to convince them I was sane, the more they said I

3

was crazy. Then Doctor Ruth, the Bitch, promised Arlene she could cure me. "Just sign an extension," she told her, "give me some more time with Mervyn. I want to try electroconvulsive therapy."

They strapped me down and put something in my mouth. "Bite down," she told me. Then...seething, white-hot agony erupted inside my head. I broke my teeth, and the pain went on and on...and on, like maggots chewing my brain.

That's when the voices started whispering, "Kill the bitch, kill the bitch, kill the bitch."

Chapter 1

The Invitation

Recently promoted Detective Sergeant Patricia Holmes peered through the windshield as her Mercedes hurtled along the highway heading north in the early evening. The rain was squally, driven by a howling wind, and Pat was conscious of the possibility of a kangaroo darting out in front of the car. *That's the last thing I need,* she worried, rapidly followed by, *"What the hell am I even doing here in weather like this?"* But Pat knew what she was doing and why; it had been boredom.

Her police work had been humdrum for a while, with no compelling murder cases in which she could utilize her unique psychological profiling abilities. Her love life? What love life would be a better way of describing the lack of anything substantial for the previous few weeks? Lawrence, her ex, a Mauritian restaurateur, hadn't worked out. Derrin, who followed shortly after, displayed definite possibilities, and he *was* damned sexy. He could hold a decent conversation, liked jazz, and the nights they had spent in bed were…well, incredibly satisfying. There only one thing that spoiled it. Derrin worked on an oil rig for long periods and wasn't due back in Perth for another week. They talked on the phone now and again, sometimes erotically, but Pat yearned for physical and intellectual contact while he was away.

She had been ready to climb the walls when the mailman brought some respite in the guise of *The Invitation.* It was from one of her friends from Graylands Psychiatric Hospital, Helen Markovic, whom she hadn't seen for ages. Back then, Pat lectured in clinical psychology at the University of Western Australia and also utilized her psychiatric doctorate by consulting the worst patients of the state hospital for the criminally insane. Then, the call came to join the police force as an investigator to help find a serial killer, which had long been her dream. She had been with the police ever since.

Tumultuous events occurred, and Pat had lost touch with most of her friends from those more carefree days. The invitation, outlining the details for the dress-up murder mystery reunion dinner party, sounded like fun, and before she could talk herself out of it, she accepted and sent an RSVP.

The theme for the night was *Friday the 13th. Dress scary* was the instruction. Her character's name was *Doreen Samuels.* Pat never saw herself as a *Doreen,* but she read the three typed pages containing details of her alter ego, likes, dislikes, and history. Pat was pleased to learn she was not destined to be the victim for the night's entertainment, but whether she was to be the murderer, she would not find out until she checked into her room and read the envelope which would be waiting for her. She smiled to think of the ironic role reversal in the game, a detective cast as a killer; she relished the opportunity and thought she could bring some realism to the part.

The venue was a one-hundred-year-old restored nunnery called The Priory, now a luxury thirty-roomed hotel and function center, an hour and a half outside

Perth in the historical town of Hamlyn Pools. The owners specialized in catered dinner parties, murder mystery nights, treasure hunts, and fundraising car rallies. Pat looked up the venue on the internet and loved what she saw. A sprawling, ivy-clad building full of atmosphere with a sweeping gravel driveway, swimming pool, Jacuzzi, and sauna, Pat envisioned herself being massaged and pampered when she wasn't at dinner or drinking red wine, reliving old times.

The pictures of the rooms looked beautiful and romantic. *Shame I don't have a current man to take as my plus one,* she thought ruefully. *Oh well, there might be a single one for me there.* She cast her mind back to when she worked with psychotic patients, so evil and damaged they would never be released, and smiled. She treated them, yet now she captured them. Were any male doctors at Graylands partnerless, or who had been married back then, like her, and were single now? *Knowing my luck, no, there won't be. Oh well, I could always return when Derrin comes back and have a dirty weekend then.*

Pat's car approached a slow-moving truck laden with cattle, and at the same time, the rain grew to deluge proportions. The wash kicked up from the tires, making it impossible to pass, and Pat's visibility was almost zero. *Damn, I'm going to be late.*

Chapter 2

The Priory

Pat's phone chirped when she drove into the Priory driveway. She pressed the Bluetooth button on the steering wheel. "Patricia Holmes."

"Hey, Pat, it's Rick. Sorry to bother you. I know you're having a dirty weekend away."

She grinned. Their relationship was, and always had been, complicated. They flirted, but because of their past, they would never do anything more than that. They had once become too close, with catastrophic results. "Hey, boss." He hated it when she called him that, which made her do it all the more. "How's Juliet coping with her final trimester?"

"Handling it like a trooper," he replied, and Pat could tell he hadn't phoned for a friendly chat. Like both of their bosses, Rick went straight to the point when he was focused. "Do you remember Mervyn Biscain?"

Pat parked the car in a vacant slot in the car park as close to the building as possible and drummed her fingers on the steering wheel. "Nope, should I?"

"He *was* a patient at Graylands. I thought your paths might have crossed."

"You emphasized the word *was*. I don't remember him. Again, should I?"

She imagined his trademark shrug as he replied, "Probably not. We need to talk to his doctor, and I'm guessing there is a fair chance she will be there with you at the Graylands psychologist's reunion. Mervyn's mother died, and he had a day release to go to the funeral. He got away from his minder, murdered his wife, and has disappeared."

"Ouch. Who was Biscain's doctor?"

"Ruth Hawthorne."

"Oh, yeah, I know Ruth. I'm not sure if she is on the guest list, but if she's here, do you want me to talk to her?"

"Would you? That would save me from sending someone because we've checked, and she isn't at her home. With Colin Harris away on holiday in the US, it falls to me to run the department, and I want to catch this guy before he goes completely off the rails. I doubt Ruth Hawthorne is going to have any clues as to where he might be hiding, but it would be good to know why he killed his ex-wife, Arlene. She was living with his brother, and he got stabbed five times, but it looks like he will pull through. He's very lucky."

"I can talk to her if she's here and call you back. There's a big dinner party tonight; it's a themed murder mystery, would you believe? I've arrived late, so it might be difficult to get her alone, but I will see what I can do."

"I see, a real busman's holiday for you then." He laughed. "Look, if you can talk to Ms. Hawthorne and ask her if she has any idea where we can look for him, call me with anything relevant. Ask her to return to Perth as early as possible in the morning so we can conduct a formal interview. We need to know why he escaped and what he hopes to achieve beyond murdering his ex-wife. We must get this nutter before he kills someone else."

Pat grimaced. She hated words like nutter, head

case, loopy, or any other derogatory names to call people with mental health issues. She also knew Rick did it intentionally to tease her, so she chose not to rise to the bait. "Will do, call you later."

A porter was waiting with an oversized umbrella to protect her from the rain. She opened her door, smiled at the young man, and thanked him. "Do you have any bags, ma'am?"

"Just the one in the trunk."

As if by magic, he produced a second umbrella for her to use. Once she had it open, he walked to the back of the car. Pat pressed the release button on the remote for him, then hurried to the entrance, dodging puddles as she went.

****

The entrance was grand, with crystal chandeliers, lots of natural timber furniture, and a massive open fire in the center. Once the check-in formalities were done, Pat had to laugh. She had been allocated room thirteen; *lucky I'm not superstitious.* She asked what room Ruth Hawthorne occupied. The receptionist, wearing a name badge announcing she was Tabitha, told her that Mrs. Hawthorne and her husband were in room number ten and that they had arrived during the afternoon.

Pat followed the porter to the elevator and climbed to the floor above, then down the corridor to room thirteen at the end of the wing. "Oh my, this is just beautiful, thank you." She handed him a tip, and he nodded his thanks.

"Enjoy your stay with us, ma'am," he said quietly, closing the door behind him.

The room was dominated by a king-sized brass bed adorned with a delicate white linen bedspread. The furniture was impeccable: plush carpet, walls decorated with expensive prints of the local countryside, and exquisite antique furniture. *This will do very nicely,* she thought, then followed up with, "M*aybe I will bring Derrin here.*" She shivered at the thought of a romantic getaway when he returned from the rig in the Gulf of Carpentaria.

Pat crossed to the wardrobe, studied the instructions for the personal security safe, and opened it using her code of 2713, the birth dates of her daughters. She unclipped the pistol, spare magazine, and holster from her belt, placed them inside, closed the door, and watched the dancing lights to make sure it was locked.

An hour later, Pat had showered and dressed. *Dress scary* had been her instruction, and she had agonized over what that meant. In the end, Pat had found a white silk Dior blouse, which she hadn't worn for a long time, and attacked it with scissors to replicate stab and slash wounds, being careful not to make it too revealing. Then, she liberally applied theatrical blood to the cuts and left it to set. She stood in front of the full-length mirror, having matched it with black pants and four-inch heels. Pat thought with a chuckle how much she resembled a murder victim. *Yeah, I think that's scary enough.*

Grabbing her clutch bag, Pat left her room, making sure the door locked correctly behind her, and went looking for suite ten and Ruth Hawthorne.

Chapter 3

Ruth Hawthorne

Pat knocked on the door of number ten and hoped she had caught Ruth before she went downstairs to the bar. From inside, she heard a muffled woman's voice. "Can you get that, Tony?" The next moment, the door was yanked open, and a tall, distinguished-looking man wearing a tuxedo performed a double-take when he saw her.

"Jesus Christ, are you all right?" he said with concern in his voice, and Pat realized the effect her slashed and bloody top had on him.

Pat gave a small laugh, which grew louder when she glanced again at his face and threatened to become hysterical. "I'm fine, thank you. *Dress scary,* the invite said, so I did. I've got to say, your tuxedo isn't scary at all. I'm Patricia Holmes, and I would like to have a few words with Ruth if I can before festivities get underway."

He grinned and stepped back, beckoning with his head for her to enter. "Yeah, we don't do fancy dress-ups, sorry. We're far too dull in our old age. Come in. Ruth is applying her makeup with a trowel. I'm Tony. I don't think we've met?"

"Thanks, Tony. Please call me Pat; everyone does. I left Graylands quite a while ago, and even when I was there, I was only part-time. I consulted with the criminally insane, the lifers, and the worst of the worst.

By all means, call me morbid. These days, I'm with the police."

He pointed to the chair by the desk where she could sit and turned his head to the bathroom. "Hon, it's Patricia Holmes. She wants to speak with you before we go downstairs. Do you want me to hang around, or can I go down and mingle?"

Ruth Hawthorne stuck her head around the doorway, clutching a lipstick in her right hand. "Hello, Pat. Bloody long time no see. How are you doing?" She turned her glance to her husband. "You can leave us girls. We can go down together. Is that all right, Pat? My God, I love your outfit."

"Thanks, Ruth. I thought I'd have a bit of fun. Going down together works for me. I need a private chat anyway…"

"Sounds ominous. You get off, Tony. Pat joined the dark side and is with the police now, but I don't think she is here to arrest me."

Pat shook her head and smiled as Ruth disappeared back into the bathroom. Pat sat down on the seat to wait, and Tony acted like most people do around detectives: nervous and in a hurry to get away.

"Righto, see you downstairs. Nice to meet you, Mrs. Holmes." He scampered out the door quickly, eager to either get away from her, find a strong drink, or both.

****

"What's this all about, Pat?" Ruth asked as she perched on the end of the bed.

"Mervyn Biscain. Without breaking any privilege, can you tell me anything about him?" Pat raised an eyebrow.

"What's he done? He had permission to leave the

facility yesterday to go to a funeral."

"He didn't return. While out, he's murdered his ex-wife and very nearly his brother. He's still missing, and my colleagues are hunting for him."

Ruth visibly blanched and shook her head. "I warned against this, but oh no, the bleeding, lily-livered, do-gooders granted him compassionate leave. Trust me, Mervyn is one man who should not have been given a break."

"What was he in for?"

She sighed. "Mervyn had a terrible accident. A crane fell on him at work and, among other injuries, damaged his front temporal lobe. He'd already begun to exhibit early signs of extreme paranoia and uncontrollable rages. He heard voices, which he said were urging him to kill his neighbors. After he recovered from the accident, he got so much worse. In desperation, his wife had him committed after all other attempts to help him failed. We've tried everything with him, and if anything, treatment made him worse. Chlorpromazine didn't help, but for the last six months or so, he's been calmer after we finished two courses of electroconvulsive therapy. But nothing works for long. These days, we keep him quiet with psychotropics and keep an eye on him. He's a lost cause, I'm afraid, though I keep trying."

Pat nodded. She couldn't see anything wrong with the diagnosis or treatment. "Do you have any clues as to what he might do now that he's out and free?"

"I'd put a watch on his neighbors. He was completely paranoid that they were watching him and reporting him to *the authorities*. Which particular authorities he would never say, just touch the side of his nose as if the answer was obvious. Otherwise, maybe his work colleagues. He blamed a man named Conroy, Samuel Conroy, for the accident. He was driving the crane that crushed the utility Mervyn was in, and, coincidentally, they had an argument over football scores the day before."

"Anyone else, or anywhere you think he might hide out?"

Ruth stared for a while until her face began to tinge red. "Naturally, he hates me for refusing to sign his release. That comes with the territory sometimes, as you know, Pat. He blames me for keeping him at Graylands, not understanding that once he was committed for his own good, it would take a court order to get him out and only if three psyches signed off on it." She shook her head emphatically. "That's never going to happen. He couldn't get one, let alone three."

Pat stood up. "Yes, I know what you mean. I still have the scars from being the focus of a psychotic rage." She patted her stomach where PPP, a serial killer she had helped capture, had stabbed her. "Are you heading back tomorrow morning? The police will need to take a statement."

"We were going to stay here and make a weekend of it, but if they need me, I can go back and then return here in the afternoon. Tony wants to do some fishing at the Pools, weather permitting anyway, so he won't mind."

"I think it's best if you do. Go to headquarters and ask for Detective Inspector Richard McCoy. He can also arrange protection if you're worried. Stay away from Graylands, just in case Biscain is watching for you. Let's go and have a drink. You look like you need a stiff one."

"I'm going to have more than one." She stood and then stopped abruptly. "Does Helen know? She's here, and I'm surprised she hasn't come to see me about it."

Helen Marcovic was the chief of staff and had been at the hospital for many years. "I'm not sure. I only got the call because my boss knew I was coming here to the reunion and wanted me to chat with you. It's not one of my cases, so my information is limited. C'mon, let's go and get that drink. I'm sure Helen is downstairs, and we can ask her."

Chapter 4

Where's Helen?

Pat took a glass of champagne from a waitress at the entrance to the function room, which had been impeccably decorated and had a long dinner table in the center. Ruth walked ahead of her, and Pat said she would see her later. Before Pat followed to mingle with people she hadn't seen for a long time, she searched the crowd for Helen without seeing her. She walked to the foyer and asked what room Mrs. Markovic was booked into. Tabitha, the same receptionist who checked Pat in earlier, consulted the register. "We have reserved suite four for her, but she hasn't arrived yet."

"Has she phoned to cancel or say she was delayed?"

Tabitha shook her head. "No, there are no notes here, and the room is paid for in full."

Warning bells rang in Pat's head. "Thanks," she murmured. She crossed to the vacant open-fire area, taking her phone from her purse as she walked. She called Rick's number.

"Hi, Pat, how's it going? Do you have anything I can use?"

"No, not really. But I'd like you to check up on Helen Markovic's whereabouts. She's Graylands' Chief of Staff and hasn't shown up here for the social. Maybe she stayed in Perth because of the escape, but if she has, she hasn't canceled her room. As tonight was her idea, and she is the convener, I'm worried."

"Leave it to me. Did you speak with Ruth Hawthorne?"

"I did. Biscain was admitted by his wife, suffering from apparent paranoid schizophrenia, after a workplace accident from which he suffered brain damage. Though I suspect that just exacerbated an existing complaint. Treatment didn't help him, and from what you've told me, it would appear he blamed his wife for the committal, hence the attack. If she was living with his brother, Biscain might have thought they plotted to have him committed so they could be together. He was extremely paranoid about his neighbors, who he thought were spying on him; that's standard behavior in cases like this. You might want to check on them and have someone stake out his old house. Ruth is going to head back tomorrow morning to make a statement. I've told her to stay away from Graylands, just in case, so she will come to the station to make a complete statement and then return here for the rest of the weekend. If you haven't caught Biscain by Sunday night, I urge you to get her protection."

"That sounds like good advice. Pat, what are your thoughts on what Biscain will do? We've had no sightings of him since the murder at the brother's house."

She paused and thought about what little she knew of the escapee from Ruth. "I have a bad feeling about this, although he was not my patient, so I can't speak of his case specifically with any certainty. Serious paranoid schizophrenics can spiral toward violent behavior quickly when they are off their medication. Everyone is against them, plotting and planning. Often, the patient believes people intend to kill them, so they have to attack first. Logic flies out of the window, and the things they worry about can make no sense whatsoever. As he has now murdered his ex, no doubt fueled by his delusions, I'd say he thinks he is on a mission. Whatever that mission is, he will not stop. I think you should also check up on someone by the name of Samuel Conroy, whom Biscain blamed for his accident at work."

"Okay, I've made a note of that. When you say Biscain's on a mission, do you mean like Bobby Cornhill? He had schizophrenia, didn't he?"

"He did. He, too, was delusional and murderous; however, he wasn't paranoid. His problem was with the type of people whom he held responsible for the death of his sister. Different psychosis altogether. Biscain's schizophrenia is more personal. He hated his wife for having him committed, so she was the focal point of his paranoia. Remember, to him, he is normal. The rest of the world has the problem, and everyone is out to get him and keep him from achieving his mission. According to Ruth, Biscain heard voices telling him his neighbors were spying on him, and so they would be on his radar, though I feel to a lesser extent. I don't think they will be his primary target now his ex-wife is dead."

"Who then?"

"Ruth Hawthorne. Again, I don't know the specifics, but if Biscain hated his wife for having him committed, once he got even with her, he must then shift his hatred to the person who kept him there, his doctor. You must watch Ruth Hawthorne once she returns to Perth. He won't stop until he's killed her."

"Hmm, okay, I hear you loud and clear. Well, you enjoy yourself. We'll put in a late night here chasing down Samuel Conroy and Helen Markovic."

She sipped from the flute in her hand. "Well, the champagne is good, and don't forget, I'm off to catch a murderer here too; it is a murder mystery dinner party. Though with Helen not turning up, the instructional envelopes haven't been delivered to us, the players." She laughed as she ended the call.

Pat went back to the function room and swapped her empty glass for a full one from the same waitress. She was worried and couldn't help but ponder, *Where is Helen Markovic?*

Chapter 5

The Gathering

Pat didn't take longer than thirty minutes of mingling to remember why she used to avoid social gatherings with her work colleagues in the past; most of them were boring. Tom, her ex-husband, refused point-blank to attend university dinners after going with her to two and never once went with her to a Graylands staff function. Naturally, she had to participate in all of his work functions as the dutiful wife, and they were boring with a capital B. With Tom, it had always been a one-way street.

Most people she stopped to speak with had not *dressed scary*, so Pat continually had to explain the cuts and blood on her top. Next, they were interested in her job with the police, particularly her role in tracking down *The Biblical Killer*, Bobby Cornhill. But continually being asked the same questions, which, granted, were interesting to others but no longer to her, was tedious at best. At every opportunity, Pat tried to steer any conversations toward work at Graylands, and specifically, Mervyn Biscain, but those she spoke with couldn't add to what little she already knew; most didn't even know of his escape.

Pat was still concerned that Helen hadn't shown up, so she asked those she spoke with whether they knew if Helen had canceled or was still attending, albeit very late. Everyone believed she was coming, and since she had the envelopes with the attendees' roles for the mystery night, everyone agreed it would be a fizzer if she didn't show.

At eight, a gong sounded, and the hostess asked everyone to take their seats. Pat found her place and was pleased to be seated alongside the only single man, Joseph O'Rourke. He was a senior psychiatric consultant well into his fifties, with gray hair, a slim build, and half-round glasses. Pat only knew him slightly, but heard that his wife had passed away two years before from complications after surgery to remove stage one cancer from her stomach.

"Patricia, I'm so pleased to meet you after all this time," he said, then indicated her glass. "A woman after my own heart, drinking red wine. Nice they put the widow and widower together to restore the balance of happy, or maybe some not-quite-so-happy couples, don't you think?"

She was instantly drawn to him and liked his irreverent manner. It's a *shame about the glasses; they don't suit him at all.* "Joseph, the pleasure is all mine, but I'd prefer not to compare our personal tragedies if that's okay with you?"

He laughed uproariously. "That's a deal, and it would be a game I'd lose anyway, from what I've heard of you. How are you enjoying life away from academia, hospital life, and working with the police?"

Before she could reply, a fork tapped against the side of a wine glass to gain attention. It was Brenda Biggins, Helen's office manager, on her feet. "Could I have everyone's attention, please?" she asked meekly, and Pat had to strain to hear her words. The guests stopped talking and turned toward her. Pat noted the empty seat by her side.

"As some of you may have heard, Graylands has had one of our patients, Mervyn Biscain, flee from a day release visit to his mother's funeral yesterday. Our special guest and former staff member, wearing the fantastic blood-stained blouse, is Detective Sergeant Patricia Holmes." She pointed toward Pat, who felt her face tingle with redness for being singled out. "Ruth Hawthorne tells me that Pat and the police believe he has attacked his brother with a knife, murdered his ex-wife, and is still on the run. No doubt, these serious events have caused Helen, our fearless leader, to cancel tonight, or she is still in transit to us, but I suspect even if she does arrive, it will be too late for the murder/mystery game."

The groans echoed around the table, but Pat wondered how many were genuinely disappointed. As soon as the murmurs died down, Brenda continued, "I've phoned Helen's mobile, but it's not answering, and she is not at Graylands. Patricia told Ruth she isn't with the police, so I'm just hoping she hasn't had her car break down on her way here, and she is out of cell phone range. Her old green Volvo has always been reliable, but as we know, it is getting on in years."

"Just like the rest of us," Paula Smithers' husband, Nigel, said, and a couple of people politely guffawed.

"Anyway, I guess we will have to postpone tonight's planned frivolities, enjoy a lovely meal and each other's company instead, and hope Helen turns up soon. Yes, Michael?"

A young man at the far end of the table had his arm up like a schoolboy in class. "Brenda," he began nervously, "I'm obviously mistaken, but when Michelle and I got here, I thought I saw her car in the car park right down the end near the trees."

His wife, clearly embarrassed that everyone was looking at them, nudged her husband and said, "Shh, sit down."

"Look, umm, it was raining hard at the time, and I'm maybe getting her car mixed up with a staff member's, sorry. I just thought maybe she was having a lie-down in her room and had fallen asleep. Has anyone checked she hadn't done that?"

Pat felt everyone's eyes on her and thought she had to respond. "Before dinner, I checked with reception, and she hadn't arrived from Perth, nor had she canceled her booking. Brenda's thought is good; the weather was bad, so perhaps she did get stuck on the side of the road somewhere and will turn up soon." Pat paused, then continued, "Look, I'm here purely socially; however, if anyone has any information about Mervyn Biscain, or if they hear from Helen, would you please come and talk to me? It's a grave matter for the hospital, and of course, he is still free, and we don't want him to harm anyone else. Any assistance would be very much appreciated."

"Well said," Joseph said out of the corner of his mouth, trying not to move his lips.

"Can I suggest to everyone we eat the fabulous dinner we're about to be served, enjoy the fellowship and the wines which Helen selected, and let's have a ball," Brenda added and sat down to a smattering of applause.

Pat's phone hummed and vibrated from inside her purse. *That will be Rick,* she thought, and whispered to Joseph, "Excuse me, please." As discreetly as possible, she stood from the table, removed the phone, and pressed the answer button as she left the room once more.

Chapter 6

Samuel Conroy

"Patricia Holmes," she said into the phone microphone as she exited the function room.

"It's Rick."

She could tell by his abruptness and tone of voice that everything was not going well. Usually, she knew he was smiling whenever he spoke to her, but not this time. She dispensed with calling him boss. "What's wrong, Rick? Talk to me."

"Everything is wrong. No, scratch that; everything is fucked up royally. Tonight is one of those times when I wish to God you were here. We need you to try to get a read on this guy. It's like something out of a horror movie."

"What's Biscain done?"

"I'm standing in Samuel Conroy's garage. He is divorced, by the way; apparently, he became moody after losing his job after the accident, which almost killed Biscain. His wife put up with his bad moods and temper tantrums for as long as she could, but finally, she took the kids and moved to Melbourne to live with her sister to get away from him."

"Go on. Why are you in Conroy's garage?" Pat knew where this was heading, and it wasn't anywhere good.

"That's where we found him dead."

Pat suspected as much. "Are you suggesting he was depressed and killed himself, carbon monoxide fumes, or something?"

"I wish that were the case. You mentioned it was a workplace accident that sent Biscain over the edge. Did it have something to do with him getting crushed?"

"I didn't get the full details, but according to Ruth, it was an accident between a crane and a vehicle he was driving, so yes, I guess you could say he got crushed."

"Inside the garage, at the far end from the roller door, is a steel bench. Conroy had one hand tied to a leg. The other was clamped into a vice, crushing it. He'd been gagged, in case you're wondering, to minimize the screams. He was then driven into by a car repeatedly until his chest was a bloody, crushed mess. We assume Biscain used Conroy's car because it's not here for us to check now. We tracked down the cab driver who dropped off someone who resembled Biscain here last night, so he's hardly hiding his tracks."

Pat sighed and shook her head. "You're suggesting Biscain is driving Conroy's car now? Jesus, he could be anywhere."

"There are a million fingerprints here, but I'm betting forensics find Biscain to be a match, yeah."

"Rick, you must find Helen Markovic. She has not checked in here, and she hasn't called anyone. Can you get a patrol car to check the highway between Perth and here? I'm hoping that maybe she's had a mechanical breakdown and is outside the mobile phone reception. That's the only thing that makes sense because tonight was her idea, and she has all of the information for the entertainment. Without her here, there is no murder mystery night, and she wouldn't miss it with no word or reason."

"Yep, I can do that. What does Markovic drive? Do you have any idea?"

"One of the guys here says it's a dark green Volvo, but I don't know the plate number. Helen lives in Mount Claremont, but she must have broken down outside the metro area in a cellular blind spot. Otherwise, she would have called someone here."

"I can tell you she isn't at Graylands, I've phoned there, and they haven't seen her all day, which is worrying. Unless she intended to make a long weekend of it and got away a day early. If that's the case, she could have car trouble anywhere. Ask around, can you? See if she had any other plans for today that would explain why she wasn't at work. It's a good thing Ruth Hawthorne is there. Biscain would have no idea where she is. That's the safest place for her to be right now. I'd like you to watch her. Make sure you keep a *close* eye on her, and I think it best you accompany her here tomorrow, just to be safe."

She nodded. "Yes, I agree. Ruth will be the focal point of his rage, but the missing link is Helen."

"I will get an alert out for her car as soon as I get a plate number from the computer. Did you take your firearm with you?"

"Yes, I was late getting away from work and had my overnight bag already in the car, so I didn't go home. My Glock is currently locked up in the room safe, here in my suite."

"Good, get it out and keep it with you. I can't see any way Biscain would know about your murder mystery social night, but it's best to be on the safe side, hey? Don't let her leave there for any reason. If Ruth

Hawthorne gets a call from someone telling her to come home because there is a death in the family, her cat has died, or her child is missing, phone me immediately so I can check it out. I have Tyler Dundass and Brooks out in front of her home as we speak, keeping watch. So far, it's quiet, but stick to her like glue. You're an hour and a half away. Do you want me to send someone to assist you, or can you cope as her babysitter?"

Pat flinched. *Why won't everyone trust me not to get hurt? Just because I had two lapses in judgment before and was wounded doesn't mean I need a minder every time.* "Rick, trust me, I will go straight to my room and get my gun. I do not need a male detective with me to protect me like a big brother. As you said, there is no way Biscain can know Ruth is here, and I will bring her back with me in my car in the morning."

"Calm down, Pat, there's no need to get angry with me. This maniac has killed two and almost fatally wounded a third. With Colin Harris away on vacation, I'm in charge and trying to do this by the book. Any serious protection job would call for two detectives to guard a witness; it's nothing personal." Before she could reply, he spoke again. "Pat, we have his neighbors and his old address under surveillance. We're staking out Helen Marcovic's house, and you're with Ruth. Is there anyone else he will go after, or is he likely to stab random strangers because he can't find his principal target?"

Mollified by his response that his concern wasn't personal, she took a moment to think. Eventually, she began. "Rick, once again, Biscain wasn't my patient, so I'm diagnosing from afar. That said, he is displaying all the signs of a full-blown paranoid schizophrenic. He has now been off his meds for forty-eight hours, and his paranoia is driving him. Will he attack a random stranger? No, but will he attack a random stranger whom Biscain thinks has it in for him? Most likely, yes, but there would be a reason for him to do that, even though that reason could be obscure. However, his number one focus is to kill Ruth, and he will not stop until he has. If he believes he has failed, he may commit suicide."

"We couldn't be that lucky."

Something was nagging at the periphery of her mind, something she should do. What was it?

"Pat, are you still there?"

Suddenly, it came to her. "Yes, I was just thinking about Helen. Have the boys knocked on her door to see if she's home?"

It was his turn to pause. "We're not that dumb; of course we have."

She giggled. "Yeah, okay, stupid question, but hear me out. She's not at Graylands, home, or here, and her mobile is not answering. You should break into her house."

"I can't get a court order on your feelings, and we don't have just cause without one. What do you think we'll find inside if we do break in?"

"Helen."

Chapter 7

Dinner at the Priory

Pat hurried up to her room, swiped her card, and walked in, distracted by her thoughts, which were in turmoil. The bed had been turned down, and there was a warm glow from the lamp beside the bed. She flicked the overhead light on and crossed to the wardrobe, where she opened the door to reveal the safe. Her mind wandered as she entered her code, yanked the door open, removed her pistol, and clipped the holster to her belt at her hip.

Am I worried about nothing, or has Biscain got to Helen? She ran through the likely sequence of events since he escaped from his minder at the funeral. *Clearly, he went to his old house and discovered his ex-wife no longer lived there, which would have fired up his paranoia. His next port of call was to his brother's house, where, lo and behold, he found his ex-wife had moved in with him. Nothing could have stopped him from murdering her once his paranoid fears were realized, which would also have fueled all his other delusions. So, from there, he went to the man who caused the accident and crushed him, but then what? He stole Patrick Conroy's car. Why? Well, the next person on Biscain's hit list would be Ruth, so he went to her house, and thankfully, she wasn't home. What would he have done then? Hang on a second. How would he know where Ruth lived? He would need to find out where that was.*

Hmm, I need to ask Ruth if she is listed in the phone book.

Pat donned her jacket to hide the pistol and raced out of her suite back to the dinner party. She opened the double doors to the function room, and everyone turned in their chairs. Pat blushed and nodded an apology. She crossed the room to her seat as a waitress placed her entree, consisting of a seafood medley, on the table.

"Are you cold?" Joseph asked her. "Your jacket," he murmured when she looked at him questioningly.

She grinned. "Yeah, and I felt a bit self-conscious with my blood-stained shirt." She wasn't willing to admit that she'd donned it to hide her weapon. She glanced around the table and noted everyone was conversing in small groups, some animated, some mumbling quietly so as not to be overheard.

Pat hurriedly finished her first course, which she had to admit was delicious, while trying to catch Ruth's eye. She was talking to Leslie Moncrief to her left, so wasn't looking in Pat's direction. Meanwhile, Joseph kept up an attempt to talk to her. At any other time, Pat would have been flattered and enjoyed not only the chance for intelligent banter but an apparent effort from a handsome man, albeit one considerably older than her, to seduce her.

Her mind wandered back to her earlier thoughts. *If Biscain didn't know where Ruth lived, and most likely, wouldn't, how would he find out?* The answer became obvious: *Helen, that's how. But how would he know where she lived?*

Pat's heart sank. Helen Markovic was in the phone book. When Pat worked at Graylands some years before, she had been invited to a dinner party at her boss's house. It was only after she and Tom dressed and were ready to leave their Applecross home that Pat realized that she had left the address on a slip of paper on her desk at work. Rather than embarrass herself by phoning to ask, Pat used the phone book, and there was Helen's Mount Claremont address. *Would Biscain be smart enough to look there?* She knew he would. A paranoid schizophrenic didn't lose their intelligence or their ability to problem-solve. They gave in to delusions that everyone was out to hurt them. In some cases, she knew they became more cunning in planning ability if it stemmed from a misconception of personal danger. *I have to talk to Ruth.*

She pushed her plate away and leaned on her elbows. "Joseph," she began, "I'm so sorry if I seem distracted. Please don't take it personally, but a lot is going on with this escape. I can't go into it, but I'm concerned for Ruth and Helen's safety while Biscain is at large."

He nodded sagely. "It's odd that Helen hasn't shown up. I suppose everyone has checked her office at Graylands? She's dedicated, so I could understand her camping at work until you cops caught him. That said, she would have let us know if she wasn't coming tonight; I think you're right to be concerned."

"We've checked her work and home. She's not at either."

"Pat, can we catch up for lunch or dinner sometime when you're not so distracted?"

She stared at him, startled by the sudden shift in conversation. She considered his offer. He had a good ten years on her, not that his age was a bad thing. To counterbalance that, he was educated and, by all accounts, an excellent psychiatrist, so they had plenty in common. He was a widower and dashingly good-looking. She warmed a little at the thought. "Joseph, I'd enjoy that. Please do give me a call."

Pat looked back toward Ruth's seat alongside her husband and saw it was empty. She jerked her head around, searching the long table, expecting to see her crouching down, talking to another colleague, but she had disappeared.

Chapter 8

The Broken Mirror

Without a word to Joseph, Pat leaped to her feet, raced around the table to Ruth's chair, and sat down. She placed a hand on Tony's arm and squeezed, trying to interrupt the conversation he was deeply into with a woman Pat had never met. "Tony, I'm sorry to break into your conversation. Where did Ruth go? I need to talk to her."

"Oh, hello, Mrs. Holmes. She just went up to the room to use the bathroom. Must be all the stress, and she's come down with a headache."

"Thanks." Without another word, she raced out of the room, desperate to find Ruth.

The elevator seemed to take forever, but eventually, the doors hissed open, and Pat stepped inside and repeatedly jabbed the first-floor button. *"Come on,"* she urged the doors, *"can you go any slower?"*

As if to tease her, the doors closed as slowly as they opened. Pat felt the lurch as the car moved upward. Without thinking, she unclipped the tab, which retained the Glock in its holster, yanked it free, and pushed the safety to the off position in one practiced, continuous movement. As the doors slid open again, she hid the gun under her jacket in case she came across another guest, but the corridor was empty.

Pat slipped off her stiletto heels outside the elevator

and silently sprinted on stocking feet to Ruth and Tony's suite. The door was slightly ajar, and the striker plate hung broken on the frame. Someone had kicked it in.

As quietly as possible, Pat cranked the slide on the Glock back and released it to chamber a bullet. Inside her chest, Pat's heart pounded, but her hands were steady as she used the barrel to push open the door and took her shooter's stance.

The light inside the room was off, so she was only backlit from the corridor. Silently, she stepped inside and, to one side, her outstretched arm swept her gun through its arc to cover anywhere a man might hide. Nothing. The door had come to rest against the wall, so Biscain wasn't hiding there. That only left the bathroom.

Pat noted that Ruth's bedclothes were turned down as she walked past it, which told her the lock had been broken after the maid had visited. Her heart pounding, Pat turned the handle and pushed the bathroom door violently open, ready to shoot a crazed intruder.

The bathroom was empty, and she slowly released the lung full of air she'd been holding. Then Pat noticed the mirror above the sink was broken. Across the jagged shards, the word *BITCH* had been written in what looked like blood.

With dawning horror, Pat realized Mervyn Biscain was in the building.

Chapter 9

The Plea for Help

"Rick," Pat yelled the moment he answered his phone. She stopped to put on her shoes. "Biscain is here; send the cavalry." She was back at the elevator, gun still in hand, feeling a mixture of fear and excitement.

"Slow down, Pat. What's happened?" he asked frantically.

Pat took a calming breath. "He's got Ruth. I took my eye off her for two minutes during dinner, and she disappeared. Her husband told me she'd gone to her room, but the door had been kicked in when I got there. Her mirror is broken, and the word '*bitch*' is written across it in what looks like blood; his, I hope. He must have taken her somewhere because the room is empty."

She jabbed the call button for the elevator, and the doors didn't open immediately. She glanced at the indicators and saw it was on the ground floor. *Hurry up,* she screamed in her mind.

"How the hell did he get there, and how did he even know where Ruth was?"

Pat froze as she heard Rick's muffled voice calling out to get attention from another detective and realized the nearest help from any police officer would be an hour away at best if they used sirens all the way, but the weather was still atrocious, more like an hour and ten minutes minimum. By then, it could be carnage.

Suddenly, Pat saw it all as she remembered a comment from earlier. "Rick, he must have got to Helen, and she told him where Ruth was, and he's stolen her car to get here. I bet, inside Helen's garage, you find Patrick Conroy's vehicle and possibly Helen's body. Someone said they thought they saw her car in the staff car park earlier. I need to check it out in case he takes Ruth there to get her away. Send help. I've got to go."

Pat thrust the phone back into her pocket as the elevator doors opened. Rushing inside, she collided with Ruth as she was emerging.

Chapter 10

A Glimpse

Where is the bitch?

No one is going to stop me from killing her; anyone who tries will die, too.

I killed her boss, Helen. She was pathetic. She thought she was smarter than me and said she would help me. But what she meant was she would lock me up again, put those electrodes on my head, and shoot the electricity through my brain some more. But I showed her who was in charge.

I could feel it melt my insides every time they did it before, and they wouldn't stop. I cried and begged them not to do it anymore, but they wouldn't listen. That bitch Doctor Ruth, if it's the last thing I do, I will get her tonight. They're all evil; all the doctors, and especially the head bitch Helen, but she's attended to. I heard them laughing in the passage outside my room when I was strapped to my bed as they plotted and schemed to electrocute me some more. They're so horrible, I bet they put it on TV so everyone could see them torture me. That is why when people look at me on the street, they all smirk. They know they've seen me have my brain fried on prime-time TV.

But no more.

If I kill them, they won't be able to do to other innocents what they did to me.

I'm coming for you, Doctor Ruth, and as many other Graylands' doctors as I can take with you. No mercy, no quarter, no forgiveness, kill the bitches, kill the bitches, then kill some more bitches.

I saw them through the window, partying, drinking, and clapping each other on the back. I will make them doctors pay. Every last one of them. Hmm, what is the collective noun for a group of psychiatrists? I don't know, but I'm going to call it a murder. A murder of psychiatrists. Oh yes, I like that.

****

"What the hell?" Pat screamed in shock as the gun was knocked from her hand in the collision with Ruth. She stooped to pick it up, muttering to herself that she needed to calm down if she was to save anyone from the madman.

"Pat, what are you doing here?" Ruth asked, apparently equally annoyed at running into her.

Pat took a deep, calming breath and slipped the gun back into the holster at her hip. "It's Biscain. He's here, Ruth. He's broken into your room and smashed your mirror. I was afraid he had taken you; thank goodness he didn't."

"Mervyn, here? He can't be. You're mistaken. There's no way he knows where I am. Maybe the cleaner broke the mirror." She shook her head as if she were dealing with an unruly child. "For goodness' sake, Patricia, calm down." Ruth pushed past Pat and began walking to her room.

Pat's hackles prickled. "Ruth, if it was the cleaner, why didn't they use their room key to enter instead of kicking your door in? And why did they write bitch across your mirror in blood after they broke it?"

Ruth stopped suddenly, with one foot in the air, then lowered it and turned back. It would have been comical in another situation. "That's what he called me: the bitch Doctor. How did he find me here?"

Pat noticed the edge of barely controlled panic creeping into Ruth's voice rather than the assuredness of earlier. *Now she believes me.* "Remember earlier when Michael said he thought he saw Helen's car here near where the staff park? I've got to check it out. I think he got to Helen, made her tell him where you are, and used her car to drive here. He wants revenge, and you are his main target."

"Call the police."

"I am the police, armed, and have called for backup. I want you to go to my suite and hide there until they arrive, where you will be safe. Here's my keycard." Pat pressed the plastic strip into her hand. Pat took her arm and forcibly led Ruth to her room. "Do not come out. Don't answer the door to anyone until I come back. Can you do that, Ruth?"

"But what about Tony, and what about the others downstairs?"

"After I check to see if Helen is in her car, I will gather the staff and get everyone into the function room where I can guard them until reinforcements arrive. But you must stay in my room where he will never find you."

Pat thought Ruth resembled a scared rabbit caught in the hunter's spotlight. She fumbled with the lock and pushed the door open. Ruth nodded, her eyes brimming with tears, as the door slowly closed on its spring, leaving Pat in the corridor and Ruth safe in the room.

Pat thought, *one down, fifteen to go*, then sprinted for the elevator.

Chapter 11

The Green Volvo

When the elevator doors opened, Pat turned left toward the after-hours entrance rather than going through the foyer. She had noticed the sign earlier when she arrived and saw that the door at the end of the passage led to the outside and seemed to be a shortcut to the car park. With her gun clenched in her hand, she looked frantically in every direction for Biscain, expecting him to jump out at any moment.

The exit door was glass, and with the outside well-lit, Pat searched the shadows for the lurking killer. Nothing moved except the trees shaking violently in the wind, which drove the rain ahead of them. It seemed to Pat that even a paranoid schizophrenic was intelligent enough to stay out of the storm, but she had no such luck. She had to see if Helen was in the car, possibly injured, and Pat knew she would get drenched before getting halfway.

Pat slid an umbrella from the bucket to help keep her dry. She kicked the door wide and opened the umbrella as she stepped through. She felt the wind blow raindrops on her legs and shivered from the sudden cold. Within three paces, a sudden gust almost wrenched the umbrella from her grasp, and while Pat could hold on, it turned inside out and became useless.

In disgust, Pat threw it aside and took off through

the car park, away from her Mercedes and the harsh lighting poles, toward the darkened area at the rear. She kept low, crouching between the gleaming guests' vehicles, ever alert, hoping not to stumble over Mervyn Biscain. She knew that if she were being filmed in a Hollywood horror movie, she would run right into him, as she had with Ruth in the elevator.

Her short, once perfectly-styled hair soaked through instantly, and water ran in rivulets down her face into her eyes. Pat squatted alongside a gray SUV, the last car before an open stretch across the wide driveway. Using the tip of her index finger, she wiped drops away and searched for anyone hiding. Pat took a deep breath and was about to stand when the sound of the phone in her jacket pocket rang, making her jump in fright. Her nerves jangled as she squatted back down and snatched it out, desperate to silence the noise, knowing it was already too late. Her position had been given away to anyone watching.

"*What?*" *S*he hissed, turning her head left and right, waiting for someone to run at her with a knife.

"Pat, it's Rick. The nearest traffic patrol is at least thirty minutes away. Until then, you're on your own. What's happening?"

"For God's sake, Rick, don't phone me again. You frightened the crap out of me and could have given my position away to Biscain. Ruth is all right. She went to the restroom before going to her room, so she missed him. I've got her hiding in my room. I can see Helen's car. It's twenty meters away, and I'm squatting here in the pouring rain on my way to check it out in case she is inside and hurt. I can't talk. Once I check the car, I'll let you know what I find. Then, I must get back and protect

everyone in the function room. Christ knows where our man is. Just get that patrol car to break the speed limit and get here, and please, don't phone again." She jabbed at the call-end button and thrust the phone back into her pocket.

Well, if he's outside, he knows I'm here. No point hiding any longer. Pat stood and held the gun at her side, hopefully out of sight of a watcher, but cocked and ready if she needed it.

The rain splattered upward from the puddles as she ran across the driveway to the row of cars on the other side. The Volvo was three cars away, and she approached stealthily, flicking her head to clear drips from her eyelashes. Fueled by adrenaline and her heart pounding, Pat wished for a flashlight so she could see inside the vehicle. The light shining from the car park poles wouldn't have reached the Volvo on a clear night, let alone during the worst downpour she could ever remember.

After a quick glance around, Pat jerked on the driver's handle, and the door swung open with a creak. The interior light flooded out from inside, and, at one glance, Pat saw that the car was empty. She breathed a sigh of relief and then noticed the stains on the carpet and rear seat. A thought crossed her mind, accompanied by a dark sense of foreboding. Blinking away her temporary blindness from the sudden light, she scanned the dash for a button or lever that would open the trunk.

There, on the right of the steering wheel. Pat pushed it and heard the sound of the trunk lid opening from behind her. Urged on by the howling wind, the lid was nearly torn from its hinges and almost slammed shut again. Fearing what she would find, Pat walked to the car's rear and looked inside. She didn't need to search for a pulse to know Helen Markovic was dead. She lay on her side. Her throat had been cut, and her clothed body was a mess from multiple stab wounds.

What will he do now when he won't be able to find Ruth? Pat wondered as she closed the trunk to keep the rain from ruining any forensic traces. Not that she thought they would need forensics for a conviction, but it didn't hurt to be prudent. *He'll go for the psychologists at the dinner party if he hasn't already. Yes, but one at a time as they go to use the bathroom, or all at once?* Pat shook her head. She had no time to ponder. She had only one course of action open to her; she had to try to protect the people in the function room.

Using the light from the car, she redialed Rick's number. "It's me," she said without preamble. "Helen Markovic is dead, stuffed inside the trunk of her car. With Ruth safe, I'm returning to the function room to try to save them. For God's sake, get that patrol car here quickly."

"Pat, wait for them to arrive to help you. I've also got the police helicopter in transit. There is a marksman on board."

"How long before they can get here?"

"Ten to fifteen minutes, tops."

Pat squinted through the rain at the beautiful ivy-covered building, blinking away water from her eyes. She wished she could do as he asked, but knew she couldn't. In ten minutes, the madman could slaughter everyone. "I can't, Rick; you know that. I have to try to help them."

She turned off the phone, put it back in her pocket, and took off as quickly as her stiletto heels would allow.

Chapter 12

Where is the She?

Where is the bitch hiding?

It's been ten minutes, and Doctor Ruth hasn't returned to the dinner, and I know she's not in her room. So, where is she?

The receptionist was no help. She looked blankly at me when I asked where Doctor Ruth had gone, but she had a look in her eye that told me the moment I turned my back, she would phone the police. Why is everyone out to get me? Why can't they just let me do my job without interfering? Is that too much to ask for?

I checked the downstairs ladies' toilet, but no luck. Well, not good for me in finding the bitch, but terrible for the other psychologist I found in there. Talk about being caught with your pants down! She won't be giving any more patients electric shock treatment. She said she didn't know where Doctor Ruth had gone, didn't even know she'd left the dinner table. Oh well, nothing for it but confronting them all and slashing anyone who refuses to help me. What does a few fewer psychiatrists in the world matter anyway? Good riddance, I reckon.

I check my knives, which are tucked into the leather belt I stole from my late brother, the bastard wife stealer's house. All seven of them are here, and I've cleaned the blood off the one I just used. After all, I don't want to scare everyone unnecessarily, just the ones who are out to hurt me or people who want to stop me from killing the Bitch.

In the mirror of the lady's bathroom, I give myself a little grin. I suppose with seven different-sized knives sticking out the front of my belt, I do look a bit scary, and then there are the blood spatters all over me. Oh well, it can't be helped now.

I run through my hastily-made plot in my mind as I admire my tough-looking reflection. For some reason, as I look at myself, I am reminded of freedom fighters or mercenaries. Yeah, I like the thought of me being a freedom fighter. I shrug. It's not much of a plan, I suppose. Go into the dining room, bar the door so the evil doctors can't get out, and demand someone tell me where Doctor Ruth is hiding. Then, start cutting one at a time if they don't talk.

I calmly rinse my face and hands, getting the last of the blood off them, then dry myself with paper towels. I'm calm, ice calm if I'm honest, and I know that's because my cause is just. How dare these people zap people's brains, telling them it won't hurt when they are well aware it burns like hot acid being dripped into your ears? And they don't just do it once. That would be bad enough, but they do it over and over again. They call it a course of treatment, torture more like it. So when you're strapped to the bed, pissing your pants with fear, biting down on the leather knob, you know what's coming, and there isn't anything you can do about it. They turn the dial, and a million biting insects invade your brain. I don't care if I kill the lot of them tonight. I'm certainly going to take as many of them as I can.

****

I leave the bathroom, cross the foyer, and halt

outside the function room. I pull two knives out of my utility belt, as I like to think of it, open the door, and step through. With glee, I note that the conversation stops momentarily as I grab an unused chair and jam it under the door handle so it will be impossible to get in without me hearing the attempt.

That's when the noise starts. It's almost a panic as the frightened doctors realize who I am and why I'm there. I hold the two butcher's knives up in the air and ask for them all to shush. Then, I smile patiently and wait for them to do just that.

Some old codger with silver hair wearing a tuxedo, obviously, an overpaid torture merchant, approaches me. His hands are outstretched, waving in front of him, almost like he is trying to get me to sit down. "Mervyn, isn't it?" he asks in one of those sickly sweet voices they use when they think they are dealing with a brain-dead moron. "I'm Doctor Joseph. Let's talk about this; I can help you. No one else has to get hurt."

I bury the butcher's blade in his chest, all thirteen inches of it, and luckily, it goes through a gap in his ribs. I try to twist it and yank it out, but the weight of his body dropping to the floor pulls it from my hand, so I grab another from my belt.

I grin as he twitches on the parquetry flooring, blood spreading out in an ever-increasing puddle around him. I step away so I don't get any more blood on my brother's beautiful shoes. That's when the screaming starts.

"Anyone else want to help me?"

Chapter 13

Mervyn's Last Stand

Pat entered through the main doors from outside and searched the foyer, but couldn't see anyone. Her intended first port of call was the reception desk. She had to warn staff to stay away from the dining room or enter it with her. Though she acknowledged that they wouldn't be a part of Biscain's paranoid fantasy, they were still at risk if they confronted him.

Once again, Pat kicked off her heels and soaked jacket, tossed it onto a couch, and sprinted to the welcome desk.

The blonde-haired woman who booked Pat in earlier was nowhere to be seen, and Pat thought she might be in the office behind. She stepped through the counter's opening, and that's when Pat saw the blood. There was a trail of it across the floor to the door to the office. Using the tip of the barrel of her gun, she pushed the door open. The blonde had been stabbed repeatedly and lay in the middle of the room.

Pat sighed. She wanted to cry. It was a nightmare she couldn't wake up from, yet some of her was thrilled. All her adult life, Pat had dreamed of being a psychological profiler and police detective hunting down people such as Mervyn Biscain. Pat told herself she should be happy, but only felt horror, sadness, and fear.

Pat knew she had to stop other staff from

approaching the function room. She looked at the phone on the desk and studied the row of buttons. There, Pat saw one marked *Kitchen.* She grabbed the handset, pushed the tab down, and saw the red light illuminate.

"Yeah, what's up?" a man replied.

"Listen carefully. This is Detective Sergeant Patricia Holmes of the West Australian Police Force speaking. We have an escapee in the building who is armed and dangerous. Keep all staff away from the function room, get everyone together, and lock yourselves in a room somewhere if you can."

"Yeah, right, good one, Tabitha. This is a much better joke than you usually play on us. Even your voice sounds different."

Pat raised her eyes skyward, angry. "You listen to me, dickhead. This is not a joke; this is deadly serious. Tabitha is dead, along with several other people. It's not a drill, so don't be part of the problem; if you want to live through this, be a part of the solution. Get all your staff together, and if there is a back door, get out now. Find somewhere safe that you can lock from the inside. Now, don't argue with me; just go."

As she hung up the handset, Pat heard screams from the dining room and realized time was up; she had to act and act fast. She spared a glance at her reflection in the mirror, and if the situation hadn't been so dire, she would have burst out laughing. She looked like a drowned rat, but the funniest thing was the shirt with the cuts and bloodstains. Now it was wet, her top had become translucent, and her white bra showed clearly through it. The cuts sagged open, and the blood looked like it was fresh because it was so wet. Pat *really* did resemble a murder victim.

Suddenly, she had an idea. Rick had gotten the better of PPP by concealing his gun. Pat looked like a murder victim and was about to confront an insane killer. Maybe she could confuse him with her looks for long enough to save everyone.

Pat replaced her gun, pulled the holster from her hip, and placed it on the desk. Next, she jerked the shirt from inside her pants and left it hanging out. Then she tucked the holster inside her belt, under her shirt, in the small of her back. *Jesus, I look as insane as Mervyn does.*

****

As Pat suspected, the function room door was jammed shut. She took a deep, calming breath and then slapped it repeatedly and screamed as loudly as she could. "Help me, help me; there's a madman out here trying to kill me. *Help*, he's got a knife." She kept slapping the door with the flat of her hand, thinking a knock would be too authoritative. She was trying to put Biscain off his stride, not startle him into killing someone else.

"Is that you, Doctor Ruth?" Pat heard the trembling male voice shout back from inside.

"Let me in. Hurry before he gets me." She kept slapping the door harder and more insistently, deliberately not confirming or denying she was Ruth. *Let him worry if I am or not.*

****

I told them I wanted Doctor Ruth and demanded someone tell me where she was. I walk toward them, and they cower away, but the screaming stops at least. They're panicking, but not screaming, panicking. I guess, being psychologists, they should be able to handle their emotions. I grab a woman by the hair and put the knife in my other hand near her neck. "Where's Doctor Ruth?" I shout. And that's when the damned slapping and shouting on the door starts.

I'm confused. How can someone be outside attacking doctors? Is it a trick, or am I not alone in hating these people who toy with our brains? Ah, maybe it is a trick, and it's The Bitch trying to fox with me. "Is that you, Doctor Ruth?" I shout.

Whoever is out there doesn't say who she is. She just wants to come in to be safe. I don't think it's the Bitch. It doesn't sound like her voice, but I'm so confused with it all. It wasn't part of the plan to rescue someone, just kill them. What do I do?

I point at the man sitting next to the woman I've grabbed. "You, go and let her in." Then I half-drag, half-carry the woman by the hair backward, using her as a shield, still thinking it's some trick, but not one hundred percent sure.

****

Pat heard a noise from the other side of the door. It sounded like a chair being dragged out of the way. *It's showtime, she* thought as the door opened wide, and Professor Roger Martinez stood in the doorway as if he had soiled his jockey shorts. Pat didn't want to give anyone time to think, so she hurtled past him, pushing him to one side, then slammed the door closed behind her. She grabbed a chair and slid it under the handle. "For God's sake, don't let him inside; he's mad."

Pat glanced around as if in a maniacal trance and noted that everyone stared at her in shock. Then, she saw Biscain holding Betty Martinez with a knife at her throat. Pat forced herself to stop perfectly still, then slowly raised her hand to point at Biscain. "What are you doing in here? You just tried to stab me out there. How did you get in here so quickly?"

"No-no-no, I didn't. Who are you? Where is Doctor Ruth?"

"I'm Doctor Ruth. You just tried to stab me in the car park when I got out of my car. Why are you threatening Nurse Betty?"

With glee, Pat could see her plan was working. Biscain looked disorientated and scared. "You're not Ruth, and who is Nurse Betty?"

Pressing home her advantage, Pat took three steps toward them, grabbed Betty Martinez's hand, and pulled her free of Biscain's grip. Pat shoved her violently toward her husband, who looked equally stupefied. "You're a nurse. You shouldn't be here, Betty; this is for psychiatrists only. Now get out. And you, what do you mean I'm not Doctor Ruth? Who are you, and why are you trying to kill me?"

"I, what? What's going on?"

Pat took two steps backward, reached behind her, and pulled her Glock free of its holster. "You're under arrest, that's what's going on. Now drop the knives and lie on the floor with your hands clasped behind your head." She pointed the gun at him, her hand steady, and she stared deep into his eyes.

Biscaine didn't speak, but his face became a mask of pure malevolent evil. He screamed and ran toward Pat. His hand raised to bring the knife down in an arc.

Blam-Blam-Blam. Pat shot him three times, dead center of his chest, as she had trained to do.

The soft-nosed shells killed him almost instantly, but his momentum kept him coming at Pat. She tried to avoid the knife by twisting away, but the blade caught her upper arm, putting another slash in her shirt, but this one was real. She fell, with Biscain on top of her, just as she heard the approaching siren from the patrol car.

Epilogue

An hour later, Pat sat on the foyer couch as a paramedic bandaged her arm. "Let me through," she heard the familiar voice from the crowded entrance.

Seconds later, the couch shifted as Detective Inspector Richard "Rick" McCoy sat beside her.

"You've been wounded in the line of duty again, Pat. What is it with you?"

Pat felt like crying, crying and sleeping. She thought she could sleep for a long time, but was so glad he had come. "This?" She glanced at her arm. "It's just a scratch, five stitches, and a tetanus shot, and I will be as right as rain."

"I like your shirt," he said with a grin.

That's when she cried for the first time. She clung to Rick and shed tears as a release for fear, adrenaline, and for taking a human being's life. Mervyn Biscain had been damaged by an accident that wasn't his fault and became psychotic. Doctors had tried to help him, but he had been beyond help. But, for all his sins, Pat knew he was still a human being, and she had killed him. There would be many a sleepless night ahead for her. *Maybe I should consult a psychologist?* She thought. *I wonder where I can find one.*

Thirteen Past Midnight

Is it a nightmare, or is it real?

Foreword

Many years ago, more than I care to remember, I saw a movie that captivated me so much that I bought the book it was based on. The book was titled *The Devil Rides Out* by Dennis Wheatley. Spoiler alert for anyone who might want to look it up: the final scene features a group of people huddled in a chalked pentagram on the basement floor, battling the Devil incarnate with spells. To this day, I remember that scene, and at the time, it ignited a deep interest in all things occult. I spent some time in museums exploring witchcraft, astral travel, and other things that go bump in the night.

I have written two stories as an homage to Mr. Wheatley, who sadly has long since passed away. *Thirteen Past Midnight* is one of them.

Whether you, dear reader, believe in the occult or not doesn't matter so long as I can entertain you with what might be true for the protagonist, Jonathon, who is about to enter a world he doesn't understand.

Does Jonathon battle something evil from the dark arts, or is he insanely jealous, causing madness and hallucinations?

Chapter 1

I awoke suddenly, drenched in sweat and terrified, but for a moment, I couldn't understand why. The bedroom was dark except for the luminous green glow from the electronic alarm clock, which flashed at *12:01 a.m.* That was odd because it usually flashed only at *6:00 a.m.* when the alarm sounded to get me up for work. The rest of the time, it just shone weakly so as not to disturb me.

A droplet of sweat dribbled down my side from my left underarm. In the distance, I heard approaching thunder, but it seemed like the storm was a long way off. I jumped, startled again, as the rattle and thrumming of large raindrops hit the eastern-facing window.

Slowly, the remnants of the dream came back to me, and I remembered the cat.

I'd been walking through the evening fog in Scottsdale Park. Why was I in that park? I have no idea, except that I knew I had to be somewhere for an appointment, and I was running late. I usually pride myself on punctuality, so I was hurrying, and that's when I saw the cat for the first time. Pale gray, ghostlike almost, and it was big. "*A keeper,*" as my mother would have said if she were still alive. I am generally not prone to being hysterical, but the cat looked evil for some reason. Is that too strong a word? No, I don't think so, and you wouldn't either if you'd seen it.

The damn thing was sneering at me. Yes, I know what you're thinking, but I swear it was. It sat in the middle of the path as if waiting for me, twenty feet away. I veered to my right to go around, and it got up and took three steps to its left, then sat down again to block my path.

A tremor ran through me. It just felt like, for want of a better word, Kerflooey. Like all my senses were tingling as if the damn cat could look into my soul, and it didn't like what it saw.

Please remember, this was a dream, *but I didn't know that until* later when I woke up.

I stopped in my tracks, staring into the feline's Lucifer eyes. Then, crablike, I took four steps to my left. It slowly shook its head as if saying, "N*o, no, no, my bucko. You will not pass."* I watched it stand, turn to its right, and take up another position in front of me again.

I admit I was frightened. I never really liked cats because my family had always been into dogs. My grandparents used to breed award-winning Terriers, and people came hundreds of miles to buy them. Dad had a beautiful Irish Red Setter as we grew up, and my elder brother and his wife much later had two gorgeous poodles, so none of us ever had cats.

Oh, this is ridiculous. I'm running late, so I'm just going to kick the bloody thing out of my way.

I took two steps forward, and the cat stood up on its hind legs, hissed as if flames were about to come out of its mouth, and bared its claws at me. I thought it was going to leap at me, rip my throat out, and eat my larynx. I stepped back, tripped, and landed heavily on my ass, and that's when I woke up.

****

Why did that dream scare me so much? Even as I sat in bed, the raindrops sounded heavier by the minute, and I *knew* I was awake and safe. I could feel my heart pounding. Was it the cat? No, I realized it wasn't so much the animal as the fact that it was trying to stop me from getting to my appointment—but what appointment and why?

I swung my legs out of bed while my right hand reached for the base of the touch-sensitive lamp, and the room flooded with light. I took a deep breath, then another. *For goodness's sake, grow up, you chicken shit. Hello, it was just a stupid dream.* I got up, went to the bathroom, relieved myself, and returned to bed. The clock glared *12:03*, but it was no longer flashing.

****

The rest of the night was uneventful and true to form; the alarm woke me at six with a pop song. I did all my usual chores and was out of the apartment by seven. Driving in the early morning traffic, I attempted to remember more about the dream, but it was as if the closer I tried to get, the farther away I felt myself sliding. *Typical of bloody dreams,* I mused. *They never make much sense, and when they do, you can't remember them half an hour after waking.* I'm not sure why it bothered me, yet it did. That damned ghostly-looking cat had scared the bejesus out of me, though I wouldn't admit that to anyone out loud.

I consider myself to be normal in most senses of the word. I'm twenty-six, single, well, at least for another two weeks, and then I'm getting married to Amber Golightly. Weird name, Golightly, and I think Amber will be delighted to become Amber Cousins, which is my name. I guess I'm reasonably good-looking. I don't smoke, take drugs, or get violent when drunk. I work out three times a week at the gym, and I eat healthily, so I am not overweight.

I'm not saying I am a significant catch, though Amber tells me I am. Of course, she is biased. We've been seeing each other for three years, and I adore her. We had already set the date and announced our plans before Amber discovered she was expecting our child. Being a strict Catholic, she was not taking birth control pills, and we used condoms. How did it happen? We have no idea, but we were both delighted with the news. She is a physiotherapist and is currently in Sydney working with the National swim team at a training camp for the next Olympics.

All too soon, I arrived at my job as an architect at Michael Jones and Sons, and the dream did what all bad dreams should do: faded from my memory as I became engrossed with my tasks.

Chapter 2

"For God's sake, get that cat away from me!" I screamed out loud both in the dream and, I realized on waking. At least, I think I said it out loud because I was sitting up and had no recollection of doing that.

I became aware of an eerie flashing green glow and turned to the alarm clock. This time, it wasn't flashing *12:01*, but *12:02*. Did that mean I woke up one minute later than last night, or had the clock been flashing for two minutes?

I shook my head to clear it of inconsequential babble. The damned clock wasn't the problem. The recurring dream with the cat from hell terrorizing me was.

I flopped back onto my pillows, rubbed the sweat from my forehead, and took a deep breath as I remembered.

I was back in Scottsdale Park, and that's the first problem right there. I've never even heard of Scottsdale Park, let alone been there. *It's just a dream, you idiot, not real life; get a grip.* Thus began a conversation between the pragmatic side of my brain and the more hysterical.

Okay, I get it, it's a sodding dream, but it didn't feel like a dream, and what is it with the continuation from last night? If you can answer that, tell me what is with the fucking cat attacking me again?

He didn't attack you. He jumped at you, and you

woke up.

That's semantics, and you damn well know it. If I hadn't woken up, the fucking cat would have clawed my throat out.

Jonathon, do you think you're being a little bit overdramatic? It's a dream, nothing more. You do know dreams aren't real, don't you?

I shook my head to clear it. Yes, I knew dreams were some sort of rationalization between the conscious and subconscious sides of the brain. But the fact was, tonight's dream was not just a recurrence of last night but a continuation.

"Oh my God." I sat up once again. "Yes, it's a continuation; that's why the clock flashed one minute later. That was the extra time it took the cat to jump at me when I fell."

Okay, the train is now leaving the station for the lunatic asylum. Are you listening to yourself, Jonathon?

All right, smart ass. What's your explanation?

I've given it to you, but let me repeat for the feeble-minded among us. It is nothing more than a dream. Now, go back to sleep. You have that meeting with the Cuthbertsons tomorrow to build their McMansion.

I glanced at the clock: *12:05.* Thankfully, it had stopped flashing.

****

Somehow, I did go back to sleep, and the cat left me alone for the rest of the night. Before I knew it, the alarm was playing another pop song, birds were singing in the trees, the sun was shining, and it was a brand-new day. But when I looked in the mirror as I shaved, I saw the hint of shadows forming under my eyes.

****

Last night, before the second installment of my nightmare, after a hasty dinner of lamb chops, fries, and baked beans, I spent over two hours on a video call with Amber. I won't go into specifics about our sex life, but suffice it to say that we got hot and heavy, and it was satisfying for us both.

We spoke about the upcoming wedding and how Amber's mother had commandeered the final arrangements during Amber's absence, for which I was grateful. My parents had died in a car accident four years ago. I liked her mum, June. Amber's father, a Catholic priest, had passed away several years before, and June seemed to approve of me as a suitor for her daughter. For me, June had become my surrogate mother, and we got along well. We still hadn't decided on a name for our baby, but as we had almost six months before the birth, we had plenty of time.

I hadn't mentioned my dream to Amber for a few excellent reasons. She was a cat lover, so some sort of evil talisman cat haunting my dreams could have caused her to think I was not quite the husband material she previously thought I was. Amber was also superstitious. For example, she wouldn't walk under ladders. If Amber spilled salt, she'd toss a pinch over her shoulder, and, worst of all, she had to have her *lucky mascots* with her before any of her "swimmers" took to the pool. Amber had *lucky panties* she had to wear before a meet, always put her left sock on before the right, and had to listen to a particular piece of music before a race. No, Amber was not the kind of person to share bizarre dreams of devil cats with, even though I had only had one dream at the time we spoke. The second came an hour or more after we hung up.

****

Somehow, I was able to go back to sleep, but it was a long time coming as my mind raced with what it all meant. I woke five minutes before the alarm and leaped out of bed as if it were on fire. I showered and dressed, not bothering to eat, as I don't think I could have kept it down.

I went to work, as usual, and my boss, a notorious "ladies' man," Tim Jones, asked if I had enjoyed a heavy night out on the town with my fiancée being away. I shook my head and asked why he thought that, and he replied it was because I looked like *death warmed up.* I thanked him for the compliment with a good-natured smile, not bothering to tell him about my recurring dreams of a maniacal cat, deciding to let him think whatever he chose.

Chapter 3

The clouds were gray and threatening as I walked through Scottsdale Park, hurrying to get to my appointment. At the feel of the first raindrops on my head, I clicked the latch of my umbrella, and it sprang open. I stopped suddenly. The gray cat pranced on the path ahead of me. Suddenly, I knew I had seen it before, but didn't understand at that point where. Somehow, I just knew it was evil and meant me harm if I tried to pass.

The cat stopped its pacing and glared at me with malevolent eyes that glowed red. Do cats have malevolent eyes? Trust me, this one did.

We stared at each other, sizing up each other's weaknesses. I took a moment to look around and noted nothing had changed as the recollection of my previous dreams flooded back. The lake was to my left, and the surface shimmered with the ripples caused by ducks searching for their next meal. A children's playground was to my right, and everywhere stood majestic blue gum trees that attracted an assortment of parrots and galahs.

I turned back, and my heart leaped from my chest to my throat. The cat had covered half the distance between us and calmly and steadfastly walked toward me. Suddenly, I remembered in my last dream how the damned cat had leaped at me, intending to scratch the heck out of me, and I was able to wake up before it did. Well, this time, I was armed. I closed the umbrella, never taking my eyes off my nightmare stalker, and shook it menacingly toward the gray ghost.

It stopped, stood up on its hind legs again, and screeched a long-drawn-out noise, the likes of which I had never heard in my life. It was a warning for me not to go any farther, but how I knew that was beyond my comprehension. I was running behind time for my appointment, and the stupid cat would make me even later, though I couldn't recall the purpose of the meeting I was hurrying to.

The umbrella had a metal prong on the tip. Sure, it wasn't sharp enough to stab someone to death, but I thought one good solid jab into the cat's flank should show it I meant business. This decrepit animal that looked like it hadn't eaten regular food for a week wasn't going to keep me from getting to...where? I hesitated while I struggled to remember that one thing...where was I going in such a hurry?

The cat darted at me as if it sensed my indecision. It flew under the umbrella, and before I could do or say a thing, it sank its teeth into my ankle, just above where my leather brogue ended.

"Fuck, fuck, fuck!" I screamed as the white-hot poker of pain lanced upward from my ankle.

****

The alarm clock flashed 12:03 as I sat up in bed and threw back the bedclothes with my left hand while my right hand hit the lamp, almost toppling it off the cabinet. The light radiating from it showed the puncture wounds in my skin—four perfect tiny holes with blood oozing from them.

****

If I said I freaked out, please understand that would

be one of the greatest understatements of all time. It doesn't even come close, but it's the only word I can think of.

I'm an architect. I deal in facts, numbers, linear equations, engineering specifications, and the like. What I do not hold any stead in is the supernatural.

How the hell can a bite in a dream appear in real life? I asked my other self to calm my pounding heart.

It's not a bite; it's stigmata.

It worked. Somewhere from my university period, submerged in my memory, was something I'd read or a movie I'd seen about demonic possession, where the protagonist had symbols that appeared on his skin. Could that be an explanation? What else made any kind of sense? Okay, I didn't have raised welts in the shape of satanic pentagrams. I had what looked remarkably like a fucking rabid cat bite, but still, it was an explanation I could live with, couldn't I?

Then, a much more severe thought from something else I dredged up hit me like a sledgehammer. An ex-girlfriend, Naomi, a wild child at heart, spoke to me about dreams. She insisted, and honestly, I had scoffed at the idea that you always woke up before you hit the ground when you were falling during a dream. If you didn't, you died in your sleep. With some sort of conspiratorial theory certainty, she said there was much evidence supporting that some people who died in their sleep did so because they had died simultaneously during a dream. Because she was in true wild child character and outstanding in bed, I didn't laugh at how ludicrous she sounded, but now, I wasn't so sure she was delusional. I had received a bite in a dream, and I was bleeding from it in real life.

I shook my head, noted the bloody clock had stopped flashing, and got up to find some antiseptic ointment.

Before I edged back into the realm of sleep, my last thought was: *Am I going stark-raving mad?*

Chapter 4

When I saw the cat sitting on the path ahead of me, I took off running—well, limping hurriedly, which would be more accurate—as I favored my aching foot toward the playground. I was determined that the bloody animal would not stop me from going to my destination, wherever that was, so I thought I would go around it.

I heard the cat screech in obvious anger. Yes, I know screech is not a descriptor you would associate with a cat, but it was neither a meow nor a hiss, so trust me, an angry screech describes the sound excellently.

The moment I left the path, I realized my mistake. The earlier torrential downpour had turned the grass into a quagmire, and it was like I was running through molasses. Time seemed to fragment. I was loping along in slow motion and getting more sluggish by the second. The harder and faster I tried to run, the thicker the mud I was wading through seemed to become.

Then I heard the patter of rapidly approaching cat paws.

I dropped my attaché case in a blind panic and pinwheeled my arms to get more purchase. I had to get away from the cat.

I heard a sibilant hiss just as the sound of charging paws on mud stopped. Then, I felt a solid thump in my back, and razor-sharp claws pierced through my jacket and shirt and entered the skin on my back.

70

The cat's momentum hit me like a pummeling linebacker, and the depth of mud that felt knee-high combined to drive me forward. I fell face-first into the squishy grass and dirt, and I knew the cat would likely rip my neck out with its teeth.

****

The clock flashed *12:04.*

I lay, bathed in sweat, heart pounding, and I feared I might suffer a coronary. *What is going on with me?* For once, my other self didn't reply, so I posed a second question: *Am I going mad?* Silence was the only response.

****

After unsuccessfully finding sleep, half an hour later, with my laptop in front of me, I sat at my desk, contemplating how to pose the question to which I desperately sought an answer. How do you ask the all-knowing Internet Search Gods if a dream cat could be a harbinger of impending doom? Eventually, I typed:

Can dreams ever come true?

Oh, my good God! I was shown seven hundred and sixty thousand results. I just read a few headings, such as: *Dreams, Nightmares, and Lucid Dreaming; Why Dreams Can Come True;* and *Dreams Don't Come True-They Are True.* Even a popular news site had one titled *Hidden Truths in Dreams.* Right then, I suspected I was lost.

****

"What's wrong with you, Jonathon? Are you sick or something?" My boss asked when I arrived.

"Not sleeping well, Tim," I replied listlessly.

"Doh, you're just missing your lovely fiancée, or is it pre-wedding jitters?" He winked.

"Bit of both, probably."

"Well, she'll be back soon, mate. By the way, you must have made a big impression on the Cuthbertsons. She asked that you phone her this morning." He slapped me on the shoulder like I was a good puppy dog, and I smiled faintly, not wanting him to know how much I didn't particularly appreciate working for him. A job is a job, and in the current climate, architectural jobs are not growing on trees.

"I'll call her later. She probably just wants to change the kitchen layout for the thirteenth time."

****

In the sanctity of my office, with a coffee mug beside me, I opened the search pages on my laptop again and carried on reading where I'd left off at home.

There seemed to be a considerable amount of information about dreams, though not all of it was factual case studies. Still, enough knowledgeable people had done some serious work to make me sit up and take notice. The articles made me feel better about my situation. It was not that I understood what was happening to me, but at least I didn't feel like I had to be committed to the funny farm anytime soon.

I read about sleep disorders and studies, recalling that I'd seen an ad on a notice board for volunteers to attend a sleep study when I was at university. Successful candidates would receive forty dollars per night, and the program ran for a month. I didn't have a girlfriend at the time, so I was one of the four hundred students who thought it was fantastic to be paid to go to sleep. Sadly, the professor only needed thirty people, so I didn't get to be a Guinea pig.

There was a wealth of research on sleep, quality, and

quantity required for a healthy lifestyle. As interesting as that was, I didn't think I had a sleep problem, just a dream one. I wasn't particularly stressed or worried about anything in my life. I found my soul mate in Amber and was excited to be getting married soon. That meant I couldn't see any possibility of the dreams being part of psychosis or a mental health problem I was facing, which my research led me to believe could have been a cause. So what did that leave? It was back to the supernatural realm.

The word "Astral" kept popping up on Google, and I reluctantly opened an article by Professor Samuel Peabody titled "*Astral Travelling: Controlling Your Dreams.*"

I have to say, when I began reading, I was a skeptic, and when I finished, I still was, but it was true I felt myself wavering. Mr. Peabody said that while dreams are the subconscious part of the mind trying to sort out the day's events, you can reach the Astral Plane through dreams, which is something else entirely. He suggested that practitioners could direct their travels and decide whom they wished to meet and what they wanted to achieve there. It is possible to choreograph your dreams. It was an instant kind of travel, meaning you could, if you wanted to, go to Russia, Birmingham, or Outer Mongolia to meet a similar practitioner if you directed yourself.

Was it all rubbish, as I rather suspected it was? Even if it wasn't, how could understanding Astral Travel help me? I had no idea and was already dreading the thought of going to sleep later that night.

****

"Jonathon Cousins," I answered the phone,

reluctantly dragging myself from my reading of dreamscapes and nightmares.

"Hello, Jonathon, It's Martha Cuthbertson. I left a message for you to call earlier."

She sounded a little peeved, and when I looked at my watch, I realized why. It was 11:35. "Hi, Martha," I responded. "Please forgive me. I've had a bit of an emergency here and was just about to pick up the phone and call you, but you beat me to it. How can I help you?"

"I forgive you, Jonathon." I imagined her smiling because Tim was sure she fancied me. "Max and I are so impressed with your work on the home you're designing for us that we wondered if you could remodel an old house we've bought, which we want to give to our daughter as a wedding present."

A house for a wedding present? Amber's mother could barely afford a toaster. I sighed silently, not wishing one of the wealthiest women in the West to think I was rude.

"Martha, we tend to do large home and commercial new builds. We're not set up for renovation projects. I could recommend someone I think would suit you."

"Yes, Mr. Jones said the same thing when I asked if he wouldn't mind if we asked to consult with you privately. He agreed and said your time was limited now with your wedding and honeymoon coming up. He tells me you are also expecting a baby. We want to meet your bride-to-be. The thing is, Max and I are extremely impressed with your vision and imagination, so we agreed to ask if you could look through the place and tell me what you think we could do with it. Of course, we would be willing to pay you directly for your time. We're not trying to be cheapskates. Bill us whatever you think is a fair consultancy fee. Money is no object because we know you will be honest."

Well, what could I say to that? I asked her to email me any building plans and drawings, and I would talk to her in a day or two to arrange a site visit. Some time later, Martha's comment about wanting to meet Amber came back to me, and I wondered why she had said that. But with the nightmares going on, causing loss of sleep, I decided it wasn't important.

Chapter 5

Perhaps because of my excessive study time on all things Astral, I knew I was dreaming when I peered around the trunk of an ancient Red Gum tree in the park to see if I could spot the cat before he saw me. He or she, I had not been able to discern its sex and didn't care either way, was prancing back and forth across the path. It looked like it was waiting for me, and it looked pissed. Suddenly, it stopped and jerked its head around, and I ducked back behind the trunk, my heart pounding.

The fucking thing saw me. How the hell did it know I was here? Now, what do I do? My mind raged in overdrive.

Why not just wake up? I replied, then closed my eyes, shook my head, and opened them again.

Nope, it's not working; I'm still here. Any other bright ideas?

Look, dummy, it's just a cat. What are you so scared of? Just walk up, kick it out of the way, and get to...to...wherever the fuck I'm going in such a hurry?

I took a long, slow, calming breath and took another peek around the tree again.

Hissssssss. *The cat had crept up on my hiding place and launched itself at me, claws out. It would be on my face in a second, biting and scratching.*

****

The green numerals flashed their welcome call:

12:05. I was back in the land of the living, sweating profusely and very glad to be alive. I raised my trembling hands to my face, expecting them to come away covered in blood, but it was just sweat. I released the pent-up breath I didn't realize I was holding, swung my legs out of bed, and shook my head.

****

The sun rose agonizingly slowly as I sat on the balcony sipping coffee. I had not gone back to sleep, not just because I feared meeting the cat again. I had been studying because I knew I had to find some way of fighting back, but I didn't know how.

No amount of logic brought me comfort, but I had to try. Firstly, Scottsdale Park: I found it. It comprised around three acres in Blencowe Heights, one of the oldest locales in the city, and not an area that I was overly familiar with. My family hailed from the rural town of Wutherington, three hours north of the city, where I came to study for my degree and stayed when I won the position at Jones and Sons. I had never visited anywhere in Blencowe. I didn't need to; it is North of the River, and my apartment and workplace are South.

Next, I researched the subject of cats known to attack humans and found some surprising tales. Generally, the attacks were carried out by feral felines or abandoned domestic cats, which had to learn to fend for themselves. Often, their jaws had grown longer, their teeth sharper, and they possessed more muscle tone because they had to hunt for food. I had noticed no such aberrations on my nightmare monster. For many years, the legend of a black panther, an escapee from a circus, had been a popular myth. It had supposedly been seen roaming the forest county around Pembroke at various times. It had been credited with attacks on children and one abduction of a baby, which led to a famous trial when a young, depressed mother was charged with murdering her baby but blaming it on the Pembroke Panther. What did that have to do with a cat attacking me in my dreams to keep me from my appointment? I had no idea, but it was a place to start and showed me that cats could be fearless and fight human beings in some circumstances.

I also searched under the subject line: *cats warning of impending danger,* but that hadn't been overly helpful.

****

Much to Tim's annoyance, I took some personal time off work and drove to Blencowe Heights. Nervously, I parked the Toyota Corolla in the gravel car park, locked it, and walked toward the lake. The weather was cloudy and cold, with the threat of rain, so I carried my umbrella. If the cat was waiting for me, I didn't have any plan to deal with it, but I knew I had to confront my fear rather than run away from it. Plus, I had to discover what appointment I was trying to get to in my dream that the cat was insistent I miss.

An hour later, a gentle rain began to fall, and I was alone in the park as I headed back to the car. I had discovered nothing of interest. There wasn't anything different or unusual about the gardens. A marauding feline, intent on ripping me apart, didn't confront me, so all in all, I felt depressed. For the hundredth time, I asked myself why I was dreaming of this place and why the cat was trying so hard to force me to miss an appointment in the dream. Shrugging once more, I decided to go to work.

Just as I got back to the car, a heavier rain started to

fall, and as I opened the door, I heard a long, drawn-out *meeeoooooowwwwww* coming from the direction I'd just left. I stopped as the raindrops fell on my head, wondering if I had imagined it or whether I should go back and investigate further. A sudden flash of forked lightning decided me, and I hurried inside my car and started the engine.

Chapter 6

"My God, Jonathon, you look terrible. Are you unwell?" Amber asked that night after dinner as we began our video call.

"Thanks, darling. You look fantastic, too. Pregnancy agrees with you," I said, smiling because she *did* look fantastic. I felt more tired than at any time in my life. "To be honest, Amber, I'm not sleeping well. For some stupid reason, I've been having some bad dreams night after night since you've been gone."

"Awww, do you miss me that much?"

I grinned. "You know it, babe. I need one of your special massages to help get me to sleep."

"Hmmm, well, I'm not back for another few days for one of those, but let us see what we can do tonight by remote control. Let's get naked."

Amber peeled her top off, and I marveled at her beautiful breasts.

****

During our very satisfying call, time flew, and by the time we ended, it was after ten thirty. I devised a plan to break the cycle and decided not to go to sleep until after midnight. I figured that six hours of quality sleep, if I went to bed after the witching hour, would be better than going before and waking up terrified, as I had for the previous few nights.

Granted, that wasn't perhaps the best idea in the

world, and I felt a bit like I had become a coward, but it made sense. I figured if I could disrupt the dream flow, which always seemed to happen around the same time but incrementally increased one minute a night, I could enjoy going to bed once more. Indeed, I knew I had to get some closure before Amber and I started our married life together, and we shared a bed again.

I made some popcorn in the microwave, settled on the couch, and switched on the TV. I found a science fiction movie I hadn't seen and settled down to watch it.

****

The fog had rolled in on the back of the earlier rain, and I pulled my coat tighter around my body as I hurried along the path. Somewhere off to my left, a duck landed in the lake, making a splashing noise. To my right, a cat mewed as if to reply. I stopped in my tracks, suddenly feeling a sense of dread, and realized if I went any farther, the cat would once again know I had arrived and would no doubt attack me.

Wait, wait, wait a minute. I'm not asleep. I'm on the couch watching a movie. Then I groaned as it dawned on me that because I had been so tired, I had nodded off. I closed my eyes and could see my inert body leaning back in the corner of the couch, head lolled to one side, softly snoring. You bloody idiot, now what do I do?

I looked back along the path, and there sat the cat, twenty meters away, and I swear it was smiling. Slowly, it stood and began walking toward me, a look of pure evil in its burning eyes.

I turned and ran like the hounds of hell were chasing me because, so far as I was concerned, this was a cat from hell.

I dropped my case, which caused me to run

awkwardly and unbalanced. As I did, my right foot trod on a felled branch. My ankle twisted, and I fell face-first. My hands took the brunt of my weight as I slid along, and I felt the instant heat from the graze across my palms.

****

I woke, my body jerking upright on the couch, and staggered to my feet. The movie was still playing, and the flickering light from the TV illuminated my way to the bedroom doorway. I rounded the doorframe and stared at the clock, knowing the time it would show. The green display flashed *12:06.*

****

I bathed my aching hands, which fortunately weren't bleeding under the cold running tap, but they hurt as if they were. I stared at my reflection in the mirror above the bathroom sink and was shocked at my red and puffy eyes. I had to get some sleep.

I dried my hands, turned off the light, and stumbled to bed. Surprisingly, I slept until the alarm woke me with its happy music.

Chapter 7

I've always been a logical-thinking man, so as I ate my toast and drank my coffee the following day, I attempted to find some reason for what was happening. If I took any form of supernatural occurrence out of the equation, what did that leave? Mental instability? I shook my head and discounted it. There was no history of any mental health issues in my family. I'd not suffered a blow to the head and couldn't think of a reason why, suddenly, I should be admitted for psychological evaluation. I then reasoned that maybe my mind was playing tricks on me without necessarily becoming a schizophrenic or anything serious of that nature. Was it because Amber was away, and that was linked to stress about our upcoming wedding? Maybe the impending birth of our first baby was causing a sleep disorder? I decided to consult a doctor that day, just in case, but it still didn't feel like that was the cause of my recurring dreams and the devil cat's part in them. As an explanation, it seemed too trite, too perfect, but I shrugged and bit another piece of toast off. What did I know?

The next question I asked myself was, why a cat? Not that I hated cats, but I certainly didn't overly like them either. Could it be a symbol for something else in my subconscious? Suddenly, a vision hit me like a slap on the face. *Noooo, it can't be. That is just too stupid to contemplate. No, no, no, that's ridiculous.*

****

I tried my best to forget the stupid notion during the day at work, but it came roaring back to me just after lunch when I noticed I had an email from Mrs. Cuthbertson. I grinned at the stupidity of it all and opened the message.

Dear Jonathon

I have attached the building plans for the property we bought for Sylvia's wedding present, and would be delighted if you could take a look and give us your thoughts on how we can make it beautiful and restore some of its former glory. You see, the house hasn't been lived in for several years after the previous owners died (apparently in a murder-suicide), and the children who inherited it spent years in litigation.

The building has three floors and a huge cellar that we thought might make a unique wine cellar, bar, and entertaining room—though, knowing you, you will have far better ideas than that. Typical of the area, it is of stone construction with a slate roof and comprises fourteen rooms. Naturally, before settlement, we had a structural report done, and we're pleased to report that the house's "bones" are solid.

We hope our daughter and her husband will spend many happy years here and give us lots of grandchildren, especially after you bring it back to life with your incredible design ideas.

We know you will wonder what budget you have. We were thinking about around three hundred thousand, plus your project management fees, but if you think we need more, say the word.

King regards

Martha and Max Cuthbertson

I sat back in my chair, still feeling the grin on my face, and thought about Martha. A glamorous woman, trying to hold on to the last vestiges of her looks, was overweight but had the money to dress to hide it. I recalled the first time we met. She wore a gray fur coat, which made her look more rounded than she was, and she had recently had her hair done in an ash-blonde color. The sunlight streaming through from the windows made it look gray. When we shook hands, I noticed her nails had been manicured but were long and claw-like. All in all, in a weird way, she resembled the cat from my dream. I laughed at the absurdity and opened the attachment.

The plans reflected a typical mansion of the era. It had high vaulted ceilings, large open reception and entertaining rooms, four bathrooms, and two dining rooms. The bedrooms looked reasonable in size, and the entire house had a huge footprint. I wondered if Martha's comment, "Restore some of its former glory," meant they had hopes of restoration rather than modernization. I hoped for a combination of the two: a modernization in keeping with the romantic era of when it was built. The plans didn't highlight the cellar definition well, but the thought intrigued me. One thing was for sure: I needed to perform a lengthy site visit, but I wasn't sure when I could do that and not let it interfere with my day job. I decided to let it rest for a few days and worry about it then. In the interim, I replied to the email and asked Martha if she could arrange a courier service to deliver a set of keys to gain access.

****

Inevitably, as the day wore on, my thoughts returned

to *the dream* and what tonight's installment would entail. I realized there were two other reasons why the dreams were so unusual, at least to me. For all I knew, many other people could remember every detail of a recurring dream and *knew they were dreaming it at the time.* Was that normal? Thus far, before the first night, I could never make sense of my dreams, and that was if I even remembered them. Often, they had jumbled-up things that defied all logic, and I certainly couldn't remember a time when I knew I was dreaming. I debated returning to the internet for more research, but couldn't see the point, despite my worry. Whatever I was going through, I believed the only way to understand it was to take the bit between the teeth, get back into the dream head-on, and confront the cat.

****

I stood behind the gum tree again and shivered as the mist swirled around my legs. The rain fell ever-present, threatening as if it might pour down any second. In the distance, there was the peal of thunder, and the wind suddenly picked up. I heard the mournful tolling of a bell at midnight. That was a first. There had been no sound of a bell before in my dream. Yes, I knew I was dreaming, almost a dream within a dream. For the first time, I didn't fear the cat, which I knew was waiting for me. I wondered why.

My right hand felt heavy, and I realized it wasn't due to holding my briefcase, as I had in the past. Now, I held something different, something cold, solid, and cylindrical. I lifted my hand, and in the glimmer of distant streetlight and filtered moon between the storm clouds, I saw I was holding a baseball bat. Come and get me, Martha. I'm ready for you.

Martha? Where is that coming from? I asked myself with a stupid grin on my face.

I gripped the bat in both hands and made a couple of small practice swings. Baseball and softball were not my favorite sports during school, but the bat felt strangely comforting.

"C'mon, you bitch, come and get me now!" I said as I stepped around the tree to see nothing.

The path lacked a maniacal gray cat, and I felt disappointed. I took two steps, holding my bat in a ready position like a samurai swordsman, but I was alone—or so I thought.

Suddenly, I heard the cat's screech of rage—yes, pure, unadulterated anger—coming from above me. I looked up as the beast leaped from an overhanging branch, claws reaching for my face like a gray Puma, and I knew I had made a terrible mistake in underestimating Martha.

****

The clock flashed its eerie green light as I sat up, screaming, fighting the imaginary cat off my shredded and bleeding face: *12:07.*

Chapter 8

There was no more sleep for me that night. Quite simply, I was terrified that if I did drift off again, I would not wake up because I would be flayed alive. Yes, I know that was ridiculous, the logical part of my brain told me, but the more powerful subconscious knew better.

Yeah, try sleeping again tonight, it said in a smug, all-knowing voice. *Even if you do wake up, try repeating your wedding vows with a bleeding, disfigured face— that is, if Amber will still marry you with a face that looks like it had a close encounter with a cheese grater.*

The mental image of a cheese grater shredding my fingertips as they held the cheese block had always been a phobia of mine since childhood. I got up, made a pot of green tea, and sat at my desk, pondering the insanity of my situation. *How long is this going to go on?*

Suddenly, I knew the answer somehow, and the realization chilled me from head to toe. *At thirteen past midnight, you will die if you don't solve the mystery by then.*

Nonsense, utter rubbish! But was it? Why would I even think that I would die in five days at thirteen minutes after midnight? Yet, I knew it was true. Worse than the chilling certainty, I didn't have the faintest idea of how to avoid it.

Around 3:00 a.m., I recalled something from the dream that made me sit up suddenly. As horrible as it had been, I replayed the scene frame by frame, like a slow-motion movie. As the cat sprang its trap and jumped from the branch, I distinctly remember thinking I had underestimated Martha. *Martha? Martha Cuthbertson?* That was just a stupid throwaway and humorous thought I'd had because of the gray fur coat she wore at our first meeting. Maybe my subconscious was pulling a gray cat from somewhere, but it could not be Martha. After all, she liked me, even Tim said that, and I wasn't sure he was my biggest supporter. *Nah, it was just my overheated imagination, nothing more than that.*

I spent most of the night scouring the internet for more help, but didn't find anything conclusive. At some point, I rested my head on my forearms, and the next thing I knew, it was seven in the morning, and I realized I had slept without dreaming. Startled, I jumped up, fearing I'd be late for work, but then remembered it was a Saturday, my day for doing my bachelor's chores. Breakfast first, then cleaning, washing, and later I would do my shopping.

****

Sometimes, things happen for no reason; other times, they happen because they are supposed to, or so it seems. On my way back from the mall with my week's worth of groceries, I passed a traveling circus and fair, and a gaudily painted sign took my eye: PSYCHIC FAIR - *ALL WELCOME.* Then, below it, in smaller letters, it said: *FORTUNE TELLING AND TAROT READINGS.*

Well, it can't hurt, can it? I asked myself, but for once, the other side of my brain refused to answer. I had tried all the logical searches for information; why not check out the silly ones, I thought, grinning.

I found a convenient parking spot, locked the car,

hoping my groceries wouldn't spoil, and strode with purpose to the entry and paid my fee. There were large and small tents, carousels, funfair games of skill, and smaller marquees on each side of the path, along with stalls that sold hot dogs, popcorn, and doughnuts. I felt good, as if visiting the fair had lifted my spirits. There were laughing children with their parents, eating ice cream or candy. Everyone seemed to enjoy a day at the fair. I spotted a tent that announced twenty dollars for a palm reading and thought that was as good a place to start as any.

A rather elderly but attractive woman stood out front, wearing a long black dress that billowed around her like a wedding dress would, although there seemed a minimal breeze to move it. She saw me heading toward her and smiled. I noticed her somewhat oversized emerald-green eyes. "C'mon in and let Lady Violet tell you your future, young man. Only twenty dollars. Learn what the gods tell me they have planned for you." She grabbed my upper arm in a vice-like grip as I drew level.

I decided to have a little fun with the gypsy-like woman. "How about ten dollars?"

She laughed uproariously and pulled me inside her tent before I knew what was happening. "Man," she began, "would you haggle with someone who can foretell your future? Me might just tell you the bad things coming and forget about the good."

"Okay, twenty dollars it is. I could do with some good news."

She pointed to a wooden chair on one side of a small vintage round table for me to take while she sat on another chair opposite me. I removed a crisp twenty-dollar note from my wallet and placed it on the table without waiting to be asked, somehow knowing I had to pay before her act, not after. Lady Violet tucked the note into a small bag at her waist, then reached across the table, pointing at my left hand.

At first, she looked puzzled as she studied the lines in my palm, but that soon became a look of pity, which then changed to horror. "*Psssst*," she wailed and dropped my hand as if it suddenly became hot. "Sorry, sorry, me no help you, here take your money back, leave my tent, pleeeeze." She yanked open her bag again, took the note back out, and almost threw it at me.

"Hang on, Lady V, tell me what's wrong. Why isn't my money good enough?"

"Nothing wrong, you go, leave me be, me have to close up, have headache." She crooked her fingers in a sign that I recalled from somewhere, meant to give protection from the evil eye.

I folded my arms across my chest. "I'm not going anywhere until you tell me what you saw that's wrong with my future."

She looked frantically from side to side, looking for help or an escape, but I sat between her and the opening in the tent. There was no escape there. She shook her head, but I just sat and stared back. Eventually, she sighed, then beckoned me to give her my hand again. Her grip was cold and hard enough to draw blood if she extended her nails. With her other hand, she pointed at my palm. "You no have a lifeline, you already dead, you just don't know it. Take your money back, you no have a future."

****

After an early dinner, I spoke with Amber briefly. She was going out to a function with the swim team and would be late back to the hotel. "Jonathon, you look like death warmed up on a plate. What on earth is wrong?"

I didn't want to burden her with my woes when she was going out to dinner with dignitaries on a Saturday night, so I glossed over it. "Nothing, babe. I'm not sleeping well because I think I'm coming down with the flu. I will drink a hot lemon and honey and go to bed early. I've got to get better for the wedding." I gave her my best smile.

"You better be well for our wedding night, Buster. I have big plans for you in bed that night; you'll need all your strength."

We chatted about things for ten minutes, and then she went to prepare for her big night out, leaving me alone with my thoughts. I had avoided overthinking about the fortune teller's words since I stormed out of the tent. Besides the dreams that plagued me, I was as fit as a fiddle, so what did a missing skin crease in my palm matter? Indeed, fortune-telling was all stuff and nonsense, surely? Still, it had been a scary experience in a week of frightening events. The only correlation I could see between my lack of a lifeline and the dreams was the deep-seated fear that it would all end when I wouldn't wake up from the thirteenth nightmare if I couldn't solve the mystery.

While driving home, I devised a plan of sorts, though I had no idea how successful it would be. Recalling my previous studies on Astral travel and the fact that I had unknowingly taken a baseball bat into my dream the night before, I remembered that exponents could imagine whatever they wanted. In the dream world, it became real, so I would go to bed and imagine with all my willpower that I had a gun. If it worked, I was going to shoot the damned cat dead and get my life back.

****

I was back behind the tree, my heart pounding, a stiff breeze in my face, as the dappled moonlight filtered through the branches. I felt different, heavier somehow, yet more confident. My head felt strange, as if there was a binding around it. I reached up and discovered I was wearing a cowboy hat.

"What the hell?" I looked down and almost laughed out loud. I would have if I hadn't been so scared of the cat. Before bed, I had watched an old Western movie on the Classics Channel, Gunfight at El Dorado. I had wanted a gun in my dream, and I now had two of them in leather holsters at my hips. I also wore chaps over denim jeans and a checkered shirt. I was a fully fledged cowboy. Despite my fear, I realized how funny it was and how typical of dreams that things were rarely straightforward.

Remembering the night before the cat had leaped at me from the branches above, I hurriedly moved away from the trunk onto the path as I drew the ancient-looking Colt .45 from the right-hand holster.

The cat sat on its haunches twenty meters away, and I swear it had a smug, self-satisfied look on its face. It stood, shook its head from side to side, and hissed at me. Suddenly, it lurched to its paws and ran at me. Calmly, I raised the pistol and pulled the trigger. Nothing happened. I panicked and pulled the trigger again, but still nothing.

The damned cat had covered half the distance, and it sneered at me, still hissing, and suddenly, thank goodness, I recalled that this model pistol was a single-

action. I had to cock the firing pin first. I did that with my thumb, but now I was trembling as I pulled the trigger. The gun boomed, the cat zigged to the left, and the bullet missed by a long way. I jerked back the firing pin again, telling myself to calm down. I shot and missed yet again. For the third time, I yanked back the pin just as the cat leaped at my throat, and I fired point-blank.

****

The clock flashed *12:08* as I woke, sweat oozing from every pore. I only just made it to the toilet to vomit.

Chapter 9

It was Sunday. I had eventually drifted back to a night of dreamless sleep, woke at ten, then groggily got up and made a breakfast of bacon and eggs. I was ravenous. I sent Amber a text message of love, hoping she had a fantastic night and hadn't had too much to drink. Her lack of immediate reply suggested she might have still been sleeping, and I grinned because Amber did love red wine. Although being pregnant, she hadn't had alcohol and promised she wouldn't. At least, I hoped she was sleeping off a late night, alone, and not in bed with a muscle-bound swimming champion. I shrugged. Of course, she was alone, wasn't she?

****

I drove to Scottsdale Park at lunchtime on a whim, though it was considerably out of my way. The day was one of those incredible spring days that made you glad to be alive, even as tired as I felt, with the temperature warm and the sun beaming.

I drove around the outside of the park, and I must admit to feeling safe inside the Toyota, knowing no matter how fierce the cat was, if it existed in the real world, it couldn't get at me. Stupid thought? You bet, but I was running on ragged nerves. I was also unsure whether I had successfully killed the damn beast or, more likely, missed as I woke up before the bullet hit.

I was driving along Edwards Street, which bordered

the park's northern side, alternating my view of the rolling green grass that stretched toward the lake, gum trees on my left, and the road ahead in case an errant child ran out in front of me. I slammed on my brakes. *Noooooo, it can't be, can it? No way, no freakin way,* my mind screamed.

I put the car into reverse and carefully returned the way I had come. I swerved into a parking spot and looked at the street sign on my right: *Ivanhoe Crescent*. Now, where had I seen that street before? I knew, of course, but I didn't want to give in to paranoia without being entirely sure of my facts. I remembered reading the address on Martha's plans: 19 Ivanhoe Crescent, Blencowe Heights, the house she wanted me to remodel.

I don't know how long I sat in the car, my mind racing, questioning, disbelieving, and yes, panicking. Nothing made sense, but eventually, it dawned on me that it did make sense in the stupid way dreams have. Throughout my life, on the occasions I could remember my dreams upon waking, they were always oblique, like they were *trying* to make sense but failing dismally. And that was the situation I thought I had here. Martha wanted me to design and project manage a significant home renovation for their daughter. In some stupid, subconscious way, she resembled a gray cat at our first meeting, and now a cat was trying to stop me from getting to the house. Weirdly, it worked when viewed in the way that dreams have of being mixed up and disjointed.

Okay, Jonathon, but here's the big question: Why?

Well, obviously, I don't know why, I replied to my other self, *but I'm going to find out. Tomorrow, Martha will send me the keys, and then I will check the house out for myself.*

****

Back at the apartment, I used my trusty laptop to research number nineteen Ivanhoe Crescent. Instantly, a newspaper story popped up from nine years ago:

Friday the 13th of February 2012

Bizarre Murder/Suicide in Blencowe Heights - the Home with a Colorful History.

by

Stephen Blaine

Last night, police and ambulance officers were called to a historical home in Blencowe Heights and found a chilling scene more at home in a horror film than a stately area of founding fathers' houses. Number 19 Ivanhoe Crescent has stood for over a hundred years and has had a checkered past of excess society parties, murder, and witchcraft.

Police are not giving many details, but sources have informed us that Mrs. Malcovoy was discovered tortured and chained to the wall in the cellar, and Mr. Malcovoy died kneeling in front of her. Police believe he murdered his wife before taking his own life in remorse.

The original owner, self-proclaimed "Witch" Lilian Pancras, had the home built to her specifications, including an extensive cellar adorned with mystical symbols and a mosaic floor including a pentagram. It is reputed that the basement was the scene of Black Sabbaths and other magical ceremonies while she resided there, though much was shrouded in secrecy. She was found hanging from the first-floor balcony, an apparent suicide victim after twelve years in residence. Various owners followed, including Lucy and Simon Balmoral, who disappeared and have never been seen since. The most notable owner, Gordon Lighthouse, son of famed newspaper magnate Hector Lighthouse, held many wild socialite parties, including the Halloween event where actress Marlene Snowden was found murdered and left in the fountain. No arrest was ever made for her killing. Lighthouse was a reputed drug dealer who died in a gun battle with rival criminals in the driveway of the house.

Brian Malcovoy purchased the home for his new wife, Delores, eleven years ago, but neighbors noticed the relationship was not going well within the last six months. Mrs. Malcovoy appeared at times with evidence of abuse, including bruises, and twice was hospitalized, though she refused to accuse her husband of mistreating her. Police have not revealed a motive but say inquiries are continuing.

I wasn't sure what to think after reading that and other articles of a similar bent. It appeared the house had some sort of mystical past, possibly even evil, though I hate to use that word. I'm not religious nor believe in spiritualism, so I couldn't see why or how the house had any bearing on the dreams, but something was going on, so that was as good a place to start as anywhere else.

****

Before going to bed, I watched a war movie, hoping it would influence the weapon I could wake up with while dreaming. I wished for a machine gun, automatic pistol, or even a bazooka to ward off the cat rather than the cowboy revolver from the previous night.

Earlier, I had caught up with Amber by phone, and she told me all about her night and her overindulgence without red wine. She enjoyed herself and made some excellent contacts with the Sports Institute and government officials, ensuring her tenure would be made permanent rather than contractual as it had been thus far. Amber was due to return before what I continued to think of as D-Day for me, or should that be D. Night? I missed Amber terribly and was determined that I would not succumb to whatever forces were trying to keep me from the house, and when she arrived at the airport at 3:00 p.m., I would be alive and able to meet her.

*****

The distant bell tolled midnight once again. I felt cold and realized the pouring rain had soaked through my clothes, and that's when I noticed what I was wearing. I almost laughed out loud, shaking my head as I recalled the film I watched before bed was a war film between America and Japan. Like the unpredictable dream building I was getting used to, I went to sleep hoping to be a heavily armed American, but instead, I was wearing a kimono with a sheathed sword in the sash at my waist.

I drew the blade out of its scabbard and stepped around the tree trunk, ready to face my nemesis. Strangely, I was confident with the curved sword in my hand even though, at the same time, I felt ridiculously dressed, especially as it was pouring with rain.

The cat was waiting for me, sitting in the middle of the path, but this time, it did not sprint toward me; it just sat and stared. Do I really want to kill Martha, the cat? I asked myself, and the answer came in a faint whisper: yesssss.

I took one step forward, and the cat turned to its left and hissed. I saw movement in the corner of my vision, turned, and out stepped another gray cat. It, too, hissed, and a third beast appeared from the other side of the path. Fear raced up and down my spine, tingling and making me feel even colder. One cat I might have dealt with, but three? I remembered an adage about bringing a knife to a gunfight. I had dreamed up a sword when a Kalashnikov would have been better. As one, the three cats bounded at me. I dropped the sword, turned tail, and ran.

****

I woke, panting. My ragged breaths lanced my chest as if I were being stabbed repeatedly. I sat up in bed, gulping air, and turned my head to the flashing clock: *12:09.*

Chapter 10

When I arrived at my office, I phoned Mrs. Cuthbertson, but my call went to her voicemail. I requested she call me as soon as she was able, and that I had some questions about the house after viewing the plans. Then I got down to work, desperate for a distraction.

Before I knew it, it was twelve and time for lunch, and she still hadn't called back. For some reason, that bothered me, but my logical brain said: *she's just busy, moron. A woman like that can't drop what she's doing to phone you.* I was probably right, so I left my office and went to the cafe around the corner for tacos and coffee.

****

When I got back, I asked the receptionist, Claire, if I'd received any messages. "Sorry, Jonathon. There was nothing for you. Were you expecting something?"

I shrugged. "I was, yes. Has a package with keys arrived for me?"

Claire had the biggest, darkest eyes I had ever seen. With her short black hair and bright red eye makeup, she was devastatingly beautiful and incredibly efficient. She shook her head slowly. "I will buzz you the moment anything turns up. That's the best I can do. Sorry."

Back at my desk, I tried again to call Martha, but it went to her voicemail again, so I left a second message. I hoped to go to the house after finishing work, but there was little point without keys, and with a sinking heart, I realized that would mean facing the cat again when I went to sleep.

****

I was about to leave the office just after five when my mobile phone sounded its cheery tone. "Hello?" I answered while tucking papers into my case.

"Jonathon, it's Martha Cuthbertson." Her voice sounded as if it were coming from the moon, so faint it was almost inaudible. "You left a message for me, but we are away in Bordertown, back in two days. What did you want?"

"I wanted to go and look at the house," I replied loudly, assuming it would be as hard for her to hear me as it was for me to hear her. "I like the plans you sent me and want to get a feel for the place from the inside. You were going to courier me a set of keys, but I haven't received them."

"Ahh, yes, sorry about that. Max made us leave before I could send them. How about we meet you there the day after tomorrow, say around eight? We will be back by then."

I nodded and was about to agree, but I suddenly realized that I couldn't do that. "No, I can't do it then. I'm sure I mentioned it to you, but my fiancée Amber flies back, and I'm keen to meet her at the airport. What about the following night, at the same time?"

"All right, I can do that. Max has his hellfire club get-together, but I will meet you there at eight. Why not bring your lovely wife-to-be? I'd love to meet her and get her feelings about the house. From what you've told me, she is around the same age as my daughter and is with child, so her mother's perspective will be invaluable."

"I will see if she wants to do that. I haven't mentioned it to her yet, but I think she will be interested to see such an old and prestigious house. See you then, Martha."

****

A peal of thunder shook the ground as it rocketed across the sky. The wind chilled me to the bone, though it hadn't been raining so far. I looked down at my attire and once again was shocked. I was wearing a black three-piece dinner suit with a white ruffled shirt and could feel a bow tie at my neck. My shoes glittered because they were highly polished, and I thought I resembled one of those sophisticated British spies. I raised my right hand and reached inside my jacket on a whim. Under the armpit sat a shoulder holster with what felt like an automatic pistol inside it.

Now you're talking. I grinned, took it out, and studied it in the next flash of lightning. I found a safety catch, clicked it off, slid the slide back, and heard the unmistakable click-clack noise of a round being chambered. Taking a shooter's stance, which I'd seen in TV shows and movies numerous times, I stepped around the tree.

The cat sat there, waiting for me, and calmly, I shot it dead. One bullet, dead center of its gray chest, and it toppled over. I was assailed by two competing feelings simultaneously. Firstly, I was euphoric; I had won, and the cat was dead. But I was also remorseful because I had murdered an animal. Yeah, okay, I was dreaming about that animal, and by the way, I knew I was dreaming, but I had cold-bloodedly shot it dead.

From my left, I heard a maniacal hiss. I turned my

head and saw a second cat, and boy, did it look pissed. Then, another screech from the right; there were two of them, and a further hiss from behind the dead one confirmed my worst nightmare. An additional three cats wanted me dead.

I shot at the one on my left as it advanced and missed. I fired again and hit it this time, but I knew it wasn't a kill shot. The one on my right was almost upon me, and as I turned, it was leaping for my throat. I fired point-blank, and while its momentum meant it hit my chest, it was dead when it did.

I breathed a sigh of relief just as the last cat landed on me. Its claws sank through my suit and shirt, and its teeth bared as it reached for my throat.

****

The clock flashed 1*2:10*.

Chapter 11

Further sleep eluded me until after 4:00 a.m. when I drifted off on the couch, laptop open at my latest time-wasting search for information. There wasn't anything that I could point to and have a "eureka moment," and so understand what was happening to me. There was nothing I could find to help. I was on my own.

When I shaved in the morning, I looked into my bloodshot eyes and realized the depth of my troubles. I could not go on this way. Something had to give, and I hoped and prayed it wouldn't be my sanity. I tried to focus on Amber's face and found that I felt *normal,* whatever that was. She was my rock, my reason for living, and she was coming home tomorrow. I couldn't let her see me like this. While she did have her apartment, which she shared with her girlfriend, Sasha, undoubtedly Amber would want to spend her first night back with me, as I did with her, but what did that mean for tomorrow's dream? I shrugged the fear off and got ready for work. Nightmare or no nightmare, I wanted to make love with Amber. I had missed her terribly, and maybe that was the heart of my troubled sleep.

Somehow, I got through the day and only dozed off twice at my desk. Luckily, I didn't get caught doing so. That would have been too embarrassing.

Amber and I had a brief call, but it was her last night, and the senior coaches planned a special farewell dinner and an awards ceremony. I mentioned Martha Cuthbertson's invitation to come and look at the house, and as expected, Amber was very interested in a period home that required modernization. She agreed instantly, and I summarized my initial thoughts and included the unique cellar, complete with a mosaic pentagram-designed floor.

"A pentagram? Was the house originally used for black magic ceremonies?" she asked, and I noted the change in tone of her voice.

I told her of my research on the house, but not the dreams that caused it. She ended the call rather abruptly, saying she had to dash to get to the dinner venue, and I felt as if there were things she wanted to say but hadn't the time. For a fleeting moment, I wondered if she wanted to tell me she had been unfaithful while away, and the doubts I kept buried tried to surge to the surface again. Why had she been uncontactable the night of the dinner? Maybe she was late to rise in the morning because she had "company."

****

"Where are we?" Amber asked me, squeezing my hand as we walked along the path.

"Scottsdale Park," I replied as if she should know that. As I did, I realized I was back in the dream, and Amber was with me. I became cold, and not just because of the weather. "Amber, we have to get out of here. We are in danger."

"Well, I must admit a park at night is scary, but you brought me here, I thought, because you were being romantic. Though, as you know, my favorite place to make love is in our bed, not outdoors where someone might see us."

The screech of a wild cat pierced the still of the night, then came another and a third. Before I knew it, we were surrounded by a continuous wall of sound of meowing cats. I pulled Amber's hand and turned back to the way we had come, but the gray cat was sitting in our path. Its eyes glowed like burning charcoal. It was as if it could see into my very soul. "What do you want?" I screamed.

Leave us the girl, and you can go free. She has something we want. The cat didn't speak out loud, but I promise it spoke directly to me, inside my mind.

"Oh, look at the gorgeous cat, Jonathon. Can we take him home with us?" Amber asked.

"No. The thing is evil. We have to run now." I yanked her hand to the left. But there were now four gray cats there waiting for us.

"Wow, there are more of them. Let me pet them, Jonathon," Amber said.

"No way. We must get out of here—now." I spun around and started to run toward the lake. But Amber's hand slipped from my grasp, and I took several hurried paces before I realized I was alone. I stopped and turned back and felt chilled to my very core. Amber had stumbled with the sudden change of direction, and the gray cats had surrounded her. As one, they leaped at her with claws bared.

****

The clock flashed *12:11*. My heart pounded inside my chest as what I thought could be an impending heart attack hurtled its way toward me. I was petrified that I had brought Amber into the dream and somehow put her at risk because the cat had told me it was her they wanted, not me.

107

Chapter 12

Amber's flight arrived on time, and my heart swelled with excitement and happiness as I watched our state's contingent of the national swim team walk through the automatic doors in the arrival lounge ahead of the staff, as was their right, being the stars. Eventually, I saw her walking with the other coaches and physios, her head bobbing from side to side as she searched for me.

I gave her the biggest hug ever after she ran toward me, dropped her backpack, and wrapped her arms and legs around me as people milled around us, looking for their loved ones. "God, I missed you," I whispered, and she squeezed me tightly. She would have been too busy working with her swim stars to have worried as much for me as I had for her, but it felt so good to have her back.

I must admit to secret worries about Amber's fidelity, especially when she traveled with young, fit, healthy men overloaded with testosterone. There is no doubt that Amber is a stunningly beautiful woman, and what she ever saw in me still mystifies me. Late at night, I often woke, sweating, suddenly realizing Amber's love for me had all been a joke, and I couldn't possibly measure up to the men she worked with. I felt puny, almost wimpish, whenever I met any of them at social functions. During several conversations when she sought to reassure me, Amber said that the men and women she worked with were her clients, and she valued her career far too much to risk it for a meaningless *fling* with a man whose ego matched his superb fitness level. Somehow, those words never made me feel comfortable, but I idolized Amber and enjoyed basking in her beauty. I made a conscious decision to make her believe I trusted her implicitly.

After the hug and a long kiss that took me to paradise and back, Amber looked into my eyes and said, "What on earth is wrong, Jonathon? You look like you haven't slept in a week?"

"I haven't slept well in over a week," I replied. "I will tell you about it later. Have you eaten?"

"No. I considered it, but thought that with my arrival time, it would be better to eat with the man I love than have soggy pasta or very ordinary meat pies on the plane. What do you feel like?"

"Other than eating at the 'Y,' I don't mind." She smiled at the innuendo. "I picked up some stuff and put it in the fridge after I finished work, so we have options for later." I raised my eyebrows, letting her know I wanted to make love with her more than anything else.

****

"Jonathon," Amber asked as we cuddled naked in bed after both enjoying earth-shattering orgasms. "What's *really* going on with your lack of sleep? I've never seen you look so tired."

I had worried about this earlier, knowing she would see the change in me, so I told her the truth. I abhorred the thought of having secrets from my bride-to-be.

"So every night, you wake up one minute later from the same dream?" she queried.

"And the alarm clock is flashing when I do," I

agreed.

"And it's always the same cat?"

"Sometimes more than one, but when it is, it's like they are identical twins, yes."

"Well," she hugged me tightly, "that's all strange enough, but then it takes a sharp left-hand turn and goes right into the weird zone because you think the cat somehow represents this client of yours. Possibly, it's a warning that something supernatural is wrong with the house she wants you to renovate. But if she wants you to work on the house, why is she warning you off in your dreams, and how would that even be possible?"

I shrugged because my answer made no sense, and I did not want to mention that the previous night, the cats had wanted Amber, not me.

"Tomorrow, I'm taking you to the doctor. I think your problem is possibly the stress of the wedding, and my being away these last couple of weeks has upset your…equilibrium. Jonathon, you *do* still want to marry me, don't you?"

"More than anything in the world, Amber. Yes, I'm willing to go to the doctor with you, but honestly, I can't wait for us to get married. I'm not the least bit stressed. I don't know the answer to this riddle, but I don't believe it's that."

****

The dream was different again that night.

I was back on the path, and there was no hint of rain this time. The moon was full and bright, and while it was cool, there was no biting wind. I looked to my left and saw Amber walking by my side, her hand in mine. She smiled at me, but the smile died on her face when she noticed the look of horror on mine. I stopped and pulled her back by the hand. "Amber," I hissed from between clenched teeth. "You're in my dream again."

She stared blankly. "What dream?"

"The one I told you about earlier. About the cat who tries to stop me from getting to the appointment."

"What appointment?"

I felt myself becoming exasperated. "Amber, I explained this to you before we went to sleep. I'm dreaming, and you are here in my dream, in the park, and any minute now..." A long, drawn-out mmmeeeeeeoooooowwww sliced through the silence of the night. "Too late. You're about to meet the cat again. Make sure you stay behind me. This thing is evil and will rip you apart."

"Jonathon, what is the matter with you? You asked me to come to the park with you to meet, umm, umm, damn, I can't remember, but it was your idea to come."

I was stunned and more than a little angry. How could Amber be in my dream and not know it? Last night, she hadn't known about them, which made some sense, but now she did, and her lack of understanding seemed ridiculous.

A second cat screeched from near the lake, followed by an answering call from the trees. Then, another came from the playground. "We're surrounded by angry felines looking for their next meal, and we're on the menu. We need to get out of here." I urged.

"I don't understand. You drag me out in the middle of the night and then want to run off because of a cat? What's going on here?"

Over Amber's shoulder, only twenty-five meters away, three gray cats were stalking across the grass toward us. I pointed. "There, now do you believe me?"

"Aww, aren't they cute?" Amber squatted down and pursed her lips in a kissing sound.

"Amber, please, we must get out of here now." But it was too late. As if they were synchronized dancers, the three cats bounded, and as one leaped at Amber's face, three bundles of fur-covered, scratching, biting things, intent on disfiguring my fiancée.

****

Amber screamed, and we both sat up in bed as the alarm clock flashed *12:12*.

Chapter 13

I held Amber's quivering naked body to me as she cried. "Shhhhh," I whispered, "it was just a nightmare. You were in my dream. I'm sorry. I didn't mean to drag you in there."

She leaned away from me and stared intently. "But that can't be right. I wasn't in your dream; you were in mine."

"The Park, full moon, three cats that you crouched down to pat, and they jumped at you?"

Her look of horror intensified, and she stammered, "How could you know that? How could we both share the same dream, and why were the cats attacking us?"

I shook my head. "I don't know, but I have done some reading up, and apparently, there is a state called the Astral Plane, which is like dreaming in that it's a state of consciousness, but exponents can direct where they go to dream, who they meet, and what they do. As I've had a few nights of practice, I'm getting better at it, but I didn't intend to take you into this nightmare. You could have had your face ripped to shreds."

Amber raised her hands, touched her cheeks, and stared at her palms. She breathed a sigh of relief that they weren't covered in blood.

"This, this, this, is just madness," she cried, and I hugged her tighter. I'd had over a week to get used to the craziness, but this was Amber's first experience. I knew

I had to give her time. I also felt bitterly mad with myself for dragging her into my apparent psychosis, but then, with that thought, I wondered how on earth I had done that. If I suffered some sort of breakdown, how could I infect my love so that she shared the same fate? It made less sense now than before, and that worry, that sense of helplessness, could be the final act that sent me into lunacy. I shook myself mentally. *That is not going to happen,* I extolled. *And what of the previous night's dream when the cats wanted me to leave Amber?* No, I was not going to tell her that, no way.

When she stopped crying, I eased her away from my shoulder and looked at her tear-streaked face. Amber had not removed her makeup, so her mascara had run. "How about I make us a cup of green tea while you wash your face, and then let's talk about this mess I seem to have inflicted on you."

She nodded, and with one last squeeze, she swiveled around, grabbed one of my T-shirts she always used as a nightie when she slept over from the bedside drawer, and headed for the bathroom. I swung my legs out of bed, found my underwear, slipped them on with my T-shirt, and then padded out to the kitchen. I clicked the electric kettle on and glanced out the window to see tiny, drizzly raindrops hitting the panes. I sighed; it was going to be a long night.

****

We spoke at length but didn't get anywhere, which wasn't a surprise to me. Amber was the most down-to-earth, pragmatic woman I'd ever known, so I believed she was ill-equipped to think supernatural thoughts. In comparison, I'd had several days to get used to the dreams: I'd been thinking outside the box for quite a while.

"Tomorrow night," I explained, "as I told you, I am meeting Martha and visiting the house. She invited you, and I've told her so much about you, but maybe it's best if you don't go."

"After that horrible dream, if you think you can keep me away from that place, you don't know me at all," she replied, as I feared she would.

After an hour of discussion, I held Amber's hand and led her back to bed, reassuring her that dreams had only come once a night in the past. We slept fitfully. Each time I awoke, I saw that Amber was dreaming, and her moans and groans told me they were not pleasant, but at least she slept.

****

It seemed like before I knew it, the alarm was playing music from the local FM station, and it was a new day.

I called Tim on his cell phone and explained that I needed a personal day off work because Amber was back. He was angry, of course, though he tried to hide it. I was determined to spend time with her and try to reassure her of my love, and that whatever had happened to me wasn't because I subconsciously didn't want to marry her.

We went out for breakfast at the Luna Diner, our favorite. Amber had her usual eggs Benedict, and I had the full English breakfast because I felt famished. We hadn't spoken of the dream when we woke, but we did make love again, slowly, and I held off my ending until I was sure Amber climaxed powerfully. It was as if I had to reclaim her after her trip away with super- fit hunks and prove my love for her. Was that silly? Probably, but that was how I felt, and making sure Amber enjoyed our lovemaking made me happy, so it was a win-win. Deep down, in a place I didn't want to visit, was the fear that if Amber took a lover from the swim camp, I wouldn't, or couldn't outperform him.

We sat outside on the verandah to eat, as the morning was warm. When Amber finished, she pushed her plate away and sat back in her chair. "Jonathon, you know, of course, that my father was a Catholic priest, and I was raised in the strict catholic faith." She shrugged as she sipped her coffee. "These days, I like to think of myself as a thoroughly modern woman, and since my dad passed away years ago, my faith has slipped. But you should know deep down that I do believe in the Bible and that there are forces of good and evil in the world. You told me the history of the house, and I think that possibly there is some form of malevolent evil residing there, and it is causing the dreams through Martha because her subconscious is picking up on it."

I sat open-mouthed, unsure how to respond. I wanted to laugh, but I could see Amber was serious, and belittling her beliefs would not go down well. At the same time, I had no better rational explanation, so what did I know? "Residual evil?" I eventually asked.

She nodded. "There is lots of evidence of hauntings, demonic possession, and evil influences. Some say that Adolf Hitler was profoundly spiritualistic, and he had a medium who advised him of the optimal times for battles, which was why he was as successful as he was in the beginning. I think we would both agree there wasn't a more evil person in our history."

I didn't know how to respond. Amber was the woman I loved, adored, and wanted to spend my life with, but she was showing me a side of her I had never seen. Worse, I knew she was serious, and while I didn't have a better explanation, I wasn't yet ready to believe in some sort of demonic being inhabiting a house that didn't want me to renovate it. "But Hitler eventually lost?" I queried.

She smiled. "Well spotted. Some believe that when Hitler's spiritualists consulted Germany's astrological chart and found it favorable to invade Poland, they didn't check if Great Britain's chart was more powerful."

She gazed at me over her coffee mug as if daring me to challenge her, which I wasn't prepared to do a few days before our wedding.

"Okay," I said cautiously, "even if that's true, what's it got to do with the house in Blencowe Heights?"

She smiled at me. "Jonathon, you have to believe that there is a negative for every positive in the world. Night and day, dark and light, good and evil, white and black. If you even remotely believe in Jesus being good, you must accept that there is an opposite?"

"You mean The Devil?"

"The Devil is the name we call him, but he has many others, too. Every religion has the antithesis of good, but surely if there is a God, there must be an opposite?"

"Amber, you're kind of freaking me out here. I thought I was going mad with these dreams, but it seems you have an explanation for them. No matter how wacky it seems, it's better than anything I can come up with."

She reached across the table and took both my hands in hers. "It's imperative that you have an open mind when we go to the house tonight. In fact, it would be better still if you believed not only in me but have *faith* in me and Jesus. In my soul, I know we can get through this nightmare, but only if we have *faith.*"

There was the problem for me, belief. My parents weren't the slightest bit religious, so my upbringing, while not agnostic, meant that we only went to Church for weddings, christenings, Easter, and Christmas. True, I had to go and have lessons with Amber's Catholic priest and be baptized so he could marry us, but being completely honest, I thought it was all so much mumbo-jumbo and was a means to an end so that I could marry Amber.

I leaned back in my chair and gazed at the woman I adored more than anyone else in the world. "No matter what, I will *always* have faith in you. You are the single most important person in my life. You are good and kind, and I love you. I have no explanation for what has happened to me, and you do, so I'm inclined to believe you; at least, I want to. But you have had an upbringing that helps make sense of this mess, and I don't. You'll have to forgive me if I'm not as committed as you are to the Church."

Amber looked worried, raised a thumb to her mouth, and began to chew her nail, a sure sign she was upset.

"I'm sorry, hon," I said softly, "I can't suddenly deny my life thus far and immediately become religious. That's not who I am."

"I know," she whispered, "that's what bothers me. Look, the Church has many icons, such as the crucifix, which people wear to ward off evil. But it only works if you believe it will work. We have had evil creatures throughout history, such as vampires, though the Church believes they are no more than minor demons. In Eastern Europe, particularly, to this day, villagers hang fresh garlic to ward them off, and they would never step outside their home without wearing a cross because they *know* it will work if confronted at night."

I was lost and must have conveyed that to Amber. It seemed to me she was getting almost hysterical, all because she had shared a frightening dream with me. "Amber," I said cautiously, "what are you even talking about? So, I've had some scary dreams, and last night I sucked you into one. What has that got to do with vampires from Eastern Europe?"

"Nothing at all directly, my love." She squeezed my hand across the table. "I'm just trying to show you that when we enter that house tonight, if you don't believe in the power of Christ to ward off evil, you could become possessed by it, and then, you may be lost. That is possibly what the fortune teller meant by your lack of a lifeline in your palm. Jonathon, I'm scared."

"Don't be, honey. If it means that much to you, then we won't go. I will refuse Martha's commission; simple."

She shook her head sadly. "I don't think it is that simple. I believe if we do not go and face the evil at the house, then the cats will kill us in our dreams tonight."

****

After breakfast, Amber left me to return to my apartment alone while she visited with her father's dearest friend, his Bishop. She said she wanted his blessing and advice about what evil might lurk in the house's cellar and how we might combat it. I still felt it was stuff and nonsense, but I dared not tell Amber that.

Once home, I went back to researching the house's history and found more articles referring to the supposed ceremonies held in the basement. Lilian Pancras seemed to lead a coven of witches and warlocks. Their parties were described as debaucherous affairs comprising wild sex, sacrificed animals, and blood ceremonies. There was no further information on what constituted *blood ceremonies,* but my vivid imagination filled in the blanks. *Maybe Amber has a point, and I need to get with the program if I'm going into a den of iniquity. Okay, but how do you suddenly believe in things you've spent a lifetime denying?* For that, I had no answer.

****

Amber called my cell phone around six. "Jonathon, have you eaten since breakfast?"

"No, love, I was about to make a ham sandwich, though," I replied, wondering why she would ask that.

"Please don't. The bishop has given me some salads and blessed them. We mustn't eat meat before going to the house, and certainly no alcohol."

Shit, I thought as I glanced at the almost empty beer bottle on the kitchen bench, which was my second. *If only she'd called half an hour ago.* "Okay, darling, no problem. Will you be much longer?"

"No, I'm on my way. I'll be there soon. Bishop Dumfries was helpful. He offered to come with us, but I explained that we could hardly bring a Bishop to exorcise a home without the owner's permission, as it wasn't our house."

****

We ate a bland vegetarian salad that Amber served, and I held my tongue at how distasteful it was because I knew it meant so much to her. She had arrived carrying a cardboard box with dinner under one arm and a leather satchel in her left hand, which she left by the front door.

Once we had finished eating, it was approaching seven o'clock and almost time to leave. "Jonathon,"

Amber said quietly, "have you given any more thought to what I said earlier about having faith?"

"Yes, and I am willing to give you my total commitment. I researched the house more, and the original owner seemed to have some awful black magic ceremonies in the cellar. I'm still unsure about residual evil, but if you believe in it, so do I."

She nodded and smiled. "That's good, my love. My biggest fear is that the house seems evil. It wants you to leave it alone, and Bishop Dumfries agrees. To that end, he gave me something very sacred. Will you trust me to give it to you to help protect you?"

"Of course."

She got up and went to get the bag she'd left at the door, then sat back at the table. Firstly, she took out a wooden cross on a sturdy gold or brass chain that looked positively ancient. Amber placed it on the table and then took out a glass bottle with a cork stopper, larger than a perfume vial but smaller than a water bottle. "Jonathon, this may freak you out, but demonic possession can take place by a spirit entering the body through one of its openings. Bishop Dumfries gave me some Holy Water, and with your permission, I will make the sign of the cross with it on yours to protect you."

I mentally ran through all the openings she was referring to and felt like laughing until I noted how serious her face was. No matter how ridiculous I thought this nonsense was, Amber believed it, and this was a side of her I'd never seen. "Hon," I said softly, "it *was* just a dream. I don't understand it all, but it was just a dream."

"If that's all it is, then you have nothing to fear from being cautious and following my advice, do you? Now, let's get this done. Humor me, okay, then we can go."

****

I parked the car in the driveway, alongside Martha's near-new BMW. The lights were on in the house, but they did nothing to brighten up the dreary façade, which looked like it would be more at home on the movie set of a horror film, although I had to concede, maybe that thought was just my overactive imagination.

Amber and I walked hand in hand, our shoes crunching the gravel underfoot, until we climbed the stone steps to the grand entrance balcony. "Goodness," she whispered, "it's beautiful. You could turn this house into a palace."

I didn't reply because I didn't see a palace; I saw a medieval castle. Then I mused, was that because of the apprehension from the dreams? It was, after all, just a house.

The door flew open before we could knock, and a jubilant-looking Martha welcomed us. "Jonathon, I'm so pleased you came, and this must be Amber. When Jonathon said you were beautiful, he wasn't kidding." She hugged a mesmerized Amber and pulled us both inside the house. In some strange way, I felt my life had come to an end.

****

Martha led us upstairs first, exclaiming we must start at the top and work our way down. Her mood appeared distracted and hurried as if showing the top of the house was a waste of time, but again, I wondered if it wasn't all my imaginings. Glancing sidelong at Amber, who seemed intrigued by the potential renovation, I decided to just go with the flow.

We saw larger-than-average bedrooms and bathrooms. The original owner had designed the ground floor for entertaining, with an enormous ballroom and three separate dining or entertaining areas. The kitchen was dated and required a total makeover, as did the downstairs bathroom and powder rooms, which was all as I expected.

"Are you ready for the cellar?" Martha asked after looking at the diamond-encrusted watch on her left wrist. "It is *amazing.*"

"Lead on, Martha," I responded, dreading what was to come but feeling reassured by Amber squeezing my hand, who had been strangely silent thus far.

"There are no lights downstairs, but I found some candles and lit them so you can see the beauty. Max is waiting for us down there with a few friends from the club. He is drawn to it, and I think you will be too."

"Which club is that, Martha, Rotary or Masons?" We descended the spiral staircase, which, as far as modernization went, had to go as being too old-fashioned. At the bottom, Martha held a stout wooden door open, embossed with black iron studs and a long draw bolt. "Oh, neither. The Hellfire Club is much more exciting than those boring old groups of people with too much time on their hands."

We stepped through, and I felt we had entered a new dimension.

The room was huge, a vast oblong with cast iron candlestick holders placed every few feet, which Martha had lit. The walls were black, as were the floor and ceiling, so the candlelight highlighted the impressive medieval pentagram in the chamber's center. In front of the pentagram was a solid slab of stone, waist-high, which I imagined was some sort of altar. To the side of that was the most enormous, ornate mirror I'd ever seen, with what looked like carved serpents entwined around each other. It was hung on the wall, but with only the candlelight, it appeared suspended in midair.

Max and a group of others—it was hard to tell if they were men or women—stood in the center of the pentagram, wearing black robes with hoods. Max smiled as we entered. "Welcome," he said, with arms outstretched. "You have entered of your own free will."

I wanted to go home immediately—Max's remark about using free will to enter inferred that we could not leave. I had never felt so scared. Martha turned a key in the lock in the center of the impossibly thick oak door behind us. Before I could say anything, she bounded past us to join her husband, whose outstretched palms turned to stop signs as if to forbid us from entering the circle on the floor.

"What's going on?" I asked, and even I could hear the tremor in my voice. I knew the answer somewhere in my soul, and it wasn't good.

****

Max started speaking softly, still with palms facing us, though it sounded like gibberish. The others joined hands inside the pentagram and repeated some words and phrases. Martha smiled, and I noticed her canine teeth were extraordinarily long and pointed. Suddenly, I didn't see her, but the gray cat. I turned to the door and yanked at the handle, but it didn't budge. I was about to insist that we be let out when I noticed the outer ring of the pentagram turn red and pink smoke emitted from it.

My gaze locked on Max's, and his eyes glowed red as if fire streaked from his irises. Instead of demanding our release, I was struck dumb. My limbs suddenly felt as if they were made of iron, or the floor had turned to quicksand—either way, I couldn't move.

"The house *demands* a sacrifice to bring it back to life," Martha screamed. "The sacrifice of an unborn child. *You* will perform the ritual foretold to us, *his loyal disciples*. Lead the woman, the vessel of the unholy sacrifice, to the altar."

Max's voice rose several decibels, my grip on Amber's hand increased, and I took an unintended step toward the altar. *Why am I doing this?* I screamed silently, though my other self didn't reply. I became two people. One was the rational-thinking man, and the other was the more dominant trancelike zombie who had to follow orders.

"No, Jonathon," Amber hissed as she tried to free her hand from mine. "Remember, you love me, and your love is pure. The child I'm carrying is yours."

Is it? I wondered, *or is it a gift from one of those muscle-bound swimmers, and am I merely your cuckold?* I took another step toward the altar, dragging her with me because it seemed the right thing to do, though my other self knew it was wrong.

Max's voice rose again, and the others began chanting something in a foreign or ancient language. The pink smoke became cloying, and the candles flickered in a breeze that I was beyond feeling. Then I heard Martha yell with glee, "Look, *he* appears to us now to give us *his* blessing."

Amber screamed as the pink smoke began to solidify into a shape of extreme height and proportions on the right-hand side of the altar in front of the mirror. Every fiber of my being screamed at me to get Amber and run, that I should protect her from harm, but suddenly, it was as if my mind could decipher the hypnotic chanting, and it was telling me to kill her and her adulterous child. I took another step.

"No, no, no, no nooooooooooo. I will *not do it,*" I shouted, but my feet wouldn't obey me, and my feet slid toward the altar once more.

"Fight it, Jonathon, please fight for me. Remember, Jesus died for our sins; God sent his only child to us so we might learn that love is the only way."

The smoke had almost finished forming into a hideous, horned, goat-like monster. With Amber's words, it roared a fierce guttural sound that seemed, just for a moment, scared.

Amber tried to break free of my grasp without success, and I dragged her another step forward. From the corner of my eye, I saw her yank open the front of her blouse. Buttons flew in all directions as she drew out the wooden cross she had shown me earlier. She raised it above her head, and it glowed in a golden light.

I could no longer squeeze her hand. It burned like I was holding a hot poker after stoking a fire. I let go, and suddenly, although the chanting was now deafening, my feet no longer led me to the altar.

I shook my head, knowing my eyes were playing tricks on me. Amber herself glowed from within. Her eyes and mouth exhaled an eerie, wispy candy floss of iridescence. The wooden cross floated in the air, upright in front of her face, the chain anchoring it to her neck, and she slowly began to spin three hundred and sixty degrees.

Amber raised her arms as Max had earlier, but Amber was filled with light where he was dark. Her voice was loud yet melodic, harsh yet dignified when it came.

"Because my love for my baby is pure, I know I have God's blessing, as he loved his only son. FUNDAMENTA EJUS IN MONTIBUS SANCTIS!"

I shuddered at the strength in her voice, the power only a mother could have to protect her child. Suddenly, lightning bolts leaped from the candles, streaked across the cellar, and converged on the ornate mirror, smashing it into a million sparkling shards. From there, the forks hit the altar. The stones exploded, and I felt myself picked up by the blast and flung across the room.

****

I sat up, searching for Amber, and found her lying beside me, asleep in bed. The alarm clock flashed at *12:13.*

Suddenly, I had a thought and raised my left hand. The flashing, eerie light revealed the deep, pronounced lifeline stretching across my palm. I laughed out loud as I realized the date: Friday, the 13th of October. We were safe, and I was loved by the most amazing woman in the world.

Amber stirred. "Jonathon, why are you laughing?"

Epilogue

Amber and I married on a perfect spring day, four days after my final nightmare. She was my beautiful bride; her face glowed, and I admit, my voice broke with emotion when I recited my vows as we held hands.

I had phoned Martha and refused the commission to renovate the house. No matter how much money she offered, I had no desire to put one foot inside it. Amber agreed, though she had no recollection of sharing my last dream. As for the nightmares, they didn't return after I made the call.

One thing was for sure. I had seen a side of Amber that I would never forget. I no longer had any doubts about her love and loyalty. Were the dreams a warning of bad things to come, or bred from feelings of angst and lack of confidence in her love for me? I do not know to this day and have no desire to find out. I am comfortable remembering my school studies of Shakespeare and the line from Hamlet that there are stranger things in Heaven and Hell than are dreamed of in anyone's philosophy.

I am happy in my ignorance and eagerly await the birth of our son; yes, I absolutely believe he is ours. We have decided we will name him after Amber's late father.

I still hate cats and have made Amber promise we will only ever have dogs in our home.

Laney's Last Day

On his last day as a cop, Gordon "Laney" Lane is on his way to right a wrong.

Foreword

I have written several police procedural books about the hunt for deranged killers. I have always tried my utmost to respect our police officers because, in real life, I think they do an amazing job. When you think about it, what kind of world would we live in if they didn't perform the thankless job they do? In my attempt to get the investigative side of things as accurate as possible, I have spoken to several serving and retired policemen (and women).

After my first book, *Forever Night*, was published, I wanted to write a story about a fifty-year-old car dealer (Yes, I was a fifty-year-old car dealer at the time) who, through his internet dating habits, suddenly became the prime suspect in a series of murders. The book was called *Domin8*. I was fortunate to meet and chat with a police sergeant who was about to retire and was a wealth of knowledge. He requested to remain anonymous, so let's call him…Gordon. He helped me in more ways than one. Gordon taught me how such an investigation would work in the "real world." He also expressed his frustrations about everything he believed had gone wrong in the force over the years, from political correctness to what he called the shift from "real policework" to being a "pencil pusher." He said he couldn't wait for retirement.

And so, dear reader, thanks to Gordon's rambling, this story was born. It is the thoughts of a simple man who, on his last day of work, decides to take the law, which has become a joke in his mind, into his own hands to right a terrible miscarriage of justice.

Senior Sergeant Gordon "Laney" Lane strolled through the drizzling rain on the evening of his last day as a cop. After thirty-seven years of service, he was not only retiring but also planned that it would be the last day of his life.

Since he first joined as a rookie at age twenty-three, following in his father's footsteps, he had witnessed many changes in the Police Force, not all of them positive. To be honest, he felt that hardly any of them were right. Times had changed significantly, and they had not really brought old-timers like Laney along into the Brave New World.

In his day, walking his *beat*, he could give a misbehaving youth a good sla*p around the ear* and send him home crying, realizing he had done wrong. Then, his father would give him another one to ensure he learned proper respect. These days, when a party gets out of control, those same thirteen, fourteen, and fifteen-year-olds throw rocks, empty bottles, and even Molotov cocktails at the police. Respect? Oh no, not anymore. That was a joke and as non-existent as a sixteen-year-old virgin in King's Cross on a Friday night. Laney had become sick and tired of the nonsense that came with wearing a cop's uniform and was glad his days were coming to an end.

These days, it was all about political correctness; you were expected to call the drunken louts sir as you helped them into the back of the police van while they swore at you and questioned your parentage. It was about trying to subdue meth heads who wanted to fight and kill you and had the strength of three men to make it easier for them to achieve that goal. It was about kids stealing cars and driving on the wrong side of the road, so the cops had to break off a chase, so innocents weren't hurt, but the joyriders then carried on doing as they liked.

Worse, it was about making a solid bust, only to spend hours on paperwork, ensuring all the i's were dotted and t's crossed. Then, the offender would be let off with just a warning by a cowardly judge who believed the perpetrator was merely misunderstood or had a tough upbringing. Laney himself had a difficult childhood, but he didn't turn to a life of crime because he had been *disciplined*.

Laney's job involved handling domestic disputes, often occurring nightly, that threatened to spiral out of control as an enraged husband believed it was acceptable to beat his wife senseless and then turn on the attending police for having the audacity to try to intervene.

It was about trying to avoid being bitten by a drug addict who might have AIDS, hepatitis *A, B, C*, or any other letters that get added these days. It was about enduring verbal abuse or facing physical assault and risking your life every single shift simply because he wore a uniform. The job had turned into a pile of crap and drained the decency from good officers until they either resigned, fell into violence and alcoholism, or tragically used their service pistols to take their own lives due to depression.

Laney sighed as he walked past an Indian restaurant that was closing early. Mr. Singh, the elderly owner, waved from across the street, and Laney nodded distractedly. *Okay, maybe I'm exaggerating just a bit. But am I, really?* he wondered.

The final irony, as far as Gordon was concerned, and the last nail in the coffin of modern policing, was that everyone wanted more police officers, but no one wanted to pay higher taxes to fund them. Furthermore, the public certainly did not want additional officers if it meant risking a speeding ticket or running a red light because they were late for work. It is impossible to issue too many on-the-spot fines in a "user pays" society or to expect real criminals and offenders to finance more police officers who are supposed to serve as a visible deterrent. No, that was just seen as revenue-raising, as many a speeder had accused Laney of doing. How could the police hide speed cameras behind trees and use unmarked cars to catch reckless drivers who clearly do not care about the safety of others on the roads? It was absurd.

While Laney managed to stay married and resist the urge to end his life, the divorce and suicide rates among active and recently retired police officers were alarmingly high. But did anyone truly care about that when they could simply bring in more officers from the UK or Ireland? They continued to arrive in droves to replace local officers because if we thought it was bad here, just try being a cop there. For them, it felt almost like a working holiday, as many migrant cops shared this with Laney during their time in the patrol car.

If a cop did something wrong, like made an error in judgment, lost their temper, and hit some ignorant, loudmouth, insulting thug back? The law came down on you three times harder than it did on a criminal who'd done far worse things. Where was the justice in that?

Imagine being a cop, doing your best, but then making one mistake and being sent to jail with many people you put in there. Life wouldn't be worth living. The criminals would make sure of that.

Of course, Laney could have applied to become a detective and escaped the patrol cars and foot duty. Over the years, he had opportunities for advancement, but he just didn't want to wear a suit and look like a well-dressed jerk. Laney wanted *genuine policing* and believed that *real police officers* wore a uniform. Local residents respected their presence, knowing they were there to help, and simply being visible would reduce the crime rate. In the past, you could walk the beat and meet the local shop owners, who might offer you a leg of lamb for your Sunday dinner, a spare pack of smokes, a half-priced hamburger for lunch, or other ways to show their gratitude. Did they have to do that? No, they didn't; they just wanted to say, "Thank you, Gordon, for helping keep the crime rate down in our area."

Slowly, over such a long period, you hardly noticed it happening; the beat cops had been phased out. Was it any wonder that incidents of muggings, break-ins, and violent crime had increased? Nope, not to Laney, it wasn't.

Of course, the days of police walking the streets alone are over. These days, officers must wear stab-proof vests and remain vigilant for any stray extremists who might want to behead an officer simply for doing his job. He felt that trying to uphold the law every time he left the station was sometimes dangerous, primarily because we are often viewed as infidels in our own country. Naturally, expressing that opinion aloud was considered racist; no one should get Laney started on being labeled as racist when he didn't believe he was.

Was it any wonder that attracting young people to join the police force was challenging? If you could keep them from playing violent video games long enough, they probably still wouldn't pass the physical exam or might fail the drug test for smoking too much weed. Where was it all going to end? Laney wondered several times a day.

Laney paused under an overhang as the drizzle shifted to a brief, intense downpour. He adjusted his belt, securing the pistol, handcuffs, and Taser back over his hips, and readjusted his rain poncho while scanning the street, just in case his imagined rabid extremist was out searching for a victim to sacrifice.

Life was tough as a cop. But after a lifetime of service, what else could he do? He and his wife, Joyce, raised two kids and put them through college. One became a doctor working in a Brisbane hospital, while the other was a mining engineer who worked one month on and one month off in Africa. However, during his month off, he typically spent it in Thailand or Bali with his Asian wife. Therefore, on average, he only saw his children if he went to visit them, which meant very, very rarely.

It hadn't always been that way, of course; they used to want to visit home and frequently did. But then Joyce had her stroke, and though she fought valiantly and held on for three long months, a second stroke hit her even harder than the first, ultimately taking her away from Laney and their two children.

Joyce had been the light of his life, the constant that kept him grounded, his rock. He had never been unfaithful and had no desire to be, though he could have easily done so in his younger, fitter days. Back then, his six-foot-three frame was athletic and rippling with muscle, quite different from the rotund appearance that Laney had taken on in more recent times. Moreover, he had to admit he cut quite a figure in his uniform back then, attracting the ladies' attention. But although he could have, and even pondered it once or twice, he never strayed; Joyce was more than enough woman for him.

He couldn't recall a single argument from the last ten years of their marriage. They might have had some, but they were quickly resolved when they arose. Simple disagreements never simmered below the surface to be used later as weapons in a subsequent dispute. No, they both followed their parents' old saying: you should never let the sun go down on an argument, and a bed is for loving and sleeping, not fighting.

The rain was easing, and he set off down the city street he had once patrolled on his date with destiny. He knew he would die that night, and he accepted it because it would mean something. At sixty years old, he felt it was time to stand up for something. Then, when he met up with Joyce again—as Laney believed he certainly would—he could look her in the eye, and she would understand his sacrifice.

He had never been able to forgive himself for Joyce being alone when the stroke struck. She had been in the laundry, washing his clothes after he returned from a fishing trip with Roger and Wilfred, two other cops he knew, coming back late on a Sunday night with two lovely-sized snappers and a smaller bream.

He had left for work, as usual, on Monday morning, and Joyce had set her daily cleaning tasks, which she performed diligently. On this occasion, that included washing the dreadful fishing clothes that smelled of mud, fish blood, and bait. Joyce used a brightly colored plastic laundry basket to hold the dirty clothes, and when she experienced her stroke, she collapsed onto it, crushing the basket. If there was any blessing, it was that she had fallen that way, and the basket cushioned her fall; otherwise, she might have hit her head. In the three months following her stroke, seeing Joyce in a vegetative state—unable to speak properly or feed herself—he sometimes wondered if it would have been kinder for her to have fallen the other way. It would have been quicker and more humane had she banged her head on the way down. She had been such a strong woman; witnessing her decline in the last three months of her life was heartbreaking. It was also a constant reminder that she had lain on the cold, unyielding laundry floor all day until he returned home from his shift.

The doctors told Laney to hold onto hope, explaining that sometimes people recover from strokes worse than the one Joyce had suffered. However, Laney was doubtful. She constantly dribbled, gazed at him from one good eye, and looked pitifully sad. He recognized that there was no way back for her, and deep down, he hoped she wouldn't return permanently in that state.

Joyce needed constant care; she couldn't wash, feed, or dress herself. She couldn't even go to the bathroom, and where was the dignity in that kind of life? A woman so strong and proud shouldn't have to live a vegetative existence. She had raised two beautiful sons and never missed their sports carnivals or award ceremonies as they grew up. While Laney worked alternating day and night shifts, Joyce took the boys to football practice, wiped their tears, and cheered for their successes while Laney did his best to keep the streets safe. It wasn't fair that she had been struck down so young, far too young when they had so many plans for after Gordon retired.

Laney felt tears in his eyes as he remembered how the kids gathered around, spending as much time as possible with Joyce during her final days. He recalled their heartbreak at the funeral. Both boys wished they hadn't moved away and had spent more time at home, when they could have cherished their mother more. However, Laney understood that real life gets in the way, and after the funeral, they both returned to their lives, promising to come back as soon as possible. Unfortunately, since they buried Joyce, he had seen James only twice and Rupert, named after Joyce's paternal grandfather, three times.

They often called him to check if he was okay and managing on his own, and, of course, Laney assured them he was doing just fine. He secretly wept most nights in the bed he and Joyce had once shared. Tears arose from loss, boredom, and the misery of what his life had become after losing his whole reason for being—Joyce. He didn't want to burden his children; they had their own lives to lead, so he pretended to be in a good headspace, and they believed him, leading them to call less frequently as the months turned into years.

Laney did get better, or at least showed a semblance of improvement for a while. He got back into fishing with his old friends and even took up lawn bowls with his neighbor, Bruce, a fellow widower. But then came what he referred to as *The Chelsea Incident*. That situation truly summed up how terrible life and justice had become, not just for Laney but for everyone, in what football commentators loved to call *the modern era*.

Chelsea Graham lived with her parents on their street, and he watched her grow from a spotty-faced, pigtailed, skinny girl into a young, beautiful woman. Chelsea was always polite, addressing them as Mr. and Mrs. L with a smile. To Laney, Chelsea was a gemstone in a world of granite. Once Chelsea finished school, she knew what she wanted to do with her life and spoke to Laney at all hours of the day and night. She sought information about the police force, particularly investigations, forensics, and police psychology. She aspired to study criminal psychology and work as a profiler or with the prisoner parole board. She was drawn to crime like a moth to a flame, and how ironic it was that crime ultimately took her life away.

While Chelsea went to university to study for her double degree in Justice and Criminology, she worked nights at the local, small, family-owned supermarket. She was working on the night that three thugs burst in and demanded the money from the cash register. Being a good person, she tried to talk them out of it and pleaded with them that they didn't have to turn to a life of crime and had other options. One hit her across the face with something thought to be a fence picket, while another slashed at her with a straight razor.

She opened the register, distraught and terrified, as the three masked young men dashed off into the night with three hundred twenty-six dollars. However, Chelsea recognized that two of them had tattoos during the scuffle and knew who they were. Since she was familiar with two of the men, it followed that she also knew the third, who always hung around and completed the notorious trio they were known as.

They spent most of their time with a group of other

no-hopers at Rosie's Seven-Eleven, where, in a side room, some old-fashioned pinball machines and Space Invader console games could be found for fifty cents per play. According to Chelsea's statement, the three men were arrested in Rosie's, and at that moment, things went from bad to very bad, and then even worse for Chelsea.

The parents of the accused could afford a decent lawyer, who argued that Chelsea could not possibly identify the third man simply because he associated with the other two. This argument would not hold up in court, and the judge agreed, subsequently ordering his release. Next, the lawyer presented affidavits from tattoo parlor operators within a ten-kilometer radius, stating that the tattoos in question were not unique but rather very common. In the past five years, it was estimated that more than two hundred similar tattoos had been inked on young men of comparable build and height. Since the men had all worn masks, the cunning lawyer contended that Chelsea could not identify the men with absolute certainty, and when it went to trial, her evidence would be shredded to pieces.

Without a confession, and with each party providing the other with an alibi, it came down to Chelsea's testimony and the tattoos. The prosecutor, Darren Blake, told Laney that although he believed the men were guilty, there was no way to achieve a conviction. The judge dismissed the charges and released the men. Once again, from Laney's perspective, this highlighted what a mockery the law had become.

A week later, Chelsea was walking home after work, as she had done since she started, when three men set upon her. They dragged her into the bushes in the park, where she was repeatedly raped before being strangled and left for her body to be found by a jogger the following day.

The offenders wore condoms and left no DNA or evidence; naturally, there were no witnesses. Laney and everyone else in the vicinity knew who committed the crime, but the three men were reportedly at the Seven-Eleven that night. Numerous witnesses, mostly their friends, claimed to have seen them there, although Rosie herself couldn't be sure they were present all night and might have slipped out for a while, though she doubted it was long enough to commit such a crime. Laney believed the offenders had threatened Rosie with the same fate to coerce her statement that exonerated them. That belief was evidenced by her inability to look Laney in the eye again.

Chelsea's murder was ultimately classified as a *cold case*, which prompted Laney to decide that enough was enough. As he approached retirement, he felt it was time to stand up for all that was decent in the world, believing that the streets he had patrolled for so long shouldn't be left to thugs and bullies. He smiled, knowing he could help his community, right a wrong, and join Joyce in whatever awaited them in the afterlife.

So here he was, on his last shift—officially retired when it ended—walking his old beat. Laney was heading toward Rosie's to make amends for a life taken too soon. He passed the old butcher shop that had been closed for several years because the big supermarkets made it unprofitable to stay open. On the other side of the street stood the take-out Chinese restaurant, with mesh and steel bars over the windows, further illustrating how the neighborhood had deteriorated.

Earlier in the afternoon, Laney had placed two

letters for Rupert and James in the mailbox, explaining his actions and asking them not to judge him too harshly. He mentioned Chelsea, sure they would remember her freckled, smiling face from their childhood before they left to build their own lives and shape their futures.

Senior Sergeant Gordon "Laney" Lane had no regrets; it had been a good life, regardless of how you defined it, until Joyce left him alone. He had been a good husband, father, and an honest cop who dedicated his entire life to doing his best for others. Now, it was time for it to end.

He looked through the window of Rosie's Seven-Eleven and saw three men leaning over a brightly colored pinball machine that chimed heavy rock and roll songs. Laney thought that was very fitting. He removed his rain poncho, hung it over a nearby bicycle, straightened his hat, and ran his index finger along the brim to wipe off the rain droplets. Laney drew his revolver and stepped through the door as a buzzer announced his entrance.

The sound of screams preceded four gunshots that rang out through the damp night air. The screams stopped as the last echo died.

Two minutes later, a fifth gunshot sounded, followed by a loud thud as Gordon Lane's body hit the floor.

The Curse of the Manitou

Some spirits are best left alone.

Foreword

This story is dedicated to Geoffrey Boyes. Geoff is a true friend—the best I've ever had. He is a kind and generous man who took nearly a month off work to host me during my trip to the U.S. Geoff has narrated all my audiobooks and done an amazing job. One of the highlights (and there were many) was when he took me to the Native American Museum in Washington. I was deeply fascinated and moved by their history and the indignities inflicted upon them.

I was reminded of a movie and book by Graham Masterton, The Manitou, which fascinated and entertained me many years ago. At the museum, I learned about Native American spiritual beliefs, particularly about Manitous.

Manitous are spirits that inhabit everything and protect the environment as well as the people who believe in them. They are not meant to be scary entities that seek revenge….or are they?

In writing this tale, which is meant to entertain, I wanted to pay my respects for the trials and tribulations of those great people. I hope I have done so.

Thank you, Geoffrey, for a wonderful vacation and the inspiration for this story.

Prologue

Silver Stream knelt in the icy, crystalline waters of The Great Lake just before dawn. Though she didn't realize it, this would be the day that the women and children of her village, along with the few men who were too old or infirm to have gone with the war party, would be slaughtered. Trained by her mother since birth, she was a gifted seer who regularly helped others with their relationships or guided the braves on their hunting trips. But that she did not foresee the massacre that was approaching haunted her for the rest of her life.

It was the usual time of day when she expressed her gratitude and attempted to communicate with the Great Manitou, the Spirit of the Lake, who had cared for the nearby Shawnee Tribe for centuries. Whenever the Gitchee Manitou chose to speak with her, it was only at sunrise, as its radiant first rays illuminated the sky above the mountains to the east. He didn't visit every day, sometimes not for many days at a time. After all, he was a Great Manitou who did as he pleased; only he decided when the tribe, through her, could receive his wisdom.

Silver Stream, or Sampata in her native tongue, had learned the language of the white-skinned intruders from a former Indian brave who had become a tracker for the soldiers at the fort, sustained by a steady supply of alcohol. She had served as a translator between the tribe and the white men at the request of her chief, Gray Wolf, ever since the invaders multiplied like bull ants, spreading their nests after their initial appearance years ago and gradually creeping across the plains. She reluctantly accepted the role at Gray Wolf's urging. Since then, the soldiers and a representative of the white man's government had started discussions with the tribe about relinquishing its territory and relocating further west.

The negotiations with the men wearing blue had recently become more intimidating. Threats had been made to move them by force. One of the young squaws had been violently raped, and, on two separate occasions, braves had been ambushed and beaten. The Shawnee elders had no intention of leaving and would fight to retain the land of their ancestors, though they had always been peaceful and welcoming. They made plans to make a stand against the increased intimidation and feign an attack on the fort that housed the *bluecoats* to show they would not be pushed around any longer.

Sampata sought the Manitou's advice and wisdom during this critical time, fearing that the whites might retaliate and were possibly looking for a provocation to do so. However, he hadn't spoken with her in a long time. She had done everything she could: cast spells, made sacrifices and offerings, and came dutifully to his home by the lake each dawn, but nothing changed. It was as if the Manitou slumbered while the tribe fought for survival.

Silver Stream was tall and slender, with angular features framed by her long black hair. Having recently turned sixteen, she knew that Gray Wolf would soon announce the time of her marriage, possibly at the next full moon. Silver Stream believed she knew the identity of the man to whom she would be given. There were three possibilities, but she hoped it would be Chinatook, a tall, muscular, and fearless brave. They had been exchanging furtive glances regularly, and he once discovered her bathing naked at the lake. She blushed demurely, feeling a thrill of excitement at the desire in his eyes. It was clear to her that he wanted her to be his woman; he had made no secret of his feelings, nor had she toward him. However, Chinatook still needed to confront his two rivals in hand-to-hand combat, as Shawnee tradition required, to win her heart.

The Shawnee Tribe insisted that Sampata maintain her bloodline's strength. She had followed in her mother's footsteps, as well as those of her ancestors, serving through the generations as a Shaaman—a seer, healer, and spiritual guide for the tribe. Now, as her mother approached old age, Sampata was expected to assume her mantle, meaning her future children must be of the strongest lineage.

At dawn each day, Silver Stream would swallow some ground herbal powder made from a recipe known only to her and her mother, then walk to the lake's shore, remove her clothing, and wade into the water. The weather conditions were irrelevant. Sampata never felt the cold; she believed the Great Manitou saw to that. Silver Stream also recognized that the mildly hallucinogenic herb she consumed first could also be a factor. It didn't matter how it happened; the temperature of the water had no effect on her state of mind or willingness to serve the all-powerful Manitou. When she reached the correct depth, she would kneel so the water lapped at her neck and chin; then, she would utter her chants in a soft, sibilant, sing-song voice to summon the all-powerful Manitou from the depths. When he chose to, he made himself known immediately, though Sampata thought he needed long periods of sleep, and that was all the explanation she required for his long absences.

The Shawnee war party left the camp three hours before Silver Stream took her position in the water and began the first chant. A wave formed in the mirror-like surface before her, rising as though it would cascade down over her face, but it didn't. It grew taller yet remained in place as if frozen in time. This had never happened before, and for the first time, Silver Stream feared the power of The Manitou. She wondered what she had done to anger the Great Spirit and provoke him to threaten her. She believed that was his intent since he had never shown his might before.

Pleading, she spoke soothing words from her heart and mind, apologizing for anything she had done to displease him, when his voice erupted in her mind, compelling her to stop.

"SILENCE, my child. Open your mind to me."

Silver Stream bowed her head so that her lips entered the water, and she breathed through her nose. Images suddenly appeared to her. Dreadful, shocking pictures of the womenfolk and children of her tribe lying dead and mutilated among the teepees of her village. Sampata knew she was awake, but the mental images were so vivid she shuddered with dread. The spilled blood and gaping wounds screamed at her as she saw herself running from body to body while all around her, men wearing blue uniforms laughed and hacked at bodies with their *long swords.* Others used their rifles and pistols to murder every member of her tribe.

"Go," The Manitou urged her, "go before it's too late. Try to stop the violence, save your people."

The wave suddenly folded back on itself and then was gone. Sampata was alone, shivering for the first time in the water, but not from the cold. That was when she heard the first shot from a carbine rifle in the distance. Within minutes, there were more, lots more, and she scrambled from the water and ran. By the time she reached the village, still naked, the men had gone, leaving dead bodies lying in puddles of blood in their wake.

Silver Stream fell to her knees by the headless body of her mother. She wept, screaming a curse against the men who brought death to her people. In particular, she cursed the man she knew as the Colonel, the leader of the bluecoats, and his family for all time.

Chapter 1

Arrival
Friday the 13th September 2024

"We're all going to die out here," Martin intoned, as if his voice were not his own but borrowed from an old-time horror movie, from the late-night films of my youth. He leaned against the gate, staring down at the valley below and the enormous lake. Nestled on the shoreline was the beautiful cabin I had inherited from my grandfather, whom I hadn't seen for many years. He and his wife had died in the cabin below us in what the authorities described as natural causes. Just how *natural it was for* two people to die at the same time in the same house, I couldn't fathom.

I glanced at Miriam, my wife, whose face had turned a ghostly shade of pale, which told me she had heard not only the words uttered by our fifteen-year-old son but also his tone. Before I could respond, Charlotte, our daughter, shrieked, "Mom, Marty is trying to scare me; tell him to stop."

I decided it was time to take charge before things got out of hand. "Martin, please don't say things like that; you're frightening your sister. Miriam, put Charlie back in the car; I will talk to him."

I had always called our youngest Charlie, while her schoolteacher mother never missed a chance to use the full name of Charlotte. She shot me one of her *You need to have a serious talk with YOUR son* scowls and ushered Charlie back to the wagon as Martin stood frozen, leaning on the top rail of the five-bar gate, staring at the lake in the valley below. In any other circumstance, it would have been a picture-perfect vista, but Martin's eerie voice and warning that we would all die had stolen the moment. I had faced significant challenges getting Miriam to agree to visit the house, and now it seemed Martin had thrown another spanner in the works of convincing her to accept my inheritance.

"Why did you say that, Champ?" I asked as I sidled up beside him, but he didn't respond; he just continued staring at the shack as if it were filled with crawling insects that only he could see. "Martin," I called a little louder while gently squeezing his shoulder.

"Wh-what?" He jumped as if I'd touched him with a cattle prod.

"Why did you say that? You scared your sister and mother."

He turned a confused, blank expression toward me, raised an eyebrow, and said, "What are you talking about, Dad? I didn't say anything. I was just wondering if there were any fish worth catching in the lake and if they were within casting distance from the balcony."

Okay, I admit, his change in demeanor and innocent expression freaked me out a little. I knew Martin sometimes had a devilish sense of humor and had been known to tell us the odd lie or two if he thought he could escape punishment, but this time, he seemed so sincere. Yet, we had all heard him. "Bud, you said quite clearly that we were all going to die out here, and you used a *really* odd voice."

He looked as though I had just slapped him. He

appeared to search my face to determine if I was serious, then he grinned. "Yeah, sure I did, Dad. Good one." He shook his head and turned toward the car. I debated whether to stop him and ask him more questions, but I was too eager to finish our journey and see our new vacation home up close.

I soon came to regret that decision.

****

We returned to the car and continued our journey down the valley. No one mentioned Martin's outburst, and each time I glanced in the rear vision mirror, he caught my eye and smiled, which I took to mean he genuinely believed I had joked with him.

We drove down the winding road surrounded by spruce, poplar, and maple trees, with gravel spitting out from the tires as we navigated the curves. The area was a scenic wonderland, and I understood why my grandfather chose to live here. I could feel the nervous excitement radiating from all of us inside the car as we eagerly looked through the windscreen, hoping that, at any moment, we would catch a glimpse of the house.

We rounded a blind curve, and I hit the brakes and jerked the steering wheel as there was something: a big, gray lump in the middle of our path on the road. The wagon slewed almost sideways, and my daughter screamed. Just for a moment, I thought our family wagon would roll onto its side, and we would be injured. The vehicle lurched, but just before it reached its tipping point, it hesitated and then jarred back on the tires, coming to a shuddering, bone-jarring halt.

"Is everyone okay?" I asked, realizing I was shouting. I took a deep breath and tried again, looking at each in turn. "Miriam, Charlie, and Martin, are you okay?"

Everyone nodded slowly, seemingly feeling as shocked as I was. "What happened, Dad?" Charlie yelled.

"There's something on the road. Everyone, stay here while I check it out."

"Not on your life," my wife said as she unclipped her seatbelt. "I'm coming with you. Kids? Stay here."

"Why does Mom get to go, and we have to stay behind?" Martin demanded. "That's not fair."

"*Everyone* is staying here, including you, Miriam. Let me see what it is, and if it's safe, you can all come to check it out. In the meantime, stay here and keep the doors and windows shut." *Why did I say that?* I had no idea, except that somehow, I felt we were in danger.

I didn't wait for an answer or any more arguments. I got out of the car, shut the door, and walked back in the direction I had come from, my heart pounding. I noticed the antlers first and realized it was a deer, immobile and presumably dead, lying in the middle of the road. My heart sank. It was a big one, *a hunter's delight*. I crouched down and wondered how it had died, and even more oddly, why it was in the middle of the road. It didn't take long for me to find out.

I shuffled around to the other side of the animal and crouched again. Someone had cut the beast's throat. Its breast was caked with blood, most of which looked to be still wet, so it was recent. I heard the crunch of footsteps behind me and knew the family had come to investigate.

****

Dragging the deer off the road was challenging. It was big, and while perhaps not the biggest dead deer in the world, I thought if there were the biggest deer

Olympics, this one would surely get a podium finish. Miriam refused to touch it and told me to leave it alone, stating it was probably diseased, and that was why it was dead. I thought she was being ridiculous; the severed throat stated otherwise, but it wasn't worth arguing with her; we were all in an emotional state.

"Hon, we can't leave it here; the next car that comes along might not be able to avoid hitting it. Someone could die, and I wouldn't want that on my conscience. Marty, are you able to help your old man drag it to the side of the road?"

"Sure, Dad. You grab the front legs, and I'll take the back."

Together, we did it. Huffing and puffing, we hauled the deer off the road, rolled it down the embankment, and then trudged back to the car, sweating.

Miriam glared at me with an "*I told you so*" look. I shook my head as if to say, *"Not now."*

****

"Wow," Miriam said. I could hear the awe in her voice, which brought me a flood of relief. *Maybe this will work out, after all,* I hoped.

"Wow, indeed," I agreed, grateful that after her earlier reluctance to inherit the house, she now seemed, if not happy, at least intrigued. I parked the car on the gravel near the wooden pier and looked around. To our right was what appeared to be a triple-car garage made from the same logs as the enormous house, which rested on thick wooden stilts rising from the lake. The side facing the water featured a rack holding four canoes in different colors, with buoyancy vests hanging from the bows. Paddles protruded from a barrel.

The garage appeared sturdily built with a well-thought-out design, but it paled in comparison to the house. We were looking at what seemed to be the back of the vast cabin, which sat about six feet above the water on stilts. Access was through a narrow jetty that led from the shore to a landing platform near the rear door, approximately twenty feet away. The architect sensibly designed the building so that the rooms along the front of the house overlooked the lake. The main room featured front and rear panoramic windows, allowing us to see right through it from our location.

I noticed something strange. Hanging from the roof eaves every few feet were dreamcatchers. Each one looked different from the next, featuring intricate threading, bird feathers, and what seemed like small animal and rodent tails. It created a disquieting impression that the previous owners believed in ghosts and things that went bump in the night, using these artifacts to ward off evil. I hadn't believed in that sort of nonsense before the letter from my grandfather, and I hadn't been convinced since, but a chill crept down my spine nonetheless.

"Oh my goodness," Miriam whispered, "it's magnificent."

The kids' silence proved they agreed. Her reaction shook me from my malaise. I grabbed the bunch of keys from the console. "Let's go see inside." My words forced action, and everyone scrambled with their seat belts, opened the doors, and ran for the house.

Martin and Charlie bolted ahead while Miriam and I took our time, taking in the cabin's beauty, the lake, and the surroundings. In the distance, a fish rose with a splash, interrupting the incredible sounds of the native birds nesting in the surrounding trees. The sky was patchy, with clouds racing across, causing alternating beams of sunlight and dark patches on the lake's surface.

Miriam stopped momentarily and tugged my arm. "That's one of the first jobs you can do tomorrow; put all that crap hanging from the roof in the garbage."

Before I could respond, the loudest clap of thunder I had ever heard reverberated across the sky. It was so deafening that my eardrums rang in pain, and I covered them with my hands, fearing another strike; I noticed Miriam doing the same. Then, the clouds opened up, and a deluge of Biblical proportions poured down on us. Huge drops fell with the force of hailstones, but fortunately, they weren't ice, or we could have been seriously injured. Miriam shrieked loudly and dashed to the house while I closely followed her, splish-splashing in the small puddles that quickly formed on the pier planks.

We joined the kids who watched our approach open-mouthed from the alcove by the heavy entrance door. Miriam, first, then I ducked under the overhang, absolutely soaked to the skin and shivering. Suddenly, as we found cover under the roof above the entrance, the rain stopped as quickly as it had started.

"What the f—" I began, but Martin grabbed my arm and interrupted.

"Dad, the rain, it was crazy; it was only raining on you and Mom."

I shook my head, angry that Martin would again play around at an inappropriate time. Then, I noticed he was right; the planks from the gangway to the alcove were soaked, but the rest of the jetty behind the house was dry.

Chapter 2

Inheriting the House on the Lake

Six weeks earlier, I had been in my office reviewing one of my more prominent clients' tax returns, making sure everything appeared legal before emailing it to him for his signature. Just then, Claire, my receptionist, buzzed the intercom. "Yes, Claire?"

"A Mr. Bamforth from Bamforth, Reading, and Hoggit is on the phone asking to speak with you. I asked him what it was concerning, as I know he isn't an existing client, but he said it was an important personal matter."

I searched my memory but couldn't recall whether either company director was a client or an acquaintance. I shrugged; there was only one way to find out what he wanted. "Put him through, Claire."

After a pause, I heard the usual click as Claire transferred the call. "Robert Harford, how can I help?"

"Mr. Harford, Trent Bamforth here. Can I please confirm you are Robert Henderson Harford, grandson of Mitchell Harford? I must tell you that I am a lawyer representing Mr. Mitchell Harford's interests."

I was taken aback and felt stunned. I hadn't seen or spoken to my grandfather since childhood. My mother and father, who were not known for their liberal attitudes, had ostracized my paternal grandfather sometime after my grandmother passed away under

mysterious circumstances. Within a year, he became
involved with another woman, and if that didn't
disappoint my parents enough, she was a Native
American from the First Nations. Now, I'm not saying
Mom and Dad were racist; in fact, I don't recall either of
them ever saying anything that would remotely be
considered politically incorrect. But I guess the
combination of my dad's mother being replaced so
quickly by a Native American woman was just too much
for them. An acrimonious argument followed, with
neither party willing to back down and admit they were
wrong, leading to their estrangement. Grandad sold his
city home, where Dad had been born, which worsened
an already bad situation, and moved away. I was never
told where he relocated, and when I inquired about my
grandfather, I didn't receive any explanation that made
sense. Eventually, I stopped asking.

"Yes, I am he, and Mitchell was my grandfather,
though I haven't spoken to him since I was a boy. How
is he doing?"

"Ah, well, I am sorry to be the bearer of bad news.
I'm afraid your grandfather has recently passed away. As
your parents are no longer with us, you are the last
remaining relative and have inherited a substantial
legacy. I would like you to attend my offices so I can
discharge my duties and administer his last will. I can
also let you have the keys to the lakehouse."

"Lakehouse? What lakehouse?"

"The one he built on the shore of Lake Manitou
about thirty years ago. It's a stunningly beautiful place
on twenty acres of prime land. When I prepared his will
a few months ago, I visited him and his common-law
wife, Navina. They invited me to spend the night with

them, which I gladly accepted, and Navina shared stories about the lake and the history of the surrounding hills. Apparently, many years ago, the 7th Cavalry murdered all the women and children in a nearby village while the men conducted a raid on the fort. It's a fascinating story, especially when told from a Native perspective. I'm sure if I'd heard the same tale from a descendant of one of the soldiers, it would have been completely different, but Navina seemed entirely genuine. I remember waking up during the night after having the oddest dreams. Honestly, I couldn't wait to leave in the morning despite the breathtaking beauty of the area and your grandfather's wonderful hospitality."

"They explained over dinner that your grandfather received a special charter from the traditional Shawnee landowners to build the cabin, which was approved due to his relationship with Navina. Her family has been tribal elders for generations. As the rightful heir, you now own it and can inspect it whenever you wish. If I were you, I would pay your respects to the Council during your visit and always be mindful of their culture. Since you are a non-indigenous person, there may be some resentment regarding your living there, although legally, they can't prevent it. A caveat states that while a direct descendant can inherit the land and house, the home can't be sold to an outsider unless the Council declines to purchase it after an independent valuation. Your grandfather was a brilliant man and an excellent negotiator, but of course, Navina influenced the Council's decision. She and her family have served as tribal healers and, some might say, spiritual advisors for centuries. I hear she was a Shaman, somewhat akin to a witch doctor, though I don't subscribe to all that myself.

I must say, she seemed to be a wonderful woman—bright, bubbly, and amiable. I was very impressed when I met her, especially because she welcomed me into her home. However, she was a Shawnee through and through, and she never made me feel like an interloper. She died along with your grandfather, so she has no claim to his will.

I was too stunned to speak. I'd heard every word the lawyer said but had trouble comprehending. After a pause, as he was no doubt waiting for my response, he said, "I have taken the liberty of transferring the deeds for the cabin into your name already and taken care of all the government fees and taxes from the estate, but we *do* need to meet for the formalities. This cabin is only a part of your inheritance."

I felt overwhelmed and wasn't sure how to react. After many years without contact, my grandfather felt like a stranger; in fact, he could have died ten years earlier, and I wouldn't have been surprised. Sure, blood is thicker than water, but naming me as his sole beneficiary felt surreal. I couldn't remember when my mother or father last mentioned my grandfather.

"Forgive me, please, Mr. Bamforth; I am in shock. You mention the cabin is only part of the inheritance?"

"Yes. There is a portfolio of shares, stocks, and bonds that I have valued at one point seven million dollars, along with a substantial amount of cash. Additionally, I have a letter to you from your grandfather, given to me during my visit to them at the lake. My instruction was to deliver it to you after he passed away and not before. Since it is sealed, I have no idea what it contains. Are you able to come to my office at ten tomorrow?"

Chapter 3

Learning about the Inheritance

Miriam and I were punctual. A very prim, proper, matronly woman who introduced herself as Mr. Bamforth's assistant led us to a comfortable couch. She insisted we have coffee, and she brought us two steaming glass mugs and set them on the coffee table.

"Mr. Bamforth won't keep you waiting too long," she said, returning briskly to her desk.

The reception area was what you would expect— modern glass and chrome furniture and brightly colored prints adorning the walls. *Chic but not opulent,* I decided, and sipped my excellent coffee.

Miriam had been strangely silent since I had told her about the inheritance the night before, which surprised me. Not just because we now owned a holiday cabin on a lake in the South of the State, only a couple of hours' drive from home, but we were almost two million dollars richer.

We weren't poor by anyone's definition, but we certainly weren't wealthy. Miriam had stopped working before Martin was born and never returned to the workforce, choosing to be a full-time stay-at-home mother, just like her mother did when she grew up. I must admit that Miriam did a fantastic job, and I had no complaints. She was a great mom and an excellent wife. The house was always neat, clean, and tidy. She was a wonderful cook, and our clothes were always fresh. Even though I was an accountant, she managed to keep a perfectly balanced home budget without my assistance.

Sure, we had arguments from time to time, and to be honest, the frequency of our love life had declined over the years. However, I understood that was typical for a couple our age and maturity. While we certainly didn't need the money, it wouldn't hurt. Our children needed funding for their college education, and there was about one hundred thousand still owed to the bank for our house. My car was four years old, and Miriam's was seven. As for the inheritance? We could enhance our family vacations and have some money set aside for a rainy day. I couldn't see a downside, yet Miriam acted as if it were toxic.

I asked her about it in bed, and she paused for the longest time—so long that I thought she had fallen asleep. "I may be being silly," she began, "but I have a bad feeling about this. My mother always said that money you didn't earn was a gift from the Devil and came with strings attached to the repayment plan. Can't you see that something is wrong? Your grandfather, whom you haven't seen in thirty years or more, dies, and out of the blue, you're a millionaire. Bad luck always follows good; that's another of my mother's maxims."

"Miriam, you can't be serious. Are you suggesting we refuse this and give it all to charity or something?"

She paused, and I could almost hear her brain working overtime. *She does, she really does; what is wrong with her?*

"Would that be so bad, Bob? We don't need the money. Sure, it wouldn't go to waste, but… oh, honestly, maybe I'm just being overly cautious. I don't know why

I feel this way, but I am afraid that something terrible will happen if we take it."

I took a slow, deep breath. This was a side of Miriam I had never seen before. She was the least superstitious person in the world, yet she spoke as if a sudden windfall was terrible. *Maybe she just needs a little time.* "Hon, I'll tell you what. Let's have the meeting tomorrow, get the keys, and go see the house. If we like it, great, but if we don't feel good about it, we can hand it back to the Indians."

She didn't answer, and I hoped it would not be the last I heard of her fears of a house she'd never seen.

****

"Mr. and Mrs. Harford? Thank you for coming in. I'm Trent; please come through to my office. By all means, bring your coffee."

He waited for us to stand and then gestured toward the doorway. The man was short—barely five feet six, I estimated—and dressed in a gray pin-striped suit. He wore round glasses, was bald in the middle of his head, and had a slightly ridiculous-looking comb-over.

He herded us into his office, pointing toward a black leather couch behind a low coffee table. "We will be more comfortable here."

We sat together, and Miriam intertwined her arm with mine as if to stop me from fleeing. I still couldn't understand why she was so worried about our good fortune, but we hadn't discussed it since. He opened a folder on the table and handed me a blank, sealed envelope. "This is the letter your grandfather gave me for you. You don't have to read it now; you can take it home and study it at your leisure. There won't be a formal reading of the will, so to speak, because you are the only beneficiary. I have taken care of all the formalities, transferred the share certificates into your name, and covered all the taxes from the cash portion of the bequest. Everything is in this folder for you to take with you, along with a cashier's check for the remaining balance of the liquid funds. I have a standard form for you to sign, releasing me from my responsibilities under the terms of the will. Do you have any questions for me?"

Before I could answer, Miriam spoke up, "I have one. What if we chose to decline this inheritance?"

The lawyer's expression was almost comical, and if I hadn't been so embarrassed by her question, I might have laughed. "I'm sorry, Mrs. Harford. I don't understand."

I glanced at Miriam and noticed her face had turned red. I decided not to answer or help her. The question reflected her silliness, not mine, so she was on her own as far as I was concerned. *Did she mean to say that out loud?* I wondered, but her answer indicated she did. "What I mean, Mr. Bamforth, is: if my husband and I decide to refuse the bequest, what can we do?"

He bit his lower lip as he struggled to keep a calm demeanor, clearly contemplating how to respond to the most ridiculous question he had ever heard. "Why would you want to refuse an inheritance worth about three million dollars, including the value of the house on the lake?"

I thought *that got her,* yet she still refused to save herself from her own foolishness. She shook her head. "The reason isn't important, Mr. Bamforth; that's for us to decide. Let's just say, in my family, we believe that accepting unearned wealth can bring bad luck, so please tell us, what if we choose not to accept the inheritance?"

He removed his glasses and cleaned them on his tie, as if he needed time to think. I caught his glance and shook my head imperceptibly to signal that I had no intention of siding with my wife. He put the glasses back on. "Mrs. Harford, forgive me for being blunt, but I don't work for you. Your husband's grandfather commissioned me as the trustee for his estate to distribute the bequest according to his instructions, and I have now done that. You must understand that the law clearly defines what an executor can and cannot do. I have performed my duties with due diligence, and my job will be complete once Mr. Harford signs the acceptance document I have prepared. What y*ou both choos*e to do with the proceeds from the will is up to you. You could donate the money, stocks, and bonds to charity and return the property to the Native American tribal elders. I'm sure they would appreciate such a gesture and find a meaningful use for the magnificent house. If you don't mind my saying, I would consider this windfall good luck, not bad.

"How did they die?" Miriam asked, undeterred and sounding annoyed by his inference.

"Miriam," I admonished.

"We have a right to know, Bob. What if they were murdered? We could meet the same fate if we go there."

I raised a questioning eyebrow at Mr. Bamforth. For once, Miriam made a good point. I hadn't asked for the cause of death, and we did have a right to know. I was in shock when he told me the news the day before, and I hadn't thought to ask.

"I have viewed the death certificates, and they both state natural causes."

"How can that be?" I asked incredulously. "Are you

saying they died together, or did one outlive the other?"

Bamforth shifted uncomfortably.

"According to the coroner's report, which I requested along with copies of the death certificates, the time of death was the same day. I can't say it was simultaneous, but both passed away within a short time of each other." He seemed to need to justify further and blurted out, "You must understand it wasn't an exact science. The medical examiner did not perform autopsies because the family doctor on the scene determined it was natural causes, with their advanced age being a contributing factor. They had been dead for a few days before being discovered by a visiting friend, which may have complicated the determination of conclusive times of death."

That sounded unbelievable to me, and I could see Miriam about to explode, so I jumped in again. "Hang on, Mr. Bamforth, surely that can't be right? I remember Navina being considerably younger than him, so if we accept his passing due to old age and deteriorating health, she couldn't possibly die in the same way at the same time; that defies belief."

He spread his hands wide and shrugged as if it were irrelevant. "I am simply the executor of your grandfather's estate, not a police officer, coroner, or medical examiner. If you seek more information, I suggest you visit your new property and conduct your own investigation."

****

Naturally, Miriam expressed her opinion vehemently on our way home: "Bill, this is wrong on so many levels. I want you to give it all away, at least the house. Maybe it's cursed or something."

I took a deep breath. I was angry with my wife and decided her petulance had to stop. *"For God's sake, Miriam, you're acting like a hysterical teenager."* I took another breath and calmed down a bit. "This is a wonderful gift from my grandfather, and if you think I'm going to give it away without even seeing the place, you don't know me. Come to think of it, I wonder if I understand you anymore. I've never known you to be superstitious or afraid of bad luck disguised as good. If you don't want to come with me to visit my inheritance, that's your decision, but make no mistake; I am going, and if the kids want to come, I will take them with me."

I couldn't remember speaking to Miriam that way in our marriage before, and I dared not look at her directly because I knew she would explode with rage if I did. From the corner of my peripheral vision, I noticed her staring at me as if I'd grown a second head. She folded her arms across her chest, a sure sign she felt incensed with me, then turned away and looked out of her window. She didn't speak for the rest of the journey home, nor did I.

Chapter 4

My Grandfather Wrote Me a Letter

I dropped Miriam at home, intending to go back to work. She didn't say a word as she got out of the car, but made her feelings obvious by slamming the door behind her so hard the car shook.

I drove to work feeling distracted, angry, and confused. I had never seen Miriam act so illogically. A part of me wanted to respond with equal anger and stubbornness, digging my heels in. But another part wanted to understand her and ease her fears if possible. After all, Miriam was my wife and the mother of our children. Sure, we had our ups and downs, but I loved her, and if she was truly terrified, my job was to protect her. Yet, how could I rescue her from her fears? I wasn't about to discard a three-million-dollar inheritance because she was scared it would bring bad luck. I touched the envelope in my jacket pocket and hoped something in the letter my grandfather had written to me might help alleviate Miriam's worries.

In the sanctity of my office, with a mug of steaming coffee within reach, I used my pewter letter opener to slit open the envelope, pulled out the many neatly handwritten pages it held, and read my grandfather's words from the grave. A tear came to my eye when I saw the salutation he began with words I hadn't heard for many, many years:

Dear Billy-Boy

As you are reading this, I have passed away, and there are some things I need to tell you. You are now the senior surviving member of our family, which dates back many generations to the early settler days. The responsibility of keeping The Manitou from returning now falls to you. I know you have many questions and will not understand what I am talking about, but I hope you have an open mind and can take over the mantle as I no longer can.

You are a direct descendant of Colonel Ramsay Harford. He led the attack by the 7th Cavalry against the Native Indian Tribe, which lived near and hunted at the Lake now known as Lake Manitou. While the Braves were away from the village on a failed raid on Fort Wilson, Colonel Harford attacked, killing every inhabitant, including children, bar one, whom he left as a warning to others. The survivor was named Silver Stream, a healer; I guess you could call her a medicine woman or spiritual guide, though I know she was much more than that. She cursed the Colonel and his descendants in the name of the Great Gitchee Manitou.

I know your parents would not have told you, but Helen, your grandmother, died in mysterious circumstances. The investigation into her drowning decided she was of unsound mind and took her own life, but I know that to be untrue. The Manitou murdered my wife in an act of revenge against our family's bloodline, as he has numerous times before through our generations. I learned this when Navina, a direct descendant of Silver Stream, approached me at the funeral and told me of the history of her tribe, the Shawnee Nation, and her beliefs, which are as relevant today as ever. However, modern science seeks to discredit the past ways of Indigenous Americans, as other countries do with their Natives.

I know you will be skeptical, as was your father. Indeed, I, too, took a lot of convincing from Navina, who disagreed with her family's actions over two hundred years before. Navina showed me things technology cannot explain until I reluctantly believed in her sincerity and truthfulness. Your father thought I had lost my mind and suspected Navina of somehow harming his mother to be with me. We fought, and he never forgave me for becoming close to her despite many attempts to convince him it was untrue. He refused to speak with me further and forbade me from having any contact with you.

The first question I know you must have is: What is a Manitou?

The First Nation Indians have inhabited this land for thousands of years, living in harmony with nature and its creatures. Unlike us, who exploit and destroy the natural order for selfish gain. The Indians believe everything has a life force, including trees, rocks, lakes, and birds. They refer to this spirit as a Manitou. Some Manitous are minor, while others possess greater powers. Lake Manitou, as we now call it, is aptly named as it is a vast body of water, and its Manitou is immensely powerful. It is this Great Spirit that seeks revenge on our family for the murders of the tribe's women and children years ago.

Over time, the Manitou rests and regains strength. After each slumber, he is more powerful than before, and I fear you may have to face him at some point, so you need to be prepared.

You probably don't remember, but before she died, your grandmother and I often went camping and sometimes took you along. We visited Lake Manitou and had a campsite right by the shore. A Tribal Elder came to see us and warned us not to camp there, but we did anyway since we had arrived late in the day and had already set up our things. We promised we would leave the next morning out of respect. I remember the man departing with a dark look, and I wish we had listened to him. I had the best night's sleep in the tent, listening to the gentle water lapping, although I recall having a strange dream during the night. In the morning, I couldn't find Helen or our canoe. The police discovered it upturned in the center of the lake and later recovered her body from where it was tangled in the river grasses and weeds below. They came to believe she had woken during the night and, wearing nothing but her nightdress, paddled out and either went for a swim and became entangled or deliberately swam into the weeds to end her life.

I experienced an icy chill coursing through my body as I read his description of my grandmother's death, which I had never heard before. My father refused to speak about it, only saying she had passed away and that I was too young to understand more. My memories of that time were hazy, but I always thought my grandparents had been very happy together. Her death came as a great shock, so how could my father believe he had an affair with Navina and conspired to murder his wife? It was simply too fanciful to be true, yet it seemed my father believed that and cut off all ties. I turned to the next page and kept reading.

Navina befriended me and was an incredible

support in helping me cope with the unimaginable grief I experienced. The fact that she was a First Nation Native from the area where Helen died was comforting. At no point then, or at any time since, was there any romantic involvement between us, despite what your parents believed. To this day, as I sit at my desk overlooking the lake writing to you, she is beside me, her hand on my shoulder, providing support as a friend. She has never attempted to replace Helen in my heart or my bed. She was as heartbroken as I was over Helen's death, though for entirely different reasons. Throughout her life, she has sought to appease the Manitou of the Lake and protect any white people who come near the Lake, especially me and my descendants. Navina was visiting her ailing mother in the hospital when The Manitou took your grandmother from me. Her death, being my loving wife and a descendant of the man responsible for the massacre of his tribe, calmed The Manitou's vengeful spirit, and he returned to rest for several years. Meanwhile, we prepared ourselves for his return under Navina's guidance and instruction.

The Tribal Elders, understanding the dangers as Navina explained, allowed us to build the house on the Lake to keep watch and be ready to confront him when he awakened again, as they too wished to end the vendetta.

We believed that when he returned, he would want to take my life, and Navina taught me some powerful incantations and remedies so we could face him together with a chance of defeating him and ending the war against our family.

Sadly, The Manitou was far too clever for us. He attacked in a way, place, and time we could not have predicted.

I know this is difficult for you to understand, and you probably think I have lost my mind. I pray you do not believe that, as what I will tell you next explains just how devious and powerful this Manitou is, and that you and your family are in great danger sometime in the future when he returns because of the curse laid many years ago.

This Manitou is a water spirit, and the Lake is his home. The Lake is fed by tributaries from other rivers and waterways, including the River Wyde. Yes, Billy-Boy, the River Wyde. On Friday, the 13th of November, your mother and father were returning from a week away and crossed the River Wyde via the bridge at Hampton Rock. There were no witnesses, but for some reason, your father drove through the crash barrier into the water, and both drowned. The coroner's report said they were unable to open the doors. I believe The Manitou traversed the waterways and murdered your parents by using the river water to force the car doors closed as they fought to escape.

"Oh my *God*!" I exclaimed, standing up suddenly. My chair shot backward on its castors and crashed into the wall.

Claire came running in. "Are you okay, Mr. Harford?"

"What? Oh, yes, thanks, Claire. I'm fine; it was just a stupid accident. I don't know my own strength."

She looked from me to the chair, lying on its side, then to the pages in my hand. "Are you sure? You look like you've seen a ghost."

I forced a smile to my lips, took a deep breath, and held up the pages. "A letter from beyond the grave from my grandfather and some revelations about my parents, which took me by surprise. Honestly, I'm fine, Claire, but thanks for checking on me."

She left, closing the door quietly behind her, and I retrieved my chair. My coffee had gone cold, but I took a deep sip to calm my nerves. I could not believe what I was reading; surely it was nonsense? Native American spirits have been murdering my forebears for centuries? No way was that true or even feasible. Yes, my grandfather had taken up with a First Nation Native American after the tragic drowning of my grandmother. Yes, that event estranged him from my parents due to their fear they had somehow engineered the death to be together. That much I could accept, but the rest? Hogwash, so far as I was concerned. And some demi-demon traveling from lake to river and forcing a car to crash and drown the inhabitants? It would have been almost laughable if my parents had not been involved.

Yet, somewhere deep within my psyche, something jarred. I had read enough of the letter for one day; it was too unsettling. I am a Chartered Accountant; I deal with numbers, tax havens, legalities, and refunds, not Native American folklore. I shoved the letter into my top drawer, planning to finish it another day. I needed to get back to Tom Malcovich's accounts. I opened the folder with one hand, booted up my computer with the other, and then halted when a thought struck me like a sledgehammer to my chest. Beyond my grandfather, whom I hadn't seen since childhood, I didn't know my family history. Maybe I should make a start and find something that discredits my grandfather's claims.

I went to my search engine and typed in Colonel Ramsay Harford. The screen lit up with several historical articles. I spent the next ten minutes reading about his great leadership, his cavalry exploits during the Native uprising, and his role in quelling it. Several minutes passed reading until I sat back in the chair and thought. *Okay, so my ancestor did fight the Indians and was instrumental in bringing peace and moving them farther west, albeit by forcing them into submission by murdering women and children. What does that prove? Certainly not evil spirits.*

I amended my search by looking at his death, and what I read was disquieting, so I leaned back in the chair once more to think. *Coincidence, surely? He and his troop camped on the shore of a lake, though the article doesn't say which one. The men used the lake to bathe in after several days on horseback, and Ramsay was the last to do so. Being the senior officer, he let his men go first. When dinner was ready, an underling went down to the water to tell the colonel, but instead found his body floating in the shallows with his throat cut. His men loved him, so the army decided a roving Indian Brave had committed the murder, though investigators could never prove it. Was it Lake Manitou, and did the Great Spirit finally catch up with him,* I wondered.

I laughed out loud, almost hysterically, but controlled myself before Claire returned to check on me for a second time. I wish I hadn't done the search because I hoped it would discredit my grandfather's assertions, but it hadn't. If anything, it had strengthened them, and I still didn't want to believe such poppycock.

Miriam's phobia came to mind, which seemed even more ridiculous. As if her female intuition, masquerading as bad luck, could prevent us from inheriting a house on the lake, along with all the investments and cash. That wasn't going to happen. I decided to forget all about the letter, and that was final.

It's funny how things we think are final rarely are.

Chapter 5

Preparations for Visiting Lake Manitou

Miriam was oddly silent when I arrived home, but I decided not to take the bait and instead knuckled down to act as if nothing was wrong. I placed my jacket, keys, and briefcase on the hall stand, kissed her cheek, and attempted a peck on the lips, but my loving wife turned her head at the last moment. Undeterred, I smiled and inquired about the rest of her day as I went to the drink cabinet. I poured a larger-than-usual measure of scotch and asked if she'd like to join me. I looked back when Miriam didn't respond, but she had left the room.

Hmm, so that's how it will be: the silent treatment.

I decided that *discretion was the better part of valor,* so I planned to treat Miriam as if nothing were wrong. I thought that would either annoy her, leading to a good old-fashioned, drag-out screaming match, resulting in make-up sex—always my favorite part of any fight—or she would cheer up, and we could get back to our normal lives.

Unfortunately, she remained gloomy throughout the evening, speaking to me only when necessary. When the kids returned home, I sensed they could feel the tension in the air as Miriam barely acknowledged them. We exchanged glances, and I shook my head, silently urging them not to say anything but to *go with the flow.* I suspected they thought I had upset her, as I had clumsily done in the past, prompting them to vanish to do their homework. They, too, understood that discretion was preferable to valor; they knew their mother well.

At dinner, I'd had enough and decided to bring things to a head. I've never been overly patient and thought it was time to force Miriam to show her colors to the kids. I took the bull by the horns and brought my loving wife into things front and center. "Kids," I began, "has your mom told you about *our* fantastic inheritance?"

Martin dropped his fork, and Charlotte gasped loudly while Miriam glared daggers at me. I'm sure she would have gladly gouged my eyes out with the steak knife she held in her hands if she could. But it was too late, and she knew it; I had outmaneuvered her.

"What inheritance, Dad?" Marty asked.

I told them, and, unusual for them, they kept quiet and listened intently until I finished.

"So, we're rich?" Charley said as if she would burst with excitement.

"And we own a house on a lake?" Martin exclaimed. "Can we catch fish off our balcony?" he added.

I grinned, glanced at my wife, and saw her smiling at our children's excitement, particularly Martin's dream of being able to catch fish without leaving the house. So maybe I'd done the right thing in bringing it up.

My hope for any kind of makeup sex that night was dashed, though. When we went to bed, Miriam had her back to me and wore her winter nightdress—a clear signal not to bother trying.

****

Life returned to normal for the next few weeks. I was extremely busy at work and chose not to provoke

Miriam about our windfall. She seemed to warm to the idea gradually, or perhaps she simply tolerated it. Sometimes, I wondered if she might one day tell me, *"See? I warned you it was a bad idea."* But over time, I think she accepted the concept of a vacation home on the lakefront. The money stayed in the investment portfolio, and I didn't mention it, nor did Miriam.

I timed my announcement that we would visit the house on Lake Manitou at a family dinner again. Miriam hadn't brought up her belief it was bad luck, and I hadn't goaded her further, choosing to let things lie. So, when I announced we were all going to the lake during the next school vacation, I received whoops and hollers from Martin and Charlotte but only a stony silence from Miriam.

That night in bed, I cuddled close to her, savoring her warmth and presence. "Babe?" I started, "You know I love you and would do anything to protect you and our children. I wish you could find some happiness about the lake house and recognize that, for once in our marriage, we've experienced some incredible luck. I've never seen you act superstitious before, and I'm concerned about our marriage if this inheritance creates a divide between us."

"It's already come between us, Bob. You acted like my beliefs were to be ridiculed and not taken seriously. I've never known you to treat me so disrespectfully."

My first reaction was to shout at her and tell her she was the one being ridiculous. Fortunately, my better judgment took charge, and I bit my tongue. As an accountant, I decided to approach the situation with logic rather than emotion because I've learned from past experiences with Miriam that shouting rarely ended well for me.

"Sweetheart, it has nothing to do with a lack of respect, and after all our years together, I'm shocked you could say such a thing. Surely, you can see that if I stopped a thousand people on the street and asked them whether such an inheritance was good or bad luck, I believe they would all agree with me rather than you."

"Maybe. But if a thousand Wildebeest leaped off a cliff, should number one thousand and one do the same?"

"Let me get this straight. You believe that my grandfather's home, which has been on a lake for the last thirty years, shouldn't pass to me as his closest living relative because it will bring bad luck to our family?"

"It didn't bring him good luck, did it? Or the woman he lived with? They both died there. And what's more, they both died at the same time. Explain that, Sherlock, if you can."

"Sherlock? Why are you being so insulting? Look, it was left to me by my grandfather, and if you don't want to go see it, that's fine, don't. But our kids and I want to, so we are going. I will respect your thoughts and agree you should stay here if you believe it's bad luck, but by the same rules, you should respect my beliefs and stop treating me like I'm your enemy."

"Bob, I'm sure you'd prefer to leave me here while you go with the kids and have a wonderful time. It will help turn them further against me as the big bad witch and you, their knight in shining armor. No, I will be going with you, and I promise to keep an open mind. But remember, you promised me that if it doesn't work out, you agreed to return it to the natives."

What could I do but agree? Unsurprisingly, we didn't make love that night, and I eventually fell asleep after wondering if and when we would again.

Chapter 6

The Lakehouse

I fumbled for the keys in my pocket, my body trembling from the cold as my clothes were drenched from the sudden downpour. I opened the ornately carved wooden door, and the children vanished into the house. Just as I was about to follow, Miriam's voice cut through the air, her words laced with a hint of nervous uncertainty. "Do you still believe this is a good luck inheritance?"

Without waiting for an answer, she glided past me and disappeared into the house, leaving me to ponder her question.

I followed, shaking my head at her stubbornness. My heart filled with anticipation and trepidation as I stepped into the entrance hall. The house's grandeur, with its high ceilings and intricate chandeliers, hit me like a wave. It was one of the largest and most beautiful rooms I had ever seen, and I couldn't help but feel a sense of awe and wonder.

The log cabin look continued inside, with the internal walls constructed of oak planking to match the flooring. The furniture suited the decor, manufactured from cherry-colored timber. The walls were adorned with Native Indian pictures, feather-clad ornaments, bows and arrows, tomahawks, and other weapons. The feel was comfortable, soothing, yet respectful of the local indigenous culture. I felt deeply moved and impressed.

To the left of the entrance was a cozy lounge area featuring luxurious leather seating for eight adults. A dining table with ten chairs was positioned in the center of the room, nestled between the living area and the opulent kitchen. The kitchen resembled something out of a magazine, boasting oak cabinetry with white quartz marble countertops complemented by high-end appliances. To the right of the entrance, a sweeping staircase led up to the loft area, alongside a doorway that I presumed led to the main bedroom.

Everything was situated so that the view looked out over the lake. I had to ask myself if that was for the view or so the previous occupants could see the menacing Manitou approaching, intent on murdering the inhabitants. The ridiculous thought made me bite my lower lip to stop myself from laughing.

A dreamcatcher hung from each window frame, dangling in the center of each pane of glass. Some segments held different-colored glass, so looking through them gave a kaleidoscope effect. The entire room contained so many native Indian artifacts that it almost made me feel dizzy. I knew Miriam would not be happy and would want it all cleared out, and my first thought was that I did, too, but then, in the back of my mind, a nagging thought that I shouldn't.

Charley's head appeared over the balcony. "Mom, Dad, there are three bedrooms up here, all with balconies facing the lake. It's really nice. Can I have the red room?"

"I want the blue room," Martin shouted above us.

I shook my head and smiled. *At least they're not fighting over who gets the biggest one.*

****

I noticed a sheet of notepaper on the countertop and crossed to pick it up.

Dear Mr. and Mrs. Harford

I've had the entire house cleaned for you by a local cleaning service. Their business card is on the desk in the study, alongside the main bedroom, if you want to use it in the future. They have also laundered all the bedding and topped up the refrigerator and pantry.

Enjoy your stay.

Trent Bamforth

I held it up and read it to Miriam, saying, "What a nice gesture. I must remember to call and thank him when we get back. Well, Miriam, what do you think? Isn't it magnificent?"

"Hmmm. Yes, it was a nice thing to do, but it was probably to get the smell out of the place from the bodies. Washing the sheets might have been necessary if they died in bed. I'm not really comfortable sleeping where two people died."

I sighed, knowing I was in for an uphill battle. "We never found out where they passed away; it could have been on the couch or the sun loungers out on the deck. Come on, love. Let's give the place a fair chance. You have to admit it's stunning, isn't it?"

She stared at me briefly as if trying to understand me. Eventually, she shrugged. "I grant you the architecture and scenery are beautiful, but even you must accept that with all this native paraphernalia around, your grandfather was scared of boogeymen. So maybe we should be, too."

I hadn't discussed the contents of the letter my grandfather left me or my internet search on the massacre that had supposedly started the curse with Miriam because I did not want to make her more paranoid. Her words shook me, and not for the first time, they made me worry she might have a point. But there was no way I could tell her that now. Call it stupid male pride, but I felt I had to get Miriam to back down.

At the same time, I knew her well. If I argued, it could start World War Three, so I had to press on diplomatically. "I agree, some of this stuff is a bit...weird, and we should bring the house into this century and put most of the things into storage. But let's not bother this trip; we'll just enjoy this little break from the city, spend some time with our children, catch some fish, drink some wine on the deck, and watch the sunset before going to bed and reliving our honeymoon."

She smiled impishly, and I saw a glimpse of the old Miriam, the coquettish one who could turn me on like no other when she wanted to. "I make no promises, but play your cards right, Buster, and just maybe."

"C'mon, let's check out the main bedroom and study, then the back deck. I hear the first glass of wine calling our names, so long as that rain doesn't return."

****

The rest of the home, including the three bathrooms and laundry room, was as magnificent as the large family and living area. I thought the valuation of the house for the estate tax that Trent Bamforth had paid on my behalf could have been understated, and I wondered if I should get an independent valuation to ease my conscience. I am, after all, a chartered accountant, and I would rather pay Uncle Sam more than necessary and sleep peacefully at night than worry about a knock on the door someday from an IRS investigator.

I commandeered Martin to help me grab our bags from the car, and he good-naturedly agreed. I loaded him with his and his sister's cases and sent him ahead of me. I was about to pull out Miriam's oversized, over-packed trunk and my much smaller bag when I looked up through the windscreen and saw a man standing near the garage.

Our eyes met across the gravel parking area, and I sized him up as a potential threat. He seemed elderly, well into his sixties, tall and thin with long gray hair down to his shoulders. He stood, staring at me, with hands in his denim jeans pockets, and for a moment, I worried whether the man held a pistol in his hand. He gave me a ghost of a smile and an imperceptible nod in greeting. I let go of my grip on the suitcase and stood slowly, intending to go and speak to him, but when I moved from the back of the vehicle to the side, he had gone. I looked around frantically, yet there was no sign of him anywhere. Did I imagine him? Noooooooooooo, I hadn't, had I?

Chapter 7

Miriam Explains

I couldn't find any sign of the gray-haired man, so I shrugged, blamed my overactive imagination, and headed inside with the bags. I distributed them to the correct bedrooms.

In the large double-chilled refrigerator, wrapped in butcher's paper, I found four beautiful steaks that I knew would be perfect for dinner. Unaware that Trent would handle provisions, we had brought food in an ice cooler and drinks in another, which I placed in the kitchen. Before leaving, Miriam had made her famous potato salad, and we had the ingredients for a green salad to go with it, so dinner was set for our first night in what I fervently hoped would be our new vacation home.

Once everyone unpacked, the family gathered on the back deck, overlooking the lake with a breathtaking view of the open lake and surrounding trees. The water was crystal clear, and leaning over the railing, we could see the bottom and the hundreds of small fish darting in and out of the weeds and grasses. An incredible outdoor kitchen was located under the main roof, featuring a BBQ, a wood-fired pizza oven, a char grill, bar fridges, and a sink. It felt special, and I could imagine cooking many meals here.

Martin asked if they could go for a walk and explore, and I readily agreed so I could talk with Miriam.

My grandfather had a small room next to the study that was converted into a temperature-controlled wine room. One wall featured racks of excellent red wines, imported and from The Napa Valley, while the opposite wall held a bank of refrigerators filled with white wines. I grabbed an Australian Barossa Valley Cabernet and two glasses in one hand, then found Miriam unpacking the icebox into the fridge. I led her through the sliding glass doors out to the spacious deck, where I poured two measures, set the bottle on the twelve-seat outdoor dining table, and handed one glass to my wife. "Here's to our new vacation lake house," I toasted, "may we always be happy here."

Miriam was about to sip from the glass, but she paused and stared at me over the top. "Bob, I have my reasons for being against this inheritance, and I understand that people may consider me mad in today's world. The house is beautiful, there is no argument there, but I am against owning it, and if I had my way, we would not be here; we would hand it back to the natives."

I shook my head, determined not to get angry but needing to understand her reasons. Thus far, I have always believed Miriam to be a grounded, down-to-earth, pragmatic woman, and this was, to my mind, so out of character. "But why, love, explain it to me so I can understand."

She finally took a long drink of the wine, and I followed suit. It was remarkably good. I detected Blackberry notes, and it was smooth, almost syrupy.

Finally, Miriam said. "It's because my sister died in a car accident."

I was aware of the tragedy that occurred when Miriam was twenty-three. I attended the funeral with her, and she was understandably devastated by the loss.

She blinked back tears of remembrance. "What I never told you is that the car she was incinerated in was inherited from our grandfather. He restored the 1968 Mustang, and it was beautiful. Audrey would go to his place on weekends to help him rebuild it. When he passed away from cancer, he left it to her in his will. The first time she drove, it was after eleven at night. She was crossing the Wyde River, well within the speed limit on the Goodman Bridge, when, for no apparent reason, the car hit a guardrail and burst into flames. Audrey had no chance to escape."

I had heard the expression before; my *blood ran cold,* but I never truly believed it. Yet on the deck, with the warm afternoon sun beating down, I shivered and realized I was freezing from the inside out; *my blood had truly run cold.* I had never before connected the death of Miriam's sister on a bridge over the River Wyde with my parents' death in the same river. Granted, it was a different bridge and different causes of death, but still…Had Miriam made the same connection, or was her phobia about inheritances being unlucky the root cause of her unease?

"Sweetheart, we've never talked about this, but surely you can see that a restored classic car could have had a mechanical fault. I remember that Mustang; it was beautifully finished, but it was still an old car, and it might have had mechanical issues that could not be foreseen."

She nodded as if she expected my response. "And my Uncle Mathew and Aunty Silvia?"

I couldn't think what she meant by that; I couldn't remember ever having met them. "What about them, love?"

"They inherited their parents' home and planned to move in, but both fell ill with a nasty flu bug before they could. Aunt Silvia passed away from her fever, and Uncle Mathew followed three days later."

"I'm sorry to hear that. However, you must recognize that every year, millions of bequests are made, and hundreds of people die from influenza."

"You know where my family's heritage hails from?"

"Yes, you've told me many times you are a direct descendant of Sarah Osbourne, one of the original witches of Salem."

"Well, I have never liked talking about it, but my family has always had the ability, to some degree, to foretell the future. Or at least to have strong feelings about it. It seems to have distilled somewhat in me because I still get…feelings. Mostly bad ones, and over the years, I have learned to listen to them. For example, I knew my father was going to have his stroke at least an hour before it hit him. It has always been the biggest regret of my life that I ignored that warning, and he died because of it."

I felt dazed by such a revelation, though I still struggled to understand why she was against inheriting the lake house. "You've never told me that, hon. Surely, you can't seriously blame yourself, can you?"

"Yes, I do. I hide it, and the logical part of my brain tells me it's not my fault, but that feels hollow. I know it is my fault. I also understand that this house, as beautiful as it is, is cursed. I can sense the evil radiating from every wall. It means us harm. Sure, maybe not today, but I know it is biding its time, and when it's ready, it will strike. When it does, it will be catastrophic. I urge you, please, Bob, give it back to the Indians, sell it, gift it—whatever you choose—but please do not put our family at risk."

I shook my head, dumbfounded, and felt I could scream at the absurdity. Then, I had a thought that might help. "Are you saying the house is the problem, not the inheritance?"

Miriam closed her eyes and tilted her head to one side as if someone were whispering in her ear. After a few moments, she nodded, "Yes, any inheritance can bring bad luck, but I know this house specifically is the problem in my soul."

I saw an opening, a chink in the armor she had covered herself in. "So if we sold it to the Indians and used that money to buy another house, that would be okay?"

"I think so, yes."

That made no sense whatsoever, but then, nothing she'd said did.

Chapter 8

The Shawnee Elders

Before I could answer, a loud rapping sound came from the front door.

"Maybe the kids locked themselves out," I murmured, setting my glass on the table before walking back into the house, cursing that I was about to lose the best vacation home in the world if I wanted to stay married.

Absentmindedly, I jerked the door open and saw two people waiting. One was the gray-haired man I had seen earlier, accompanied by a younger woman. Behind him was a bright red truck adorned with chrome bars and spotlights.

"Mr. Harford, my name is William Ford, and this is Magenta, my youngest daughter. We are elders of the Shawnee Nation, traditional owners of this land. We have come to speak with you. Your grandfather was a good friend, and Navina was my oldest daughter."

"Please come in. I'm glad to meet you both, and I'm sorry for your loss. We're having a glass of wine on the deck; would you like something to drink?"

"Thank you. Some iced water would be welcome."

I guided them through the house, pausing in the kitchen to pour them water from the refrigerator dispenser. I took them outside and introduced them to Miriam. We sat at the table, and I asked how we could assist them.

"Firstly, as your grandfather's heir, we welcome you and your family to our land and assure you that, despite your heritage, the Shawnees hold no ill will toward you. We harbor no grudges and want you to know that your family is welcome to live here in peace and harmony with our people, as far as *we* are concerned."

At first, I felt welcomed but then sensed an undercurrent beneath his words, as if there was something grim that he hadn't mentioned yet because he had emphasized the word *we*. "Thank you for the welcome. We are pleased to be here and had intended to seek the elders out and pay our respects tomorrow; we only arrived an hour ago."

He nodded in acknowledgment and smiled. "You have children, I believe. Did you not bring them with you?"

"We did," Miriam added, "they have gone off exploring. You know what children are like."

William exchanged a glance with Magenta, who had not spoken a word so far, then turned to survey the lake's surface. "They aren't in canoes out on the lake?"

"No, exploring in the forest. Why do you ask?" Miriam sounded worried, which matched how I felt.

He shook his head as if the question was inconsequential and glanced at me. "I believe you were estranged from your grandfather for many years?"

"Yes, unfortunately." I didn't want to go into why and admit my parents had been bigoted.

"Are you familiar with the Shawnee history in this area?"

"Some, yes." I wanted to avoid going into detail in front of Miriam. She opposed keeping the house, but if she learned about the curse placed on my family due to the massacre, I knew I would have no chance of convincing her to do it.

"My people have lived near the lake for thousands of years, and when the white men came, we offered peace and even some land concessions. But the more we gave, the more the whites wanted, and they pushed and pushed us to leave our homeland and travel west. Meanwhile, we looked to our protector, The Manitou of The Lake, for guidance and help, but it was too late. The soldiers attacked our village when our men were away. It was a genocide, and all our women and children were murdered. Your forebear led the men who did it."

Miriam gasped and turned an accusing gaze to me. "Did you know this, Bob?"

I sighed and nodded. There was no point in lying or denying it. At that moment, I realized again that we wouldn't be keeping the lake house if I wanted to stay married. "The letter Mr. Bamforth gave me was from my grandfather; it explained the attack. But, Miriam, that happened over two hundred years ago."

"Your grandfather was a good man," William interrupted. "With Navina's help and guidance, he did his best to appease The Manitou, hoping the curse would end with him. He sacrificed himself to the Great Spirit so that you and your family could live in peace. However, The Manitou chose not to forgive, punishing both Navina and your grandfather for what he saw as her treachery. Magenta believes The Manitou is not finished with your family yet, so I asked if your children were out on the lake. You must not let them go out there alone."

Miriam's cheeks turned red in anger, and she glared at me. "You should have told me this, Bob. How did they die? Can you tell us, please? Mr. Bamforth couldn't or wouldn't tell us."

William looked down at his gnarled, arthritic hands, and I noticed his eyes clouding with tears. "No one else was here, so we can only guess at some things. It seems they were both on the deck at night. Somehow, Navina fell into the water and drowned. Your grandfather couldn't save her and suffered a heart attack." I watched him wipe away the tears from his eyes. "I found their bodies two days later. I've never known two finer people. I miss my daughter every day, but feel proud that she did everything she could to end a curse that shames our nation."

I looked at Miriam, who was crying, and I felt I could join her. Whether or not I believed in the mumbo-jumbo curse, my wife was upset, and I knew I finally had to concede to her beliefs or lose her. "William, we have decided that as beautiful a house as this is, it is not for us. We want to offer it to your people."

He nodded. "That is a wise and very generous decision, and I thank you for it. Do not remain here any longer than necessary; you are in danger from The Manitou's vengeance." He raised his hand to halt any interruptions. "In today's modern world, I understand you may not believe in ancient curses, Manitous, or anything spiritual, but in our culture, we do. Magenta has implored The Manitou to end his revenge, yet he has ignored her requests. He could be sleeping right now, or he may have chosen to dismiss her plea. I do not claim to understand his thoughts. We made a treaty with your grandfather stating that neither he nor his heir can sell without our explicit permission and only if we elect not to purchase it. Please obtain three independent valuations, and we will agree to pay you the average price."

"No!" Miriam exclaimed. She turned to me, half pleading, half demanding. "I believe Bob needs to make amends on behalf of his family, who wronged your people years ago. We also have an opportunity to make a gesture on behalf of all the whites who came and stole your lands. We should gift this home to the Shawnees, not sell it."

Chapter 9

Trying to Make Peace with The Manitou

When Miriam proposed giving away our lakeside house, it felt like she had lifted a heavy burden off my shoulders after William's comments. During his speech, I felt ashamed. A smile spread across my face. They say you can't miss what you've never had, and I had never been a millionaire. By parting with the house, I knew I would be one with the rest of the inheritance and our current savings. It seemed that donating the house was the right thing to do.

"I wholeheartedly agree with my wife," I said, smiling at Miriam. "We would like to make this goodwill gesture to the Shawnee people. The truth is, William, for the last thirty years, I didn't know my grandfather, and I certainly didn't know he lived here. I regret that, but due to events that occurred years ago, my mother and father enforced the separation. This building is one of the most beautiful houses I have ever seen, but honestly? It doesn't feel like home, especially since my wife feels so uncomfortable here. And if my family is in any danger from this Manitou, even if I don't personally believe in it, it isn't worth the risk as far as I'm concerned. Please take the house and do as you wish—turn it into a fishing and hunting lodge, a hotel, a rental, or a home for the head of the tribe. We don't want a single cent from the Shawnee Nation for it: it's our gift to you. I'll have our lawyer prepare the transfer of ownership documents when we return to town. Please give me your lawyer's contact details as we won't visit here again."

The euphoria that filled my soul was indescribable. I knew, without a doubt, that this was the right thing to do. And if, in some small way, it could make up for the terrible things done to Native American Indians over the years, then that was a bonus. But beneath the surface of our decision, a complex mix of emotions was brewing: hope, fear, and a deep sense of responsibility. These emotions, like a bittersweet symphony, played in my heart, reminding me of the weight of our choice. We were giving away a home worth over a million dollars, and suddenly, the value didn't matter—not in dollar terms, anyway.

Magenta stood up suddenly and spoke in a trembling, emotional voice. "Mr. and Mrs. Harford, your generosity reflects your good nature. I knew your grandfather well. Navina was my sister, and I spent a lot of time with them. He would be proud of you for doing this. He spent his years here trying to make peace with The Manitou for the wrongs of the past. He attempted, with my sister, not just to converse with The Manitou but also to befriend it. He did not succeed and passed away trying. While his heart was true and his intentions good, he failed because he was unwilling to make a personal sacrifice of the magnitude that The Manitou would accept. Not that he would demand a sacrifice. For it to hold any meaning, it must be offered unconditionally. True love should always come with sacrifice. You have made an earnest offer, and I hope this will appease The Manitou and allow him to release the curse and finally let the past remain buried."

She opened her purse and pulled out several leather strands adorned with baubles. "I have made you four amulets," she said, her voice infused with reverence as she handed them to me. "These are more than mere trinkets; they are symbols of protection. I would like you and your children to wear them whenever you are near the lake or inside this house. I carved them from pebbles collected from the lake and blessed them, hoping they would provide some protection from The Manitou if he struck. The Manitou sleeps for long stretches, so he may not even be aware of your presence; I sincerely hope that's the case. I will take my leave now; I need to try to communicate with our protector, express your generosity, and ask that he put an end to the feud with your family that has persisted for two hundred years. Thank you for the water and your kindness. I can see myself out.

I realized that the charms were not merely physical objects, at least not to Magenta, but symbols of our willingness to confront the supernatural and protect our family. I stood and walked with her, the amulets swinging from my hand, uncertain if I would wear one but not wanting to appear rude.

At the door, she turned to me and smiled. "I sense your skepticism, and I understand it. You do not know the ways of my people or our beliefs. May I ask a personal question?"

I shrugged. "Of course, ask me anything."

"Are you a Christian?"

I nodded. "We go to church on Sundays, and I believe in God."

"In your faith, you believe that wearing a crucifix will help ward off evil, do you not?"

I knew where this conversation was heading and that she had boxed me into a corner. "Yes, the image of Jesus on the cross is a centuries-old symbol of good."

She smiled, and her emerald eyes sparkled. She was an extraordinarily beautiful woman. "Your religion is centuries old; ours spans thousands, but both share iconography. We believe that our symbols are good and meaningful and that faith protects us, not the item itself. Please wear the amulets and believe that if The Manitou appears, they will protect you. If you believe they will work, then they will. I am going now to a special place in the lake to try to summon The Manitou. If he comes, I will tell him of your generosity and hope he agrees to a lasting peace. The Shawnee Nation has always favored peace over bloodshed. You've done a wonderful thing for my people with your gift, and I hope it is enough to atone for the evil deeds of your forebear."

"Thank you, Magenta." I held out my hand, and she shook it. I still wasn't sure I believed in the curse or that there was any credible danger to us, but I also figured it couldn't hurt to cover all the bases. I watched her leave on foot toward the trees and thought: *Have faith in blessed stones on a leather thong? I don't think so.* I left them on the hall table as I walked back to the deck.

Chapter 10

Charlotte Harford

Thirteen-year-old Charlotte, or Charlie as she preferred, came home from her walk in the woods with her brother, wet, cold, miserable, and angry. Martin, who surely had to be the most obnoxious brother in the world, had started their walk being *almost* normal. She had to add the word *almost* because Marty was always unpredictable. He could be nice one moment, then her tormentor the next, seemingly for no good reason other than he wanted to be a pig at her expense.

For all his faults, she loved him, and it was true that throughout her life, he had been kinder and more considerate than a terror. But it seemed to Charlie that the older he got, the worse his jokes that belittled her became. Charlie hoped it was a passing phase, maybe linked to his raging puberty hormones, but sometimes she could just…well, in the best-case scenario, disown him, and in the worst, stab him in the eye with a dinner fork.

Today was a perfect example. Martin started with that creepy voice when they paused for a break at the top of the hill and saw the lake house for the first time, which terrified her. Her friends once showed her a clip from *The Exorcist*, where the possessed girl spoke in a demon's voice, and Martin sounded just like that. She wasn't sure why it was so frightening, but his voice felt ancient and sinister, not like the fifteen-year-old A-grade student he was.

After they returned to the car, he seemed normal, almost human again, as if nothing had happened. He laughed and joked with her, which was unsettling, too, because it was as if he were two different people. He acted normally right up until her father nearly crashed the car while avoiding a dead deer. Once again, Martin became her favorite brother when he volunteered to help move the carcass without any complaint, even though Charlie herself could not bear to touch the filthy, bleeding animal. He huffed and puffed, sweated, and grunted until they dragged the dead deer to the side of the road so that another car wouldn't have an accident.

Martin was usually a good brother, so she thought it would be a good idea when he suggested going for a walk to explore the woods and give their parents some alone time. And it was fun—until it wasn't.

The weather was lovely, neither too hot nor too cold, and peaceful, with only birdlife breaking the silence. After half an hour, Charlie and Martin came across a bubbling brook, a small tributary that fed into the lake that seemed to come from the heart of a giant redwood tree's roots. It was a picturesque spot, and they stopped to sit on a fallen log for a while. Martin trailed his fingers in the water as it rushed to join the vast body of water below.

Suddenly, he jerked his hand toward her and threw something that hit her throat and then slid down the front of her shirt. It was slimy and wriggling. Charlie shrieked and stood up, stomping, yanking at her clothes, trying to get rid of it. Whatever it was, it was moving inside her shirt, slithering, making her scream in terror. Charlie didn't know what the hell it was: a spider, small snake, lizard, or heaven knew what. Frantically, she tried to dislodge it by pulling the shirt out of her jeans and ripping the buttons apart while Martin sat on the log, laughing his head off. A bright green frog leaped from her stomach, no doubt as frightened as she was. *"You horrible pig, I hate you!"* she screamed at Martin and then stormed off back to the house, leaving him giggling hysterically.

****

Her parents were still sitting at the table on the deck, talking to an old man who looked like a cross between a farmer and a cowboy, so Charlie stormed past without a hello and went upstairs to her bedroom. On arrival, she had unpacked her bag, so after slamming her door shut, she grabbed fresh underwear and a change of clothes and headed into her bathroom, locking the door to keep her brother out.

Charlie reached into the shower cubicle and turned on the taps. She waited for the water to warm up, undressed, and stepped inside, closing the glass door behind her. The moment she stood under the rainmaker shower, the water flow slowed to a trickle, and a strange, sloshing noise echoed in the cubicle.

"God damn it, will anything go right today?" she cried, turning the taps forward and backward in frustration, but no more water came out, and the scurrying noise increased. *Must be a blockage in the shower head,* she thought.

Charlie considered getting dressed again and asking her father to fix the shower, but that felt like too much effort. Besides, he had company and wouldn't want to leave to attend to it, so she would have to endure the slime from the frog on her skin for who knew how long, which was unacceptable. Groaning in frustration, she yanked the taps to the off position, reached up, gripped the shower head, and turned it counterclockwise. Slowly, it moved, then picked up speed as it unscrewed. Charlie smiled; *soon,* she thought, *I can wash away the scent of that filthy frog from my tummy.*

She felt proud of herself for being an adult and not needing her father until the shower head came apart, and a plague of tiny wriggling, hopping, creepy, slimy frogs spewed from the pipe. Hundreds of the creatures rained down in a torrent of obscenity.

Charlotte Harford had never been so terrified in her life. This was worse than any nightmare she could imagine. She screamed in utter terror and fainted, collapsing onto the marble-tiled floor as the frogs continued to pour out of the pipe, raining down and covering her bare body.

Chapter 11

The Coming of The Manitou

William stayed for over an hour, and they talked about the area's history and the attempts by the Shawnee Nation to not only welcome the first white people but also work toward a peaceful cohabitation. Over many years, the Shawnees, despite their best efforts, were coerced into giving up more and more of their lands for towns, mines, and farms. The buffalo herds were slaughtered almost to extinction by hunters who only took the pelts, leaving the carcasses to rot and feed the vultures. Waterways became polluted by silver mining, and the Natives were pushed farther and farther west. And then, after three braves, including the chief's son, were beaten to death by townspeople, apparently drunk, according to the local sheriff, the tribal council decided they could take no more. A vast war party came together from surrounding tribes and, led by Gray Wolf, amassed at the village by the lake to go and confront the blue coats. They believed that only a show of strength could make the whites take notice and desist. They did not want to attack the fortress; they merely surrounded it to show there would be a war if things did not improve.

But while they circled the fortress, the soldiers came to their village and massacred everyone. When the braves returned, they found Sampata naked and ranting maniacally, cursing and screaming. She wanted not only every white man in the area killed but also future generations. Gray Wolf, realizing how far the invaders would go to steal their lands, understood that if he didn't move farther west as the government man had ordered, the white men would obliterate the Shawnee Nation. Reluctantly, despite Sampata's bitter complaints, they moved west.

Much later, the tribal elders sent a delegation to Washington and negotiated with the government to return to the lake, which had fed and sustained the tribe for thousands of years. When they succeeded, the area was designated a reservation.

****

Miriam and I saw Charlotte come home alone after her walk in the woods with her brother. She crossed the family room with an angry determination and headed straight for the stairs. In my heart, I sensed that Martin had done or said something to upset his sister, judging by the look on my daughter's face. Miriam shook her head and glared at me. For the hundredth time, I wondered why Martin could be so unkind to her at times. I realized I needed to have a serious talk with him. Miriam stood up and said, "Forgive me, William, but I need to check on my daughter; she seems upset about something."

He glanced up, looking alarmed. "Is she hurt?"

"No, I don't think so," Miriam replied. "Charlotte seems like she's fought with her brother, which isn't unusual considering he's fifteen and acts like he's eight. Please stay. I should be back soon."

"No, I've taken enough of your time. I should go and leave you to pack. You need to get on the road if you are leaving today."

"We will go home tomorrow, William. We might as well stay at least one night, though our children will be upset about leaving such a beautiful home. Staying tonight will help us explain it to them," I said.

He looked down at his hands as if searching for the right words. "You have both been incredibly kind. I feel I must caution you against staying. I know our beliefs and folklore are difficult for you to understand, let alone believe, but The Manitou is as real to my people as the sun is to you. Your family has been cursed, and if you stay, you may be at risk from his wrath unless Magenta can appease him. The Manitou is the spirit of the lake, and his power is immense. While distance can lessen his influence, it is that very distance that has kept you safe so far. Here, in this house, you are perched over his domain. He may be sleeping and not know you are here, or Magenta may be able to persuade him to leave you alone. But it is possible that he will take his revenge regardless."

I felt a mix of sadness and anger. I had been polite and respectful of William's culture, agreed to hand over a million-dollar house, listened to his stories of days gone by, and accepted stones on strings to wear, supposedly to protect us. But this was too much for me to endure. "William, we will stay tonight and leave before lunchtime tomorrow. I believe the deaths in my family's past are nothing more than coincidences. I don't believe in ghosts, voodoo dolls, black magic, or Native American Manitous, I'm sorry. We will be fine. Thank you for coming. My lawyer will be in touch soon to arrange the transfer of ownership."

I held my hand out for him to shake, which he did. He nodded first to me and then to Miriam and walked away without another word.

****

Miriam hugged me the moment William left. "I'm proud of you. Thank you for agreeing with me," she whispered.

I didn't want to say I completely agreed with her reasoning, but the outcome was the same. Giving back the house was for the best. Before I could respond, we heard a shriek from upstairs.

"Charlie!" I called, and Miriam and I dashed upstairs to see what was wrong. "Charlie," I shouted louder as we ran up the wooden stairs. "What's wrong?"

Silence was the only reply. I ran ahead of Miriam, got to the bedroom first, and knocked on the door. "Charlie, are you okay?" Again, there was no answer, so I turned the handle and pushed it open. The bedroom was empty.

"Bathroom," Miriam yelled and pushed past me. With one hand, she slapped the bathroom door, shouting Charlie's name, while her other hand jerked at the handle, but Charlie had locked it.

"Step back, Miriam." I pulled her away and then shouldered the door. It shook and wobbled on brass hinges but remained closed. I stepped back and hit it again with all my strength, and this time, the door swung open. The latch flew across the room and clattered on the tiled floor as my momentum carried me inside. The wall trembled, and a mirror came loose from its mounting and crashed to the floor, shattering into three pieces.

Charlie lay curled on the shower floor, water cascading down, not moving.

****

After turning off the water, Miriam and I tried to

help our daughter out of the shower. As we propped her up against the wall, she started to regain her composure. I wrapped her in a towel to spare her embarrassment. I assumed she had slipped and hit her head, although I couldn't see any bruises or bleeding.

Charlie jerked awake and frantically looked around her. "Where's the frogs?" she demanded in a maniacal voice.

I glanced at Miriam, questioning, but she looked back as perplexed as I was. "What frogs, sweetheart?" I coaxed.

"The ones that came out of the shower head, hundreds of them." Her head jerked from side to side, then back to us. She burst into tears. "I didn't imagine them, I didn't."

Chapter 12

Martin Harford

As Martin's laughter at his sister's shock subsided, a wave of guilt crashed over him, its intensity mirrored in his pained expression. Though his sister's fear had been amusing, it had been genuine. He felt a pang of remorse for relishing in her distress, but their typical sibling banter was a force he found hard to resist. After all, what were younger sisters for if not to be teased and annoyed?

He watched his fiery sister, a young girl with a quick temper, stomp away from him through the trees, cursing and muttering about him being a child. Slowly, his joyful mood ebbed away. *Maybe I should go after her and apologize? Nahhhhhh, she'll be okay. For Christ's sake, it was only a tiny frog, not a poisonous spider.*

He wasn't ready to head back to the house, and he assumed Charlie would rat him out to their parents, so he decided to let things calm down before returning. Plus, there were acres and acres of lakeside forest to explore. Maybe he could find another deer, a live one this time, rather than the dead one on the road earlier.

An hour later, Martin realized he was completely lost. Panic gripped him as his heart raced and sweat dripped from his forehead. He paused and slowly turned three hundred sixty degrees, hoping to spot a landmark to guide him back home. Nothing. All he could see were trees and bushes, and more trees and bushes beyond those.

Martin wrestled with the rising tide of panic that began in his stomach, climbed to his chest, and threatened to engulf him. He fought to remain calm and think rationally. *Where is the sun? When I left the house, I remember feeling the heat on my left shoulder, so if the sun is now on my right, I should be heading in the right direction.*

The only problem with that theory was that he couldn't see the sun through the thick tree canopy and clouds. He tried to stop the echoing sound of his frantic heartbeat so he could listen for any sounds that might give him a direction to follow. *Cicadas...leaves rustling...birds whistling...a splash like a fish jumping...wait, a fish jumping? That must be the lake. All I need to do is get to it, then follow the shoreline to the left, and it will lead me back to the house.*

Martin felt a surge of relief as if the world's weight had been lifted from his shoulders. He trotted toward the splash sound, believing he had found his way to safety.

A stiff breeze suddenly sprang up several minutes later, which Martin felt on his face. With it came a slightly unpleasant smell. A cloying, decaying odor assailed him, and it seemed like the farther he went, the stronger the scent. Fifty yards farther on, sweating even more now from exertion and the humidity under the canopy of what Martin thought of as the endless forest, he almost gagged from the smell of rotting vegetation, or was it something else?

Martin stopped, placed his hands on his knees, and tried to take deep gulps of air without breathing through his nose. He watched a bead of sweat drip from the tip of his nose and hit the mud.

That's when Martin realized he was no longer standing on solid ground as he had thought; his once-white trainers were submerged in thick brown slime up to the laces. *Mom's going to kill me. These shoes are only three weeks old.*

He lifted his left foot and repositioned it, then did the same with his right. However, the change in his leg angle and the suction of the marsh forced his foot out of the shoe, leaving Martin balancing on one leg like a stork until he lost his equilibrium.

"Shit, shit, shit," he yelled as his foot sank into the mire up to his ankle bone. He bent down, grabbed the heel of the errant sneaker, and yanked it out. An almost invisible cloud of methane gas wafted up, and Martin took a deep breath through his nose.

First, his eyes watered, and then his brain recognized the terrible smell. Before he could comprehend or halt the feeling, Martin projectile vomited again and again. Each time he attempted to stop, thinking he was done, the smell overwhelmed him again, and the retching resumed.

Martin fell to his knees, weak and sweating profusely, feeling as if he were dying. Being on his knees brought him closer to the mud and its putrid odor. *Oh my God, what could be buried here to smell this bad?* His vision swam; drool dripped from his lips down his chin. Martin felt as if he could die there, and part of him felt so weak that he thought he would welcome it.

That's when he noticed the water collecting around his knees. It appeared to be lapping in ripples from the direction of the lake, which he realized must be very close. The rising water was reminiscent of the tide coming in on a shallow beach. *But surely, a lake isn't tidal, is it?*

As his foggy mind cleared, Marty realized several things at once. He was sinking deeper into the mud as the influx of lake water transformed the marsh into quicksand, which spiked his panic again. He also noticed that the skin below the muddy surface itched intensely. Martin understood that it might not have been sudden; he just hadn't noticed it earlier. Martin yanked his hand out of the slime—which had sunk deeper during the minutes he spent on hands and knees—reached down and rubbed the outside of his calf. He felt a wriggling sensation. He gripped whatever was causing it and raised his hand to inspect it.

Martin screamed as he saw his cupped hand contained a mound of pink, seething, jostling worms with curved pincer-like jaw appendages that clicked together as the worms tried to bite anything they could. Each one was around five inches long and translucent as if swollen from drinking blood, his blood. Martin couldn't move, frozen in time, rocked to his core with a chilling terror as he realized the worms were trying to eat him.

Panic set in, and Martin struggled to escape the mud, but the more he struggled, the deeper he sank. Terrified, he screamed again and again as he struggled to break free. It was a race to see if he drowned in mud before the worms ate the flesh from his bones.

A crashing noise echoed from ahead, and he saw a torrent of water rushing toward him. His mind struggled to comprehend everything happening around him, and his body was sinking deeper into the muck. At the same time, worm-like creatures attempted to burrow beneath his skin, and the approaching wave of lake water threatened to engulf him.

He screamed for help once more and looked up at the wave that he was convinced would inundate and possibly drown him. Yet the wall of water, a mini tsunami, halted as if frozen in mid-air, just three feet in front of his struggling body. There, as part of the bubbling surface of the water, a Native Indian's face displayed an evil smile at Martin's helplessness.

The mud held Martin in its deathly grip and was up to his hips while the lake water climbed up his chest. The worms burrowed into his skin, now causing agony rather than the itching before. He felt one creature crawl up his neck, over his chin, and enter his mouth. Screaming louder and louder, he bit the worm, which exploded against his tongue. The foul taste made him gag, and he spat the remains out. He dry retched once more, but there was nothing left in his stomach to vomit.

Martin sobbed as he noticed the water was now up to his neck. More worms tried to get inside his lips, and he could hear the mocking laughter from the face in the wave.

Martin knew, without the shadow of a doubt, he was about to die.

Chapter 13

The Manitou

I left Miriam to help Charlie dry and put on comfortable clothes. I went downstairs to wait and was relieved to see Charlie looking a little calmer when they came down to join me, though her skin was still pale. She wore pink gym track pants and a T-shirt featuring her favorite pop star on the front. Her blonde hair was brushed and tied up in a ponytail.

"Are you okay now, sweetie?" I asked my daughter softly as she sat on the leather couch across from me in the rocking recliner.

She nodded, but Miriam interjected. "Apparently, Martin scared Charlotte by throwing a frog at her during their walk in the forest. It landed inside her shirt and upset her, so I think when she got home and took a shower, she somehow imagined more frogs coming out of the pipes. Martin has a lot to answer for, and I expect you to punish him when he returns."

My anger at my son rose like the mercury in a thermometer dropped into boiling water. "Oh, you can be sure I will have words with him," I muttered.

"It seemed so real," Charlie gasped as fresh tears appeared. "I've never felt so scared in my life; they poured out when I removed the showerhead, hundreds of them, wriggling and crawling all over me. I will never go into that bathroom ever again."

I must admit that I couldn't imagine how a hallucination could be so frightening, but Charlie's distress was genuine. She wasn't usually hysterical, so whatever had happened was certainly real to her. "Sweetheart, we're leaving here in the morning, so you will never need to go into that room again. Your mother and I have decided to give this house back to the Native Tribe; it's the right thing to do."

"I want to leave when Martin returns, not in the morning. This house is evil, and I don't want to spend the night here," Miriam said firmly, using the tone of voice she always used when I knew from experience it would be impossible to change her mind.

I sighed. It was pointless to argue, and the fact that I was already tired from the long drive here wouldn't sway Miriam's decision, even though it was after five. "All right, let's get packed up and head out as soon as Martin returns." I stood and patted my pocket for the car keys, but they were missing. "Where are the keys, Miriam? Did I give them to you?"

"No," she replied curtly. Charlotte, come with me and help remove the bags from the bedrooms while your father works down here." Then she asked me, "Did you leave them in the car?"

"Maybe. I'll go check."

****

The keys were neither inside our wagon nor hanging from the tailgate. I knelt in the gravel, looking underneath in case I had dropped them while unpacking, but they weren't there either. *They must be in the house,* I decided.

I headed back inside, trying to remember the last time I'd seen them. I searched the kitchen, then outside on the deck—still not there. *Our bedroom! I thought with relief that I must have left them on the bedside cupboard*, even though I couldn't recall doing that. When I checked, they weren't there either.

In the next ten frantic minutes, I searched every inch of the house, inside and out, but I couldn't find the keys. I went back to the car, convinced that I had just overlooked them during my earlier search, but I had no more success than before. Back inside the house, I found Miriam and Charlie putting the food back into the ice chest in the kitchen. "Miriam, I can't find the car keys anywhere. Are you sure you haven't seen them?"

She glared at me with a look that could peel paint off the wall. "Bob, I do not have the keys; why would I? If this is your scheme to get us to spend the night here, I promise I will never forgive you."

I suppressed an angry reply, took a calming breath, and tried again. "No, Miriam, this is not a trick. I've searched the house and car from top to bottom and can't find them anywhere. The only thing I can think of is that when we got caught in the rainstorm and ran along the jetty, they must have fallen out of my pocket and into the water."

Silence reigned as the three of us considered that possibility and what we could do about it. Eventually, Miriam said, "You better call the auto club then. I mean it, Bob, I will not spend the night here."

"I tried, but there's no cell coverage here. Have you seen a phone anywhere in the house?"

She shook her head, and her face took on a scared little girl look. "There is one in the study. I saw it there earlier, but the line was dead when I picked it up. Bob, what now?"

My heart sank because I knew what I had to do. "I suppose I need to look for them in the water before it gets dark."

****

Miriam sighed and then exhaled explosively. "You can't swim for shit!"

I recoiled, tempted to retaliate with as much anger as she'd aimed at me. Yet, I realized she was stressed about being in a house she never wanted and the mental state of our daughter. I bit my tongue because, throughout our marriage, I'd always played the peacemaker. It's also true that she'd been a track and swim team superstar in college while I had been a nerd. "It looks shallow near the walkway. I'll be okay," I said through clenched teeth. But it sounded feeble, even to me, since I wasn't a good swimmer and never would be. Still, as the man of the family and undoubtedly the one who had lost the keys, it was my responsibility to find them.

"Do you think you can manage to look after Charlotte while I get changed and go find the keys *you* lost? Hopefully, the water isn't too cold, and I don't turn blue."

Before I could respond, she stormed off. Her emphasis on the word *you* wasn't lost on me. I was in the doghouse. I glanced at Charlie. She looked back and gave a crooked smile. "I'm okay, Dad. I don't know what happened to me in the shower, but I'm fine now. If you want to go in the lake with Mom, I'll be good."

I smiled. God, how I loved my daughter. "Sweetheart, if I even suggested leaving you alone, your mother would skin me alive." I reached for her and hugged her. "I love you, kitten." She hugged me back but didn't say she loved me, too. What teenage daughter would admit to loving her dad? I knew she did, and that was enough. "Come on, let's see if we can see the keys so we can direct your mom to them when she comes out."

We walked back outside through the door and onto the walkway that connected the house to the shore. I paused to consider which side I was on when Miriam and I ran as the rain started, and decided I was on her right. "If they are in the lake, it will be on this side. Your eyesight is better than mine. Remember, they have my lucky rabbit's foot on the ring."

She paused and giggled, which filled my heart with joy. "Didn't bring you much luck, did it, Dad?" she asked, then erupted with laughter again.

"Okay, smarty-pants, come on, let's see if we can spot them."

She seemed to be back to her old self, and we walked to the side rail and leaned over, trying to see the misplaced key ring. The water was crystal clear, and I could see the bottom well enough; however, it was covered in weeds and grasses. A sudden wind appeared out of nowhere as if to taunt me further. Ripples formed on the surface and flowed toward the shore, making visibility more difficult.

Just then, Miriam appeared in a black one-piece swimsuit with a large white fluffy towel draped over her shoulders. If the mood had been better and Charlotte hadn't been with us, I would have wanted to take my wife and make love to her; she looked so good. But that wouldn't happen, given her current frame of mind.

She walked past us without a word, continued to the end of the jetty, turned left, and dropped her towel. "Where were we when the rain came and we started to run?" she called.

I looked around, recalling our headlong dash when Charlie said, "I think it was somewhere around here." She pointed, and I agreed that seemed about right. We sprinted to the spot, and I waved to Miriam. "I think it's around here, and Charlie agrees."

Miriam nodded and started walking into the water, visibly trembling—perhaps too much, I thought—creating even more guilt for me than I already felt. She succeeded; I felt like the worst husband in the world.

****

Despite her age and having two children, Miriam still possessed the grace of an Olympic swimmer. I marveled at her effortless strokes and how she glided down to the bottom, remaining there for what felt like an inordinate amount of time before streaking back to the surface. Once there, she shot me a glare before duck-diving back down again.

I realized the water was deeper than I thought it was and well beyond my swimming abilities. I was glad Miriam had volunteered, although I felt certain I'd never hear the end of it. I glanced toward the middle of the lake and noticed what looked like a wave of water or a fallen log. I thought, *That's odd; maybe it's a school of fish jumping*, and I returned to watching Miriam's progress.

The next time I looked up, the wave was closer and appeared taller. It was moving toward the house. Suddenly, I felt uneasy. Had there been an earthquake that caused a small tsunami? I wondered, fearfully, though I certainly hadn't felt any disturbances. Would the wave damage the house? Was my next concern. Then, I thought about Miriam in the water. I looked down and, with dismay, saw she was below the surface.

"*Dad,*" Charlie screamed, "a wall of water is coming; we have to help Mom."

I glanced back at the approaching wave, which now looked at least ten feet high and was racing toward us. Miriam was still searching the bottom for the car keys, running her hand through the weeds, and the deluge would soon be upon us. I had to act.

"Charlie, run. Get to shore, now!" Without a second thought, I took a deep breath, leaped over the rail, and hit the water feet first in front of Miriam. The water was so cold it shocked me, but I had no time to worry. I sank like a stone, feeling the lake's sandy bottom connect with my feet. I couldn't see anything due to the bubbles and the silt cloud I'd created, which engulfed me.

I felt hands gripping my arms and shaking me. Miriam put her face close to mine and made her *WTF* expression. I pointed up, wrapped her in my arms, and pushed off the bottom. When we broke the surface, I gulped air and shouted, "Get out of the water now, Miriam. We are in danger."

I pushed her away from me with a rough shove and sighed in relief as I watched her powerful Australian crawl stroke propel her through the water toward the shore. I knew I didn't have the swimming skills to outrun a tsunami wave, but I didn't care what happened to me as long as I could save my wife. I kicked to tread water and used my hands to spin around.

I felt paralyzed with fear. The top of the wave rose higher than the railing on the jetty, and I knew I would be overwhelmed by the weight of the water when it crashed over my head, which it would do in just seconds.

But the strangest thing happened. The deathly wall of water stopped three feet before me as if Moses himself had parted the waves. I was so stunned that I stopped kicking, and before I knew it, I took a mouthful of lake water, which made me choke. In a blind panic, I waved my legs frantically again, and using my arms, steadied myself to face whatever I was about to face.

****

I had never witnessed anything like what stood before me. I say stood because I can't think of any other way to describe hundreds of tons of water held in place by God knows what. The water wasn't frozen because, in its depths, there was movement, like a million tiny ripples in a monster wave on a surf beach. I felt petrified, but then things took a major turn for the worse.

The minute ripples within the mother wave seemed to dance around each other, gradually forming the shape of a body—a tall, muscular man with a bare chest and long, straggly hair. The apparition's eyes glowed like flaming diamonds as he stared at me, arms folded across his chest.

Impossible. Not only is he standing on water, but he's also within it. I must be dreaming. Yes, that's it. I've fallen asleep, and this is just a dream. But somehow, I knew it wasn't that. I was awake, and before me stood the fabled Manitou. He had come to kill me, just as he had my parents, grandparents, and probably many more members of my family tree over the last two hundred years.

"What do you want from me?" I shouted, noting the pleading tone of my pathetic voice.

There was a long pause, but when The Manitou spoke, it was with a clear, powerful baritone—the opposite of the whine I had used. *"You must pay for the sins of your forebear."*

"Why?" I shouted back. "That was something that happened over two hundred years ago."

"Time has no meaning to me. You are as guilty as those who came before you. You must die."

"I inherited this house from my grandfather and have donated it to the Shawnee Nation today. We will never return here again. Please, spare my family. Take me if you must, but allow my children and future grandchildren to live without the curse of you hanging over their heads.

The Manitou unfolded his arms and stretched a ghostly, disembodied hand toward me until his icy-cold fingers wrapped around my throat and squeezed.

"You white men lie. You have always lied, and you always will. You stole from my people, murdered them, and cheated them of their lands. You are not worthy to receive my mercy."

I couldn't breathe. I stopped treading water, but The Manitou's strength held me in place while his hand choked the life out of me. My vision darkened. I reached up and tried to dislodge the fingers that were throttling me, but they felt as if they were made of stone. Resistance was futile, and I resigned myself to the fact that I was about to die. I cursed that I might not have found myself in this deadly situation if I had listened to Miriam or William. Or even if I'd put the protective amulet Magenta gifted me around my neck, I might have been saved. But it was too late. I was a victim of my own foolishness and stubbornness. I stopped struggling, too weak from lack of oxygen and the cold water. It was time to give up. As long as Miriam, Charlie, and Martin were safe, I could let myself go.

****

I heard splashing and shouting behind me, but I was too weak to turn my head. I slipped below the surface before bobbing back up. I heard a woman's voice: "Stop, Great Spirit of the Lake. I call on the Great Gitchee Manitou to command you to stop."

The chokehold on my neck loosened, and I drew a breath, coughed it out, gagged, and took another. White spots danced in my vision as I struggled to stay conscious, afloat, and breathe. I felt arms wrap around me from behind and heard Miriam's voice. "I've got you, Bob. Don't panic; let me support you."

"No. The white man must die," The Manitou roared.

The hand reached for me again, but Miriam pulled me back into the water, away from his grasp. I felt her lean back into a lifesaver position and kick her legs to propel us toward the shoreline.

But The Manitou wasn't done with me. His arm seemed as if it were elastic as it stretched farther until his fingers touched me again, the long, jagged fingernails digging into the skin on my neck. That's when I realized the first voice I had heard commanding The Manitou wasn't Miriam's; it was Magenta's.

She swam in front of me, took The Manitou's hand from my throat, and kissed it. As Miriam propelled us backward, I noticed Magenta was naked, and she caressed the hand as if it were her lover's.

"Look into my heart, Great Manitou of the Lake. I am a descendant of Sampata, who laid the curse all those years ago, and I rescind it in her name. This man is good. He speaks the truth; he gave, not sold, the house back to our people and was willing to sacrifice himself to save his loved ones. I beg you, please, it is time to end the curse. You have been a great Manitou, cared for our people, and protected us, but now it is time to let this family live in peace."

The wall of water seemed to shudder and grow even larger. Then it collapsed, sending a surge of water cascading over us like rapids in a river. I choked again, but Miriam pulled me back above the surface, and I saw that The Manitou had vanished.

I felt mesmerized by what I had witnessed but, at the same time, suddenly wide awake after being nearly choked to death. I began to help Miriam swim us into the shallows, where we both collapsed, panting.

Magenta stood, unashamed of her nudity, and I noticed she was crying. "It's over. You will be safe now. Come, you need to get to your son. Martin has had a bad scare, and he needs you."

****

We didn't bother to dry off but waited while Magenta got dressed. She ran ahead and led us to where Martin lay motionless under a maple tree. My heart sank, thinking he was dead, but then he stirred weakly and waved. He was covered from head to toe in foul-smelling mud and looked as if he had been buried alive and then dug up. Miriam and I knelt beside him while Charlie stood crying next to Magenta. Martin was barely awake. He offered a tired, crooked smile.

Magenta told us she had gone to the lake to speak with The Manitou, but he hadn't come to their usual sacred meeting place. She waited in vain and then heard Martin scream. Magenta raced to where he was struggling, stuck in a bog, and being sucked deeper by the second. She reached a hand to Martin, helped him break free, and slowly helped him back to solid land.

"I'm sorry, Mom and Dad. Sis, I apologize for

throwing that frog at you. I promise I won't ever do anything like that again."

I hugged him. "It's okay, son. Let's get you cleaned up. We were going to leave the house tonight, but I lost the car keys, so we're stuck here until tomorrow."

"Oh," he said with a rueful smile. Slowly, he reached into his jeans pocket. "You mean these keys? When I picked up the last bag, I noticed you left them in the ignition, so I put them in my pocket. After that, I forgot and set off with Charlie for our walk in the woods."

I glanced at Miriam, and she looked back. We had gone to hell and back, searching for the keys he had in his pocket the whole time. I wasn't angry; I was just grateful we had all survived The Manitou. "It's getting late. Do you want to stay one more night?" I asked Miriam, knowing what her answer would be.

"Not on your life," she replied, and I smiled, letting her know I didn't want to stay either.

Epilogue

The family had packed and was ready to leave. They sat in the four-wheel-drive wagon, prepared for the long drive home, happy to be departing. Each silently gazed at the sparkling water as the last rays of the pink sunset reflected on the lake. Suddenly, the engine rumbled to life and lurched into gear. But it wasn't in reverse as intended; it was moving forward. As if possessed by a mind of its own, the vehicle accelerated, gaining momentum, then flew over the embankment and into the water, continuing until it became fully submerged. Only then did the motor gurgle and cut out.

Water rushed through the door seals and gradually rose higher. The frigid water replaced the air as the family struggled to open the doors, but it felt as though they had been welded shut. Panic set in; Charlie screamed simultaneously with Miriam while Martin curled into a fetal position in the back seat, moaning incoherently.

Bob looked through the windscreen and saw the grinning face of The Manitou. He screamed a blood-curdling scream while pounding the door window, trying to break free. The water reached his mouth and poured in.

The Manitou had won.

****

I sat up in bed, screaming, drenched in sweat.

Miriam woke and immediately cuddled into me. "Shhhh. It was just another nightmare, Bob."

The Boy in the Bubble

Timothy's mental powers are limitless

Foreword

As the General Manager of a large new car dealership, I often receive invitations to sporting and entertainment events at a corporate level. I enjoyed the hospitality in the box at an Australian Rules football match on one such occasion. My team wasn't playing particularly well and was significantly behind at halftime, but the wine was fine, and the food was excellent, so it was enjoyable. My wife and I weren't feeling much pain (if you know what I mean?).

A woman I knew, Sharon, who worked as a stock controller for a rival dealership, asked if she and her husband, Tim, could join us at our table, and of course, I eagerly agreed. When Sharon mentioned to Tim that I was also a published author, he claimed he could share a story from his life that I wouldn't believe. Comments like this aren't unusual, many people I meet want to pitch me ideas for stories, and frankly, not many of them interest me, though I am always polite.

Tim mentioned that as a child, he was one of the original boys in a bubble. He had so many severe allergies that he had to live in a plastic bubble while growing up. I was deeply fascinated as he shared stories about his childhood. Some of the allergies he grew out of, some he didn't, but as an adult, he could lead a relatively "normal life" as long as he was extremely careful. He got a job working outdoors and ate only food meticulously prepared by first his mother, then later, when he married, by Sharon.

As if that weren't enough of a burden to bear, Tim had to go to the hospital for a minor procedure: a hernia operation. However, something went wrong. When he woke up, he experienced excruciating pain and has had to live with it ever since. Although he underwent several operations to correct nerve damage, nothing worked. He had an electronic device attached to his spine to send voltage to nerves to reduce the pain, but it was a long process as they had to get the right combination of shocks to specific nerves.

He lived on the strongest painkillers available, yet, for all his troubles, Tim was humble and not at all self-pitying. He was a gentleman and incredibly interesting to talk to, and I am eternally glad I met him.

I had one of my *what-if* moments as I lay in bed that night. *What if Tim developed incredible telekinetic powers while living in a bubble? And what if he unleashed those powers on the incompetent surgeon who performed the operation incorrectly?*

And so, dear reader, this story came together. I dedicated it to Tim, a superhero in my eyes, and Sharon, his wonder woman.

Chapter 1

4:00 p.m. Tuesday, 13th April 2023

Thirteen-year-old Timothy Bergendorf woke and screamed in pain and confusion.

The confusion was overwhelming; he was surrounded by an opaque plastic film that allowed light to filter through and vague shapes to emerge, but that was all. It was akin to lying at the bottom of a murky swimming pool, gazing at the surface and only catching glimpses of shimmering, indistinct shadows swirling around. Timothy had no idea where he was, but that wasn't the worst of his troubles. He felt a blinding, crippling, unbearable pain radiating from his groin, and he had never encountered anything in his life like the white-hot agony that came in wave after wave.

Tears streamed down his face as Timothy reached down with both hands to rub the area, causing him so much pain, but he only found thick bandages. He pressed against the swollen spot, hoping for relief, but touching it only made it worse, if that was even possible. He screamed louder in shock and horror.

Suddenly, there was movement at his side, beyond the plastic barrier. Something white was shuffling and fussing around out there. He heard a voice—a female voice—urging him to calm down. "It's okay, Timothy. I'm here to help. I'll give you something for the pain. Please stop screaming and try to stay still, or you might tear your stitches and make it worse."

"Worse? Worse? Nothing could be worse than this," his tortured mind told him as he shouted, "Help me, oh my God, help me."

He heard more footsteps and a male voice, "Timothy, calm down; it's Doctor Mendez here. We are about to put more morphine into your IV, but you must calm down."

"It burns, it burns, stop it burning," Timothy yelled.

"We will. The nurse is injecting you now, so please stop screaming; you are upsetting the other patients in the ward."

Above the doctor's head, the fluorescent light tube hidden within a diffusing panel exploded with a loud *bang*. The doctor and nurse flinched as if they had heard a gunshot and feared for their lives. They looked up, anxious that the ceiling might collapse, and felt relieved to discover it was just a blown bulb, as indicated by the sudden dimming of the room's light.

Timothy didn't care at all about upsetting the other patients. Didn't they realize he was experiencing more pain than he could have ever imagined? He had no idea where he was, what was happening, or why some kind of opaque tent surrounded him. Another wave of pain shot upward through his stomach, and he tried to sit up and find a position that might ease the intense agony.

"Timothy, no, you must not sit up. You've had an operation, a minor procedure for a hernia. You're disoriented and feeling some discomfort due to the medication, but you need to try to stay calm and lie still. The nurse has injected you; please remain still and let the morphine do its job. I promise you will feel better very soon."

****

But Timothy didn't feel better for a while, although his memory came back regarding why he was in the hospital and why an oxygen-fed tent surrounded him. His nightmare persisted, the pain only slightly relieved until Doctor Mendez approved more medication, which the nurse injected into the drip tube that snaked beneath the opaque shroud, keeping Timothy in isolation. Timothy didn't stop screaming for another twenty minutes, which everyone within earshot believed was two hours, until he slowly slipped into blessed unconsciousness, bringing a welcome silence to the nurses and patients.

"What is wrong with him?" Nurse Hartley asked the doctor as she rubbed her temples; the constant noise from her patient had frayed her nerves and given her a headache like no other she had ever experienced.

"I don't know; I'm not the surgeon, just the sap dealing with the aftermath. I've paged Mr. High-and-Mighty Beltrane, but he may be botching another poor victim in the operating room. Keep our patient sedated, and let's arrange for the portable ultrasound to check if there's anything obviously wrong."

"Yes, Doctor."

****

Two and a half hours later, Timothy woke once more, screaming. The fluorescent bulb the maintenance man had replaced earlier exploded again, sending a cloud of glass shards tumbling onto the opaque cover.

His parents, Luke and Belinda, jumped at the sudden noise. The attending nurse explained that the hospital must have received a bad batch of light tubes, as it was the second one that day to explode. His parents sat by

Timothy's bed and tried to talk to their son and ease his mind. Still, nothing they said got through the veils of agony invading Tim's body, and eventually, they watched as more drugs were administered and knocked him out again.

Luke Bergendorf was anxious about his son's welfare and was prepared to confront the surgeon, William Beltrane, when he later arrived and attempted to reassure the terrified parents.

"What's going on here?" he demanded of the overwhelmed nurse, who tried to explain the medications prescribed by Doctor Mendez and that an ultrasound had been performed to determine the cause of the patient's pain.

"An ultrasound? What on earth for? It was a perfectly routine hernia removal operation that went off without a hitch. Show me the results, Nurse, although I know they won't indicate anything wrong; I've performed thousands of these procedures."

"Well, if everything went as planned, why is our son screaming in agony?" Luke shouted.

"Yelling at me isn't going to help your son, Mr. Bergendorf; it will only result in security escorting you from the premises. Everyone has a different threshold for pain. What feels like a minor paper cut for some can be a life-altering catastrophe for others." He snatched the envelope from the nurse and pulled out the scans. He held them up to the light and murmured, "See, as I told you, everything is normal. There's no internal bleeding, nothing out of place, and no reason for him to scream for the hospital staff. Nurse Hartley, keep him sedated throughout the night, and we'll check on him in the morning. Mr. and Mrs. Bergendorf, I assure you that everything is fine, and there's no reason for concern."

Three hours later, Timothy Bergendorf woke up screaming once more.

Nurse Hartley was at home, sharing her day with her husband. She considered the surgeon, Beltrane, an arrogant jerk who had clearly done something wrong and was trying to cover it up. Her headache had only recently subsided after she took painkillers at the hospital and when she got home.

The night nurse, Alison, reviewed the notes and observed that the day shift nurse had consistently recorded the boy's pain levels as extreme. Alison called the doctor on duty and received permission to resedate her young patient. She proceeded with the injection while Timothy's parents watched in anguish, overwhelmed by their only son's clear suffering.

She injected morphine into the drip tube, shaking her head from side to side to clear the sudden cloudiness in her vision and ease the throbbing pain that lanced through her head just above her left ear.

Chapter 2

7:15 p.m. Thursday, 14th of May 2010

After seven and a half hours of labor, Belinda Bergendorf gave birth to Timothy. Her husband sat by her side, holding her right hand and sobbing with joy as he gazed at his beautiful boy against her breast.

Belinda felt tired yet content. They had been trying for a child for four and a half years, and their dreams had finally come true. "What should we name him?" she asked softly.

Timothy Gerald Bergendorf has a nice ring to it."

She smiled with love for her husband. Timothy was her father's name, and Gerald was her grandfather.

"I love you," she replied.

****

A month later, Timothy developed a rash. The home nurse believed it wasn't too serious and that Timothy might have an allergy to the laundry detergent she used. Belinda switched products, but the rash didn't go away, so she changed again.

Then Tim stopped taking his feed, which he had eagerly drunk until that point. He cried when Belinda tried to offer him her breast, and the more she attempted to feed her baby, the more he sobbed and turned his head to escape.

Belinda called her husband, who hurried home from his job as an insurance assessor. He brought his wife and son to the emergency department at their local hospital, where they waited to see a doctor. Timothy continued to cry and appeared increasingly agitated. His screaming disturbed the other patients in the waiting room, who were on the verge of starting a riot to escape the incessant cries of the baby. The triage nurse took pity on the family and guided them to an examination room.

A quick but thorough inspection showed the rash seemed to have spread all over his body and to the inside of Timothy's mouth, tongue, and throat. The doctor injected a mild antihistamine into the beleaguered baby to calm him down, fitted a saline drip to hydrate his body, and then took blood and other samples. Timothy woke screaming before the results were ready, and Belinda tried to feed him again with the same lack of success.

The nurse guided the frantic mother and father away while a doctor inserted a feeding tube and administered additional medication to relieve the symptoms of the rash and help their poor child sleep. Later, Timothy appeared calmer as the intravenous line satisfied his evident hunger.

Luke and Belinda met with a doctor who wanted to keep Timothy in the hospital overnight and run more tests in the morning. The doctor told them that, in his opinion, the rash resulted from an allergy. On the community nurse's advice, Belinda explained that she had changed detergent brands, but Timothy's rash worsened.

He nodded in understanding. "Mrs. Bergendorf, that was a perfectly reasonable assumption, and it may still be the correct diagnosis. However, I have requested an allergy specialist to see Timothy tomorrow because I suspect the issue goes deeper than just a laundry detergent. I believe it's a food allergy. You need to understand that whatever the mother consumes can be transmitted through breast milk."

"But I don't have any food allergies," Belinda argued.

"That's not uncommon either. Sometimes allergies can skip generations or result from a chromosomal imbalance between the parents at conception. We don't know much about infantile allergies and intolerances, so I've requested a specialist to examine Timothy and determine the best way forward. We will keep your son sedated through the night; hopefully, he will feel stronger in the morning. In the meantime, both of you should go home and get a good night's sleep."

"I want to stay with him," Belinda insisted, "in case he gets scared during the night. Luke, could you please go home and grab some things so I can spend the night here?"

****

Luke Bergendorf entered his home, distracted. He was terrified that something might happen to his son while he was away from the hospital, and if it did, he knew Belinda would be inconsolable. It felt as if he were drowning in a bath of molasses. Timothy was his beautiful son, his firstborn, and he had never experienced true happiness until the midwife placed a squawking baby into his arms, allowing him to gaze into the gray eyes that stared back at him.

As he walked through the entrance hall, he dropped his car and house keys onto the shelf beneath the mirror, which had been recommended to Belinda by a Feng Shui expert with the ridiculous name of Roxy. Luke had no interest in Feng Shui, astrology, tarot readings, or ghosts, but he adored his wife with every fiber of his being. So, if she wanted a mirror in the hall to deflect bad vibes, who was he to complain?

Three steps beyond the mirror, Luke stopped, shook his head, and exclaimed, "What the hell?" He walked backward, almost moonwalking like the late, great Michael Jackson, until he found himself in front of the mirror again, where he noticed what had offended his eyesight. A crack snaked across the surface from the top left corner to the bottom right, catching the light and refracting like a prism. Luke stared, his mind befuddled as it made no sense. That morning, when he left for work and picked up his keys, he distinctly recalled glancing into the mirror for one last look at his hair. He remembered thinking he was due for a haircut and could be mistaken for an Old English sheepdog, so he knew the crack had appeared between leaving home and returning. *Perhaps there had been an earthquake?* he wondered, then shook his head and continued.

Chapter 3

Doctor Joseph Ashworth must be in his fifties, although he speaks as if he's seventy, Luke thought when they met in the afternoon the following day. Baby Timothy had been sedated throughout the night, fed through his feeding tube, and the rash seemed to be diminishing. Belinda was excited about her son's recovery and looked forward to the family returning home. She had met with Dr. Ashworth in the morning while Luke had called into work. He needed to arrange some time off and went to his office to transfer files for claims he had in progress, so Luke had yet to meet the allergy specialist and was eager to find out the results from the barrage of tests performed earlier and the extensive questionnaire Belinda had filled out.

The husband and wife sat on one side of the desk while the specialist occupied the other. The doctor removed his half-moon spectacles and cleaned them with a handkerchief he pulled from his jacket pocket. Doctor Ashworth's gaze shifted between the parents as he rubbed the lenses. Eventually, as Luke felt ready to scream with pent-up impatience, he tucked the cloth away, slid the glasses onto his face, and began. "Mr. and Mrs. Bergendorf, I'm afraid I need you to be a bit more patient. We need to conduct more extensive tests because I fear your son's allergies are more severe than we initially thought."

"What do you mean, more severe?" Luke asked as Belinda burst into tears.

"You must understand that there is much we still do not know about infant allergies. A child's allergy can be mild, occasionally severe, and in extreme cases, potentially fatal. This is simply when a single allergen causes the issue. In Timothy's case, we have yet to identify one specific cause for the rash, but the testing indicates several reactions to different substances. It has spread to his mouth and throat, which poses a genuine risk. If we do not discover the root cause, it could fall into the category of potentially fatal allergies. If, as we suspect, Timothy ingested it through breast milk, it might be one of several items Belinda consumed in the last three days, leading to an accumulative effect. Worse, it could result from a combination of various foods or drinks, chemicals, sweeteners, preservatives, and more. Additionally, the main issue could arise from an airborne pathogen, either alone or in conjunction with something ingested. I want to put Timothy in strict isolation and conduct extensive testing to determine exactly what he is allergic to so we can decide on an appropriate course of action."

Belinda stared, mouth agape as if struck by a cattle prod. "But, Doctor Ashworth, it was just a rash, and Belinda and I don't have any allergies. Surely it can't be *that* serious, especially since the inflammation is now receding."

The Doctor sighed, removed his glasses once more, and rubbed the handkerchief over the previously spotlessly clean lenses. "I understand how difficult this is for both of you, but I assure you that while I hope this is a minor, isolated incident, I fear it is far from that. It is extremely common for an infant's allergy not to be an inherited trait from either parent. More often than not, severe allergies do not appear in any family history. We frequently see this with various allergens like nuts, sugars, certain proteins, and even bee stings. Yes, it is only a rash at this point, but I'm sorry to tell you that had you not brought Timothy to the hospital when you did, I believe he would have passed away within twenty-four hours due to suffocation. We found extensive inflammation had spread to his trachea and upper lungs. One more feed could have been Timothy's last. There is a genuine risk here: if we don't identify exactly what Timothy is allergic to, it could happen again, possibly even more severely next time."

****

Timothy was placed in an isolation room where anyone entering, including his parents, had to wear what could best be described as a hazardous materials suit, complete with a full-face mask. Doctor Ashworth assured Luke and Belinda that these stringent precautions were to prevent any chance of the baby coming into contact with a dangerous allergen before they could identify it. Given that Timothy was a baby, even the tiniest particle could be fatal, and until they could determine whether it was a specific type of food or an airborne pollutant, Doctor Ashworth was unwilling to take any risks.

Due to the strict conditions, Belinda could not sleep in the same room as her son. Initially, she resisted leaving the hospital and was offered a small room in the nursing quarters, which she reluctantly accepted. Since the nursing rooms were for singles, Luke could not move in and chose to return to work part-time in the mornings.

He would then arrive at the hospital in the afternoon to stay with Belinda before returning home after evening visiting hours ended.

Timothy's testing continued for three days, and it was mid-afternoon on Friday the 13th when Luke and Belinda met with Joseph Ashworth again. They entered his office and sat as the doctor cleaned his spectacles once more. He nodded and waved his glasses in greeting. "What news do you have for us?" a very tired-looking Belinda asked.

Luke knew all too well how much of a strain the week had been for both of them, but especially for his wife, who he realized felt guilty for passing something to their beloved son through her breast milk. Luke had tried to reassure her, but it was to no avail.

The Doctor slid his glasses back on the bridge of his nose, tucked the cleaning cloth in his pocket, sighed deeply, and began. "Mr. and Mrs. Bergendorf, unfortunately, I do not have good news for you."

Belinda clutched Luke's hand and began to cry.

"What's the problem?" Luke asked anxiously.

"Your son is an exceptionally rare case. If we had to quantify it, it would be approximately one birth every forty to fifty thousand. Timothy suffers from multiple severe allergies to substances he might encounter daily. Any one of these items could be fatal in a moderate-sized dose, individually. And cumulatively, well, you can imagine how concerned we are. Unfortunately, the list of hazardous items doesn't need to be ingested. In some instances, if one of them touches his skin, the outcome could be disastrous, especially if it leads Timothy to scratch, allowing the allergen to enter his bloodstream. Even worse, if it first contacts his skin and then Timothy touches it before putting his fingers in his mouth, it could attack his immune system on two fronts at once."

After a few moments of stunned silence, Belinda asked, "So, what is the cure?"

"I'm so sorry," Doctor Ashworth said. "There is no cure, only prevention through avoidance and an EpiPen if Timothy has an anaphylactic reaction. In such cases, Timothy would need hospitalization."

"All right. What do we need to keep Timothy away from?" Luke asked.

Silently, the Doctor slid a neatly typed sheet of paper across the desk. Belinda grabbed it and positioned it between herself and her husband so they could read at the same time. "Here are the things we've identified so far."

"So far? Oh, my God," Belinda exclaimed. "How can I avoid all these things to prevent passing it on through my milk? How many more allergies will you find?"

"You can't breastfeed Timothy again; I'm sorry. As you can see from the list of problem foods and proteins, it will be nearly impossible for you to maintain a diet that will negate the risk of transmission. Even touching him will pose challenges. We have a dietitian who will help you come up with foods he can eat later and a safe milk formula for now. You may choose to follow the same diet at home to be safe. A specialist will work with you on household products, such as cleaning supplies, detergents, and others. We must be cautious of airborne allergens and those that Timothy could directly ingest. Life, as you know it, will need to change if you're going to raise your son at home. He will need to stay with us in isolation for about three months. We need to conduct more tests and see if we can reduce Timothy's reactions to certain items so things are less critical. You will also need to make significant modifications to your home."

"What modifications?" Luke asked incredulously.

Doctor Ashworth sighed deeply, took off his glasses, and began cleaning them again. Luke wanted to reach over and knock them out of the infuriating man's hand, but he didn't. "Over the next few years, we hope Timothy will outgrow some of his allergies as he develops natural immunities. We will work with you to introduce minute particles to assist him with that, but obviously, it must be one allergy at a time. So we are looking at years, not months, to do this, and we may not be successful at all. There is simply no way to know at this point. Timothy is just over a month old, and it is far too early to determine how he will respond. In the meantime, he must live in a safe environment, protected from all the items on that list and any others we identify through further investigation. Therefore, you will need to convert a room where he will be safe. I can recommend a fine builder we've worked with who, incidentally, also has a child with extreme allergies and extensive experience in this area. I have some forms for you to fill out to apply for government assistance to help offset the costs.

Luke felt the dawning of understanding hit him, and he glanced at his wife. "He means Timothy will have to live in a bubble, Doctor. That's what you mean, isn't it?"

"In effect, yes."

Chapter 4

Joanna Mulhany had been a senior nurse for over thirty years. She raised three children, all of whom had left the nest. This left her and her husband, Zack, in a large four-bedroom home, which Zack was eager to sell and downsize. Joanna refused because the garden was her pride and joy, always blooming with flowers, regardless of the season.

Zack loved fishing and seized every opportunity to do so with his longtime friend Dean on the eighteen-foot fishing boat they had purchased together. Joanna had no interest in such a small power launch because it lacked a toilet, but she stopped complaining when she realized her husband fished as much to enjoy his time with Dean as he did to keep her off the boat. She recognized when she wasn't wanted and didn't resent Zack for needing time alone, as he had always been a great provider, a fantastic father, and a decent husband. Instead, Joanna focused on joining a wine-loving book club that met on Saturday afternoons, featuring mystery and suspense novels. Every Sunday, without fail, she spent time tending to her garden.

Joanna had always been a no-nonsense type of nurse, especially in her senior years, and she was known for being strict to the point of obsessiveness with younger nurses and students. She walked daily from home to the hospital, covering five kilometers in the morning and back after her shift, regardless of the weather. Due to her walking routine, Joanna was fit for a fifty-six-year-old woman and moved briskly as her white training shoes swished along the sidewalk while her backpack, containing her work shoes and homemade lunch, shifted from side to side with each step.

Recently, her job had involved closely monitoring a young baby with a horrifying list of severe allergies. Due to her seniority and the critical shortage of nursing staff, Joanna only worked day shifts and never on weekends. For her employer, it was Joanna's way or the highway; such was her attitude toward work and marriage, and the hospital reluctantly acceded to her demands.

Part of her did not care for looking after the baby with allergies because she had to wear a full-body protective suit to be in the same room as him. Joanna thought she looked like a cross between an astronaut and a worker in one of those germ warfare laboratories. She understood that protective clothing was necessary for the baby's continued health, but it was inconvenient, time-consuming, and uncomfortable. At home, she would take a steaming hot shower to wash away the smell of sweat mixed with plastic.

The inconvenience was made worse by the *little tyke* screaming every time she tried to take him out of his crib for feeding and changing. Timothy Bergendorf had a fully developed set of lungs, and while her years of training helped her ignore a child crying incessantly, this baby's hysterical yelling gave Joanna a headache. Yes, she knew that someone picking him up while wearing a white bodysuit and a face mask would frighten a baby, but he should be used to it after the eleven days since she had been assigned to look after him.

Joanna noticed that the screaming was decidedly better when his mother was in attendance, but only by around thirty decibels. Mrs. Bergendorf had a lovely singing voice and constantly sang lullabies to her son, which did help calm him.

Today marked the eleventh day that Joanna had been working with baby *screamy-pants*, as she had nicknamed him. She had two weekends away from the hospital and thoroughly enjoyed the peace of working pain-free in her garden. Surprisingly, while tending to the shrub beds in the blazing sun, Joanna did not experience the constant headache that plagued her each weekday while helping Timothy Bergendorf.

Being a Monday and her first day back at work, she walked home in the evening sunshine, her head pounding as if she could still hear the yelling and temperamental screaming. *For goodness' sake,* she wondered for the hundredth time, *didn't that ungrateful jerk realize all she was trying to do was help him?*

Joanna suddenly stopped walking as she felt an excruciating pain just above her temple, and her vision shifted to blinding white. She became clammy and heard the sound of a spring bouncing in her ears. Her home was only minutes away, and Joanna tried valiantly to keep moving, though it felt as if she were wading through a fast-moving stream for some reason. Then, her left leg nearly refused to obey her brain and began to drag instead. The sole of her sneaker caught on a raised edge of a flagstone on the pavement, and almost in a daze, Joanna realized she was about to fall. The ground rushed up to meet her, and Joanna's forehead struck with a sickening thud that echoed in her ears before darkness enveloped her consciousness.

Joanna Mulhany died before the ambulance arrived. A man walking his dog came across her inert body and immediately called for help. He turned her over when she didn't respond to ask if she was okay, and screamed at what he saw. Joanna's eyes were not just red; they were leaking blood, and rivulets of scarlet liquid coursed down her cheeks.

A later autopsy showed Joanna had suffered a brain bleed or aneurysm. Unless it had happened in her hospital emergency department, nothing could have saved her from the massive internal bleeding inside her skull, which struck her down like a lightning bolt.

Chapter 6

Timothy Bergendorf was seven months old when Dr. Ashworth discharged him from the hospital. His parents had undergone exhausting training to care for him and understood that this would require twenty-four-hour assistance. They maintained detailed lists of foods that Timothy could eat, as well as those that Belinda and Luke must avoid to the extent that they could not even bring them into the home. For Belinda, this meant adhering to a strict vegetarian diet, while Luke could consume some meats outside the house as long as he thoroughly showered at work before coming home. Upon arriving in the evening, Luke went directly to the family bathroom to shower again at Belinda's insistence, "Just in case," she said. He then changed into a freshly laundered bodysuit and wore a medical face mask before entering Timothy's room.

What had once been a sizeable informal dining area combined with the living room was transformed into a hermetically sealed, triple-filtered, dust-free chamber with a transparent plastic wall. Within the wall was a zip-locked arched doorway leading to a short tunnel that connected to the hall doorway, featuring a second zip-secured entrance to create an airlock. Small spray jets along the ceiling of the tunnel released a fine mist of antibacterial spray designed to eliminate any contaminants brought inside the bubble by the parents, which could seriously jeopardize Timothy's health. The builder had crafted a kitchenette nook equipped with the essentials, allowing Belinda, Luke, or both to spend extended time with Timothy and prepare meals.

Life was tough for the Bergendorf family, but Luke and Belinda loved Timothy so much that nothing was too much trouble. Yet, they hoped and prayed that one day, the restrictions could be eased to allow them and their son to live a more complete lifestyle.

A community nurse, specially trained in severe allergy management, visited four times a week to check on Timothy. She often stayed for two hours, allowing Belinda some respite and giving her time to go shopping. Each time, Belinda felt so guilty that she hurried through her chores to return to her son.

The family endured the next thirteen months until Timothy suffered an anaphylactic attack that nearly claimed his life. Briony McShane, the nurse on duty that week, had celebrated her eighth wedding anniversary the day before and enjoyed a dinner out. Their usual spot was a Chinese restaurant called *The Jade Teapot*, where Briony savored her favorite dish, Satay Lamb Fillet, accompanied by steamed rice. She found the peanut sauce exquisite, perfectly balancing chili and peanuts, warming both her mouth and her soul. While they dined, her husband, Seamus, told a joke that made Briony laugh so hard she choked, coughing into her hand. Although she wiped her eyes with the table napkin and later washed her hands, Briony missed the tiny piece of peanut that had lodged under her fingernail. The next day, while checking on Timothy, she overlooked the fact that the toddler in her care had picked up the nut crumb in his small hand when she changed his diaper. Later, as

Timothy tried to pull himself up using the couch for support, he rubbed his mouth. Within moments, he fell to the floor, gasping, sweating profusely, and screaming in pain. Briony initially thought Timothy had hurt himself in the fall, and valuable moments slipped by as she hugged and cooed at him to soothe his crying.

Horrified as the toddler let out a final ear-piercing scream, which made her blood turn to ice, she watched his eyes roll backward, his body go completely stiff, and he became unconscious. Briony realized the danger and carried his body to the white cupboard on the wall, yanked open the door, and seized the EpiPen. By the time she loaded and readied the injector, Timothy had stopped breathing.

Belinda arrived home, softly singing an Elton John song that had been playing on the car radio while clutching shopping bags under her arms. She noticed her worst nightmare through the plastic wall of Timothy's bubble: Timothy lay spread-eagled on the floor, the EpiPen by his side, with Briony McShane performing CPR on his lifeless body. She screamed and dropped the shopping bags.

Briony looked up. "*Belinda*, stop it and help me. Call an ambulance, *now!*"

****

Timothy lived, but as Doctor Ashworth put it, as he cleaned his glasses later that evening, "That was a close-run race."

Benito, the cheerful paramedic ambulance attendant, decided to check Timothy's mouth and noticed a small piece of peanut stuck under his tongue. Belinda, speaking in a panicked voice, explained her son's allergies, informing him of what to look for. After removing the offending nut, Benito rinsed the area with saline and continued CPR. Gradually, Timothy began to recover and breathe on his own. Fortunately, Benito wore latex gloves, as he always did, to avoid contracting hepatitis or any other harmful bacterial infections. Although Benito kept his hands clean and regularly used antibacterial wash, he had recently eaten lunch. He could have easily worsened Timothy's contamination and put his life at risk if it hadn't been for the gloved finger entering his mouth.

Briony endlessly apologized to Belinda and Luke for the scare she had unknowingly caused during her visit to Timothy's hospital room that night. Both parents reassured Briony that they did not hold her responsible, recognizing that her actions were unintentional. The incident also highlighted the severity of Timothy's problems and emphasized how vigilant they needed to be to ensure his safety.

At the time, Timothy lay in the hospital crib, covered by an oxygenated plastic tent to protect him from any allergens that might be in the air. Briony asked if she could see Timothy up close, and Belinda nodded, understanding how guilty the nurse must feel for coming so close to inadvertently causing her patient to die.

"Hi, Timothy," Briony whispered as she waved at the boy through the translucent tent. I'm so sorry I did this to you. Please forgive me."

Belinda smiled as she held Luke's hand and squeezed it lovingly. Timothy stopped wriggling his arms and legs in the air, a behavior he had been displaying while gurgling his apparent happiness as if nothing untoward had occurred just a few short hours earlier. Slowly, he turned his head as if to gaze at Briony and lowered his arms.

Much later, when Belinda reflected on the incident, she could have sworn she noticed Timothy's eyes widen at first, and then a moment later, he appeared to squint in concentration.

"Oh my, oh my," Briony exclaimed as she slapped her hands against the sides of her face. *"Uggghhhhhh, no, no noooooooo."*

"What's wrong, Briony?" Belinda asked as she stepped closer, only to stop as if she had encountered an invisible wall of heat.

Briony shook her head frantically, turned away from the crib, and stared at the parents. Belinda gasped when she noticed the blood streaming from Briony's nose. Luke reached for the nurse and gripped her upper arm. "Are you okay, Briony? Your nose is bleeding. You need help; should I get a doctor?"

Briony seemed to come awake and clamped a hand over her nose. She ran out of the room without a word or a backward glance.

Belinda and Luke never saw Nurse Briony again.

Chapter 7

The next few years passed with only three more allergy attacks, none as severe as the Satay Peanut episode. All three resulted in using the EpiPen and a mad dash to the hospital. Each visit ended after a week, and Timothy returned to living in his bubble.

Belinda had completed her studies and earned her teaching degree so she could homeschool her son, and he excelled in every lesson she provided, which amazed her. Belinda struggled to keep up with Timothy's thirst for knowledge, and she beamed with pride when the Department of Education officially recognized that he was at a genius level for his age.

Doctor Ashworth retired when Timothy turned twelve and visited the house to say goodbye for the final time. Joseph made it a point to see Timothy at least twice a year, sometimes three times, always preferring to stay outside the bubble, as he preferred talking to examining. As Tim grew and learned to speak, Doctor Ashworth insisted that Belinda, and if Luke was home from work, join her for a walk, leaving him to chat privately with their son. They eagerly took the chance to shop together or stop at a café for a relaxing coffee and cheesecake, confident that Timothy was in good hands with the specialist who had been there for them since their son's birth.

Joseph usually sat on a chair near the bubble wall so he and Timothy could talk comfortably. He explained that, in his advancing years, he needed to feel comfortable because his bones ached if he stood for too long. Joseph would spend an hour or more speaking with Timothy, sharing what the boy's life would likely be like as he grew into adulthood to prepare him, knowing his parents had lived in the hope of a miracle that someday their beloved son would outgrow his allergies and be able to enjoy a normal life.

During what he believed to be his last visit, Joseph sadly informed Timothy that his allergies had not decreased in number or severity, contrary to what typically happens to most boys reaching the age of twelve. Timothy's case was so serious that he would never be able to live outside his bubble, and he felt it was important to deliver the news in person. Joseph explained to Timothy that he had spent many hours each week over the past few years trying to find a cure or some treatment that could improve the boy's quality of life, but he finally had to admit that he had failed. Joseph had explored every avenue and consulted many experts worldwide, yet no one could offer a solution because Timothy's symptoms were so severe that they were unprecedented. He went on to explain that he was now retiring from medicine and that no one at the hospital would continue his search for help on Timothy's behalf. Although the hospital had not been able to find a specialist in Joseph's field, they would keep looking, and if they succeeded, Timothy would likely meet with whoever they found, whether male or female.

"I'm sorry, Timothy," Doctor Ashworth said as he polished his glasses. "I've tried everything I know and spoken to every expert in allergy research, but I've come up empty regarding your condition. Your case is so unique that significant research hasn't been conducted on it. Your allergies are numerous and varied, and sadly, there is simply no hope for a cure. I understand you want to leave this place and experience the outside world, but you need to realize that if you tried, I doubt you would last more than a day before something put you down; even with protective clothing and a face mask, the risk would be extreme. Here, you have protection; while it may not be ideal, it is still life. With the internet at your fingertips, you can study and expand your mind in fields like computer science, allowing you to work from here and still enjoy a career. Of course, nothing stops you, considering your intellect, from pursuing medical research in allergy studies yourself. Your parents have done so much for you, and I know you want to find a career to contribute to the cost of living when you're older."

Timothy sat cross-legged in front of his doctor, nodding with a maturity beyond his years. "Thank you for everything you have done. I know you did your best; I can see it in your thoughts, and I want to express my gratitude for your persistent efforts."

Joseph looked up and, for once, stopped cleaning his glasses. "What do you mean, Timothy? You can see it in my thoughts?" For the first time, he realized that although the boy was only twelve, his demeanor and way of speaking made him seem much older and wiser.

Timothy grinned. "Well, let me put it this way, Doctor. You suggested that I should develop my mind. I've focused on that for years. Understanding your thoughts is easy; I can tell when people are being truthful and when they're lying. If they lie, I can see why, whether they're being mean or trying to protect my feelings."

Doctor Ashworth snorted in derision. "Timothy, I'm far too old to let you pull my leg. No one can read minds outside of horror movies."

"Really? Let me prove you're wrong. Think of a color...Blue," he added quickly.

Joseph spluttered. "Just a lucky guess, a party trick. It's a good one, but still just a party trick. Maybe most people think of blue when you put them on the spot. Try it on your parents, Timothy; entertain them; I'm sure they'll enjoy it."

"But it was blue, wasn't it? Alright, think of another...Red. Come on, Doctor, challenge me; think of an obscure color this time...Cerise. Another. Let's make it tough...Purple. Okay, I can see you're not convinced. Let's try something more difficult. Imagine an object, anything at all, and envision it in three different colors." Timothy shook his head sadly. "I thought, being a doctor with a brilliant mind, you'd come up with something more complicated than that. You're picturing a ball with yellow, orange, and blue stripes. Pretty gaudy-looking ball, if you ask me, Doctor Ashworth."

Joseph stared back as if he were facing a monster. Everything he'd predicted had been true, including the ball he had given his grandson last Christmas, and he had to admit, it did have some very gaudy stripes. "But you can't read minds, Timothy; no one can do that."

The boy grinned again. "Oh, when I want to, I can do much more than read people's minds while they think of simple objects and colors. Perhaps Mother Nature has compensated me for a life in a bubble by giving me something extra; what do you think? Challenge me; think of something complex—a song, an instrument, or anything else; the more complicated, the better. Now you're getting the hang of it." He nodded in appreciation. "You play the guitar, and you're thinking of your favorite one at home, which you keep in a black case lined with blue velvet. A cherry red and yellow Sunburst Gibson Les Paul made in nineteen seventy-two—a beautiful guitar, Doctor Ashworth. Would you consider giving me lessons sometime?"

Joseph stood up abruptly, gasped loudly, and then sat down heavily again. "What's going on here? There's no way in this world you can read minds; it's just not possible."

"Of course not; just keep telling yourself that. Would you like another demonstration? Something even more amazing?"

Speechless, he nodded.

"Well, Mum and Dad have an inkling of what I can do, but not the full extent, so if I show you, you must promise not to tell them, please? Let this be our secret? Otherwise, they will worry, and I don't want that."

Doctor Ashworth nodded again as if he didn't trust his voice.

"Can you see my laptop on the table over my shoulder? Yes? Just keep an eye on it, and while you do, please notice that I'm not looking at it."

As Joseph watched, the laptop lid slowly opened on its own. Then, it rose and started to rotate as if on an invisible axis. Next, the cover closed and opened repeatedly while the computer spun through the air as if it were speaking silently, with the base and cover resembling lips.

"Doctor Ashworth, think of a poem or a song if you prefer; any verse will do. Oh, that's an excellent choice, Doctor. I truly appreciate your taste. Now, watch my laptop."

The machine halted in mid-air, and the lid opened as it glided across the room, stopping just before hitting the plastic wall barely three feet from Doctor Ashworth's face. As he observed, the keys moved swiftly, almost in a blur, as if invisible fingertips were pressing them. "That was the verse you were thinking of, wasn't it, Doctor?"

The Doctor raised his eyes to the screen and read:
The woods are lovely, dark, and deep,
But I have promises to keep,
And miles to go before I sleep,
And miles to go before I sleep.

"You like Robert Frost, Doctor Ashworth? I must admit he is one of my favorites, too."

Joseph turned his weary yet astonished eyes toward the boy as the laptop hung in midair. "I believe you have an extraordinary talent or gift, unlike anything I've ever seen or heard. What else can you do?"

"Oh, lots of things, especially when I'm stressed or upset about something. But ever since I was little, Mom and Dad warned me not to let anyone know. They're scared of what might happen if it ever got out. Maybe some government agencies would want to experiment on me, or they worry that people might become frightened by what they can't understand, so they might want to keep me imprisoned. I mean an actual prison, not just something like this." He waved his hand to indicate that he meant the bubble he had to live in. "I've told you this because I know, ever since I was born, you've tried to help me, and I can see the sorrow you feel, thinking you've failed me. I want you to know I don't hold you responsible. I thank you for doing everything you could to help. Nature compensates, doesn't she? I have to live with chronic allergies, but my *party tricks,* as you called them, well, I feel like I've only scratched the surface of what I can do if I *really* put my mind to it."

"You seem calm and wise beyond your years, your speech is that of a fully grown mature, yet you say you've met my wife in my home? You can't be serious; I know you've not left the bubble unless to go to the hospital."

"I can see you still doubt me. I didn't say I met your wife, merely that I watched her. She had no idea I was there. Let's see if I can make you believe I was there in spirit. Your couch and matching chairs are old-fashioned brown leather. Miriam, yes, I know that's your wife's name. Miriam wants to get rid of it, but you find it too comfortable, so you won't let her. You have a tortoiseshell cat older than the couch; his name is Clive. Cute name for a cat, by the way. You have seventeen pictures of your two children and four grandchildren on the wall above the TV. Clive's basket is to the left of the television, but Clive prefers to be on your lap when you watch it. Shall I go on?" Doctor Ashworth stared back, seemingly incapable of speech, so Timothy shrugged and continued. "Life has dealt me what it has. I have the world's most wonderful, loving, and kind parents. Sure, I can't leave my bubble physically, but in my mind, I can. For example, I know where you live. I've seen inside your home. I've seen your wife; I watched as she cooked your favorite meal last night, Lasagna with cheesy garlic bread on the side, and you shared a bottle of Chianti.

There is nowhere I can't go, though my body never leaves my bubble." Suddenly, he laughed. "Maybe I could become a hitman for the mafia as a career? I'd have the perfect alibi every time I killed someone."

Joseph stopped wiping his glasses, which he had been doing automatically, and suddenly looked at Timothy. "Could you murder someone, Timothy? Is that even possible just by you thinking about it?"

The boy shrugged again. "I'm not sure; I haven't tried. Why, is there someone you want out of the way?" He laughed again. "It's okay; I'm just kidding. Look, Doctor, I think…if I tried or wanted to badly enough, yes, I could hurt someone, even kill them. I could visualize their beating heart, flick a switch, and turn it off. Or I could be much more violent if I truly wanted to. The question is, why would I want to? The idea of causing someone else pain is abhorrent to me."

"And you could do that from any distance? What if, for instance, you actually wanted to hurt someone in Vienna, Berlin, or Russia?"

"Probably; again, Doctor, I haven't tried to, though I'm confident I could."

He shook his head in amazement. "Timothy, your parents are absolutely right; you must tell no one about your abilities. You know, don't you, that if you lived two hundred years ago, they would burn you at the stake as a witch?"

Timothy laughed loudly. "I have no intention of doing that. I only told you because you've come to say goodbye and have always been kind to me and my parents. They've been through hell for me, and you've helped them more than anyone else could. I appreciate all you've done for us. Enjoy your retirement, Doctor. I believe you are off travelling the world, starting in Africa."

Joseph nodded, once more amazed at how the *boy in the bubble* could know that.

"Doctor, if you ever need my help, please let me know, will you? I know you might not understand what I mean. All you need to do to reach me is call my name along with the word help in your mind; I will hear you."

Ten minutes later, Luke and Belinda returned home from their shopping trip. They insisted that Joseph Ashton join them for coffee, which he happily did before saying his goodbyes.

Later that week, he and Miriam were leaving for a well-deserved holiday on an African Safari because Miriam had always been an animal lover. The three talked about his upcoming trip while sipping their hot drinks. Doctor Ashworth did not tell Luke and Belinda that Timothy already knew of his retirement vacation plans.

Chapter 8

2:12 p.m. 13th December 2022

The streets of Johannesburg were filled with cars and pedestrians. Everywhere the Ashworths looked, people were bustling about. After six weeks of experiencing the best the African savannas had to offer, they were on their way to the airport to catch their flight home. The weather had been spectacular, the scenery breathtaking, and the wildlife incredible.

Joseph and Miriam had been part of a twelve-member tour group and felt they had made friends for life. They had gotten particularly close to one couple from Britain, partly because he was also a retired doctor. At dinner the night before, they agreed to reconnect for a cruise down the Rhine the following year.

"Joe," Miriam said as the cab slowly edged toward the next set of traffic lights in the worst traffic jam the couple had ever seen. "It's been the most wonderful vacation; thank you so much for arranging it, but you know what?"

"What's that, my love?"

I can't wait to get home, sleep in our own bed again, cuddle with Clive on the couch while we watch a movie, and enjoy a nice cup of tea.

Joseph laughed and nodded. He was also looking forward to a cup of tea he could enjoy. He thought m*aybe it was the water, but tea in Africa doesn't taste the same* *as it does back home.*

The cab lurched to a halt, and the driver sounded his horn in frustration. The next second, the window next to Miriam's head exploded in a thousand sparking shards, which imploded inwards, showering the couple as a man hit it with a crowbar. An arm reached inside, found the door lock, and pulled it up before dropping to the handle and yanking the door open.

Miriam screamed, and the cab driver jerked his head around to see why his window had suddenly broken. A dark-skinned young man leaned in and seized Miriam's handbag sitting on her lap. She grabbed the strap and tried to wrestle it away from him. "Bitch," the man exclaimed with a sneering tone.

Joseph saw the sun glint off the knife blade, which appeared suddenly in the robber's hand. "Miriam," Joseph yelled, "give him the bag!" But with dismay, he saw her try to wrench it away from her attacker even harder. The man grunted and thrust the stiletto-bladed knife toward her chest. Joseph knew his wife of forty years was about to be killed in front of him over a handbag that contained hardly any money, and he screamed for help.

Time slowed down in Joseph's stressed brain as he watched the knife arc through the air, wielded by a man who clearly held his wife's life with little or no value. In a split second, Joseph imagined Miriam dying with a seven-inch blade in her chest while he could only look on as the mugger made off with Miriam's handbag.

But then the strangest thing happened as Joseph watched helplessly. Barely an inch from piercing the sky-blue cotton blouse Miriam wore, the knife tip seemed to hit an invisible barrier. The man jerked his hand back and thrust it again with a curse, aiming higher to cut the woman's throat, but his effort ended with the same result.

The man suddenly staggered backward as if he'd been tasered or hit with a baseball bat from behind, yet Joseph couldn't see anyone else around. Joseph lunged toward his wife and wrapped his arms around her, trying to protect her from certain death by pulling her toward him. The taxi driver gunned the engine, trying to swing the vehicle into the next lane to escape, but it was already occupied by a yellow school bus full of children. There was no escape for the cab driver to take, and the children watched the attempted mugging go wrong.

Much later, when Joseph recalled the incident, he realized their attacker suddenly resembled a marionette operated by a manic puppeteer. As the man reeled backward away from the cab, his hand, which held the switchblade, trembled as it turned toward his own stomach. The man seemed to be fighting with an invisible bodyguard, and he grasped his right wrist with his left hand to try to stop the knife from stabbing into his own body. But he was fighting a losing battle, and the blade disappeared into his stomach as he screamed a blood-curdling yell which ended with an even louder shriek.

"No," Joseph shouted frantically as he realized what was happening. "Timothy, stop, don't kill him."

The man jerked the knife out, and a squirt of blood arced toward the open door, some hitting Miriam's skirt. "Arggghhhhhh," the mugger exclaimed and looked directly into Joseph's eyes as the knife re-entered an inch higher, then again, and again, repeatedly until he fell to the sidewalk, shaking and kicking his legs in pain before passing into unconsciousness.

A gap in the traffic jam opened, and the cabbie, who Joseph realized hadn't seen the bizarre self-mutilation performed by the mugger, seized his moment, and the car surged forward, causing Miriam's door to slam closed. Joseph turned in his seat and watched the final death throes of their attacker and the widening puddle of blood he lay in while people on the busy street turned away and walked by.

****

Joseph called Belinda to ask for a suitable time to visit Timothy, and she mentioned she planned to go shopping for dinner around three. Doctor Ashworth knocked on the door five minutes early and spent ten minutes chatting with Belinda about the African Safari while secretly eager for her to leave. She made Joseph coffee and set up his usual chair where he always sat. Doctor Ashworth spoke of trivial matters with a smile while Belinda busied herself, but his gaze toward Timothy was steely, and Timothy met his look with an almost insolent air.

"What did you do, and how did you do it?" Doctor Ashworth asked Timothy through the bubble wall when Belinda finally closed the front door.

Timothy shook his head with a blank look on his handsome face. "I have no idea what you mean, Doctor. How was your safari?"

They gazed at each other through the plastic, neither wanting to break the staring contest. Joseph was the first to look away, as he knew he would, because he had to confirm that what he believed had happened was attributed to Timothy's remarkable talent. The incident had haunted him since Johannesburg. "I called for help in Johannesburg when the mugger was about to stab Miriam, and you heard me and intervened."

Timothy initially did a double-take but then winked. "Did I, Doctor? How on earth did I do that, stuck here in my bubble?"

Joseph paused, understanding that Timothy was smart enough not to admit murder, albeit caused by telepathy. "The last time I was here, you said if I ever needed your help, I was to call you in my mind. In Johannesburg, Miriam was about to be murdered by a mugger. He was attempting to stab her with his knife to make her release her grip on her handbag. I believe you helped us, and I wanted to thank you from the bottom of my heart for stepping in when and how you did. That said, I need to know how you did it. I can't sleep at night thinking about what happened. Miriam has no idea. In the cab, I pulled her toward me so she didn't see the grizzly end our mugger came to, but I did. You made him do it to himself, didn't you?"

"I'm reminded of the Gospel of Matthew and how we've paraphrased his words to say, '*Those who live by the sword shall die by the sword.*' It's *a*n apt saying for your mugger, wouldn't you agree, Doctor?" Timothy smiled mischievously.

Joseph leaned back in his chair. "You did help us; I knew it. Thank you for saving Miriam's life. How on earth did you manage it?"

Timothy nodded and shrugged at the same time. "I can't fully explain what I did because it happened so quickly. You must understand that this is the first time I've ever intentionally caused harm to another human being. If you want my opinion, when you called, I fed off your fear, saw what was about to happen, and made the attacker turn his blade on himself. I didn't have time to think; I just reacted."

"Did he die?"

"Yes. Your mugger received thirty-seven stab wounds to his stomach. And lying on the sidewalk for over an hour until someone bothered to call him an ambulance didn't help his cause. The shocking crime rate in Johannesburg and a very low appreciation of the value of life is not a healthy combination, is it, Doctor?"

"What about the police?"

"Without witnesses, they concluded a rival gang member attacked him, or it was a drug deal gone wrong. Your cab driver didn't report the damage to his vehicle, and the bus full of children didn't either. But even if they did, who would believe them?"

Chapter 9

9:12 a.m. Tuesday, 11th April 2023

Timothy Bergendorf decided that today was the day he would test his abilities more than ever before. His mother was about to leave the house for a dental appointment, while his father was at work. Earlier, he had lain in bed and let his mind wander. Knowing when his mother would be out and that he would be alone for just over an hour, Timothy wanted to explore the extent of his telekinetic powers.

For the past three weeks, Timothy read articles and searched for government studies, many of which were conducted in the 1970s and had become declassified. He even watched some fictional movies to better understand what he could do and how he could influence things using only the power of his mind.

"Will you be all right on your own, Timothy?" his mother asked as she slipped her jacket over her shoulders.

"I'll be fine, Mom," he replied with a smile, internally urging her to leave so he could begin his experiment. He loved both his mother and father with every fiber of his being. He understood the sacrifices they had made for him; the love they offered without expecting anything in return warmed and sustained him each day. They taught him not to complain about the hardships God asked him to endure but rather to be grateful for the blessings. Yes, he couldn't leave his bubble and survive, but he was alive; his IQ was beyond genius level according to Harvard University's testing protocols, and they had even offered him a free scholarship to study from home in any field he desired. Then there were his remarkable *talents*. Was that a gift or a burden? He wasn't sure, except that he felt confident that Doctor Ashworth was grateful for his intervention. Timothy had taken a life, and he knew that was a mortal sin. Still, he believed that if he stood before God and explained the extenuating circumstances surrounding the murder, God would forgive him.

And then, there was the fact that Timothy *loved* using his powers. When he made the South African mugger repeatedly stab himself, Timothy felt like a God. Even the small things he could do, like lift furniture, open doors, and set things alight, gave him a thrill. It was like an addiction. The more he used his powers, the more he wanted to do it again. And each time, something more grandiose than the last. Today, as soon as his mother left the house, Timothy intended to use his mind to lift automobiles in the air, one at a time, to see just how many he could hold at once.

Timothy had discovered a parking lot in Birmingham, England, used by night shift workers at a steel plant. There were no CCTV cameras monitoring the vehicles, and the time Timothy intended to take the cars was during mid-shift, so there shouldn't be any witnesses.

"Are you sure you're okay, Timmy? You look a little anxious."

He smiled; it was typical for her to worry; she'd been doing it his whole life. "Mom, go to the dentist; I promise I'm fine. Now get."

****

Timothy stood in the center of the bubble, his head bowed to his chest, eyes closed, and arms outstretched. He could clearly see the Birmingham parking lot and the two hundred and forty-seven cars within its barbed-wire-topped fence. It was raining heavily, which was perfect for Timothy's purpose. He nearly laughed at the idea of a worker rushing out to retrieve something forgotten from his car, only to see several of them suspended in mid-air.

He began in the corner farthest from both the road and the entrance to the spacious workshop. A dark green sedan lurched four feet into the air, followed by a white van next to it. As Timothy held the vehicles rigidly hovering above the ground, he looked inward to assess his feelings and realized he had barely broken a sweat. He added a third car, then a fourth, and a fifth. Timothy smiled as he imagined placing them back in different spots and watching the expressions of the bewildered workers when they finished their shifts.

"How many more can I lift?" he wondered, as five wasn't challenging him at all. One after another, more vehicles rose into the air. As the eighteenth lifted off the ground, Timothy felt the onset of a headache and realized that his shoulders had dropped, as if he were a weightlifter struggling under a barbell.

He decided to stop at twenty. It was a nice, round number and a solid foundation for his experimentation. Timothy believed he could manage more, many more if necessary, but he had noticed a dull ache low in his stomach and was also feeling a slight rise in his body temperature. He mused that twenty automobiles could serve as a launching pad for lifting thirty next time, in a week or so, when his mother left him alone in the house again.

The nineteenth lifted in the air quickly enough, but as the final car rose, Timothy felt something break inside him. A sharp pain emanated from his groin and spread upward in a spiral of breathless agony. Inadvertently, he stooped to ease his discomfort and dropped his arms while in Birmingham, twenty vehicles crashed to the ground and bounced on their tires, seven of them bursting with the sudden force.

Timothy clutched his stomach, dropping to his knees before pitching forward. He struggled to breathe; searing pain surged through his body as the room whirled around him, and he slipped into unconsciousness.

****

Timothy woke up in an ambulance. He felt the oxygen mask covering his mouth and glanced around frantically, disoriented. He saw his mother, tears streaming from her bloodshot eyes. "It's going to be okay, Timothy. You must have had an allergic reaction to something. I found you on the floor, so I used the EpiPen and called the ambulance."

He shook his head as a wave of pain surged again, reminding him of what had happened. "Pain, stomach, not allergy," he said, each word punctuated by a gasp of breath wrenched from the oxygen bottle, which left him feeling lightheaded.

Belinda looked at the paramedic, perplexed; she was sure it had to have been one of his many allergies. "Timothy?" the medic said as he bent over Tim's face. Can you hear me? Can you show me where it hurts?" The man pulled Timothy's shirt open and gently pressed his hand over his appendix. "Here?"

Timothy shook his head, grabbed the ambulance attendant's wrist, and slid the hand lower before recoiling upon contact with the inflamed area.

"Okay, I think you've suffered a ruptured hernia; I'm going to give you some morphine for the pain."

****

Due to his condition, an orderly transported Timothy through the emergency entrance, bypassing the busy waiting area, on a trolley bed covered with a plastic isolation tent designed to contain an infectious patient, which also effectively protected Timothy from airborne allergens.

Although time dragged for Timothy, it flew by in terms of hospital protocol. As the paramedic predicted, he was tested and diagnosed with a hernia within thirty minutes. An ultrasound revealed his condition was so severe that Doctor Beltrane was informed his next patient would be Timothy, and the theater was prepared immediately.

When Timothy Bergendorf woke up after the operation, the pain he felt as the medication wore off was infinitely worse than it had been before. It seemed that apart from sedating him, the doctors could do nothing to alleviate his suffering. While everyone else saw no reason why Timothy should be enduring the agony he seemed to be.

Chapter 10

11:18 a.m. Saturday, 15th April 2023

Dr. Marcel Pernfours, the head of surgery, spoke with William Beltrane in his office, adopting a conciliatory tone. "I understand your perspective, Bill, but you have to admit there's something wrong with the boy. Unless you allow us to open him up again, we'll never know exactly what's going on. If you'd prefer, I can bring in another surgeon?"

Betrane was fuming. He had never had his expertise questioned before, and he was damned if he would stand by and let this French export quack start now. "I'm telling you, the operation was a success," he insisted. "It was child's play and nothing, would you like me to spell that for you? N-O-T-H-I-N-G went wrong. For God's sake, Marcel, it was a stupid bloody ruptured hernia, nothing overly complicated; I was in and out within forty-five minutes. Even the ultrasound didn't show anything wrong with my work."

"I know; I've checked. But you know, as well as I do, they don't show everything. Look, Bill, maybe you're right; I hope you are. But there's only one way to find out for sure, and let me tell you, it's going to happen. The only question is whether you perform the procedure, or I get someone else to do it."

"Have you considered this is due to one of his many allergies? Christ, he has enough of them."

"Well, anything is possible. If you're suggesting that you or someone on your team wasn't completely sterile, then it's definitely a possibility. However, even if that were the case, we still have only one way to confirm or deny that as the cause."

"I've tested and re-tested his samples, and nothing seems to be wrong. Perhaps because he lives in a bubble, he has zero tolerance for pain. Have you considered that?"

"No, Bill, I only became qualified yesterday. *Of course, I've thought about his lifestyle.*" He took a long, calming breath before speaking again in a calmer voice. "Bill, this poor kid has suffered all his life, and I've gone through Doctor Ashworth's notes; Timothy Bergendorf has never once complained. Maybe you're right, and there isn't anything wrong with the operation you performed, but I have to consider the welfare of the hospital, not your bruised ego. So." He glanced at his watch. "The boy is being prepped for surgery as we speak, and in about an hour, we will open him back up, check him out, and I will observe whoever performs the procedure. Now, the only question is, will that be you, or should I find another surgeon to review your work?"

****

"You see?" Beltrane yelled, pointing a blood-covered, latex-wrapped finger at the open wound. "Nothing. Not a single thing is wrong. Look at the stitching; notice there's no unusual inflammation. Everything is as it should be. The boy is a lily-livered, grade-*A* sook, suffering no more than the usual recovery pains, yet acting like he's been doused in molten lava. Can I close him up now?"

****

We believe there is nothing wrong with your son that could be causing the pain he reports. I personally supervised the second operation, and I assure you that Doctor Beltrane removed the hernia flawlessly. There was no excess scar tissue, and the stitching was impeccable; in fact, I must commend Doctor Beltrane for his outstanding surgical skills.

"If that's the case, why is Timothy in so much pain?" Luke asked, almost shouting.

Marcel Pernfours shrugged. "We don't know, is the short answer, but we will keep working to find out. However, yelling at me will not help your or Timothy's cause. We are his best and only hope. I've arranged for a pain specialist and a hypnotherapist to speak with Timothy. Clearly, we can't keep him on massive doses of morphine, so he needs to learn to manage his pain using more natural remedies. When he comes out of recovery, we need to reduce his pain medication, and you must do your part to help ease his mind. I've asked Doctor Beltrane to be there with us, and together, we need to make Timothy understand that he's only making things worse by screaming like this."

Chapter 11

Timothy woke slowly as the drugs in his body juggled his state from pain-free sleep to wakefulness, his stomach ablaze. He opened his eyes and glanced around, managing to make out several shapes of people outside his plastic protective tent. That was when the first wave of pain hit him, prompting him to try to raise his legs to alleviate it.

"Timothy, it's Dad. Mom is here, too. You've just had a second surgery, and you're waking up from the anesthesia now. The doctors say you'll feel some pain, but there's nothing wrong with you; it's simply recovery pain. The first surgery to remove the burst hernia was completely successful, so you have nothing to worry about. You need to try to manage the pain and learn to cope; there are specialists here to assist you. Do you understand me, Timothy?"

When he didn't reply, Belinda said, "Sweetheart, you mustn't panic. We will get through this as we have with every other problem that's plagued your life. We love you; don't give up, fight it, and we will fight alongside you."

Slowly, Timothy's mind began to clear from the fog that the drugs had created, but as it did, the pain increased in increments as well. He heard his parents and understood that they were trying their best, but it was easy to say that when they couldn't feel what he felt.

There was a raging fire in his lower abdomen, and gradually its heat intensified, and soon, he sensed it would become a blazing inferno. *What have they done to me?* he screamed to himself, but that only caused the pain to rise a few octaves higher, and he groaned loudly while shaking his head from side to side.

"Listen to me, Timothy. I'm Doctor Beltrane, the surgeon who operated on you, and I assure you, I've performed that same procedure hundreds of times. Nothing went wrong, nothing was removed that shouldn't have been, and nothing extra was added. You need to understand that fact and train your body to adapt. I know you live in a bubble, and I'm sorry for that. It's time to join the real world and stop crying whenever the pain meds wear off."

Timothy turned his head toward the shape speaking to him. His mind was ice cold, while his stomach was burning hot. He decided to give Beltrane an inkling of what pain he was experiencing. *Let's see how you deal with pain, Doctor.* Timothy's eyes narrowed to almost a squint, and suddenly, Beltrane flew backward across the room and hit the wall. The others turned to watch, shocked at the sudden and violent way he had careered into the wall. They watched spellbound as the Doctor seemed to wriggle his arms and legs and slowly began to slide up the wall, inch by inch, like a spider. Beltrane screamed and clasped his hands over his stomach. He shrieked, and at first, everyone thought it was a reaction to hitting the wall. *"It burns, it burns, I'm on fire,"* he shouted. *"Water, give me water."*

"Stop crying. Try joining the real world," Timothy grunted softly, but his mother heard.

"Timothy," she hissed, "stop it right now; release

him. He's only trying to help."

Just then, another tidal wave of pain struck Timothy, and he could no longer be bothered with trying to teach Doctor Beltrane manners. He yelled and thrashed on the bed as sheer white-hot agony raced throughout his insides. Meanwhile, Doctor Beltrane's body slid farther up the wall until his head hit the ceiling with a dull *thunk*. He screamed as flames shot out of his mouth. Then, while everyone watched, horrified yet rooted to the spot, Doctor Beltrane became a human flashlight ball of fire.

The room quickly filled with smoke caused by the burning flesh, which the smoke and heat detectors picked up. A fire alarm blasted shrilly, and water squirted out of the sprinklers.

Marcel Perfours dashed out of the room into the corridor. He yanked a fire extinguisher from the bracket on the wall and raced back into Timothy's room. He pulled the pin from the trigger and pointed the stream of foam at the burning body.

"Timothy," his mother shouted, *"stop this right now."*

Her shout galvanized everyone else in the room, except her husband, into a mass panic, and they fled the smoke-filled room. Doctor Beltrane's body fell to the floor, a blackened, charred corpse, though Doctor Pernfours continued to play the weakening stream of retardant over him, though he could tell it was too late.

Chapter 12

Marcel Pernfours threw the empty extinguisher to one side. He was soaked from the overhead sprinklers and was in a state of shock at what had happened. He had read of cases of spontaneous combustion in human beings, but never expected to witness a case. He bent and touched his finger to the neck of the body on the floor, but there wasn't a pulse, not that he expected to feel one; it was just habit.

He became aware of Luke and Belinda Bergendorf shouting at their son, who was writhing in clear distress and pain on the bed beneath the canopy that sheltered him.

"Nurse," he shouted, "bring me some morphine, stat!" But then he noticed that the nurse and other specialists had fled the room, leaving just the four of them. As the fog lifted, he realized that the parents were urging their son to stop hurting Beltrane, but that made no sense. He was inside a tent, barely conscious and suffering severe, acute pain; what on earth were they talking about?

Just then, the door flew open, and a nurse appeared. "There is a fire; we need to evacuate the patient," she shouted above the siren."

Pernfours gripped her arms firmly. "It's all right, nurse. The fire started here, and it's out now. Cancel the sirens and bring me fifty micrograms of morphine; the patient is in severe distress. This patient cannot be evacuated outside due to his allergies, but we need to move him to a new room. I need that morphine now."

She nodded and turned away, but saw the smoking body against the wall and screamed.

Chapter 13

Timothy Bergendorf had had enough. As he jerked in pain on the hospital bed, he realized that his life had always been a continuous series of problems. Something was wrong with him now, and the doctors couldn't cure it. He felt exhausted by everything. Living in a bubble that seemed nothing more than a glorified prison was not truly living. He recalled a song he had heard on the radio called "Born to Be Alive." His life was terrible, and he was certain he wasn't meant to exist in a bubble, hiding away from the world. If he were condemned to spend whatever time he had left in agony that no one could alleviate or in prison, he would choose to do so outside in the fresh air, consequences be damned.

Through the veils of agony enveloping his body, he became aware that his parents were scolding him for murdering Dr. Beltrane, even though Timothy believed he had simply taught the arrogant pig a lesson he would never forget about manners. But he no longer cared. He loved them, yet it was time to free them from their prison as well. They had sacrificed their lives to exist in his bubble, working tirelessly and spending all their money to keep him safe. Still, he finally had to ask himself, *safe for what?*

Timothy struggled to sit up as a new wave of pain surged through his stomach. He focused a small portion of his power inward and examined his abdomen, uncovering the issue that Beltrane had overlooked. Timothy was bleeding internally from a spot higher than before. He didn't have just one hernia but two, and Beltrane had stopped his examination when he found the first one, ignoring the second. Too late, Timothy realized he should have stopped at eighteen cars and not pushed on to twenty.

Timothy sensed it was too late to fix; it had been going on for too long, not that he even wanted it resolved now. He had committed murder, and it was time to end everything rather than face the mockery of a trial that would only further punish his parents. *I won't let them lock me away or subject me to tests like a hamster on a wheel; no way, he* thought, as a fresh wave of agony surged through his body. *I definitely should have stopped at eighteen cars.* He rested his hand over the area that ached so intensely and pressed down. He closed his eyes and focused, trying to use his powers to ease the pain. He felt the energy flow from him, through his outstretched palm, onto his lower stomach, and then deep inside. The warm glow surrounded the area, allowing him to breathe again without feeling like a knife had been thrust into him.

Timothy focused on the oxygen tent meant to shield him from allergens. He shut his eyes and envisioned it soaring through the air until it landed to envelop the charred remains of Doctor Beltrane. He made it happen, causing his parents to gasp. "Timothy, what are you doing?" his mother yelled.

"Lie down, Timothy. I have more morphine on its way to help with the pain," Pernfours urged, "Then we will get you to a new room."

Timothy turned to the French Doctor. "Beltrane

fixed the first hernia he found and stopped. But he missed the second one, and it's bleeding badly. My time left is limited. Now get out, leave me to finish my life how I want to spend it. And unless you want any more dead and burning bodies, keep everyone away from me."

Behind Pernfours, the door burst open, and he thought it was the returning nurse with the morphine syringe. Suddenly, Pernfours found himself moving involuntarily as if on skates. He flailed his arms to maintain his balance and tried to slow down as he realized he was being propelled backward through the open door. The senior surgeon collided with the passage wall, and the door slammed shut behind him.

"Timothy, what are you doing?" his mother cried as his father attempted to wrap his arms around him.

Timothy gasped and flinched as his father held him. Timothy used his mind to uncouple his father's loving arms as gently as possible and forced him to sit on the bed. "Mom, Dad, I've had enough; I can't do this anymore. Please, don't try to stop me. Help me go for a walk outside. I'm dying anyway; it's too late now; they cannot repair the damage. Let me enjoy my last hours in the fresh air with people around me like a healthy person.

The door suddenly swung open, and Doctor Pernfours, accompanied by two security guards, attempted to rush in. Timothy flicked his head toward them, and as if thrown by a wrestler, they careened back out, the door slamming shut behind them. Timothy closed his eyes and projected a powerful thought that forced the three men to clutch their heads in pain. *"Leave me alone, and I will leave you alone. Try to interfere, and there will be more deaths."*

"Tim, if you go outside, you know what will happen:

you will die. We've done everything we can throughout your life to keep you safe. Please, if you truly believe there's a second hernia, let Doctor Pernfours operate again," Luke pleaded.

Timothy shook his head and grimaced as another wave of pain surged from his stomach to engulf his body. He closed his eyes and allowed his mind to wander through the corridors until he found what he was looking for: a wheelchair. He maneuvered it between the panicking people evacuating the building. Pernfours was still outside, pounding on the door, even though the guards had left as the unpiloted wheelchair arrived. Timothy opened the door, and the wheelchair rolled in with the surgeon behind it.

Timothy felt himself weakening, but used sheer willpower to keep going. He knew he had little time left now, and he was certain this was his last chance to be normal. He was determined to take it.

"Doctor Pernfours, Mum, and Dad, please understand this. I caused Doctor Beltrane to combust; that's on me. I lost my temper, and I killed him for his arrogance and oversight, which caused my pain, suffering, and soon, my death. There is no time left; I am bleeding inside, and I've committed murder. Even if you could save me, I no longer want to be locked away. Let my last hours be spent experiencing something I've never been able to do in my life before. Please, help me get outside." He glanced at the surgeon, who stood mouth agape, unbelieving. "I promise not to hurt anyone else, but if you try to stop me, I will rain down destruction the likes of which you've never seen." He decided the doctor needed more proof, so he flicked his hand toward the window, and the glass burst outward.

"That's just a sample of what I can do; now let me be."

Luke Bergendorf stared at his son and saw his sincerity. Suddenly, he remembered all the minor instances of his son showing his telekinetic abilities, and he knew that if he didn't help his beautiful boy, there could be more deaths and destruction. He stood and grasped the handle of the wheelchair, maneuvering it to the side of the bed. "C'mon, son, let's go for a walk outside. Belinda, grab a blanket to wrap around him. We need to keep him warm."

Belinda looked from her husband to her son and back again. Tears streamed down her cheeks as she nodded. She loved her son dearly; she could not deny him anything, not at any point in his life, but especially now at the end of it all.

Luke helped Timothy to his feet by wrapping his arm around him. For a moment, he realized that doing so could pass on any of the multitudes of things Timothy was allergic to. But he knew, with a heavy heart, that it no longer mattered.

"Stop," Pernfours shouted, holding up his arm in a halting gesture. I can't let you go; the police have been called and are coming."

Timothy settled into the wheelchair, sweating and clutching his stomach as waves of pain surged through his body like a stallion galloping across the prairie grass. "Please, give me something for the pain, not something to put me to sleep; I will be dead soon enough. If you don't do that and keep the police away from me, I will do this..." He projected to Doctor Pernfours a mental image of his beloved hospital as a charred ruin. "I can do it; you know I can, so help me get this IV out before I pull it out myself."

He glanced at the dead body in the corner. Had this boy, who had only just reached puberty, done that? And if he had, could he destroy the hospital? He shook his head, unwilling to take the chance. "All right, wait one minute; let me get the morphine—enough to take the edge off, but not enough to knock you out. Then I will help you."

****

Timothy, Belinda, and Luke walked through the bustling city mall. Luke pushed the wheelchair while Belinda held Timothy's hand, trying not to cry. She looked at her son and, despite the pain she knew he must be feeling, cherished the sheer happiness radiating from his face.

Timothy turned his head from side to side, admiring everything and everyone around him. He wondered why those who could mingle with others in the outside world and weren't afraid of catching a disease didn't appreciate the simple pleasure of that. "Stop over there, Dad, please," he said, nodding toward a bench as the family approached it. Belinda sat on one side and Luke on the other. "Mom, Dad, thank you for everything you've done for me. You've been the most amazing parents."

Timothy looked down and noticed a tiny beam of red light settling on his chest. He smiled. Deep down, he expected this; they could never risk that he wouldn't unleash his power if he lost his temper. They feared he might hurt innocent people, and while that was impossible, Timothy understood their uncertainty.

"I love you both," he whispered as the crack of the sniper's rifle reverberated through the mall.

Timothy Bergendorf toppled sideways in the wheelchair.

The Note

Sometimes, being a good Samaritan is a mistake

Foreword

I consider myself extremely lucky, and sometimes unworthy, to have found a publisher for my first book. Furthermore, I have been continuously published in all subsequent books. Since I left school at age fifteen, I had no formal education in literature, so several years ago, I decided to take an online writing course.

The course was taught by a well-known author whom I won't name, though I respect and admire him for his body of work. I've read most, if not all, of his books, and several have been adapted into films, which is every writer's dream.

One exercise he set involved writing a short story about the protagonist discovering a note. The genre could be anything, but the note had to be the central focus. I submitted my effort and was extremely proud when I learned I was a finalist. This meant that the author himself would read my story. Did he enjoy it? Honestly, I don't know because he didn't email me. My effort did not win the competition, but I didn't expect it to. By the way, the winning entry was a superb story, and I agree it was far better written than mine. The point was that such a famous author read it, which was enough.

Did it deserve to be a finalist, dear reader? You be the judge.

Chapter 1

I very nearly didn't see the note as it lay on the wet ground, forlornly. Its bent-over corner was dipped in a puddle, which reminded me of a soggy corn chip in salsa. The rain had caused the water to travel up the paper, slowly spreading the letters, which were face down on the concrete, so they looked *fluffy.*

Sometimes, I wish I had simply stepped over it during my darker moods and kept walking. Yet, at other times, I find comfort in knowing that if I had done that, I could never have saved Simone Brereton's life. On my better days, it's a close race between regret and gratitude for having been there to help. Ultimately, that came at a high personal cost. Was that a fair trade? You be the judge.

I suppose the strangest thing about the entire episode is that the writing on the note was underneath while it lay on the ground. If it hadn't been raining, causing the ink to bloom like the petals of a chrysanthemum, the word *HELP* wouldn't have bled through to become visible. Moreover, if the weather had been dry, the wind could have carried it away to land somewhere else, and Simone would have died.

At first glance, the note seemed to have been roughly torn from a spiral notebook and appeared crumpled and discarded. The elements had caused it to unfold, and the rain stuck it to the pavement. That single word, *HELP*, was written diagonally in large, scrawled letters, with the P nearest to the corner, resting in the puddle. As it absorbed the water, much like a sponge, it made the ink visible. This phenomenon allowed it to be legible from the reverse side as I rushed from my car to reach the front door of my house.

If it hadn't been for a series of strange coincidences, I wouldn't have stopped mid-stride, ensured I saw the word in backward writing, and then bent down to pick it up. Speaking of strange coincidences, there was another. If I hadn't felt the onset of an approaching migraine, I wouldn't have left the office early. Even if I had found the note later, the rain would have washed the ink away, leaving nothing behind to see.

After years of dealing with severe headaches, I recognized the signs well. Within two hours, I would be in so much pain that I wouldn't be able to see clearly. Going home while I could still drive was crucial, so I turned off my computer, let my assistant Jane know I was leaving for the day, and headed out. That's one of the perks of owning my own business. Isn't life strange sometimes, though? With what happened later, the migraine didn't manifest at all. What I find interesting is that they say these migraines are triggered by stress. However, staring at numbers on a computer was nowhere near as stressful as what occurred later.

It's hard to describe my emotions as I stood, with the rain beating down, looking stupidly at the word *HELP* and trying to make sense of it. I had not taken an overcoat or umbrella to work earlier in the day because when I left the house that morning, it was a quite typically warm late spring day.

I recalled a practical joke we used to play on

passersby when I was younger and quickly scanned the area for any giggling children who might be watching. In my day, we took pleasure in using super glue to cement a gold coin to the sidewalk and then laughed heartily as some unsuspecting person tried to pick it up. Was this a trick in a similar vein, I wondered? There was no one else I could see hiding anywhere, which ruled out that theory. As you'd expect on such a rainy day, Tippington Close was empty, except for me.

My searching eyes returned to the paper, then darted back up to something my peripheral vision had noticed. *Why is Derek and Simone's bedroom window open when it's raining?* I wondered.

Another thought occurred: if the note had been discarded for someone to find, rather than falling from a pocket, it made sense that it must have come from a window. I glanced up and down the street again and realized two things. First, there were no other windows open that I could see, and second, even though it was pouring rain, there was no wind—not even a breeze. Therefore, the note couldn't have traveled very far, which directed my gaze straight back to the open window. I then had another realization. I had noticed, but then overlooked, a car parked somewhat haphazardly against the curb outside their home, and it looked quite out of place.

Mount Lawley, where I live, is a lovely area. It may not be the best neighborhood in Perth, but it's certainly far from the worst. Tippington Close has exactly thirteen houses, and we all know one another. One thing I can tell you is that no one living here owns the old dark blue rusty sedan currently parked outside number seven.

I'm sure you've heard the saying about the hackles

on the back of your neck. Mine rose right then, and for good measure, I felt goosebumps on my arms beneath my shirt. Somehow, and I get that this will be hard to understand, I knew Simone was in trouble. Hot on the heels of that thought—or if you prefer to call it a premonition—I had another. If she was in trouble, whoever had caused her such grief, prompting her to cast a plea for help into the rain, could be watching me through a window.

As if I had an audience, I shook my head dramatically and continued to my house. With trembling fingers that seemed reluctant to cooperate, I inserted my key into the front door slot and turned it. Once it opened, I stepped inside, firmly shutting the oak door behind me and immediately feeling a sense of relief. I leaned against the wall, trying to calm my racing heart and make sense of the chaotic whirlwind of thoughts swirling around in my mind.

Had I imagined things? *Perhaps* I had to concede. The note might be a prank from a kid, and Simone could be at the store, having opened the window when the weather was warm and pleasant earlier in the day. *Could it be that simple, and did I imagine the rest? Yes, but what about the car?* I questioned myself in response. *Well, I suppose it could belong to a tradesman working at one of the homes on the street.* But deep down, I knew that wasn't the case. Don't ask me how, I just knew, okay?

So what should I do? I wondered. My initial thought was to call the police. *Don't be a total idiot,* my alter ego replied. *Seriously, what would I even* say? They'd think it was Looney Tunes Hour, and even if they believed the note was real, there would be no way to prove it came from my neighbor's window. Meanwhile, if something bad happened inside, precious hours could be lost trying to get help while I was there.

Okay, I know what you're thinking: am I a superhero in disguise? A highly trained ex-soldier? A retired cop? Nope, I'm just a chartered accountant whose wife is away in Darwin visiting her sister, who has been diagnosed with stage three cancer. I'm just an average guy who has never been in a fight at school or rescued a damsel in distress. I don't meet very many damsels in Mount Lawley.

But something was happening next door; I could feel it in my bones, so I had to investigate. If I didn't, and something terrible happened, I would never have been able to live with myself. I walked to the closet in the hallway, removed my now-soaking wet suit jacket, and grabbed a lightweight, waterproof one. I kicked off my shoes and slipped my feet into my gardening sneakers.

The next stop was the kitchen, where the knife rack was above the butcher's block food preparation area. I slid out a twelve-inch Japanese beauty that was as sharp as my mother-in-law's tongue. Then, holding the knife as if it were a weapon, I got a fit of the giggles. *Who am I kidding?* I put the knife back. There was no way I was capable of stabbing someone, no matter what the justification was. I'm more likely to cut myself in the event of a scuffle.

I was halfway across the room when an alternative idea struck me, which I saw as a fair compromise. I hurried to the five-drawer unit and opened the third drawer. Amid the clutter, I discovered what I had been searching for: my Swiss Army Pocket Knife, which I tucked into my jacket. Somehow, I felt better about myself, though part of me thought it was a silly idea—laughable, even. Still, it felt somehow right.

Fortunately, my patio sliding glass door opened to the rear garden, an area concealed from Simone's house, just in case they were watching. I refer to *them*, which I now know is accurate, but it seemed like an ethereal *they* back then. For all I knew, *they* existed only in my imagination.

Between our two houses stood a six-foot-high fence made of Colorbond steel sheets with a cream finish. On either side, there were trees, plants, and flower beds. Both wives were passionate about gardening, filling our yards with flowering shrubs. Under normal circumstances, the only way to go from the rear of one property to the other would have been to scale the wall, which wasn't an option since I would be seen and heard climbing over a metal fence. We had been friends with our neighbors for many years and often hosted barbecues together. About three years ago, a sudden storm blew down part of the fence, and we replaced it through an insurance claim. Derek and I teamed up to offer the installer a couple of cases of beer in exchange for a semi-concealed gate. When Grace, our daughter, got married, we held the reception in our yard under a marquee, and we kept the gate propped open to use both kitchens and bathrooms, which was fantastic.

I opened it as quietly as possible, hoping and praying that the hinges hadn't rusted and would squeak. Fortune smiled at me. I stepped through the opening, closed it behind me, and stood in their garden behind a conifer tree. I listened for any sign that I'd been spotted, but all I could hear was the sound of raindrops hitting me after bouncing off the branches of the tree above me.

Then, from inside the house, I heard the unmistakable clattering of cutlery falling into a stainless-steel sink, and I breathed a sigh of relief. I had worried for nothing; Simone was home and had simply forgotten that the window was open. Shaking my head at my unfounded fear, I left the cover of the tree, crossed the flower bed along the gravel path, and stepped onto the lawn. From there, I made my way to the rear door, which led into the pantry beside the kitchen. I opened the door, stepped inside, and called out as I did: "Hey Simone, it's just me. You left your bedroom window open, and it's raining, you silly goose."

Chapter 2

I turned into the kitchen, and my heart sank for two reasons. Firstly, two men stood with their mouths agape, staring at me as though they had seen a ghost. The second thing was lying on the kitchen bench: a gun. A large, horrifying-looking handgun with what appeared to be a massive opening at the business end. How huge? I'd never seen anything like it when one of them picked it up and aimed it directly at my chest.

"Who are you, buddy?" the man with short, spiky, dyed-blond hair asked. He seemed intimidating, even though he wasn't the one holding the pistol. He wore a denim jacket that looked like it hadn't been washed in years, a black T-shirt, and faded jeans.

The taller one had dark, curly hair. Part of his right ear was missing, as if it had been bitten off in a fight. The other ear sported a large, thick gold earring. He also wore jeans and a T-shirt, this time a grimy shade of what was once white. His leather jacket was well-worn. However, his most striking feature was that his eyes resembled two lumps of coal, by which I mean they appeared lifeless.

"I'm a neighbor and friends with Simone and Derek. Where's Simone?" I asked, raising my hands. I couldn't believe how shaky my voice sounded, even to me, and I had never felt more scared.

"See this 'ere, mate?" The one holding the gun asked. "Imagine if I pulled the trigger right now. It would make an entry hole in your chest, oh, say, about half an inch in diameter, but now 'ere's the interesting bit. The exit hole out of your back would be about the size of my fist. So the thing is, buddy, when we ask the questions, it does not give you the right to bloody ask one back. Do you get me?"

I nodded frantically, unable to speak. If I said I could almost pee my pants, but thank God not quite, would you understand I'm not kidding? These men were criminals; you didn't need to be Sherlock Holmes to see they were dangerous. Worse, I feared they would shoot me without losing a moment's sleep. I was petrified, plain and simple, and thought I was about to be murdered.

"What are we gonna do with him?" Blondie asked his mate.

Here it comes, he's going to shoot me, I thought. Then he cocked the hammer back, and I heard the double click as it locked into place. I very nearly fainted as the seconds seemed like hours. Time passed in slow motion, and I had the saddest thought about my wife: *I'm not going to be able to say goodbye to Mina.*

"If you want to live, buddy, you need to be honest with me. Is there anyone else at home who might stop by in the next few hours looking for you?"

I shook my head, still not willing to trust my voice. Then Blondie sealed my death warrant when he said: "He's lying, mate. This job's gone pear-shaped. Kill him and the bitch, and let's get out of here."

Fortunately, right then, I found I could speak; in fact, I could beg. "I'm not lying. My wife is in Darwin; her sister just got diagnosed with cancer. I swear I am on my own in the house. I came home early from work and saw Simone's window had been left open. With it raining, I popped over to tell her. Please don't kill me."

The silence lingered as Curly contemplated while Blondie shifted from one leg to another. After what felt like an eternity, Curly released the pistol's hammer and lowered it.

"It's your lucky day, buddy. Let's take him upstairs, tie him up on the bed with the bitch. The husband will be home before five with the money, and then we're out of here. He's agreed to pay up, and I'm not leaving without it."

In a flash of blinding inspiration, it occurred to me exactly what the men were doing there. Derek was the manager at the Leederville branch of The Farmers Union Bank, and the men must have broken in and attacked Simone. Somehow, she threw the note out of the window for someone to find. Then I guess they phoned Derek at the bank and threatened to kill his wife if he did not bring money from the vault home with him for her freedom and life. I also realized one more sad fact. They had not worn masks. I could identify them even if Simone couldn't, leaving me with no doubt that when Derek did hand over the money, the three of us would be murdered.

He beckoned with the gun, and like a lamb to the slaughter, with my hands still held high and legs feeling like jelly, I walked ahead of them to the stairs. How I reached the bedroom door on the first floor without stumbling, falling, or begging for my life, I will never know. I don't want you to think I was anything but scared out of my wits; I'm not some super brave guy; I'm just Joe Average.

Chapter 3

Blondie kicked the door open ahead of me, and I saw Simone staring frantically up from the king-sized bed covered by a rumpled quilt. She lay on her back, tied up like a chicken, with a strip of black tape stuck across her mouth. Alarmingly, I noticed the black eye she had and the bloodstains on the side of her face from what I suspected was a broken nose. The blood had been smeared by her tears, turning the pillow, which was usually white, pink.

"Search the wardrobe and find something to restrain him with," Curly instructed his friend, then added, "Looks like it's your lucky day too, darling. We were all set to have some fun with you before your husband brought home the cash, but your neighbor here thought he would crash the party."

The next thing I felt was his hand on my back as he shoved me violently forward. My knees hit the bed, and I toppled over to land across it, my upper chest landing on top of Simone's stomach. He dropped his knee onto my backside, brutally, to hold me still as first my left, then right hands were yanked down behind my back, and I felt something soft, like a dressing gown belt, or one of Derek's neckties, wrapped around and around my wrists and tied off.

Once my feet were secured with one of Derek's leather belts, they manhandled me, so I lay alongside

Simone on my back. Then, from the bedside table, Blondie grabbed a roll of black tape, ripped a good-sized chunk off, and stuck it across my mouth fiercely, crushing my lips over my teeth as he did.

Curly sat on the edge of the bed and tapped my chest, non-too softly, with the tip of the gun barrel. "Listen up, Nosey. We only want the fifty K hubby is going to donate to us when he finishes work, which he agrees is worth it to keep his little lovely here alive. After all, it's not his money, is it? So here's the deal. Are you listening?" I nodded, eager for him to know I would not be any trouble. "You two lie here, quiet as little mice. Hubby gives us the cash, and we bring him up here to join you two. Then we leave. And you all get to play happy families again. But if you make a noise or piss us off, then we shoot you both and take the money anyway. Are we clear?"

I nodded again, even more earnestly, trying to convey my sincerity with my eyes. They exchanged glances before leaving, propping the door wide open behind them so they could hear any attempt we might make to escape.

Naturally, I struggled to free my hands from the knotted belt as I heard them walking across the shiny tiled hallway at the bottom of the stairs. Although I could gain a few millimeters, I realized I wouldn't be able to get my hands free anytime soon. Even worse, the fear and exertion, combined with my inability to breathe through my mouth, made my chest tighten. I felt the early signs of an asthma attack approaching. I had no choice but to calm myself, try to relax, and regain control of my breathing.

Unfortunately, my next idea was not more

successful. I turned to Simone and, using gestures of my eyes and head, tried to signal her to turn onto her side with her back facing me. Either she didn't understand what I meant, or she did but didn't want to risk the two men coming upstairs again to find us back-to-back, trying to untie each other's ropes.

I gave up and calculated how much time we had left on the planet, which sounds brave now, but I assure you, I didn't feel that way then. What I felt was desperation. I knew I left work around two-forty, so I would have arrived home around three-fifteen. I estimated it would now be close to three-thirty, and Derek usually got home just after five. I had no idea if he would leave work early with the cash or if he would need to wait until everyone departed before taking it. But one thing I knew about Derek: he would do anything to save Simone, and he would find the money to free her. I realized there might be very little time left before Derek burst in like a knight in shining armor with a bag full of cash, and we all could get shot dead.

At that moment, a blinding flash of inspiration struck me. I recalled the Swiss Army knife in my pocket, and a glimmer of hope came with it. But then I wondered how I could retrieve it with my hands tied behind my back. I glanced down at my body and saw the knife's outline nestled in my right jacket pocket, just in front of my hip. I could feel its weight, but when I swiveled my hands to reach it, I found myself about four inches short, no matter how hard I struggled.

Maybe, I thought, *I could lift my hips while keeping my shoulders on the bed and try to jiggle the damn thing out of my pocket.* Thankfully, I hadn't zipped it up, which was meant to protect whatever I had inside from the rain.

It was lucky, really, because I usually make a point of zipping it up, but on this occasion, distracted by my concern for Simone's welfare, it was gaping open.

Don't ask me how, but I worked my feet underneath me so I could lift my hips clear of the mattress. Then, using what at any other time might have been quite an obscene motion, thrust them up and down, and I swear I could feel the knife jiggle around. Out of the corner of my eye, I could see Simone staring at me, petrified that the two men downstairs would hear my jerky movements. No doubt, had the bed been squeaky, I'm sure they would have, but as a bank manager, I believe the bed was of excellent quality. Doing what I was doing would only have appeared worse to her because she had no idea I had the means for our escape in my pocket; she probably thought I was going mad.

It felt like it took forever, but suddenly I saw the end of the handle poking out of the pocket. Thanking my lucky stars, it only took another minute or so before it dropped onto the bed between us.

My asthma had worsened, and breathing through my nose became increasingly difficult. I was also sweating heavily, and a headache was quickly approaching, though thankfully it didn't feel like a full-blown migraine, which would have rendered everything else impossible.

I cannot describe the feeling of joy that washed over me when I wriggled my body upward and around, and I had the knife in my hand. From that point on, it was simple to open the blade, but then it got hard all over again as I hacksawed back and forth over the cloth to try to cut through it. I admit, there were two or three times I thought it was impossible and almost gave up. My wrists were getting slippery with blood, where I kept missing and cutting myself, and the stinging was intolerable. But never underestimate the extent to which a man will go to survive. Even if I'd slashed an artery, I think I would have kept cutting.

Well, all I can say is that those Swiss Army guys know their stuff because, eventually, my slippery hands broke free. God, my wrists were a mess. There was blood everywhere, but I didn't feel a thing. Adrenalin, I suppose. I sat up, bent forward, and freed my legs before turning to Simone, who looked at me with a mixture of fear and hero worship.

I ripped the tape from my mouth, wincing as I did. "Shhh, Simone, we need to stay quiet," I whispered after helping her turn away from me and cutting through the rope that bound her. I worried she might have lost the use of her hands as they looked unnaturally blue. Next, I freed her feet and noticed she couldn't grip the tape covering her lips well enough. So, I assisted her and eased it off as gently as possible.

"What if they come back and find us like this? They will kill us," she whispered.

"They're going to do that anyway, Simone. They didn't wear masks, and we can identify them. They won't allow us to live."

She pressed one very blue hand over her mouth to stifle a gasp as she realized what I said was true.

"How are your hands? Can you walk?" I watched her attempt to rub around her wrists to restore circulation and flex her feet. "I can't feel my fingers, but I think I can walk okay. What should we do?"

There was the rub: what could we do? I did not doubt that any attempt to go downstairs would be heard, and they would be waiting for us. Then I had an idea. I slipped off the bed and crept to her side, then helped her stand, holding one hand in hers and the other around her waist. She was trembling even more than I was, and believe me, that was no small feat. I hugged her for reassurance, and she whispered in my ear, "Thank you, thank you so much, George."

These days, when I feel down about my life, I remember those words, whispered softly yet sincerely. And you know what? It's not so bad anymore.

I put my finger to my lips to remind her to be quiet, then crossed the room to the window she had left open in the rain and looked down.

I quickly assessed the situation and thought: *Yes, it can be done.* I beckoned for Simone to come over, and as she hobbled toward me, my initial doubts arose. She would be slow due to the prolonged circulation loss in her hands and feet, but that couldn't be helped; I would have to try to buy her some time.

I pulled my car keys from my pants and tucked them into the checked shirt pocket she was wearing over her right breast. She gave me a questioning look, so I bent down and whispered directly into her ear, "I'm going to lower you out of the window so you can get onto the roof of the dining room below us. I know it's a sloped roof, but from there, you can jump into the flower bed, which will be soft from all the rain. Don't stop; run to my car, jump in, and start it. I'll be right behind you. Oh, and if I'm not—if anything goes wrong—drive like the wind and get help. Okay?"

"But they might hear the window opening and be up here in seconds."

"I understand, which is why I don't want you to stop

for anything. If you're out of the picture, Blondie and Curly will realize they won't get the money and get in their car and go. Derek will be safe, and they will have no reason to hurt me."

She looked at me with an expression resembling love. Not that there had ever been anything like that among the four of us; we were just good friends. As far as I could tell, it was the only plan that stood a chance of success. It didn't make me a hero; it was merely about survival. "C'mon, let's do it. We have to get you out of here before Derek gets home."

She nodded, thank goodness. I didn't think my nerves could handle a full-blown discussion. It made sense to get her out, and she understood the reasoning. "So once I get the window all the way up, climb out as quickly as you can, and let me hold your wrists to lower you down. Don't stop, Simone, not for me or anything; you need to escape and find help. Are you ready?"

Chapter 4

She shook her hands one last time to move the blood and nodded again. I grasped the upper sash window and mouthed, "*One, two, three.*"

The damn window screeched like a banshee as it opened, causing us both to jump. Good girl that she was, Simone sprang into action and pushed her left leg through the opening. She grimaced in pain as she grasped the lower sill and swung her other leg through the gap. With a sinking heart, I listened as the men ran up the stairs.

I grasped her wrists above the rope marks to support her and prevent her from falling, as her grip was too weak to hold her weight. I braced my knees against the wall beneath the window and held on for dear life. Then, I slowly lowered her down, squatting to position her as low as possible.

"Let go," she called, and I released Simone's wrists just as the men raced into the bedroom. I did the only thing I could think to do; I stood up to block their view of Simone's escape.

"What the hell?" It was Curly's voice. They had arrived and sounded pissed.

I stood frozen and watched Simone jump into the garden from the lower roof. She landed awkwardly but thankfully managed to stay on her feet. Turning, she looked up at me, and I waved her away frantically. I had the pleasure of watching her turn tail, run to my car, and climb inside.

I didn't hear the gunshot, but I felt a sharp sting in the middle of my back. My body was thrown forward against the glass, and foolishly, I wondered what the hell had happened. I slowly slid down, dazed and confused, until my upper body reached the opening, and I fell through into the void, unable to stop myself.

My last waking thought was to wonder why the roof was rushing up to meet me, and meet me it did as I swan-dived into the rain-slicked tiled surface. Thankfully, that was when I lost consciousness, so I didn't feel the subsequent fall from the roof into the garden bed below.

Chapter 5

When I woke up, I saw my wife holding my hand, and I thought, *You're in Darwin.* Then I realized I was in a hospital bed. It took a long time—and I mean a long time—to understand what had happened. But eventually, that was one thing I had in abundance.

I had been in a coma for eleven days. The surgeon, a dapper older man named Banks, operated to remove a bullet from my back where it had lodged against my spine. He also addressed a blood clot on my brain caused by my head hitting something during my rapid fall from the window. My left arm was broken, and apparently, my face was a mess of healing grazes and bruises.

On the third day after waking, Mr. Banks, it seems you don't refer to a surgeon as "Doctor," which I wasn't aware of, informed me that I was unlikely to walk again. Initially, I thought it was due to being shot in the back, but that wasn't the cause of the damage. It was the fall into the flower bed, partly in and partly over the brick retaining wall, which held back the mulch that caused the injury.

Fortunately, Simone had not seen me fall from the window. If she had, I'm certain she would have stopped to help and got caught by Curly or Michael Hampton, his real name, and Blondie, née Sampson O'Halloran. Simone had driven off in the opposite direction after sideswiping my BMW against the driveway gate.

She quickly found help, and the police responded immediately. In doing so, they likely saved my life. They prevented Derek from leaving the bank while armed officers surrounded our house and blocked off the street. An ambulance was called in case it was needed, which it was. Once the police confirmed that the two criminals had fled the scene, my unconscious body was found in the garden. Brad, the paramedic, worked wonders and kept me from dying. He recognized that the human back was not meant to be in the shape it was while I lay unconscious in the rain. I don't know exactly what steps he took, and I have not yet been able to meet him to ask and express my gratitude, but I'm told I was very lucky to be alive. How lucky I was still to discover.

Within a day and a half, the two men were arrested and ultimately sentenced to twenty-seven and twenty-three years in prison, respectively. The main charges were kidnapping and attempted murder. I'm confident that my testimony, delivered from my wheelchair, earned the jury's support; they didn't stand a chance, nor should they have. Curly claimed that shooting me was an accident. Thankfully, the jury didn't make that distinction; either way, I was left crippled because of him.

It was a long journey for me. First came the recovery, followed by rehabilitation, which was lengthy and painful. Mostly, these days aren't too bad. To be honest, I have my dark days, and whether that's self-pity or a side effect of the painkillers I constantly take, I can't say. Still, for the most part, it's okay; I manage.

The bank surprised me with a ten-thousand-dollar account. My best day was when I received the Prime Minister's Medal for bravery, with my family, friends, and work clients there to witness it. I was also nominated for Australian of the Year, likely due to the publicity surrounding the event. Thank God I didn't win because, while I enjoyed the fame for a day when I received my medal, I never truly felt deserving of it. I just did what anyone would have done, and I never thought of myself as brave. I believe most people would have acted the same way in my situation.

You know, the worst part of the whole episode for me was losing our best friends and neighbors. They moved away, unable to continue living in their house. But that wasn't the worst thing. We understood their need to relocate and create new memories. I felt that every time they saw me after I returned home in the wheelchair, they felt so guilty. In my opinion, they should never have felt that way, yet they did, and no amount of reassurance from me could change their minds.

These days, I am still working. A chartered accountant can operate from a wheelchair, and all my clients waited for my recovery and wanted me, which I found very humbling. Truthfully, I had to turn new clients away, such was the publicity. My car has hand controls fitted, so I remain mobile and independent. Personal fitness is crucial for someone with paraplegia, so I took up archery. Our bathroom and home have been modified, allowing me to manage bathing and using the toilet independently.

Of all the things I thought would never happen, they did. Mina and I bought a kayak, and we often paddle down the river when the weather is nice.

Overall, life is good, and it sure beats the alternative. I sometimes wake up in the middle of the night in a cold sweat, reliving being shot and the fall from the window, but somehow, it seems a small price to pay. Simone and Derek lived, and they would not have but for me.

So you tell me, should I have picked up the note I saw lying in the puddle?

The Grimoire of Caligari

Sometimes, it's best to let the dead stay buried.

Foreword

Okay, remember I mentioned that Dennis Wheatley's book and movie, *The Devil Rides Out,* inspired two stories? Well, this is the second one. Thanks to my good friend Alicia Dean, this is another installment in the Friday the 13th series. I won't reveal the ending, but think of pentagrams, black magic ceremonies, and the occult.

I would also like to pay tribute to the other, far more talented and famous Stephen King. In particular, his arguably most scary book, *Pet Sematary*. Yes, the clown in *IT* is frightening, and my namesake is the master of all things spooky, but to this day, I recall being in a cold sweat when I read *Pet Sematary* because of two things.

When SK wrote about a father chasing after his son to prevent him from being hit by a truck, the father in me screamed, "NOOOOOOOOOO! Don't let him die!" This scene moved me deeply. In fact, I admit it; I had tears in my eyes. Every father would feel the same way; it was incredibly well-written. The horror of losing a child is surely everyone's worst nightmare, and boy, did the author capture that fear. Yet, as I continued reading, I felt a growing dread that the protagonist intended to try to bring his son back from the dead. I knew for sure it wasn't going to end well, and I almost wanted to scream at the character not to do it. The highest praise I can give is that an author could evoke such a response from me, the reader.

Quite frankly, this book left me anxious and eager to read the next page because *I had to know how it ended.*

So, I would like to dedicate this story to two authors who entertained me for hours: Dennis Wheatley and

Stephen King. I do not pretend to be as good a writer—not even close—but I hope, dear reader, that I can make you feel something for poor Lucian as he hunts for *The Grimoire of Caligari* in an effort to bring back his loved ones from the grave.

Part 1

Through the Veils of Time

"There is more to life than simply increasing its speed."

Mahatma Gandhi

Chapter 1

I don't know why I was in that park when the little girl with rosy cheeks, resembling an antique doll, told me I would die if I didn't change my plans. I shouldn't have been there. I know it was a place I didn't usually visit; in fact, I had never been there before, as far as I can remember. Yet, there I was, sitting on a park bench, gazing at the serene lake, wondering why my life had become unbearable and what I had done to deserve such misery.

I remember thinking: *Go on, walk into the lake, sink, find a tree root on the bottom, and hold on until you drown. Go on; you can do it.*

It's interesting how, at times, it seems to me now, when you reach your lowest point and have lost all hope for happiness, you suddenly face death—an actual death, rather than an imagined one. Your perspective can sometimes shift. In the midst of your grief and foggy mind, it suddenly occurs to you that perhaps, just perhaps, there is something worth fighting for.

I won't say it was like that for me right away; no, that would be too storybook-like. Given what transpired, it was far from a fictional novel, although I wish it were. The issue was that when the girl appeared out of nowhere, looking as if she had stepped out of an antique shop, and stood in front of me, declaring in no uncertain terms that I was going to die, I suddenly wondered if that

319

was welcome or not.

"What do you mean? Why are you saying that?" I pleaded, but she stared back, her blue eyes resembling marbles. She shook her head and walked away several paces before stopping. When she turned around, her face had transformed, aging somehow; now, she looked as if she'd gained twenty years with every step.

"Let the dead stay dead and buried; whatever you do, don't try to bring them back," she intoned with a voice that sounded as if it came from the grave. Before I could do or say anything, she vanished. Then, I woke up in bed and realized it had been a dream.

****

I am fifty-seven years old and a widower. Not only *am I* a widower, but my two children—whom I loved with every fiber of my being—are also gone. There will be no college graduations ahead, no engagement parties, and dare I say it, no marriage ceremonies where I could proudly stand and, when asked, "Who gives this woman away?" shout with pride and devotion for my beautiful family: "Her mother and I do!"

Unfortunately, that's not a strong enough word; regrettably, though, "heartbrokenly" doesn't quite fit either—if such a word even exists. There wouldn't even be the waiting for my daughters to return home from their first dates. I'm sure all fathers feel the fear, even terror, that after raising girls into young women, you suddenly find yourself no longer the most important man in their lives. Now, it's a boyfriend who occupies that special place in their hearts. And as a father, my God, you worry. Will they be safe? Will the boy bring them home unharmed and with their virginity intact? And if they do fool around, will he want to see her again or break her heart?

I remember a poem by Kahlil Gibran from my younger *make love, not war* days, that always seemed corny, but I now believe it's true. It began:

Your children are not your children.

They are the sons and daughters of life's longing for itself.

They come through you but not from you, and though they are with you yet, they belong not to you.

Wow, I remember thinking as I inhaled some pot, *"That's heavy, man."* But I realize now that it was probably the most honest evaluation of parenthood ever. Yeah, the sixties. They say you weren't there if you remember them, but I remember I was at a rock festival when I first met Connie, the woman destined to become my wife. My God, she was beautiful, stunning, magnificent, and even breathtaking. As if by magic, she saw me and must have thought there was something about me that was more than just a guy to share a sleeping bag with while winding down after an acid trip. She had the longest blonde hair that shimmered and flew in all directions as she danced to a Canned Heat song about going down to the country. She wore a faux suede tasseled top that gaped as she danced, revealing the swell of her full, voluptuous breasts, bouncing and breathtaking, as if begging to be released, held, and caressed. She was a goddess among goddesses, and my heart skipped several beats. Sure, the summer San Francisco weather was warm, but suddenly I felt clammy, and sweat beaded on my forehead and poured from my armpits.

"Hey, dude," my mate George said. Are you okay, man? You look like you're trippin' into an early grave."

"I gotta dance with her," was all I could mutter as I stumbled to my bare feet, my torn fluorescent t-shirt blowing in the wind, just like the great poet Dylan once sang, and crossed the twenty yards or so to be with her. When I got there, I didn't speak; I couldn't. I was dumbfounded, but I managed to smile as I shook my head, causing my extravagantly long hair to whip around my face in the breeze. She smiled back, and at that moment, in that instant of clarity in my drug-fueled mind, I knew I was in love. Not in a soap opera, I love you kind *of way*, but in the I *fucking love you* way that said, pass me a blade and let me bleed for you. Okay, that expression worked in the early seventies, and maybe it's lost something over the years, but back then? Far out, man, it meant…well, everything.

Dancing had never been my strong suit. Honestly, I didn't have a strong suit in anything except studying ancient history. I was just one of those college students who went along to get along. I stumbled my way through half the sophomores. Okay, sure, the other half had far better guys than me to share their beds with, but I held my own, is my point. Yet that day on the commons, grooving to Canned Heat, I was the consummate dancer, hip shaking, feet moving, lord of the dance. And Connie? She appeared to be as starstruck by me as I was by her.

This tale isn't about falling in love in the sixties, dodging the draft, taking speed, and smoking dope to the most fantastic music of all time. Sure, all that happened. As I discovered, Connie was my soulmate, and I was hers. We were together for over thirty years, and I can't recall a single argument lasting more than an hour. Usually, when we were frustrated with each other and one of us was angry, a moment would come when we looked at each other, trying to stay mad but failing. Suddenly, one of us would sing, "I'm goin' down the country," the song that played when we first met. It always diffused the situation, and we would giggle, cuddle, kiss, and before we knew it, enjoy the most amazing make-up love. I can't call it sex because I don't believe we ever had it, but boy, did we make love a lot. Our bodies seemed to just "fit" together. Whether we were walking arm in arm, spooning in bed, or sharing an earth-shattering orgasm, we fit.

We finished school. Connie became a nurse, and I became a history and philosophy teacher. While sex, drugs, and rock music were my mantras in college, I adored ancient history and embraced my subjects wholeheartedly. Much to our parents' dismay, we married as they insisted we were too young. But we were in love, and we understood our feelings for each other while they could only speculate. Nothing and no one could stop us from pursuing our destiny.

We never spoke about having children. It's not that we didn't want them; we just never consciously decided to try or not to try for them. Life was blissful as it was. Looking back, I suppose it wouldn't have been easy to conceive while Connie was constantly taking the birth control pills. But one day, years later, during a holiday in Cancun, over dinner at a candlelit beach restaurant with the freshest shrimp, lobster, and local grilled fish I've ever eaten, Connie said, "Hon, I have something to tell you: we're going to have a baby."

It turned out that Connie was mistaken. It wasn't just one baby; they were twins. Several months later, she presented me with two achingly beautiful girls. I have never shed as many tears in my life as when I held my two daughters, Molly and Deborah. I thanked God and Connie for making me the happiest man on the planet.

They say a parent should never outlive their children. I consider it the worst act against humanity that my wife and daughters were taken from me, leaving me alone to carry on without them. Every day feels like a nightmare I can't escape, a horror movie on an endless loop. Every bone in my body aches as I stumble from one day to the next, wishing for an end to the torment of being alive and alone. And the most painful part? I never had the chance to say goodbye to them.

Music has always been a huge part of my life with Connie, so naturally, Molly and Deborah grew to love pop music, too. For the twins' fifteenth birthday, Connie and I bought front-row tickets to see their favorite singer, who wasn't much older than they were, but wow, she was famous and beautiful.

The girls were overwhelmed with excitement in the lead-up to the concert. As any parent knows, doing something for your kids that makes them burst with happiness is a feeling that no amount of money can buy. The night before the show, they barely spoke, and when I said goodnight to them, they both expressed how much they loved their mother and me for making them the happiest girls in the universe. Yes, I assure you they used the word "universe"; I didn't dream that or make it up; that's how excited they were.

It wasn't a show I thought I could sit through; however, I wished I had gone with them afterward. We bought three tickets: one for Connie to accompany the twins while I stayed home and watched a ballgame. I will never forget the date my world came tumbling down; it was Friday, June thirteenth.

As the sixth inning approached and the score remained tied, the police arrived. A wet road, a young man racing a friend, a red traffic light disregarded, and the three most important people in my life were gone, never to return.

As the driver was street racing at an estimated forty miles per hour over the speed limit, the police initially charged him with three counts of vehicular manslaughter. Later, the District Attorney upgraded the charges to second-degree murder.

Chapter 2

My universe went awry, for lack of a better word. I was aware of what was happening around me, but I felt shell-shocked and lived as if on remote control.

The term *remote control best* describes my state of mind during that time, a phrase I found in an article. In a nutshell, I believe it perfectly captures my existence in the months following the accident. Where does the saying, *in a nutshell,* come from, anyway? What does it *even* mean? I have no idea; regardless, I digress.

I suppose it's no surprise that Connie's father held me responsible. I know it was his grief speaking, and I couldn't blame him because I agree; I should have volunteered to drive my family to the venue and picked them up after the show concluded. How I've blamed myself for prioritizing a stupid ball game over them, but of course, I didn't have a crystal ball to foresee that they would be killed. To be fair, I did have a crystal ball, which I acquired during my studies of the Esoteric arts from the Middle Ages. My point is that while I owned a crystal ball, it never worked for me in predicting the future. I tend to have a pragmatic outlook, as most teachers often do. We can be a dull lot; I agree. The Black Arts fascinated me for a couple of years while I pursued my degree, but purely from an academic viewpoint. I can't say I believed any of it. Well, not until I met *The Dark Man*; then everything changed. My entire belief system shattered into pieces in just a few weeks as he guided me on what might be possible.

The funeral. What can I say about the funeral? First, it marked the beginning of my dreams, or more accurately, my nightmares and encounters with the China-doll-like girl.

While not particularly religious, Connie held beliefs like all the youths of the sixties and seventies. With influences from Buddhism, Catholicism, Hinduism, and whatever was "Blowin' in the Wind"—there's that song again—her core spirituality was a blend of various elements. It's safe to say that cremation was anathema to her, and considering what happened later, I'm grateful for that. How on earth could we have planned a ceremony to bring them back from the dead if the crematorium had turned their bodies to ashes?

My father-in-law, held back by his wife, threatened to beat me to death before the funeral for taking not only his daughter from them but their granddaughters, too. If I had been even half the man I used to be, I'd have punched him on the nose, but all I could do was stare at him, mouth agape. Didn't he understand that while it was his daughter and grandkids, it was my *wife and daughters*? What planet was he from?

No amount of verbal abuse from him could alleviate the guilt I piled onto my own dinner plate from the bain-marie of misery I was enduring, so I did nothing. I knew deep in my soul that the deaths *were* my fault and mine alone, so how could I blame him for holding me accountable?

Over four hundred people attended the funeral. Both of our girls were extremely popular in school, and Connie? If I said everyone who met her loved her, I wouldn't be exaggerating. She was truly an angel who lived among us mere mortals, touching each of us she came into contact with while sprinkling her angel dust.

So many of her work colleagues attended that I wondered how few nursing and medical staff were left to run the hospital. All her school and college friends were there, many of whom I didn't know. But it was clear that everyone who had come into Connie's orbit wanted to pay their respects after her passing.

When it was time for my eulogy, I stood at the podium, speechless. I gazed at the throngs of people and realized there were just as many outside listening who couldn't fit inside the chapel. The silence as everyone awaited my start was deafening and echoed around the walls. Ridiculous, I know; how can silence resonate? Yet, at that moment, it felt as if it did.

In a croaky, wavering voice, I began, "I want to thank you all for being here today to honor the lives of Connie, Molly, and Deborah." I remember gasping and taking a deep breath, trying not to cry but feeling the tears run down my cheeks, nonetheless. "I think everyone would agree that the world is a much darker place without them. For me, it feels as if the light has gone out at the world's end, and I have nothing left to look forward to in this life except hoping to be with them in the next."

At that moment, I completely broke down, and my brother, Marcus, came to my aid and helped me back to my seat.

After the funeral, I began walking the streets without a destination in mind, but I often found myself in one park or another. That was when I started to see the little girl with glassy eyes and rosy cheeks in real life, not just in my dreams. She would appear in my peripheral vision but rarely came close enough to talk to me, except in my dreams. There, she spoke to me, though I was too grief-stricken to heed her warning that I should let the dead stay dead.

Marcus came to my rescue a second time weeks later when he found me kneeling on the bathroom floor; my upper body hung over the bathtub side as my wrists bled into the drain. I had the presence of mind to care about not leaving a mess for my family to clean up, though not enough to wait until everyone left for the night after they called in to check up on me. I had tried to *soldier on*, *buckle down*, *toughen up*, and all the other cliches well-meaning people threw at me, and I had failed. Life was unbearable. It was as if I couldn't live one more minute with my sycophantic family staring at me, wondering when I would *get over my wife and daughters' passing*. Marcus saved my life that time, though I didn't want him to. I suppose I could have locked the door so he couldn't get in quickly, so maybe I was appealing for help subconsciously, though, to my mind, I just wanted to die.

I didn't want to talk about why; I didn't want to be saved again, so I kept quiet. I refused to answer any questions when I woke up in the hospital and instead made silent plans for my next attempt, determined to succeed.

What else could they do but lock me up in a psychiatric institution for evaluation? "Catatonia," they suggested, "a total and complete nervous breakdown brought on by grief. Depression, my mother claimed; it's such a shame." My family shook their heads in unison and sighed. There was no hope. Thus, they abandoned me to the sanatorium, ironically named Sunnydale. That was where I first met *The Dark Man*.

Chapter 3

Initially, I thought he was one of the doctors; I still wonder if he was, despite everyone else denying it. I saw him several times, though he chose not to acknowledge me. I need to ask: *if he wasn't one of the psychiatrists, how could he come and go as he pleased?* Interestingly, it seems to me now, when I look back, that the more I saw of the man in black, the less I saw of my doll-like girl, whether awake or asleep.

I refused to speak to anyone during my first three days at Sunnydale. My favorite place was sitting by the recreation room window, staring at the well-maintained flower beds and admiring the bluebells and daffodils in bloom. While sitting, I thought of foolproof ways of killing myself when they eventually released me, which I believed they had to.

"Lucian," he said softly that first time he spoke in his sickly, syrupy voice. "Lucian, can you hear me?"

I turned slowly, feeling as though some invisible hand was tugging at my forehead, urging me to look at him. He sat in a straight-backed chair beside me, one I didn't remember being there before. He wore a long black jacket, similar to what a Pilgrim father might wear, along with a black shirt and a black string bow tie. I glanced down and noticed his black pants, paired with Western-style boots that had scuffed toes. He held what appeared to be an ancient Bible, though I didn't see a cross embossed on its cover, so it might not have been a holy book.

"There's no need to speak if you don't want to; just think of any words you may have and project them. I can hear your thoughts just as easily as if you were speaking, so don't worry. Or you can nod yes and shake your head no if you prefer. Is that all right with you, Lucian?"

I clearly remember turning back to the window and thinking, *please, just go away and leave me alone.*

Then, something strange occurred. It was as clear as a bell tolling at midnight. I heard him speak, but this time, not through my ears, but in my mind. *"Oh yes, Lucian, I could leave you alone to suffer in your silent world of pain and angst. But if I did, I wouldn't be able to show you how you could be reunited with Connie and the twins, could I? I can help you with that, but the question is, are you brave enough to talk to me and discover how to reanimate their bodies and bring them back from the dead?"*

I stood up suddenly, causing the seat I had been on to topple backward. I wanted to…well, I'm not sure what I wanted. Maybe to scream, punch the man, or beg him to tell me how on earth he could reconnect me to the broken, burned, and battered bodies of Connie, Deborah, and Molly. But when I turned to confront him, he and the chair he had been sitting on were gone.

Chapter 4

It was two days later when I saw him next. I was again by the window looking out when suddenly *The Dark Man* appeared, bending to pluck a flower from the garden bed. He stood and gazed at me, although it felt like he was looking through me. The man in black first waved, then, holding the daffodil in his hand, beckoned me outside and sat on the brick wall as if waiting for me.

I rushed out of the common room and headed to the door leading to the outside gardens. Barry, a rotund guard who preferred to be called an orderly, was of Hispanic descent. He stopped me with his palm against my chest. "Whoa there, Mr. Brufos, you can't go outside; you're not allowed."

"Please, Barry," I pleaded, "there's someone out there I need to talk to; he's one of the doctors."

Barry looked as if I had shoved a cattle prod up his backside and given him a shock of five thousand volts. "Mr. Brufos, Lucien, you haven't said a word since you arrived until today. What's prompted you to speak up now?"

I felt frantic but didn't know what to say that wouldn't make me sound crazier than they thought I already was. I managed to slow down and take a deep breath. "I'm not upset, Barry." I even put on a fake smile. "I didn't have anything to say before, that's all. I don't know his name, but one of the doctors spoke to me a couple of days ago, and I felt a connection with him. I just saw him out in the garden, and he waved for me to come outside and join him. It's a lovely day, so can I go, please?"

He shook his head slowly. "No, Lucian, I'm sorry. Your doctor is Dr. Royce, and he is in his office with another patient, not in the gardens. You don't have permission to go outside, only to the courtyard out back. It's for *your* safety. Now, let's get you back into the recreation room, and I'll let Dr. Royce know you're talking again. How does that sound?"

Reluctantly, I let myself be led back to my seat by the window, and of course, when we arrived, *The Dark Man* had stopped waiting for me and left.

With my sudden return to speaking, Dr. Royce wanted to psychoanalyze me, so I cooperated fully, hoping for the man dressed in black to visit me again. I drove myself because I felt the need to prove to him that I was indeed brave. I showed Dr. Royce what I believed was the right amount of remorse for my failed suicide attempt and stated that I'd had an epiphany and no longer wished to end my life. When asked why I had remained silent for so long, I explained that I had felt so sick and tired that I shut down mentally. At that point, I wasn't ready to elaborate on the depth of grief I experienced from losing my wife and children. In the days that followed, I felt as if my silence had allowed my internal batteries to recharge so I could face the world again.

It was absolute poppycock. I fully intended to end my life. However, I also felt an overwhelming need to discover what *The Dark Man* meant by being reunited with my loved ones. I wanted everyone to view me as recovered and to let me speak with the man dressed in black. But I quickly learned to stop mentioning him when it became clear that no one knew who I was referring to. Everyone claimed no staff member or patient dressed that way, but I knew it was nonsense. For reasons I couldn't understand, everyone chose to deny his existence.

Late one night, I lay in bed, staring at the ceiling a million miles from sleep, wondering whether I had imagined the man or if there was some reason everyone at Sunnydale denied seeing him. Suddenly, I was overcome with fatigue and drifted off to sleep, where I had a dream about the little girl who spoke to me and said I was going to die.

I woke up and sat up, shivering with fear and dread at her prophecy. I wondered if the dream made me paranoid or if my paranoia caused the vision. Either way, I feared I was suffering from a severe mental disorder when I had thought I was sane. Sure, back in my college days, I took a lot of hallucinogens. Heck, Connie and I took them together, so I knew I could imagine some wild things, but this had seemed *so real*.

A gentle knock at my door disturbed my rambling yet frantic thoughts. I assumed it was the nurse bringing my sleeping pill for the night. "Come in," I called.

The door opened as if on whisper-quiet hinges, and *The Dark Man* slowly entered and closed the door behind him. "Good evening, Lucian. Are you ready to talk to me now?"

Part 2

The Dark Man

"Knowing your own darkness is the best method for dealing with the darkness of other people."

Carl Jung

Chapter 5

It was a further nine days before Dr. Royce released me, supposedly safe from making further suicide attempts. I knew I was sane all along, and the dream with the girl hadn't occurred since. I reassured myself it had just been an aberration of my overheated imagination. I understood my family's concern about trying to keep me from killing myself, and acted grateful to them for the intervention. I had nothing to live for before *The Dark Man* turned my life around and gave me a purpose, and that purpose made me want to live.

That first night, he calmly explained what I needed to know about the ancient dark arts, reflecting much of my study during and after college while pursuing my doctorate. It would be accurate to say that I wasn't a believer then, just a student.

"Lucian," he said in his almost hypnotic voice, "I know you were interested in black magic during your studies, but there's a difference between exploring the dark arts as a subject and being a true believer. You need a Grimoire, a remarkable one, to help you learn the ways of the left-hand path, and I'm going to help you obtain one of the most powerful books on resurrecting the dead since the dawn of Man."

I wanted to laugh in response and express my skepticism, but I noticed he was dead serious. It hit me that I didn't know his name. "What should I call you?"

He smiled, and I noticed his canine teeth were unusually long. "What's in a name, Lucian? For now, you can call me Jolly."

Then, I almost burst out laughing because that was not an adjective I associated with him. However, as that thought crossed my mind, I realized I was wrong; Jolly suited him well. He wasn't a jolly person; no, it was more abstract than that; it just fit. "I've heard of the more famous Grimoires, of course, Jolly, but most have disappeared over time. I know some are in private collections, and others resurfacing have proven to be forgeries."

"The thing about magic," Jolly responded calmly, "is that modern science has stripped away a lot of the mystique surrounding what one might call mainstream esoteric spells. However, there remains a devoted core of true followers who believe in the dark arts and practice them. Raising the dead is something only a true wizard or witch could achieve." He smiled that toothy grin again and added, "Many years ago, someone like yourself grieved so deeply that he successfully summoned his loved ones back using incantations very similar to those found in *The Grimoire of Caligari*. I know where that Great Book is buried, and I could lead you to it if you want to become a true believer."

I had read about Italy's famous wizard of the sixteenth century, Caligari. He was tried and executed by the Roman Catholic Church during one of its purges in Europe. His grimoire was referenced in surviving manuscripts from that time as being bound in human flesh and written in blood. It was said to contain hundreds of Caligari's spells and pentagrams that offered protection from demonic possession to those who wielded them. It is said that the owner of the grimoire could live forever, but if that were true, I wondered, how could the Church kill Caligari?

As a professor of Ancient History, I recognized the immense value of such a book if it existed, both financially and academically. Even if the spells didn't work—which I had previously believed would not, although now I wasn't so sure—the value was incalculable. I thought the spells would be remnants from an era when the Church had a strong hold on people's lives, and they lived in fear of all things that went bump in the night. But I now wondered, could I afford not to believe in Jolly's teachings? If there were any way I could resurrect my loved ones, wouldn't it be insane not to try?

The more I listened to Jolly, the more he made me believe that such spells were possible, and if I truly had faith in him, I could bring Connie and the girls back to life. Naturally, I agreed to be his student, but when I looked out the window, I saw a young girl with rosy cheeks by the Grevillea bushes, crying. She looked up, our eyes met, and suddenly, she shook her head vehemently before turning and running away. For some reason, I felt more alone than ever.

Chapter 6

After my release, I went home, where I had spent so many wonderfully happy years with Connie and the girls. I switched between studying with Jolly, who had moved into the spare bedroom, and reassuring my family that I no longer planned to end my life prematurely.

That period, when I look back now, is hazy, for lack of a better word. I seemed to spend most of my time in la-la land. My family had a schedule to visit me and keep me on the straight and narrow, which I appreciated to some extent, but honestly, I just wanted to be left alone with Jolly for his tutoring. Whenever I had visitors or family, like my brother Marcus or my mother, my resident *Dark Man* made himself scarce. He had no interest in meeting anyone else. If I wasn't hosting various family members or visiting them to keep them from coming to my home when they coaxed me into doing so, I spent every waking hour learning about black magic rituals, talismans, spells, and the power of pentagrams.

Waking hours, hmmm. That's the strange thing. When I recall those days now, it feels like looking through thick layers of translucent veils. I was either sleeping or awake, but when I was awake, it felt like I was daydreaming. I seemed tired all the time. I once asked Jolly if he was hypnotizing me because I constantly felt like sleeping. But he denied it.

I recall some incredible acts that Jolly performed to convince me of the existence of the black arts. He referred to them as simple spells. Jolly could gesture toward items on the table, making them burst into flames or fly across the room, crashing into a wall with a loud bang. He could point that same finger at a door, and it would open by itself. I was truly impressed.

Eventually, Jolly told me it was time to go and collect the grimoire because he believed I was ready. So, I jumped to my feet. "Let's go!" I almost shouted.

"From Sicily." He sighed, shaking his head.

"Sicily?" I yelled, shocked, and he nodded.

"Caligari's Grimoire has been buried for over five hundred years, and you thought what? Caligari hid it in Santa Monica?"

I realized I had been foolish and tried to make amends. "No, what I mean is, why Sicily? Caligari lived and died in Italy."

"That's true; he did. But Caligari escaped during his trial in Naples after being found guilty but before the Witchfinder could carry out the death sentence. He mysteriously opened a locked door despite his captors chaining his wrists to a wall. As I've shown you, locked doors and manacles would have been child's play for a wizard of his caliber. When the jailer discovered his escape, Caligari already had a head start of several hours. He crossed the Messina Straight by bribing a ferryman, who betrayed him to the Witchfinder's posse. They relentlessly pursued him. It took two weeks, but the pursuers eventually found him hiding in the cellar of a brothel. His Grimoire wasn't in his possession and has been lost ever since. They kept him hooded, gagged, and hogtied on a mule all the way back to Naples, where he was burned at the stake without delay on the same day he arrived."

"So, are you suggesting Caligari hid his Grimoire in Sicily before his capture?"

Jolly nodded. "And I know where."

"But how could you possibly know that? Surely the knowledge died with him?"

The Dark Man stared back for a few moments, then raised the extended index finger of his right hand and tapped it against the side of his nose. "How I know is not your concern, Lucian."

****

My family was thrilled when I announced that I was taking some time off and going to Italy for a break. They even drove me to the airport. I flew Swiss Air to Catania, with a short layover in Zurich, and slept most of the way. Jolly gave me lengthy and detailed directions before I left, which he insisted I follow exactly. I repeatedly asked him why he wouldn't accompany me, but he said he couldn't and that I had to make this trip alone. It was to be my initiation and also to demonstrate my faith in him and his teachings. He assured me that the solitude would aid my purification and help me become a wizard in my own right, but I could never grasp his reasoning.

Catania is the second-largest city in Sicily and is known as the place where Caligari was captured after his bid for freedom. However, according to Jolly, it was not where he hid his Grimoire. When I arrived at my hotel, I was so exhausted that I collapsed onto my bed and fell asleep within moments, missing dinner.

In the morning, I was starving and enjoyed a substantial breakfast at the hotel, even going back for seconds of bacon and eggs. Afterward, I chatted with the desk clerk, who helped me rent a small car. I wanted a nondescript vehicle that would blend in because I needed to locate the book that the wizard had buried on the grounds of a building that has since become a tourist attraction. I noticed that small white cars seemed to be everywhere during the cab ride from the airport, making that model an ideal choice.

I brought along a portable GPS navigation unit with my destination pre-programmed at Jolly's request. I set off in the mid-morning sunshine, believing that four or five hours would get me to Naxos, where I intended to spend another night. Jolly assured me it was near the ancient building that Caligari had used to hide his Grimoire, which still stood.

I thought the traffic in California was heavy, but wow, was I wrong! Cars were everywhere in Catania, and everyone drove as if they were on fire. The sound of chirping and blaring horns filled the air, and I quickly realized that if I didn't drive aggressively, I wouldn't get anywhere. I had the air conditioner set to high speed, but I was sweating profusely from the stress of navigating among thousands of reckless drivers who all wanted to occupy the same piece of roadway I was on. I became a nervous wreck, so I needed to find a shady spot to pull off the road once I got outside the city. I parked and immediately fell asleep for two hours, waking only when something fell from the branches above and hit the roof of the car like a gunshot.

I felt well enough to continue and restarted the engine. The traffic had eased somewhat, and I flowed back into the rhythm, heading for my overnight stay in Naxos. The next day, I would search for the ancient structure known as Badia Vecchia, a tower built in the fifteenth century that has been restored numerous times since. According to Jolly, Caligari buried the grimoire within the grounds.

The countryside was breathtaking, featuring towering rocky hills interrupted by trees swaying in a gentle breeze. After my restorative sleep, I relished the drive.

I arrived in Naxos late in the afternoon, checked into the Kalosi Hotel, and enjoyed a lovely evening in the town. The hotel provided spectacular views of the Messina Straits, with its azure waters and gentle waves lapping against the white sandy beaches. Even though I wasn't there as a tourist, I must admit that the city and its surroundings are beautiful. My limited experience of Sicily so far led me to view it as breathtaking. As I parked the rental car in front of the hotel, I thought that this country would be a fantastic place to visit again once I reunited with Connie, Molly, and Deborah. That thought comforted me as I dined in the restaurant, savored amazing seafood chili pasta, and washed it down with a delightful local red wine.

After the meal, the weather was warm and pleasant, and the breeze had calmed. I continued my stroll along the main street and stepped into a lounge bar with a spacious balcony overlooking the ocean. A local band played somewhat familiar songs, although the lyrics were sung in Italian. I ordered a bottle of Retsina, thinking I should drink as the Romans do in Rome, and took a seat at a small table on the balcony's edge, which extended over the sandy beach below.

I found myself tapping to the beat of the band, observing the locals and tourists engage in their dating games while savoring the richness of the wine. Of course, I had no desire to dance or try to pick up a woman, but I must admit I appreciated the atmosphere of the place. The view of the ocean, the wine, and the music made me feel better than I had in months, so I decided to bring Connie back to this same bar when she and the twins returned to life. Perhaps a family holiday in the sun, exploring the region's history, swimming in the sapphire blue ocean, and coming back to this bar for dinner. Yes, that would be idyllic, I thought.

I realized that Jolly's influence over me was so complete I no longer thought *if* I could resurrect them, it was now *when*.

Around ten o'clock, a wave of tiredness washed over me, and I decided it was time to leave the taverna and head back to the hotel. I was about to stand when I felt a tug on the hem of my jacket. For a moment, I thought I had simply caught my jacket on the arm of the chair I was sitting in. But then, I looked down and saw something that chilled me to my very core and, at the same time, caused sweat beads to appear on my brow.

Standing on the sand below me, the girl with rosy cheeks and glassy eyes reached up with her right hand and grabbed the edge of my jacket. "Don't do it," she pleaded. "Please, Mr. Brufos, don't try to bring them back to life."

I couldn't help but lurch to my feet in sheer, unadulterated terror. The near-empty bottle of Retsina spun away to smash on the terracotta tiles, and those around me also jumped up. When everyone settled down, and a young, dark-haired waitress came to clean up my mess, I sat down again, feeling faint and my heart pounding in my chest. I turned to the beach, but the mysterious young girl had gone.

Chapter 7

Despite being upset to see the doll-like girl so far from home, once back in my hotel room, I collapsed on the bed without undressing and slept soundly until the shrill ring of the phone beside the bed woke me. The room was dark, and I had no idea of the time. Groggily, I answered by grunting, "Hello?"

Jolly's calming voice spoke, "Hello, Lucian. You've made it to Naxos; well done. You're doing great, and I'm proud of you."

"Jolly? Why am I so tired all the time? Have you done something to me?" I mumbled, barely awake.

"Of course, I have, Lucian. I want you to concentrate on the task I've assigned you, so I've implanted some hypnotic suggestions to make sure you get enough sleep. Don't worry; it's all for your benefit."

"That's fine then." I set the phone back into its cradle and soon fell into a deep sleep, only waking up to the call I had scheduled with reception. Groggily, I made my way to the bright breakfast room and savored scrambled eggs on toast along with a generous mug of black coffee, which helped me regain a sense of normalcy.

I asked the concierge for directions to a nearby hardware store, who fortunately spoke broken English. I bought a pick, a shovel, and a battery-powered lantern that also functioned as a flashlight, and then headed to my destination: *The Grimoire of Caligari.*

I parked in the lower car park with several other tourists who wanted to see a building that had stood for over five hundred years, while locals had restored it. Being American, this concept was alien to me, but history had drawn me to study ancient civilizations and teach the subject to others.

Badia Vecchia was a stone tower that formed part of a fortified wall designed to defend against potential invaders, of which there were many during the Middle Ages. Great Britain, France, and Spain all vied for supremacy.

There were simply too many people visiting for me to consider digging up Caligari's book then, so I decided to act like a tourist and look for the signs Jolly had given me to follow, allowing me to return later and finish my task.

I joined a tour and rented a set of headphones to hear the guide's story translated into English. Perhaps, before the tragedy that devastated my family, I would have been captivated by the history of the building and the surrounding area. Still, to be honest, I cannot recall the beautiful Sicilian woman's words; I had far more pressing matters on my mind. The means to bring back my wife and daughters was so close I could feel it.

After setting the alarm on my phone for midnight, I had dinner at the hotel and then went to sleep. I dreamed of my beautiful wife on our wedding night. She wore a satin nightdress and was a vision of pure beauty and sensuality. We had both been drinking alcohol, of course, but were sober enough to make love for most of the night, falling asleep just before dawn, wrapped around each other. I remember waking with the love of my life in my arms and thinking: *Could my life ever be more complete?* Well, yes, I discovered it could be on the day my twin daughters were born.

The night air was cold as I carried my tools and flashlight from the car to the western corner of Badia Vecchia. Following Jolly's instructions, I counted out the required number of steps, located the marker, and then turned north, using my phone's compass feature for accuracy, before counting an additional twenty-four steps. After that, I turned east, heading toward a tall stone column that was barely visible in the moonlight and measured ten paces.

My heart raced as I set up the lantern and started using the pickaxe. I paused every few minutes to make sure I wasn't being watched and continued digging when I felt satisfied that I was alone.

After an hour, I began to worry that I might be mistaken and started to fret. *How tall was Caligari? If he was either taller or shorter than I, surely our strides would differ, and if that were the case, I might be digging in the wrong spot.* I took a break and stared at the hole while replaying Jolly's instructions in my mind. For once, I felt completely alert. I had dug a hole about a yard wide and a foot and a half deep in the rocky soil. Suddenly, with a deep sigh of relief, I remembered Jolly had mentioned that the book was wrapped in oilskin inside a metal box, two feet down. I wasn't deep enough yet.

With renewed vigor, I attacked the ground again, and fifteen minutes later, my shovel hit something metallic with a dull *"clang."* "Yes, yes, yes, yes, yes," I muttered, barely able to conceal my glee. I had a vision of being able to cuddle my daughters and, even better, hold my wife as she reached an orgasm—God, how I missed them. "Soon, Connie, we will be together again," I whispered.

I dropped to my knees and, fearing damage to the object of my quest, scraped and burrowed with my bare hands until, in the dim light of my lantern, I spotted the black iron lid of the box. It wasn't quite square, measuring just over a foot on one side and less on the other; it was the perfect size to hold a book. Tears welled in my eyes, trickling down my cheeks. Frantically, I dug, pulled, and wiggled the box until, suddenly, the ground released its grip, and it came free with a jolt. I fell back, and the box landed in my lap.

"It won't be locked," Jolly had told me. As I shone the flashlight on it, I saw he was right; it was a simple clasp and shackle. With trembling fingers, I undid the hook and lifted the lid. There it lay, just as he had said it would. Caligari had tightly wrapped the grimoire in what looked like thick material, which felt as if it had been oiled only last week instead of five hundred years ago. It was moist to my touch as I gripped it and removed it from the box. My skin itched and crawled as I held the package. I could have sworn I felt the book sigh and wriggle tighter in my grip, as if it were glad to be with me and wouldn't let go, ever.

The rest of the night is a blur when I reflect on it now. I remember putting the empty box back in the hole, shoveling dirt to cover it, and then tossing my tools into a nearby bush instead of returning them to the Fiat. The next thing I knew, I was in my hotel room in Naxos, shrugging off my clothes, too exhausted to bother with a shower. I collapsed on top of the bedspread and fell into a dreamless sleep, feeling secure knowing the grimoire was safely tucked in my backpack. My last conscious thought was a promise to Connie and the girls that I was coming for them; it wouldn't be long now.

Chapter 8

I planned to return to Catania the next day, but I didn't wake up until after three in the afternoon, making it too late to drive. I called the reception and asked if I could extend my stay for another night, and if they could please inform my hotel in Catania that I had been delayed but would arrive the following day.

Once again, I was so hungry that I could eat a horse, so I left the hotel, walked to the beach, and found a pizzeria where I devoured four slices of the best pizza I've ever had. The dough was fresh, the tomato sauce was delicious, and the garlic pepperoni took my breath away.

I wanted to return to the hotel room and study the grimoire, but Jolly warned me against it. He said it was so potent that my sanity could be at risk if I tried to read it without him to protect me. Not that I would have understood the Italian language from that era anyway. I couldn't speak modern Italian, let alone the dialect from five hundred years ago. Still, I wanted to look inside the book, and the impatient movements from inside the backpack indicated that the grimoire wanted me to unwrap it, too.

Before I left California, Jolly had me create what he claimed was a powerful pentagram with chalk and salt on the hardwood floorboards of my home's basement. Once we were inside with the book, we would recite the incantations to bring my beautiful wife back to life after digging up her coffin, or so I thought. Once Connie and I were reunited, I knew we would spend the rest of the day making love. Then, that following night at midnight, we would recover the twins' bodies from the cemetery, repeating the spells so that our family could be whole again.

As I walked along the promenade looking out over the Messina Straight, I felt the book in my backpack shift and vibrate in agreement as if promising that, yes, together, we would reunite my family, snatching them back from the jaws of death.

I returned to the taverna from the night before, but I couldn't help searching the beach for the child who had troubled me during my last visit. After just two glasses of Retsina, I left the bar and went back to my hotel room, anxious that she might show up again and try to stop me from fulfilling my destiny. Once inside, I swung open the French doors to the balcony, uncorked a bottle of wine, and savored the sights and sounds of a bustling tourist city while the radio played some Italian folk music in the background.

At one point, as the bottle neared emptiness, I glanced at the couch where I had placed my backpack and smiled, noticing that the book inside seemed to jiggle and dance to the music playing on the radio. It was then that I heard a rap of knuckles on my door. "Who's there?" I asked, but the silence was the only reply.

I turned my gaze toward the door, stood up, and suddenly felt the room grow colder. I staggered over, questioning whether I was drunk, thrust my outstretched hands flat against the wooden surface, and recoiled immediately. The door felt freezing to the touch, as if made of dry ice. Then I noticed wispy white clouds of icy steam streaming under the door and licking at my bare feet, causing me to leap backward.

"You're going to die. You're going to die," a strange, disembodied voice sang in a singsong tone, reminiscent of a child speaking in a guttural manner.

Then, my skin erupted in goosebumps as I watched the brass door handle start to turn. I couldn't breathe; terror gripped my very soul, and I began to back away, expecting any moment for someone or something to enter my room, which felt like a freezer, and murder me.

My knees crashed into a coffee table, and I flailed my arms in the air, trying to find something to grab onto to avoid falling, but it was all for nothing. I saw a thousand stars as the back of my head struck the corner of the bed, and then everything went black.

Part 3

The Resurrection

"Cancel my subscription to the resurrection."
Jim Morrison

Chapter 9

My memories of the next three days are worse than vague. I knew I had a purpose: to get the grimoire to Jolly and bring back my loved ones, and nothing would deter me from achieving that, but the rest feels like peering into pea soup. I think I was somewhat concussed from the blow to my head, though not enough to keep me from the tasks *The Dark Man* had ingrained in me.

I believe I was unconscious for no more than ten minutes or so. By that time, whoever or whatever had been trying to get inside my room was gone, and the temperature returned to normal. Somehow, I got to my feet and fell into bed, so I didn't notice the smear of blood from the small gash on my head until morning.

The next thing I recall is arriving back at Catania, checking in, and having the desk clerk confirm my flight back to the States the following day. The rest of my time in Catania is a blur.

I regained my senses while going through the airport baggage check, determined to keep my backpack as carry-on luggage instead of letting it go into the cargo hold. I felt nervous as it passed through the X-ray machine, but they likely saw a very thick book wrapped in heavy canvas-like material, and the operator hardly glanced at me.

The flight lasted fifteen hours, including another stopover in Zurich. I'm sure I would have watched a movie or two, but I can't remember a single scene for the life of me. I remember thinking about the grimoire in my bag, stored in the overhead compartment. More than anything in the world, I wanted to take it down, unwrap it, and read it. But there was the catch; I couldn't read it even if I chose to disobey Jolly because it would be written in ancient Italian or Latin.

"Anything to declare?" the customs officer asked me.

I wanted to scream *yes, the most incredible book of all time on casting black magic spells,* but all I replied was "No."

He looked at my face, my suitcase on wheels, my backpack, stamped my passport, and said, "Welcome back to the United States, Mr. Brufos."

Outside the terminal, it was raining—not quite torrential, but close enough. Without a raincoat, I stood under an overhang, waiting for a cab to become available. Finally, one arrived, and I hurried over to it, tossed my bags into the trunk, and jumped inside, at which point I'm sure I resembled a drowned rat.

The driver, clearly a master of the obvious, said, "How's this weather, Mac? Wet enough for ya?"

I mumbled my address and, for some reason, turned my gaze back to the terminal. There, standing in the rain, was the girl with rosy cheeks. Her cheeks were wet, not just from the rain; she seemed to be crying. Before I could stop him, the cabbie jerked the vehicle into the traffic, and within moments, I lost sight of her.

For the first time, I questioned whether I was wrong to try to reunite my family from the grave or if seeing the girl was a sign of a mental illness. Sure, she seemed so real, but how could she be? She had been in Sicily and then at the airport, which couldn't be unless she had been on the same flight, but that didn't feel right. *Okay, if she isn't real, I must be imagining her, but why? I want my wife back, and Jolly is showing me how; what's wrong with that? Maybe it's the last remnant of my sanity trying to stop me from making a terrible mistake,* my more rational inner self replied.

I had no answer to that and realized I didn't want one. I had the grimoire and the means to bring my wife and children back to me, and nothing was going to stop me.

Once the cab backed out of the driveway, I fumbled the key into the lock of my front door. As usual, it took some wriggling to get it to work, but finally, I swung it wide open. "Jolly," I yelled, "I'm back and have the grimoire."

There was no answer. *Strange; he must be out.* I closed the door behind me and left the suitcase in the hallway. It was a little after four in the afternoon, and for the first time since I'd left California bound for Sicily, I didn't feel tired.

I ventured into the basement and was astonished by what Jolly had created. Within the pentagram, at each point of the chalk-lined star, stood tall silver candlesticks alongside two small bowls—one filled with what appeared to be water and the other with white granulated powder, which I presumed was salt. In the center lay a pile of cushions surrounding an old-looking wooden podium, where I believed the grimoire would be placed, facing north. I knew this because Connie desired north-facing windows when we built the house.

I suddenly heard a scampering noise and realized it came from a cage. Squatting down, I saw a black rooster and a white hen scurrying around each other, and with a sinking heart, I knew these birds would be sacrificed. I have always abhorred cruelty to any animals, and my first thought was to set them free. At the same time, I knew deep down that they were an integral part of the ceremony to come. "I'm sorry," I whispered to them.

The largest, most grotesque mirror I have ever seen was mounted on the wall, directly in my line of sight if I stood behind the old lectern. The thick, carved wooden frame resembled serpents entwined, some with their mouths open and fangs bared. I shuddered, and for a moment, as I started to drag my gaze away, I thought I saw some snakes moving, but when I looked back, they were still.

I almost ran out of the basement and back upstairs to my bedroom. There, I stripped off my clothes and took a long, hot shower. The needles of water seemed to cleanse my outside and insides.

Once dried and dressed in casual clothes, Jolly still had not returned. I cursed his lack of a cell phone, which meant I couldn't call to tell him I was home and that I had the grimoire. I was eager to start the ritual he had only talked about so far, which would allow my family to be reunited once again.

I was hungry, but opening the refrigerator disappointed me, as the food I had left there had grown mold. I slammed the door, deciding that was a job for another time, and went to the pantry. There wasn't much on the shelves, but I found some crackers, a jar of olives, and a can of tuna fish. *That'll do,* I thought before ripping the can open.

Chapter 10

"Wake up, Lucian."

I jerked awake, groggy, and realized I had fallen asleep on the couch, and Jolly stood over me. "Whah, whah…where have you been, Jolly? How long have I been asleep?" I sat up and rubbed my eyes.

"I've been at the cemetery preparing for your wife's return. There's a lot to do, and you weren't in any condition, so I took care of those tasks for you. It's now a little after 11:00 p.m., and we'll begin precisely at midnight. Are you ready?"

My heart surged; at last, I could hold and kiss my wife. "I've never been more ready for anything in the world, Jolly."

"Good, give me the grimoire, and let us get to work."

I reached into my backpack and gripped the book. It felt like I had dipped my hand into an aquarium and grabbed a live fish, as the grimoire seemed eager to break free from my grasp. After a few seconds, it appeared to sigh and settle down, allowing me to reverently hand it to Jolly, who took it with barely concealed glee.

He turned on his heel, and like a lamb, I followed him down into the basement. He paused just before the chalk lines on the floor, and for the first time, I noticed a gap in the circumference lines; one motif seemed to be missing. "Lucian, make sure you only enter and exit the

Pentagram through this gap. Before we start our spells and chants, I will close the rings, which will protect us from any minor demons that might want to crash the party." He smiled and stepped inside, and again I followed.

"Minor demons?" Suddenly, doubts that our actions were safe began to creep into my mind.

"Lucian," Jolly said seriously. "You need to be certain this is the path you want to choose. You wished for Connie and the twins to return to you in this life, but that comes with risks, which is why I'm here to guide you. If you'd rather have them stay buried in their cold graves, just say the word. *Pfft* and I'll take the grimoire and disappear from your life, leaving you," he pointed at my chest with his index finger, "to spend the rest of your days alone. Yes, there are demons in the underworld that would love nothing more than to overtake and possess you, but the Pentagram and my power will protect you; you must trust that I can."

I suddenly imagined Connie, wearing her white linen sundress, running toward me through a field of long grass with her arms outstretched to hug me. God, I needed her so much. "I want them with me, Jolly. I'm not scared. You used the words minor demons being in my house, which made me stop and take stock. I trust you; please show me the grimoire and bring my family back from the dead."

****

As the witching hour drew nearer, Jolly led me outside the circle and handed me a floor-length black gown. "Take off everything else and put this on," he commanded. "Once you have it on, wash your hands and all openings in your body." He gestured toward a pail of water and a towel.

I stared uncomprehendingly at him. "Umm, every opening in my body?"

He nodded. "Lucian, if you're going to question every order I give you, we might as well stop now. Trust me when I say that what I'm asking you to do is for your own protection. Now hurry; we need to be ready by midnight."

I turned my back and did as he told me.

At 11:45, he ordered me to turn off all the lights in the house as he lit the candles. Then we entered the Pentagram, and he knelt to rejoin the chalk lines and add the motif, which looked like some sort of goblin that, even with my medieval studies, I didn't recognize.

Jolly slowly and carefully unwrapped the book I had traveled halfway across the world to retrieve. I stood by his side, gasping as the final layer came off. Jolly dropped the bindings, and there it lay in all its glory. Olive green in color, though faded as one would expect due to its age, the cover resembled the mirror's frame, adorned with brown serpents. Even as I watched, it seemed to writhe and wiggle, mouths open and fangs bared, as if any attempt to read what lay within would provoke an attack.

Jolly opened the cover, and I gasped again as I saw that the cover page featured the same pentagram Jolly had drawn on the floor. *How could that be?*

Jolly turned to me, placed his right hand on my forehead, and said, "Sleep." I stumbled as if I were drugged, and he caught me, laying me down on the cushions. My last waking thought was that Jolly had cheated me and that all he ever wanted was for me to go to Sicily to retrieve the grimoire. I realized I would never see Connie and the girls again.

Chapter 11

I awoke with the odor of burning in my nostrils. It was a cloying, sickly, yet sweet scent. *Incense?* It smelled like rose petals soaked in whiskey and then burned into ashes. Then I heard the chanting. Jolly stood in front of the podium, a dead bird from the cage in each outstretched hand, their heads missing and necks dripping blood on the floor.

The room was bitterly cold—freezing cold. I watched Jolly's steamy breath as he spoke unintelligible words in his most powerful voice. He faced the mirror, yet I could not see his reflection. The snakes writhed around the glass, seemingly maniacal with bloodlust from the beheaded chickens.

I lifted my head and noticed the pink smoke swirling and dancing around the edge of the pentagram. My eyes began to focus, and I could make out grotesque, misshapen forms concealed within the thick smoke. They seemed to reach out with tendrils of mist as they moved around the circle, but then recoiled as if burned when they contacted the invisible barrier of protection that the pentagram provided.

I sat up, feeling terrified, and realized I was trembling. the grimoire on the wooden stand radiated an iridescent green light, reflecting on Jolly's face. I had never been more scared in my life, and suddenly regretted my decision to tamper with the black arts to bring my wife and daughters back to life.

"Noooooooooooo. Jolly, stop; I don't want this anymore," I screamed.

Keeping his body still, Jolly turned his head as if he were a coiled spring. Then I noticed his eyes, which burned like red-hot coals with small flames licking his cheeks. "Too late, Lucian," he said in a low, guttural voice, "Your wife, Connie, is coming now."

That's when I heard the squelching sound of liquid coming from the direction of the stairs.

"She's coming, Lucian. She's coming back from the dead to be with you, just as I promised," Jolly exclaimed gleefully.

The pink smoke parted, forming a passage from the stairway to the Pentagram, but whatever was coming toward us wasn't walking; it was slithering. I realized the awful mistake I had made. Connie may be coming back, but her body had been broken in many places in the accident, and her skin had all but burned off her head, which was why we had a closed-casket funeral. She wouldn't return as the beautiful woman she'd been before but as a hideously deformed monster. Jolly had deceived me and reanimated her dead and decaying body. I was reminded of the worst zombie movies I'd ever seen, and knew that was how my beloved wife would appear.

Jolly's chanting grew louder and more intense, while my wife's slithering sounds as she tried to return to me intensified. Whatever creatures hid in the mist began to hiss sibilantly as they coiled and swayed, causing the smoke to thicken even more. My heart was pounding in my chest, and I felt as if I might die from a heart attack. *What have I done?*

And then I saw Connie, or what remained of her. Her blonde hair was gone, her skull exposed through the gaping burnt-out wounds the car accident and subsequent fire had left her with. She crawled across the floor toward me. She wore the white dress I had given the undertaker for her to wear, but now it was gray and grimy. Her legs trailed uselessly behind as she levered her body like a salamander, desperate to be reunited with me.

I backed away from her, pushing with my hands and driving my legs like a jackhammer, but Connie was catching up to me as I got tangled in the pillows.

Connie's hands, now claw-like, singed and deformed, reached for me, and God help me, I screamed in sheer terror. "Looshian, Looshian, I'm back," Connie rasped through heat-warped vocal cords as her body seemed to rear up at the outer edge of the Pentagram.

I scampered back even faster, frantic to keep my distance. "No, Lucian," Jolly shouted, but it was too late. My hand overturned one of the water bowls, spilling its contents over the chalk lines and destroying our only defense against the demons in the mist.

Connie wailed; the smoke cleared, and Jolly screamed as I fell backward, causing a candlestick to topple. The thick, tallow candle rolled across the floor and came to rest beneath the curtain drapes along the wall. Flames licked upward, and within seconds, the drapes caught fire. Flames leaped from window to window, and one of the curtains crashed onto the mirror. The snakes surrounding the glass hissed and writhed as they burned, and the glass shattered, sending a cascade of shards toward Jolly. I watched, spellbound, as a thousand miniature spears pierced his face, blood spraying in every direction.

I couldn't move, captivated by the flames racing away, spreading from their source. I sighed and welcomed the fire, which would end the night's horrors. I no longer had the will to live. As I sat amid what remained of the Pentagram, I felt Connie wrap her arms around me from the left, and I heard her whisper, "Looshian, I love you; please let me stay."

I turned to her and saw that her dress was now on fire, feeling the heat radiating from her body. "I love you too, Connie," I replied, hugging her tightly, knowing that in death, we would be reunited forever.

Chapter 12

The front page of the San Francisco Chronicle newspaper carried the story:

Mystery plagues the tragic life of university history lecturer Lucian Brufos.

A bizarre series of events culminated in a fire at the home of the well-respected Ancient History lecturer, Dr. Lucian Brufos. Dr. Brufos recently lost his wife and twin daughters in a car accident. The other driver who survived has been charged with vehicular homicide and has yet to stand trial. The grieving husband and father later attempted to take his own life, but was saved by a visiting relative. Since that night, Dr. Brufos has spent time in the hospital but has recently improved and been released. His family believed that while he seemed moody and withdrawn, he had turned a corner and was overcoming his depression.

A security patrol called the police to Highgate Cemetery before midnight last night after discovering that Mrs. Brufos's grave had been desecrated and the body exhumed. Officers then went to notify Professor Brufos but found the house ablaze. The fire was believed to have started in the basement.

Police hope to identify a recovered body from the basement after forensic and DNA testing, due within days, as the blaze had burned the corpse beyond recognition.

Chapter 13

"Mr. Brufos, please state your name for the record and confirm that you know this interview is being recorded."

I shifted my gaze between the two men. The one on the left had spoken, but I didn't know his name. I'd been told that today was the day I would be questioned by a police officer, yet I didn't know his name. The other man was my old sparring partner, Doctor Hugo Royce. I felt so tired I couldn't muster the energy to go through everything again, but I knew if I didn't, they would never understand that Jolly was responsible for everything, not me. It was he who promised he could bring Connie back to life, he who made me go to Sicily to collect the grimoire, and he who had dug Connie up from her grave.

"My name is Lucian Brufos, and I understand you are recording this conversation. I also understand my Miranda rights."

"Thank you. Can I call you Lucian? My name is Detective Gerald Rainer."

"Sure, can I call you Gerry?" I responded. I had so little opportunity for fun these days that I enjoyed the verbal jousting.

He didn't reply or smile; he simply continued with the questions. "I have read your written statement and investigated your claims as thoroughly as I could, and to be honest, Lucian, not much of your story adds up."

I shook my head and grimaced. "Then I doubt the veracity of your investigative skills, Gerry." This time, he glared at me, and I was pleased I got a reaction. I knew some of my claims were far-fetched, but they had happened, and my being alive was proof of that.

I had been back in Sunnydale for over a month after my release from the hospital's burn unit, and I was bored out of my mind. They had initially said I was insane again and kept me locked in a room for my safety. By now, I was hopping mad, tired of the monotony, and eager to return to my burned-out home and start over. I had finally accepted what the girl with the rosy cheeks had told me: the dead should stay dead and buried.

"Okay, let's begin with your visit to the cemetery where you claim you didn't dig up your wife's body."

"Correct," I smugly said. "Jolly did that."

"Yes, while you slept, you stated. This man, Jolly; the problem is we can find no record of him anywhere."

"Nonsense, it was here that I met him, so someone must have seen him talking to me; therefore, he must exist."

"Lucian," Dr. Royce interjected in his sickly, sweet, soothing voice. "I've asked everyone, both staff and patients, and no one else has seen him."

I sighed, feeling exasperated. "Just because you can't find anyone who saw Jolly during all this time doesn't mean I imagined him, does it? Maybe he was visiting one of the other patients at that time. He didn't mention that he worked here; I just assumed he did." I knew I had him there; let him try to out-logic me again after that well-placed tennis ace.

"No, Lucien, I agree. If that were the only issue here, we might be able to find another explanation. However, there are many more discrepancies in your story than just that. We need you to face your psychosis if we're ever going to find a way past it and help you live a normal life again."

"Fiddlesticks! I acknowledge that after my family's deaths, I went a little off the rails, but after the Black Sabbath ceremony Jolly held in the basement, I'm finally cured and ready to let the dead rest in peace." I smiled again.

The two men exchanged glances, and then the cop started up again. "Okay, please answer this question: How many passports do you own?"

I raised my eyes; my goodness, this man was a moron. "Like everyone else, just the one. Why do you ask?"

He opened his briefcase and took out a plastic zip-locked evidence bag. "Is this it, Mr. Brufos? It was recovered from the desk drawer in your study."

"It's a bit hard to tell with it in that bag, but if that's where you got it, then yes, it must be mine, especially if it has my picture inside. Wouldn't you agree?"

"Yes, we believe this is your passport. You said you recently spent eight days in Sicily, yes?"

I simply nodded, completely bored, and wondered why they hadn't sent someone with a little more common sense than this doofus.

"All right, I will return to the passport shortly. You mentioned seeing a young girl who warned you several times not to dig up your wife." He glanced at his notes. " And you described her as wearing old-fashioned clothes, with very red cheeks and eyes that looked like glass marbles?"

"Yes, what about it? Don't tell me you couldn't find

Jolly, but you found the girl?" I asked in disbelief.

"Yes, we found both of them."

"Both? Good Lord. That explains why I saw one in Sicily and one here. Thank goodness; well done, Gerry. They must be identical twins, right?"

"Mr. Brufos, when did you last go into your daughters' bedrooms?"

Suddenly, I felt cold and clammy. The room darkened, and I thought I might faint. An icy hand reached inside my chest, grasped my heart, and squeezed the life out of me. I gasped, bent my head between my knees, and took deep gulps of air.

Dr. Royce leaped to his feet, and I felt him stroke my back. "I told you to go easy," he hissed to the cop. "No sudden questions that would remind him of the sudden loss of his family. Have you no heart, man?"

I didn't hear Gerry's reply but assumed they exchanged glances again. Gradually, things came back into focus, my breathing returned, and I sat back up. "Here, Lucian, drink this." Dr. Royce handed me a paper cup of water, which I sipped gratefully.

"Sorry," I mumbled, attempting to wipe away the tears from my eyes. "My daughters meant everything to me. To answer your question, I haven't entered the girls' rooms since the night before they passed away. Why do you ask?"

Gerry smiled faintly and responded to my question with one of his own. "Do you remember your trip to England just before your daughters' twelfth birthday and the gifts you brought back for them?"

"Yes, identical twin antique dolls for two beautiful identical twins. I found them in an antique shop in Covent Garden."

"Do you recognize these?" He took out two photographs from his case and carefully placed them on the desk.

Suddenly, everything became clear. I closed my eyes and wept heartbreaking tears. The images revealed each of my daughters' pillows. On each rested one of the dolls I'd bought, resembling the girls who had warned me about my impending death and advised me against bringing Connie back to life. But how could that be? None of this made sense.

Dr. Royce spoke calmly, his hand still on my shoulder, squeezing gently. "Lucian, do you think it's possible that your tortured mind created the image of these girls warning you because they reminded you so much of your daughters? It was your subconscious trying to tell you not to take your wife from her grave, which you knew was wrong. Your grief ran so deep that you couldn't see it, so your mind attempted to warn you the only way it could: with hallucinations."

Is that it? Does that make sense? My mind raced at a hundred miles an hour. "But, but…they were *so real*," I pleaded.

"When it tries to protect itself, the mind is powerful, Lucien. There have been many documented cases of this kind of imagining. The important thing for your health is to accept the truth. Those girls exist only in your mind; they are not real people, just dolls you brought to life to prevent you from doing something you knew was wrong."

"But what about Jolly? He must be real."

"Why?" Dr. Royce asked.

"Because, well, because he was living with me for two weeks. Because he told me all about the grimoire and how I could reunite with Connie once I retrieved it from Sicily. He gave me purpose, a reason to live when I might otherwise have ended my life. He saved me."

Royce looked at the cop and nodded. He cleared his throat and said the words that felt like a hammer blow. "Mr. Brufos, you did not go to Sicily recently."

"What? Oh, this is madness. I went to Sicily and stayed in the hotels I told you about. I traveled to Badia Vecchia and dug up the damned book."

He nodded and once more exchanged glances with the good doctor. "Oh, you went to Sicily all right, just not when you claimed you did. Let me ask another question: when you earned your doctorate at university, what was your thesis about?"

The hand returned, slithering down my throat and into my chest, searching for my heart, and this time I understood it wouldn't relent until I perished. "I don't remember. It was years ago. I want to go back to my room now."

"Soon, Lucian. We're so close now, and everything will be revealed," Dr. Royce said. However, I shook my head; I didn't want to hear this.

He opened his case again and reached inside. "I have a copy of your thesis here. It was excellent, and I really enjoyed reading it. You did a thorough study of the life and death of Caligari. Your parents funded your trip to Italy and Sicily for research as part of your Ancient History studies. That was when you stayed in those hotels, not a few weeks ago. You visited the taverna you mentioned as a single man when you and Connie were only dating, because she couldn't afford to travel with you. That's how you learned about *The Grimoire of Caligari*, through your studies and not from your imaginary friend, Jolly. Your remarkable work discusses the grimoire and states that it has never been found. You theorized that he buried it somewhere along his route before his capture." He tossed the bag containing my passport so it landed in front of me. "Open it and check the immigration stamps. You haven't been in Sicily for twenty years. You imagined Jolly, and it was you who dug up your wife. We have CCTV footage from a street camera of you driving back from the cemetery. You tried to stage some kind of black magic ceremony you remembered from your drug-fueled university days to bring your wife back to life. When that failed, you set fire to your home to destroy her body and cover up your wrongdoing.

"No, no, nooooooooooo," I wailed, but he didn't stop.

"You've invented all these memories, and I believe you're just play-acting, even though your doctor thinks you're severely depressed and facing a complete mental breakdown. Your family has committed you here, and a court has ordered that you must remain until deemed sane enough to stand trial for tampering with a grave, arson, and any other charges we might think of that we can make stick."

That was when everything went black, and I felt myself falling to the floor in a dead faint.

Epilogue

I'm not talking to anyone, not ever again.

After what they did to me and the lies they spread, they can all jump off a cliff. I refuse to give the doctors here the satisfaction of hearing me speak. They can do whatever they want—talk to me, threaten me, or give me electric shocks—I don't care.

It's not enough that I've lost Connie and my beautiful girls; now they try to tell me it was all my fault, not Jolly's. Well, I call bullshit on that.

I still see him—Jolly, I mean. I haven't spoken to him since that glass hit him in the face, but I catch a glimpse of him now and then from my spot in front of the window, where I spend all my waking hours. Jolly waves sometimes, but other times, he doesn't. Occasionally, he is too busy talking to Sharon.

Sharon is as batty as a fruitcake; she murdered her family with an axe because they told her she couldn't go to a fourteenth birthday party. I can see Jolly helping to calm her down now. He is whispering to her, and I see her smile and nod at his urging.

Jolly will help her get out of here; I'm sure of that because that's what he does. She will probably be placed in a foster home where they will want to give her a fresh start. Then, one night, Sharon will murder another family, and no one will believe her when she tells them Jolly made her do it.

They won't believe her, but I will know.
Jolly is an evil man.

The Village of Last Hope

Once Michael enters, will he be able to leave?

Foreword

Some movies remain in your memory forever, don't you agree? Iconic moments like Linda Blair turning her head in *The Exorcist*, the first appearance of the shark in *Jaws,* or the scene where something bursts out of that poor woman's stomach in *Alien* come to *mind.* How about the opening of the first *Star Wars* film or the landing sequences at the beginning of *Saving Private Ryan*?

Great movies, like great books, have not only provided me with countless hours of pleasure but have also left an indelible mark on my soul. Sometimes, it's because I wish I had created such scenes. One film that made a strong impression on me was *The Sixth Sense*, and another was *Shutter Island.*

Some years after watching these two wonderful films, which were released in entirely different years, I unconsciously had the idea for a plot line for an upcoming Friday the 13th series that pays homage to both. Thus, *The Village of Last Hope* was born.

Interestingly, my first idea for this story was to set it in the US during the great depression. I had read of villages of homeless people living in parks, supporting each other during the darkest of times. As often happens, once I started writing, things took a left-hand turn and I ended up in a completely different place.

I genuinely like this story, which is not to say I don't like all my others, but I feel I achieved something special with this one. I hope you, dear reader, agree.

Chapter 1

It feels like I'm losing my grip on reality more and more every hour. I am losing my mind.

The worms have been eating into my brain, but doing it selectively, slowly, and perhaps even seductively. I tried to tell them numerous times, but no one cared.

Old Doctor Parginter, our family quack since before I was born, would listen to me describe my ailments and tell me I was imagining them unless I displayed actual symptoms. I assumed he thought I had a cold or fever, perhaps a virus that simply needed bed rest and chicken soup. He didn't take my call or return my message when I reached out three days ago. I pictured him nodding while gazing out the window at the leaves dancing in the wind like a conductor's baton, just as he had the last time I saw him. At least he gave me an appointment then, even if he mostly ignored me. My wife used to accompany me back when she seemed to care for me, but that was a long time ago, back when we were dating, and there's been a lot of water under the bridge since then.

My headaches have worsened alongside Hyacinth's growing lack of sympathy and understanding. "Get a grip on yourself, Michael," she's said repeatedly, as if I could simply flip a switch to turn the pain and feelings on and off. I know I can be moody and downcast at times, but ever since the car accident, the pain and aches are real, not imagined, and they are becoming more severe and frequent. I just wish everyone would believe me.

It used to be that the itching under my hairline was worse than the pain, but that's no longer the case. Have you ever had an irritation that you just had to scratch? An irresistible urge, like being bitten by two hundred mosquitoes, making you scratch and scratch until your skin is raw and bleeding? That's how it was at first. But my itching was worse because it came from underneath my skin, not on it. It didn't matter how much I rubbed with my fingertips or what tool I used; I couldn't reach deep enough to eliminate whatever was causing the maddening, burning sensation. My wife, Hyacinth, used to be so caring, even trying to scratch my head for me as I sat on the floor between her legs, but I don't remember the last time she helped me like that.

I use the word burning because the more I scratched my head, the hotter my skin became. At times, it positively glowed despite smothering it with calamine lotion, a remedy my grandmother swore by, which I tried when all of the drugstore recommendations failed. Still, even that didn't stop the maddening irritation and only turned my hair to a sickly creamy pink color.

I know who is responsible for how I am now: my brother, Caine. He practically told me so after I found him with Hyacinth. She had fled, clearly embarrassed to be caught, crying, to our bedroom. He didn't express it in words; no, he's much sneakier than that; he conveyed it with a glance and a knowing grin as if I were the only one not being let into the secret. He even had the nerve to deny their affair.

It was Friday the thirteenth of December when my world collapsed. I didn't see it coming. Only the weekend before, Hyacinth and I had decorated the house with Christmas ornaments, dressed the tree, and put up the outdoor lights. I thought it was a happy, fun time, and I didn't get a single headache for the entire weekend *because* I felt so joyful. We even made love that night after we stood across the street under an umbrella, a glass of red wine in hand, watching the outdoor lights glitter and blink.

Christmas had always been a family affair, a special time. I noticed the neighbors watching us as we sipped our drinks and snuggled in the rain. I was sure I detected some elbowing, disapproving headshakes, and sad faces, though my wife refused to believe it. She said I was imagining things again, hugged me, and assured me that they were not imposters sent by *them*.

****

Caine wore a patronizing smirk, making me even angrier than when I first came home early from work and found them on the couch. The same couch that had been a gift from our mother. I hope the stains will come out.

My mother's favorite actor from the silver screen was Michael Caine. Hence, she named her two children after him.

His know-it-all grin revealed everything I needed to know when I confronted them. It was clear that this had been going on for some time because in the few minutes I stood frozen, observing their intimacy, I realized they seemed so…familiar. The touches, whispers, and the fact that they were completely absorbed in each other indicated that this wasn't their first time alone while I had been working to support my wife and future family.

My rage knew no bounds. When I screamed at them, they separated like guilty children caught stealing.

Hyacinth ran upstairs to our bedroom in tears. I shouted at her retreating back that she was a lying slut. Caine spouted empty platitudes while standing with his hand outstretched, trying to calm me, but he couldn't conceal his smug tone. It seemed I was mistaken, once again imagining things that weren't real. But I saw through his lies and grasped the naked truth. They had been seeing each other for weeks, if not months, no doubt in cahoots with *them*, wanting to be rid of me so they could be together.

"Why?" I demanded. I needed to know what I had done to cause their disloyalty.

He had the nerve to claim they were meeting for my benefit and told me to stop imagining things that were not true, as I always did. What a joke! Stealing my wife of nine years was for my benefit?

That is when the itching, burning, and agonizing pain in my head, which had brought me home early from work, exploded into a million brightly colored lights, resembling our eight-foot-tall Christmas tree, now lying on its side; baubles shattered and lights that would never sparkle again.

In my mind, the lanterns were blood-red and dripping.

One thought rocketed and echoed through my mind: *Oh God, help me.*

I don't know what happened next as a mist descended in a crimson, opaque, all-consuming fog.

Chapter 2

I regained my senses sometime later, wandering the streets, soaked to the bone. I knew I couldn't go home again after what had happened. I wouldn't be welcomed anyway; I decided never to set foot in that house again. I hated Hyacinth for her disloyalty to me with her lover, my brother. When I thought of her while walking in the rain, all I could see was the color of my rage. Crimson, bright, dripping red—the reddest red ever. It seeped into my peripheral vision until it soaked my irises and seemed to run down the sides of my nose, mingling with the rain.

I still wore the suit I had on at work that day. The events at home when I discovered the lovers meant I didn't have time to change. While I couldn't remember everything that happened in the exact order, I knew I had to get away from the pain and ugliness as fast as possible, realizing that, at last, my beliefs about *them* had been vindicated. My paranoia wasn't imaginary; it was real. Even my wife and brother had conspired against me.

I ran from the house until I could hardly breathe. Then, I walked; I just had to escape. I was chilled to the bone and shivered constantly as the sun sank below the horizon. My clothes were soaked from the unrelenting rain while I wandered the streets, but I couldn't clearly remember when or how heavily it had fallen.

****

I crossed under the city Christmas lights, which

383

were strung between lamp posts on Main Street, and ducked into the doorway of Smith's Shoes. They were closed for the day, and the alcove gave me some respite from the arctic breeze blowing between the buildings. I slid down the glass, put my arms around my knees, and huddled into the corner, wanting to die. Too late, a bus rumbled past, throwing up a wall of water from the recent showers, and I realized I could have jumped in front of it and ended everything. At least I'd have been at peace. *Maybe the next one,* I decided.

"Hey, buddy?" A gruff voice called out to me as his bulk obscured the neon signs across the street. I looked up to see him extending something toward me. "You look like you need this more than I do."

He tossed it to me, and I realized it was a raincoat. Tears welled up in my eyes. On the worst day of my life, this man I had never met showed a kindness that took my breath away. I wrapped the coat around myself until it enveloped me like a blanket. I nodded my thanks, unable to speak. For the first time, I noticed the headache had vanished. My mind felt clearer, my vision returned to normal, and even nodding didn't cause discomfort as it would have at any other time.

"Merry Christmas," he said, smiling as he squatted in front of me for my first look at him. He carried his bulk in a long, dark blue coat, and his curly gray hair peeked out from under a woolen cap. He had a short, gray beard, and his eyes shone like sapphires, radiating warmth. "Bad day?" he asked softly.

I nodded, still reluctant to speak, knowing that if I did, I wouldn't be able to stop crying for the loss of my wife.

"What did you do?"

I had no idea what he meant by the question. I hadn't done anything that I was aware of; it was more about what my wife had done to me. I simply shrugged in response.

"Do you have somewhere to stay while you get back on an even keel?"

I hadn't thought that far ahead. Ever since I discovered my wife canoodling with my brother, all I could think about was escaping. I raised my hand under my jacket to check for my wallet and felt dismayed when I realized it wasn't there. I had no idea where it had gone. The next bus was looking more and more appealing for my getaway from this world. "Nuh," I managed to say. "I've got no money and nowhere to go."

"I thought so. Come with me."

"Come where?"

"We're heading to Limbo." He smiled as if it were an inside joke.

"Limbo? I've never heard of it." My mind wasn't too clear, but I couldn't remember a locale in our town or anywhere in the state called Limbo.

"We call it The Village of Last Hope, but it's meant in a positive, not negative way. When we get there, you will see why—it's where we look after people like you. I can arrange a bed so you can have a good night's sleep. Things will look clearer in the morning. Don't worry, we're a friendly bunch."

Chapter 3

"Who are you?" I asked as the man helped me get the raincoat over my wet clothes as I stood beside him in the doorway.

He stopped and gave another faint smile illuminated by the nearest streetlamp. "Call me Gabriel."

Gabriel, I wondered, where had I heard that name? It wouldn't come to me, and honestly, I couldn't be bothered to rack my brain. I was grateful for Gabriel's kindness and his offer of somewhere to sleep. My head started to ache again, but I thought it was just exhaustion. The itching and burning returned with a vengeance, and all I wanted was to lie down, close my eyes, and for a while at least, forget the images of my wife's infidelity that kept echoing through my mind. But there was one question I had to ask as I struggled to get the coat over my shoulders, "Why are you helping me?"

"The answer should be obvious, Michael, because you need it. Come on; we have a long walk ahead of us. The sooner we start, the sooner we will get there, and you can get some sleep."

I trudged along behind him, trying to avoid puddles. Despite my efforts to keep up, he always appeared to be one or two paces ahead. Time passed; I have no idea how much. Suddenly, a thought struck me like a sledgehammer. I stopped, and Gabriel seemed to sense it because he halted as well. "What's wrong?" he asked.

"How did you know my name? I didn't tell you."

"Yes, you did. When you asked for help, I came." He turned on his heel and called over his shoulder, "Let's get moving; we need to get there before midnight."

I wanted to ask why, but he had already moved on before I could. I also wanted to understand what he meant by my asking for his help and telling him my name. That hadn't happened, at least not that I could remember. However, my head throbbed again with a fuzzy sensation, and my vision drifted in and out, so I took him at his word, thinking maybe I had just forgotten, and started walking again.

Chapter 4

We reached the interstate and crossed it safely, as the traffic was light at that time of night. Gabriel guided me to a path along the highway at the bottom of an embankment while another rain shower hit us. Large, heavy droplets cascaded from the clouds, and once again, I felt eternally grateful for the raincoat, though I wished for a hat or an umbrella. My head and hair were so soaked that I thought I would have been drier in a bath, but at least the weather cooled the burning on my scalp. I felt more tired than I could ever remember.

"How much farther, Gabriel?"

"Soon, Michael, not too much longer. Be patient."

Ahead, in the distance, the interstate rose higher as an east-west road ran beneath an overpass, and that was our destination. It felt like about thirty minutes later, when we turned under the main bridge, Gabriel stopped and raised his hand. An eighteen-wheeler thundered overhead while two cars jockeyed for position, heading east toward Wilkinsburg. Once they passed, Gabriel looked left and right, then opened a door I hadn't noticed in the concrete wall under the bridge. He stepped through, beckoning for me to follow, which I did, into a vast cavern that stretched as far as I could see—not that I could see very far due to the lack of light. It seemed quite dim at first, but slowly, my eyes adjusted, and I began to discern things.

This can't be right; we're under the interstate, yet I can see stars above. Are those fireflies, perhaps? I knew I had to be in some kind of cave, but it didn't feel that way. It felt more like I was in a valley, which seemed impossible. "Where are we, Gabriel?" I asked, feeling anxious and even a bit scared."

He gave me one of his trademark warm smiles, making me feel like a silly child while he took on the role of an understanding parent. "You are right where you need to be. You are among friends, and you can rest and recover from the trauma you've experienced."

Gabriel led me to an ancient-looking, carved wooden lectern with a massive book open, perhaps three-quarters of the way. A string of red and green fairy lights pulsed slowly on and off, casting a warm, friendly glow. To its left stood a six-foot-tall Christmas spruce, resplendent with blinking white lights and what seemed to be real icicles, though I knew they couldn't be. On the right side, an artist's easel was topped with an ornate mirror, with fairy lights affixed to the edge. A jagged crack stretched from the top left corner to the bottom right, as if someone had dropped the mirror at some point in its past. Written in evenly spaced red letters on the mirror's surface were the words:

Welcome to the Village of Last Hope

I first looked at the mirror, then slowly turned three hundred sixty degrees, gazing around me. I could see the gray concrete wall we had come through, but for the life of me, I couldn't find the doorway. After a moment, I realized it must be due to the dim lighting and that it had to be there; we had come through it, so it was simply hard to see.

I was still in shock. My eyes slowly adjusted to the

darkness, and as I looked around, I noticed buildings. Some resembled large sheds, others were trailers, but all had blinds or curtains drawn. Around the edges of the window coverings, I could see the faint glow of Christmas lights, which made me feel welcomed. There was a lot of background noise, not from vehicles traveling on the interstate but from distant voices, creating a low mumble. At the far back of the valley, or cavern, I still couldn't decide which, was a set of white marble stone stairs leading upward. I couldn't see what was at the top as it became too dim.

"You have to sign in; it's a rule," Gabriel said softly.

I turned to face him. "Where are we?" I asked again, feeling lost and helpless.

Gabriel nodded at the mirror and the words etched upon it, and I realized that was the only answer I would receive. Everything felt surreal, as if I were in a different dimension or trapped in a horror story. *Am I dreaming?* I wondered. *No, this is too real. I can't comprehend how, why, or even where this place is, but it exists, and so do I.*

I headed to the podium, picked up the old-fashioned fountain pen, unscrewed the cap, and wrote my name in block letters, my hand shaking from a mix of nerves and the cold. Strangely, the ink in the pen was red, which I found unusual. I glanced at the entries above mine: *John Porter, William Henderson, Blake Lively,* and *August Moderi.* They meant nothing to me, but that was hardly surprising. Then I shook my head to clear the cobwebs away, realizing I did recognize one of the names, *Blake Lively,* though I couldn't recall where I knew it from.

"Gabriel," I asked, "I recognize one of the people on this list. When was Blake Lively here, or is he still around? There aren't any dates provided."

My companion slowly shook his head. "He moved on last week."

Something in Gabriel's tone suggested that I shouldn't ask any more about Mr. Lively, so I turned back to the book. Michael Abel, I wrote. Then, in the column for my address, I wrote: *No fixed abode.* I was never going back to number 231 East Street. I scribbled my name in the last column, barely resembling my signature. I screwed the cap back on the pen and put it back on the ledge.

"Let's go meet *the keeper,*" Gabriel said as if it were the most natural next step in the world.

I looked at him sharply, feeling more dazed by the minute. "Who's *the keeper?*" For some reason, I felt even more scared than before he spoke. There was no reason for that, yet I did.

Gabriel smiled. "He manages room and board, so we call him our gatekeeper. His name is Peter. If you prefer, he hands out the keys to our rooms here, so we also refer to him as the key master. He also determines who can stay with us longer than three days, who is unworthy of that, and those fortunate enough to move on to greener pastures."

"I don't understand. What happens to those who aren't worthy? Is that what happened to Blake Lively when you mentioned he moved on?"

Gabriel smiled faintly. "There's no need to worry about that right now. Get a good night's sleep; we can discuss more tomorrow when things become clearer. At the moment, you seem to be in shock, and you look like you might collapse."

For some reason, his words didn't comfort me, and

the thought of not being worthy troubled me. My self-esteem was non-existent; I had no wife, no home to return to, and not much to live for. Yet, the idea that I might not deserve to stay in the village worried me. I recalled the bus that had thundered past earlier, splashing a wall of puddle water, and I thought that, perhaps, death might be the ultimate release. "I'm grateful for your kindness; you've found me at my lowest point on the worst day of my life, and I don't wish to seem rude. But how can someone be unworthy of living here? Are you implying I may not be able to stay? I don't understand where *here* is, but I'll leave now if you don't want me."

Gabriel raised his hand in a calming gesture. "I invited you because you need this, and it was the right thing to do, especially during Christmas time." He smiled warmly once more, and somehow, his smile brought me comfort. He continued, "No one should be alone and feeling down as we celebrate the birth of Jesus Christ. Beyond tonight, I have no control; only Peter does. You can meet him, get a good night's rest, and let tomorrow unfold as it will. If, for some reason, you can't stay with us beyond tonight, then you won't be worse off than when I found you shivering in that doorway, will you?"

I had to agree; he was right, and I felt too tired to care one way or the other.

Chapter 5

Peter reminded me of an ancient, gray-haired, retired biker when I first met him. He wore faded denim jeans, a worn white t-shirt, and a leather jacket with chains hanging from the pockets. His shoulders were broad, but he wasn't overweight. Peter sat behind an old-school flip-top desk inside a tin shack, illuminated by a green desk lamp. Behind him stood a small Christmas tree in the corner, adorned with red and green flashing baubles, one of which I noticed was broken. The colored lights highlighted his hair from behind, making it appear as if he had a halo around his head.

As we entered, he looked up from his black leather-bound book. He showed no smile or frown. "Peter, this is Michael. He's had a traumatic day and could use a soft bed and some understanding. I found him huddled in a shop doorway," Gabriel said.

"You're late. I expected you half an hour ago."

"Michael is a slow walker, and the weather is atrocious."

I felt disoriented. Everything had a dreamlike quality to it. How could Peter have expected me half an hour ago? None of what happened made any sense. The room tilted for a moment, as if I were having a bout of vertigo.

Peter's warm gray eyes bored into mine for a minute. Then he asked, clearly and commandingly,

"What have you done?"

Suddenly, the fog in my addled brain lifted, and I felt a mixture of anger and confusion. Why was everyone asking me what I'd done when I hadn't *done* anything? I swallowed the instinct to give an angry retort and took a slow, calming breath. "I'm pleased to meet you, Peter. Thank you for having me here. I don't know what you or Gabriel mean by asking me what I've done. Today, I went home early and found my wife and brother intimate on the couch. I left them to it and have been wandering the streets ever since. Does that answer your question?"

"It doesn't." He glared at me like Gabriel had, as if I were a misbehaving schoolboy. That was strange, I realized, since he was sitting behind a school desk. I'd heard people talk about hallucinogenic drug trips, and I wondered if that was the reason. Had someone given me something like Ecstasy?

"I know you've had a rough day," he continued, "and you're tired, but you've done far more than you realize, and you know it deep down, where you don't want to go. For now, I'll give you the benefit of the doubt; I can see how tired you are. We can allow you to stay for no more than three days, that's it. You need to come and see me tomorrow morning and then each night to renew your stay. When you remember what you did, talk to me right away. I'll be here all day. I will ask you that same question tomorrow if you haven't come to see me earlier. I hope you'll tell me the truth then."

"Truth, what truth? I've told you everything. I haven't *done* anything."

He turned his gaze away, dismissing me. "Gabriel, take Michael to shack twenty; it's ready for him.

Gabriel put his arm through mine and turned me

toward the door. "Come on, Michael, let's get you a hot shower and a warm bed. Things will look much better tomorrow."

Chapter 6

The small building Gabriel took me to was located on a side street off what I assumed was the main road, although there were no roads in the traditional sense. There were also no sidewalks, yet the buildings appeared to be arranged in some semblance of order, forming a relatively straight line rather than being randomly placed. The walls of the shacks—a term that best described the squat, tired-looking buildings—were constructed from aluminum siding or corrugated galvanized sheets. Every door in my line of sight was painted yellow, and thick, opaque curtains obscured the small window to the left of the doors.

The shed we stood in front of was not the sort of building I would usually be seen dead in, but Gabriel's comforting touch on my elbow, his gentle opening of the door, and his firm but reassuring guidance inside made me feel safe and trusting.

The only light came from a small Christmas tree perched on the bedside cabinet, adorned with sparkling white crystal lights and silver crucifixes, casting a welcoming glow. The walls were painted white, and the single bed was neatly pulled back, revealing pink and blue striped flannel sheets. It was simple yet comfortable, and I had to admit it looked inviting in my tired state.

Gabriel opened a narrow wardrobe, took out a white

wool shirt and matching long pants on a wire hanger, and handed them to me. "Change out of those wet clothes and take a shower. You'll find fresh underwear in the bedside drawer and dry shoes in the wardrobe. There's a laundry bag in the bathroom for your wet items; you won't need them while you're here. I'll take them when I leave. They'll be ready for you when you go. I can get you a sandwich and coffee while you freshen up if you're up for it; you must be starving?"

I stopped to consider his question and was shocked to realize I wasn't hungry in the slightest. Goodness, I hadn't eaten since breakfast, so I should have been ravenous, yet food was the last thing on my mind. "I'm not hungry at all, thank you, Gabriel. I will do as you suggest: take a hot shower and then go to sleep. I'm dog-tired."

"That makes sense. I'll stay here while you get undressed, and you can pass the laundry bag out. After that, I'll be on my way and leave you in peace."

Suddenly, his overwhelming kindness hit me like a freight train, and I couldn't help but cry. "Gabriel," I whispered when I could, "I don't understand any of this." I gestured with my right arm to show that I wasn't just referring to the hidden village. "But I truly want to thank you for the kindness you've shown me. I was ready to end my life when you found me, but you've given me hope that I might make it through this."

He stared at me for what felt like minutes, and although he was smiling, his eyes seemed sad. Finally, he spoke just above a whisper, "You're welcome, Michael. Get a good night's rest. Things will be clearer in your mind tomorrow; they always are. I don't want you to worry about anything tonight except getting some rest. In the morning, you can meet with Peter again, and hopefully, you'll remember what you did and talk to him about it. He can help you move on. Now, go and get undressed, and give me your wet clothes."

Again, with this insistence about what I did. I sighed deeply. "Gabriel, I didn't do anything, I swear." My confusion was mounting, and I could feel the weight of the unknown pressing down on me.

"You're in shock. Tomorrow is a new day; don't worry about it tonight. A good night's sleep will restore your memory, perhaps one piece at a time, but you will remember. People always do; they have to; it's inevitable."

****

It was my wedding day. I stood next to Jason, my friend since school days, who was my best man at the altar of St. Patrick's Cathedral, waiting for my bride-to-be. The air was thick with anticipation, but something felt off. Father Dominic's warm smile did little to soothe my nerves. Suddenly, the organist began to play the wedding march, but the sound was distorted, as if it were echoing from a distant memory, which intensified the surreal atmosphere.

I could hear gasps of admiration from the family and friends on both sides in the pews behind me, but I felt rooted to the spot and couldn't turn to see Hyacinth on her father's arm, walking toward me.

Father Dominic smiled again and nodded, as if giving me permission to turn. I did, gasping as tears filled my eyes with emotion. Her white lace dress shimmered in the candlelight and the flashes from cameras capturing pictures, and I noticed the dress train seemed several yards too long, stretching out behind her like a giant white snake. Strangely, I wondered if it would get dirty dragging across the stone floor. The veil concealed her face, but I knew she was smiling. Her father, Darren, looked immensely proud as they approached.

As we had rehearsed, Darren stopped and handed me her arm, which I gladly took and guided her to stand beside me. However, instead of facing Father Dominic, she turned stiffly to me. With her right hand, she lifted her veil, revealing a face that suddenly seemed contorted in pain.

"What's wrong, Hyacinth?" I pleaded, worried that she might be unwell and that the wedding could be postponed.

"Oh, Michael, what did you do?" Hyacinth's voice brimmed with fear and accusation. Before I could respond, she screamed. Blood appeared at the corners of her mouth, then dripped down her chin, reminding me of a cheesy vampire movie. Before my eyes, the blood transformed from a trickle to a river, spilling down the front of her pristine wedding gown. The dress shifted from white to pink, then to crimson, as Hyacinth shuddered and contorted.

I reached for her, frightened and confused. I had no idea what had happened, but Hyacinth screamed again and shook her head. She raised her arms, hands outstretched to keep me away. Her father wrapped his arm around Hyacinth, guiding her away, but she faltered and dropped to her knees. Blood squirted from her wide-open mouth as she moaned the words again, "Michael. What have you done?"

I screamed and sat up in bed, terrified. It took me several long minutes of sobbing to understand that it had been just a nightmare.

I was alone, lost, and confused in a strange room in the Village of Last Hope.

Chapter 7

I got out of bed and put on the clothes Gabriel had left for me, which surprisingly fit perfectly and felt comfortably warm. I looked in the mirror, dressed entirely in white, including the shoes he had given me. I felt wired after the nightmare—way too upset to sleep again, at least for a while. The problem was, there was nothing to do in the room or the Spartan bathroom. I had no interest in reading the Bible, which sat atop the bedside cabinet next to the tiny table lamp covered by a white fabric shade that looked like it came from a garage sale. I decided I wasn't in the mood to read, especially not the Bible.

It was true; I went to church on Sundays, but the main reason was that Hyacinth had been a regular churchgoer since childhood. I wouldn't call myself an atheist, but I was far from convinced that a higher being would reward us with an afterlife for worshipping all our lives. I lived a good life. I had never broken the law, always donated to worthy charities, and never intentionally hurt anyone, either physically or emotionally. So I thought that when I died, if I needed to justify the kind of person I had been, I would *pass the test*. Therefore, the idea of sitting in bed reading the Bible because I was too afraid of another nightmare held no appeal for me.

I donned the borrowed raincoat to ward off the chill

and stepped outside. I no longer had my watch, and I couldn't recall when I lost it, leaving me without any sense of time. There wasn't a clock in the room, which felt eerie, as if time didn't exist. I guessed it was around two or three in the morning, but the light—or lack of it—when I stepped outside seemed unchanged from when I had arrived, making it difficult to determine whether I was in the night air, inside a cavern, or even in an artificial space like a major movie studio soundstage. Once again, it felt as though I had been abandoned in a dream or a make-believe world.

Perhaps this area was where the workers stayed and stored their equipment while constructing the interstate. That made sense to me, and I envisioned the massive diggers, loaders, trucks, and rollers used to build the highways that crisscrossed New York State.

As exhausted as I was, I thought a short walk might help expel my demons and allow me to get back to sleep when I returned, free from another nightmare. A look around the area could offer a clue as to where in the world I was, as I still felt disjointed and somewhat severed from reality. That wasn't entirely surprising, I believed; the day had been an emotional rollercoaster, to say the least.

I shuddered at the memory of Hyacinth bleeding from her mouth in my dream, then pushed the thought away and stepped outside my room, pulling the door shut behind me. I stuffed my hands deep into my pockets and walked toward the marble steps I had seen earlier. Although I had no desire to climb to the top, I wondered where they led; I assumed they would take me back to the outside world if I were in a cavern. But the steps reaching up to who knows where were a mystery if I was in the open air.

****

The streets were as quiet as a grave, and my footsteps clip-clopped in the white slip-on shoes I wore, echoing through the night. I tried to walk on my toes to minimize the noise since I didn't want to wake anyone who was sound asleep. When I reached the bottom of the gleaming stone stairs, I was surprised to find a woman sitting on the bottom step, hugging her knees to her chest. She was dressed just like me in white, and she glanced up as I approached. She gave me one of the most dazzling smiles anyone had ever directed at me and seemed genuinely happy to see me.

"Hello," I said, "can't you sleep either?"

She raised a hand and waved quickly, almost childlike, as her smile grew wider. It was difficult to determine her age, but I guessed she might be in her forties. She was slim, wore the same long white jacket I did to fend off the cold, and had shoulder-length blonde hair. "You got it in one," she said. "I'm moving on in the morning and can't wait."

"Sounds awesome. Where're you heading?"

She burst into spontaneous laughter, which felt so out of place that I couldn't help but join in. "You're kidding, right?" she asked. Then, she suddenly looked more intently into my eyes. "You're not joking, are you? You're new here."

I shrugged. Like everything that had happened to me that day, this conversation felt so absurd that I thought it was just another strange occurrence in a day that epitomized weirdness and wasn't worth worrying about. "Yes, I only arrived a little while ago, and to be honest, I don't even know where this place is, let alone where

I'll go when I decide to leave."

Her face turned sad or perhaps sympathetic. "What did you do?"

Before I could stop myself, I lost my temper. "Why is everyone asking me that? For God's sake, I didn't do anything. I came home from work early and found my wife in my brother's arms. I stormed out, leaving them to it, and went for a long walk. Then, when I was contemplating ending everything, I met a man named Gabriel who brought me here. That's it, end of story. If you don't want to tell me where you're going, fine. I was just trying to have a polite conversation. I wish everyone would just stop asking me what I've done. Goodnight and safe travels."

Before I could leave, I noticed her eyes, which had been so bright just a moment ago, now clouded over as tears formed and slowly trickled down her cheeks. "I was like you when I arrived, but they helped me remember. It was painful to do that, but it was necessary. It would be better if you faced things without intervention, but either way, you *will* remember."

I sighed in exasperation and ignored her. I turned on my heel and headed back toward my temporary home, muttering how insane this whole situation was.

"I hope you remember soon," the woman called out to my retreating back. "You too, can feel the rapture once you confront your inner demons."

She's a lunatic. I shook my head in restrained anger and confusion. I was too furious to continue such a ridiculous and pointless conversation with a woman who was clearly unhinged. I kept walking, quickening my pace to put some distance between us. For some reason, despite how infuriating her words were, they also frightened me, although I couldn't figure out why. *Maybe it would be best to leave the village now; everyone here seems insane.*

I stopped in my tracks, with that thought reverberating inside my mind. Wasn't it the height of paranoia to think everyone was mad and I was the only sane one? *What if...what if everyone here was normal and I was insane? Maybe I had finally officially flipped my lid. Did Hyacinth have sex with my brother as part of their ongoing affair? Did I imagine it? Did I suffer a nervous breakdown, and what I thought I witnessed was a hallucination? What did I do? Maybe everyone is asking me that because I did something I'd rather forget.*

I searched my memory, trying to recall if I had done anything untoward, but nothing came to mind. I refused to think about the love scene on the couch; that was off-limits. I only remembered wandering the streets in a daze after seeing Hyacinth with my brother, and the confrontation. I couldn't bring myself to use his name; he was dead to me. True, I'd struggled with mental health issues since childhood, which had intensified and worsened every year after the car accident, especially the *voices*. With Hyacinth leading the charge, everyone wanted to sweep my *episodes* under the rug and insisted I man up and get *over it*. That was easy for them to say; let them walk a mile in my shoes and then tell me I was imagining things when I knew for a fact that *they had* been following me. Oh, I saw *them* discussing me on their mobile phones and huddled together as I walked past. *They* made endless notes in tiny notebooks and often watched me from behind newspapers or dark sunglasses. I never knew who *they* were, but I was certain *they* were evil and wanted me dead. It took all my concentration to avoid situations where I felt vulnerable.

No. I couldn't accept that I was imagining things; everyone was out to get me. I started walking again, determined to escape the mysterious woman on the stairs, Gabriel, Peter, and this crazy village.

Chapter 8

I walked past my designated hut, embracing the shadows that lingered, wondering if I was being watched from behind closed curtains. I could have sworn I saw one or two twitch as I crept by. I continued toward the entrance beneath the overpass. I found the podium with the Visitor Book still open, indicating that my entry was the last one recorded. The cracked mirror reflected back at me mockingly, I thought, so I turned away to look for the exit.

As I approached the gray, damp concrete wall, I looked to my left and right but couldn't find the door we had entered through earlier. I shook my head and rubbed my tired eyes with my palms, wondering if I had overlooked it; after all, a solid door couldn't just disappear.

I tried to remember when Gabriel and I entered and the angle we took to reach the Visitor Book. After a minute of reflection, I realized I should be right on top of it. I was sure my initial instincts were correct, and the darned door should be right in front of me. I felt tired and confused, but I recalled that when we arrived, I was nearing exhaustion, so I could easily have made a mistake.

I stubbed my foot against the ground, creating a small trench in the hard-packed gravel to mark my position. Then, I turned left and walked away, trailing my hand along the rough stucco surface to find the seam of the doorway. I convinced myself it had to be hidden to prevent anyone from discovering it accidentally, so relying on touch was the best option.

For a moment, I imagined that while it made sense to disguise the door to prevent anyone outside from accidentally finding it, it didn't make sense to hide it from visitors already inside. Unless, of course, that was the entire point. Like Hotel California, once you're in, you can never leave. *No, that can't be right; it's too crazy, even for me.*

****

Several minutes later, I had no success. The concrete wall seemed to stretch on forever. I turned and retraced my steps to the divot in the ground I left earlier. I felt tremendous relief when I found it, as I had convinced myself while walking back that the same people who hid the door would fill in the hole I made, just to make me suffer even more.

Taking a deep breath, I set off in the other direction, sure I would find the doorway.

I had no idea how long I walked, but eventually, I realized the truth: I was trapped in the village—or should I call it a prison? There would be no escape unless Peter or Gabriel let me free and opened the door, and to do that, I had to remember what I had done.

Chapter 9

I made my way back to the welcome mirror, deep in thought and feeling frightened. I was trapped, a prisoner, but I didn't know why or what I had done to deserve it. Gabriel had seemed so genuine and caring, while Peter had been gruff—though that was a generous assessment. I wouldn't say he'd been rude; he was more forthright to the point of abruptness. The pair was almost like a good cop-bad cop scenario. I couldn't figure out why Gabriel had brought me here; why had he been so kind? Unless it was to lure me into a trap for some nefarious purpose, that seemed like the only answer.

The notion that I had been drawn in a strange way made sense, yet I kept grappling with the question of their purpose. More importantly, what could I do about my situation if that were the case? It seemed to my terrified mind that I had two choices. First, I could raise a commotion, lose my temper, threaten them with exposure, and whatever else I could think of, and create a ruckus until they let me go. Or I could pretend I didn't realize I was a prisoner and try to understand why I was there and what they wanted from me, all while feigning ignorance of their game. Perhaps that might give me an advantage. The confusion was infuriating, like a puzzle with missing pieces, but I couldn't see any other way forward. What I kept returning to was that I was just so ordinary. I wasn't a CIA spy, an ex-army veteran, wealthy—and therefore a target for ransom—or even someone trained to fight. My brother had beaten me up every time he picked on me as a kid, so what chance did I have in a physical confrontation? Mild-mannered and nearly weak was how anyone who knew me would describe my character.

As I looked around, I realized I had subconsciously started walking back to my hut. It felt as if my mind had already made the decision for me. I sighed; the choice was clear. Any attempt at physical confrontation would be futile. I also considered that if I were indeed a prisoner, the reason for my captivity would soon become clear, so hiding my awareness of the situation might prove useful later on.

In the back of my mind was also a fear—or, to be honest, terror—that the reason I had been imprisoned could only be bad for me. I couldn't think of a single reason why my abduction could possibly be a good thing. What would come next? My murder? Torture? Was the Village of Last Hope some kind of hippie Manson-style commune cult that drew in people in trouble and then killed them for their own gratification? Again, waiting to see what came next seemed to be my only option and the best way forward. I could not afford to panic or react without more information. Hopefully, tomorrow would bring more clarity, and then I could decide what to do.

****

Any further sleep after I returned to my room didn't come easily, despite my exhaustion. I lay awake, my mind a tangled mess of half-formed plans and escape ideas if my worst fears came true. I searched for anything I could use as a weapon, but nothing in the hut could help me fend off an attacker. Then, I faced a harsh truth. Even if I managed to escape, where would I go, and what would I do? I couldn't return home; I knew I wouldn't be welcomed there, nor did I want to be. Hyacinth clearly preferred my brother over me; that much was obvious. She had undoubtedly been planning to leave me for him. I had no money in my pocket, not enough to buy a hamburger, so if I did escape, I would become one of those homeless people begging on the streets whom I usually ignored. I was not only trapped, but the fact that I had no viable alternatives deepened my despair. I realized I might as well stay and let whatever would happen to me happen. When all hope is lost, carrying on regardless seemed like a fitting mindset. I had seen that slogan written on a coffee mug at work, held by a colleague who, by the way, didn't like me either.

Suddenly, I sat up. *How could they make a door in a concrete wall vanish? Surely, that wasn't possible. Maybe I had overlooked it in my agitated state and was, therefore, worrying about nothing.*

I decided to return in the morning, or whenever I could, and try again. I was confident I would see more and discover the portal in the daylight. With that thought in mind, I felt better, but sleep still evaded me.

Chapter 10

I heard a knock on my door that made me jump out of my skin. It was the closest I'd been to sleep since my failed escape plan. I paused to remember where I was and then noticed the light outside through the curtain seemed less gray. It wasn't brilliant sunshine, but it was brighter than when I went back to bed. Therefore, I decided it must be morning.

"Coming," I called out to whoever it was—friend or foe. I dressed in the same white clothes as before, momentarily wondering why everything Gabriel gave me was white, even the underwear and socks. It felt like I was a neophyte in a nunnery. If that even made sense, but it seemed apt.

When I opened the door, Gabriel was standing there, dressed just like me, which caught me off guard. In his outstretched hand was a cardboard tray holding what seemed to be a breakfast roll wrapped in white greaseproof paper and a lidded paper cup with steam gently rising from the opening. "Breakfast," he murmured, walking past me into the room and taking a seat on the end of the bed.

"Thank you, Gabriel. That's very kind of you." I closed the door but noticed another man walking on the road, pretending not to look at me. He was dressed in white from head to toe. *What is it with everyone wearing white?*

Once again, Gabriel offered the tray and nodded for me to take the roll, which I did. I unwrapped the sandwich and examined the filling, which looked like a mix of colorful salad vegetables. It wasn't the most appetizing sight I'd ever encountered, but my stomach growled, reminding me of my hunger.

I bit into the warm, fresh bread, and creamy mayonnaise oozed out of each side of the roll, running down the sides of my mouth onto my chin. The taste was divine. "Mmmm," I mumbled, and Gabriel smiled as I wiped the spillage with my fingertip and licked it off.

"How did you sleep?"

I shrugged in reply, not wanting to speak while my mouth was full.

"You went for a walk, didn't you?"

I looked at him quizzically, wondering how he knew that. "Abigail told me. You met her at The Ascension Stairway." Again, I shrugged and took another bite; the roll was just as good, if not better, than any I had ever eaten.

"Michael," Gabriel said in a serious tone. "You can roam while you're here, but you upset Abigail by yelling at her. We don't allow guests to shout at other residents. Please refrain from doing that again."

I'm being reprimanded! But I didn't shout at her! At least I didn't think I shouted. I recalled being angry, but did I really yell at her? I swallowed, cleared my throat, and replied, "Gabriel, I don't remember actually yelling. If I did, please convey my apology. She asked what I had done after I greeted her, much like you and Peter did. I freaked out a bit because, as I've said repeatedly, I didn't *do* anything yesterday that justified such a question being demanded of me."

He stared at me for a moment, then nodded. "Abigail has crossed over; she's gone. We held the ceremony earlier at dawn and watched her depart, so she will never hear your apology. The thing is, while you are here with us, our residents, like you, are in transition, so they deserve peace and quiet to reconnect with their inner spirit."

I couldn't figure out the hidden meanings behind his word choices. *Transitional*—what did that mean? Was he suggesting I was between two states, like a chrysalis becoming a butterfly? And *Abigail crossed over?* What did that mean? She had told me she was leaving, hadn't she? I struggled to recall her exact words, but I was certain she'd said her three days were up and that she was happy to be leaving. I thought about my decision during the sleepless night to learn more about my situation and avoid rocking the boat, but the problem with that was my head felt like it would explode with confusion. Was I here to reconnect with my inner spirit? My earlier idea that the village was some sort of hippie commune seemed closer to the truth, though it still didn't explain why.

The sandwich, once delicious, suddenly tasted bland. I wrapped the leftover in paper and dropped it into a wastebasket near the bathroom door. Fears that I was being led like a pig to slaughter surged in my mind, and I recognized that it was fitting. Gabriel was leading me by the nose, and I had no idea where or why. I decided to ask for more information and damn the consequences. "Where am I, Gabriel, and what am I doing here?"

He passed me the paper coffee cup and nodded for me to take it. "You are where you need to be, and why you are here will become evident once you remember what you did. Until then, I can't help you."

"Am I a prisoner here?"

He shrugged and stood. "Once you finish your coffee, we will see Abraham. He is our village doctor and guidance counselor. He may be able to help with your memory loss."

"Gabriel, I haven't lost my memory because I didn't do anything. You haven't answered my question. If I wanted to leave, can I?"

He smiled. "And exactly where would you go?"

I began to feel frantic; he was speaking in riddles and evading the thing that terrified me the most: the reality that I was trapped. "Where I would go isn't the point; the fact that I could go if I chose to is. I ask you again, am I a prisoner?"

He shook his head. "No, you're not. You can leave if you acknowledge what you did, confront your memories, and repent for your actions. If you don't, you'll leave here in two more days anyway. Michael, don't push the issue; it won't end well for you. Just face the truth and remember what you've done. You must for your sanity and future well-being."

I recognized the futility of pressing further. Gabriel wasn't going to spell it out for me, and his warning that it wouldn't end well for me was the only threat I needed to remember my earlier plans to go along until I understood what was happening and then escape. I sipped my now lukewarm coffee; it tasted bitter but not entirely unpleasant. I finished it all and felt strangely calmer afterward.

****

We walked together in relative silence, though everyone we passed greeted Gabriel cheerfully and nodded at me. Gabriel knew all their names, acknowledged them, and smiled back. The weather was warm, but it was humid and cloudy—too overcast to tell if I was outside or, as I suspected, inside a vast cavern. I estimate we encountered about twenty people on our walk, mostly men, though a few women were among them. Everyone we saw wore the same white clothing, adding to the impression that we were dressed in prison uniforms. In the distance, I could see the stone steps disappearing into the mist, with three or four ghostly figures standing at the base, engaged in conversation. It reminded me of a vampire or zombie movie, which did nothing to ease my unease.

I pointed to the steps. "Where do they go?"

"To a better place. I hope you will find out, Michael. One thing to consider regarding steps: Can you guess what?"

I shrugged and mumbled inwardly. *More riddles. Why am I not surprised? He wouldn't know a truthful, direct answer if it jumped up and bit him on the leg.* "No, I can't, what about them?"

"Well, depending on your point of view, they go both ways."

I stopped walking and stared at him quizzically. "What does that mean?"

"When you are on a staircase, you can go up or down, depending on where you want to go."

Obviously, I thought but didn't say. We started walking again, and I ignored Gabriel's cryptic answer and asked another question. "How long has Abraham been here?"

He laughed. "It feels like forever. I can tell my riddle about the steps has you stumped. It's okay, Michael.

Trust me, everything will make sense. Just give it time."

Suddenly, Gabriel slipped his arm through mine and turned left, away from the steps and down the side of a much larger shack than the one where I had spent the night. He reached through a hole in a gate and opened it, encouraging me to go through first. I stepped into a beautiful garden filled with perfectly pruned flowers, shrubs, and fruit trees. I stood there, stunned by the breathtaking scene before me, the most beautiful garden I had ever encountered. A man stood beneath an apple tree, reaching up to pluck a ruby-red fruit as large as his hand. When he turned, I noticed how tall he was. Then I saw his extraordinarily long white beard. He was dressed in white, but unlike the pants and tops I and everyone else wore, he had on a long, flowing, one-piece gown that brushed the ground. He smiled warmly and approached me. "You must be Michael; I've been expecting you. I am Abraham. Welcome to my garden."

His voice was warm, friendly, and welcoming. I felt immediately calm as if I were in safe hands. "Thank you," was all I could manage, and I feared I might burst into tears.

"You look tired; come and sit for a while; let's talk. Would you like a glass of lemonade?"

Chapter 11

Abraham led us to a small, open pergola made of deep red timber, surrounded by rose bushes. Beneath the canopy were four wooden chairs adorned with floral cushions and a matching round table. He directed me to sit and motioned for Gabriel to join me, then disappeared inside while I admired the surroundings.

From the wooden beams framing the edges of the pergola roof, several clay pots hung from white macramé hangers, interspersed with small, delicate wind chimes. Each pot contained a different plant or vine trailing from it. They all bobbed and swayed in the nearly nonexistent breeze, creating the illusion of a dance. I found myself staring, feeling calmer with each passing moment, as if I were being lulled to sleep. Gabriel remained silent, as though he didn't want to disrupt the peace and quiet.

A few minutes later, Abraham returned with a pewter tray that held a clay jug and three mugs. He sat across from me and poured the drinks, handing a tumbler to each of us. "Drink," he said softly, "it will help you feel more relaxed."

I felt myself become nervous again. *Is Abraham drugging me? If so, why?* "Why do you think I need to be more relaxed?" I asked, my glass halfway to my lips.

He broke into a big grin. "You have nothing to fear from me, Michael—quite the opposite. I'm not going to drug you, hurt you, or mistreat you in any way. I offer only to guide, help, and mentor you to accept the past and look forward to the future. If you prefer, we can swap glasses, and you can drink mine." He held out his glass as if challenging me to swap, but I took a long sip from my own instead. I had no intention of falling for the double bluff. I believed that if one glass had been tampered with, the alternate one offered was tainted, making the original one safe. He wasn't going to trick me that easily. That was an example of what people never understood about my paranoia: even if it wasn't true, it protected me from *them*.

"It's delicious. Did you make it from your own fruit?"

"Why, thank you. Yes, I did. I add just a splash of freshly squeezed lime and orange juice for flavor." He took a sip, then looked up, and as he did, the wind chimes began to tinkle softly. It was melodic and soothing. I followed his gaze and saw the potted plants sway gently to the faint jingling sounds. My earlier calm washed over me once more, and I felt Abraham take the glass from my hand before it could slip and shatter on the ground. "Michael, do you know why you're here?"

"No," I whispered, not daring my voice to disturb the gentle sounds from above. "I don't even know where here is."

"Where you are isn't as important as why you're here. You've been chosen for a reason; this is an opportunity, Michael. Talk to me—tell me about yesterday. What happened? What did you do?"

The pendulum motion of the potted plants swaying from side to side, paired with the tinkling of the wind chimes and the gentle, cool breeze on my skin, seemed to transport me back in time, and I remembered.

****

My job was in life insurance at a small, family-owned brokerage, which I disliked. However, my employment options were limited once I chose that career path, married Hyacinth, and moved to the town where she grew up. So, even though the job made me unhappy, I stayed because I loved my wife.

My boss, Murial, was a woman whose demeanor reflected the drab and gray office furniture. She seized every opportunity to micromanage my work to the point of obsession—hers, not mine. Murial appeared determined to make my life so unbearable that I would leave. I think she was in cahoots with the men in black suits who had been after me since the car accident.

I remember yesterday, the thirteenth. Well, I recall most of the day. Murial droned on and on about my latest failings for most of the morning while the rain hammered against the windows outside, and the intensity of my headache grew to the point where I no longer wanted to listen to her. I raised a hand like a cop directing traffic to stop her mid-sentence, told her I was going home sick, and walked out as she yelled it would be a cold day in hell before she let me back in the building. At that moment, the headache was so severe that I was beyond caring.

As I drove home, the windshield wipers swished excess water from side to side, and pedestrians hurried for cover. They cast furtive glances my way to report my location to the men in black suits. By the time I arrived home, the migraine had intensified to epic proportions, and I needed my pills, a dark room, and peace until it passed. Unfortunately, it was not meant to be.

Caine's car was parked out front, which was

unusual since he worked as a pilot flying out of New York City, and we lived two hours away. Something kept me from rushing inside and calling out that I was home; perhaps it was a premonition. Instead, I approached the front windows, cupped my hands around my eyes, and peered through, where I saw them laughing and joking on the couch as if they were married and I were the single brother.

All the fears and insecurities I tried to keep buried every day flooded back into my mind. Everyone conspired to make my life miserable, even my wife and brother. The mist descended as I entered the house through the garage door, pausing at my workbench. Caine, being older than me, had constantly bullied me while we were growing up, often leading to fistfights, and I always ended up hurt while he laughed at me. Not today, I told myself. Not ever again.

Hyacinth ran upstairs, screaming while Caine smirked in that way that said: I fucked your wife, and she loved it!

Then, I was running in the rain, walking when my lungs felt like they would explode, and hours later, huddled in a shop doorway, I met Gabriel.

Chapter 12

"Michael," Abraham said in his calm but firm voice. "Go back to where you were standing, watching your brother with your wife. Can you do that?"

"I don't want to; it's too painful." I shuddered, suddenly feeling cold and terrified, though I didn't know why.

"You must."

I attempted to resist, to wake up from whatever dream he was compelling me to relive, but it felt like trying to run with my feet stuck in molasses—impossible. Abraham's voice commanded me, and I had no choice but to comply.

****

Once again, I found myself standing outside my home. I was under an overhang, sheltered from the rain, and the noise must have masked my approach. They seemed so happy together, and I realized, for the first time, that they looked like a couple, as if they truly belonged together. Perhaps I was wrong to deny them their happiness. If Hyacinth no longer loved me, didn't she deserve to find joy with someone else?

No, she didn't. She promised to be mine forever, till death do us part, in sickness and in health, and forsaking all others, including my loathsome brother.

But everyone deserves to be happy, I argued with myself. And if my mental disorders led her to realize that it was just too much for her, then who was I to deny her a life of joy?

"She is so beautiful," I muttered out loud, "I love her so much."

"Concentrate, Michael, read her lips. What is she saying to your brother?" Abraham boomed into my subconscious.

I watched her lips, the ones I longed to kiss, if only for one last farewell, and tried to read them. "I don't know, it's too hard, something about a birthday?"

"Whose birthday would she be discussing with your brother? Think, Michael, remember."

I felt tears trickle down my cheeks. "No, no, no, I can't see, I don't know."

"You must. Concentrate, Michael."

It felt like the scene was replaying in my mind's eye on an endlessly spinning spool. They were talking, smiling, and happy. Hyacinth said, "Surprise birthday party." Caine nodded eagerly, placing his hand on her upper arm and stroking it affectionately, encouraging her and clearly trying to get her into bed. I realized this just before I stormed into the house, determined to make them pay for their disloyalty.

Abrahams's voice thundered into my mind. "Who do you know that has a birthday coming soon? Who is Hyacinth arranging a surprise birthday party for, Michael? Come on, you are so close now."

****

I stood up abruptly, tipping the chair I had been sitting on backward. I gripped the underside of the table and lifted it forcefully, throwing it aside and sending the jug and glasses crashing to the ground. *"No, I can't!"* I screamed and ran away in a blind panic.

I reached the gate and fumbled it open. As I ran through it, I heard Abraham calling, "Michael, come back anytime. We must finish this for your sake."

Fat chance of that, I mumbled to myself. *Everyone here is mad and only interested in driving me further insane, along with them.* I ran as hard and as fast as I had ever run in my life.

****

As I reached the wooden podium holding the guestbook, I panted, exhausted, gripping it to keep myself upright. I felt as if I were on the verge of passing out, my heart threatening to explode from my chest like an alien breaking free. Someone—Peter, I assumed—had added three more names beneath mine, as the handwriting matched: *Jenny Quatermaine, Nigel Brookes, and John Denver.* One of those names rang a bell for me. Taking deep gulps of air to steady my heartbeat, I tried to recall where I had heard it before, and then the memory suddenly struck me.

Nineteen-year-old Nigel Brookes, while intoxicated, drove his car into a group of people, including his girlfriend, who had broken up with him via text message earlier that day, citing his controlling behavior as the reason. The incident occurred outside a house where a party he wasn't invited to was taking place. His lawyer argued diminished responsibility. While out on bail and awaiting sentencing, he was admitted to the hospital for a self-inflicted drug overdose. Although he wasn't expected to survive, if he were here, clearly, he had.

That decided it for me. If this place accepted convicted murderers for a three-day stay, to—what did Gabriel call it?—reconnect with their inner spirit, then I didn't want to be here. What a load of nonsense; the Village was not the place for me. An unknown future was better than whatever this prison could offer if I had to associate with murderers, and only God knew who else.

Gradually, my breath returned, and I sprinted toward the wall, determined to locate the missing door or a spot where I could climb over it and escape this cursed place once and for all.

****

Time went by. I couldn't tell how long, but it was long enough for my run to slow to a jog and then to a walk because, once again, I could barely breathe. The damned wall seemed to stretch on forever. There was no door, portal, or crack, and at no point could I even see the top of it, let alone climb it. The surface, while not exactly smooth, offered no footholds. Maybe if I had a rope with a grappling hook, I could get over it, but without one, I realized that I was truly trapped.

Chapter 13

I sat, leaning against the rough stucco wall for a long time, considering my options. *What options?* I didn't have any. If I couldn't escape, I had to wait out my three days and presumably get evicted. *Would that be so bad?* Not that I could see. I wouldn't be any worse off than if I had found the door out. Or would I? The way that Gabriel and Peter had spoken suggested that things would not go well if I didn't recall what I had done, although I was positive I hadn't done anything catastrophic. So, what did that mean, and did it even matter in the grand scheme of things? It was only a short time ago I wanted to kill myself under the wheels of the next bus, so if they had brought me in as some sort of bizarre plot to murder me, why fight it?

My mind spun in ever-decreasing circles, and sometime later, I still had no idea how much time had passed; I was no closer to any form of resolution or concrete plan. Inevitably, my mind returned to when I sat in the outdoor area at Abraham's house, recalling the moment when I watched my wife and brother through the window. *Surprise birthday party?* What did that mean?

The skin on my arms started to prickle, my chest tightened, and fresh sweat formed on my forehead from concentration. *Oh my good God! Was that it? Could it have been? Was I mistaken?*

Think, man, I told myself, *remember, you must do this.*

Gradually, my mind cleared. I was a Christmas baby—born on Christmas Day, a fact I resented as a child because it felt like I only received one set of presents while all my school friends got gifts for Christmas and more for their birthdays. Could it be that my wife and brother were not having an affair but rather planning a surprise party for me?

The more I pondered, the more I began to believe that my latent paranoia and mental health issues may have, no scratch that, probably clouded my judgment. So, if that were the case, I had called my wife a slut and screamed abuse at my brother while he tried to tell me their clandestine meeting was for my benefit. Then, full of rage, I stormed out of the house and vanished as far as they knew. My blood ran ice-cold. I had to get home to them and beg forgiveness if it wasn't already too late.

****

After spending the last few hours running in blind panic, I slowly jogged back to Abraham's house, knowing I'd arrive faster than if I rushed and got out of breath again. What was that old saying? *Slow and steady wins the race.*

I knew I had to apologize to my beloved wife for my jealous outburst, but to do that, I needed to find a way out of this hellhole and get back home. But how? Maybe that's what everyone meant when they asked me what I'd done. Perhaps I was supposed to admit the misunderstanding, though why or how they even knew I had made a terrible decision in the heat of the moment, only God knew.

I was nearing exhaustion when I realized I'd hardly

eaten anything in two days. I believed I had to admit to Peter, Gabriel, and Abraham that I had been wrong to jump to a horrible conclusion. Perhaps it was because I was suffering from a migraine headache at the time; yes, *that must be it*—that made perfect sense.

It gnawed at the back of my mind how they knew what had happened at my house or why they cared, but it was the only thing that made sense in this senseless town. This made me pause to consider the village's name: *The Village of Last Hope*. It oddly made sense if this was my last shot at reconciling with Hyacinth.

****

When I arrived at Abraham's shack, the street was quiet, so I assumed it was nighttime. However, the ambient light hadn't changed much since I'd been there, so I did not know for sure what time it was.

Standing in front of his house, I hesitated, feeling embarrassed about my earlier outburst. It struck me that, in some obscure way, these people were here to help me, not to harm me. That realization resonated deeply within me. Even if they refused to let me leave, Abraham deserved an apology, and I needed to find the courage to offer one if I hoped to get home. With my head bowed, overwhelmed by shame, I walked toward the door, but just before I could knock, it swung open.

"Michael, welcome back," Abraham said, smiling warmly. I opened my mouth to apologize, but he held up a restraining hand, as if directing traffic. "Come on in. Let's sit in the garden again and chat. Gabriel isn't here; it's just the two of us."

I quietly followed behind as he led me through a simple living room with minimal furniture and then out through a glass door. The table had been returned to its original position, and there were no signs of broken debris from my earlier outburst. He directed me to sit, and this time, I avoided glancing at the mesmerizing swinging pots. "Abraham," I began, "I want to apologize for my behavior earlier."

"It's okay, Michael. I get it. You're scared of the unknown; everyone feels that way in your situation. I just want you to remember one thing: can you do that?"

I was unsure if I should agree to something without knowing what I was agreeing with, but I did it anyway. I nodded.

"God gave mankind free will. Because of this free will, people often make mistakes and commit wrongdoings, at times even evil acts. For this reason, God allows people to confess their sins and seek forgiveness. Since God is just and fair, He will always listen if a sinner is genuinely contrite."

I had no idea what he was talking about. Yes, I had been to church many times, and yes, I understood the gist of his message, but I couldn't see how it applied to my situation. I only needed to sincerely apologize for misreading the situation with Hyacinth and Caine. "I understand that, Abraham, but how is it relevant?"

"If a person will not admit their wrongdoing, they cannot be forgiven, and therefore must be damned forever."

I sighed and decided to ignore the veiled threat. "Because you helped me remember earlier, I now know I shouldn't have accused my wife of sleeping with my brother; I realize that now. I was wrong, and possibly because of the trauma or that I had been suffering a severe headache at the time, I verbally abused the one person I loved. I now see that they were arranging *my* surprise birthday party, not enjoying a lover's tryst. Hyacinth does love me, and I treated her abysmally. Can I please leave this place? I need to go home and beg her for forgiveness. She must be upset and distraught with concern for my safety."

Abraham stared at me with an expression that appeared to blend annoyance and pity. "Michael, it's far too late for that."

"It can't be. I need to get back to Hyacinth, Abraham; you have to help me. I understand everything now; I was mistaken. Please help me set things right."

"I can help, but you need to trust me. Remember what else you did; what occurred after you confronted your brother and your wife? It's your only hope. Let me assist you in reclaiming your lost memory. Look up at the swinging plants. Observe how they gently sway in the breeze, synchronized with your breathing. Relax, take your time, and return to the moment when you were outside the window again."

I didn't want to, but his saying it was too late to apologize to Hyacinth scared me. I figured the only way out was to play along, do what he wanted, and find a way to escape before Hyacinth lost all hope for me. I settled back in the chair, looked up at the swaying plants, watched them dance, and felt instantly better. Abraham's voice, always calm yet commanding, filtered through the fog, reassuring me that it was safe, to breathe deeply, and let the past return.

****

The rain felt relentless as I hurried past my family's dull SUV and my brother's sports car, wondering why he was here in the middle of the day. I noticed the blinds were open in the living room to the left of the front door, and I made my way toward them, needing to reassure myself that it was safe to return and that they *weren't waiting for me.*

Caine was on the couch, sipping coffee, while Hyacinth sat beside him, smiling and looking beautiful. She had always told me she didn't have much time for Caine, believing he was a narcissist who only cared about himself, but they looked cozy—too cozy, almost familiar. It was as if they were planning something. Hyacinth touched his arm, laughed, and mentioned something about a birthday. But Caine's birthday was in March, not December, unless Hyacinth meant that all his birthdays would come at once. What did she mean by that? Caine reached out and tenderly stroked Hyacinth's arm, and then I realized what was going on. They were meeting in secret because they were having an affair. Over my dead body, *I thought, and then I decided what to do.*

I gave up everything to be with Hyacinth—my hometown, my family and friends, and a promising career—all to move across the country. Now, I go to church every week to praise a God I don't believe in, have a job that makes me miserable, drive a car I hate, and I'm about to lose Hyacinth to my brother. No way, no freakin' way.

Trembling with barely suppressed rage, I silently entered my home, though I guessed the lovebirds wouldn't hear a bomb go off; they were so engrossed in each other. The living room was to the left of the front door, and our bedroom was to the right, which was where I headed first. Kneeling with shaking fingers, I used the key on my keyring to open the gun safe, which took three or four tries. Once it was open, I grasped my

.357 Magnum pistol. I always kept it loaded because I knew they would come for me one day. They would eventually tire of endlessly watching me, noting my arrival and departure times, and take action. I had to be armed; even Hyacinth agreed to my request for owning a weapon, provided I kept it in a locked safe.

It always felt just right in my hand. I glanced at the gleaming chrome steel. "Hello, old friend. At least you've never let me down, have you?"

I stormed into the main room and stood six feet away from the lovers. Thankfully, they were not kissing or undressing each other. "You slut, Hyacinth. With my brother? You're screwing my sleazy brother?"

She stood, screamed, and bolted past me while I glowered at Caine. I heard the bedroom door slam behind me. "It's not what you think, Michael," he pleaded. "This is a surprise for you; it's all for your benefit." He held up his hand as if that would stop me.

"Yeah, Caine? It's for my benefit, you fucking my wife?"

I didn't consciously pull the trigger, but I watched as the back of his head exploded in a cloud of blood and brains. The fantail of gore spread out, coating the snow-white painted wall behind the couch, turning it crimson with blotches of gray lumps sliding slowly floorward.

"It's okay, Caine, me shooting you is for your benefit." I fired another two bullets into his body just to make sure. Then I turned and headed to the bedroom.

I didn't need to try the handle to know it was locked. I kicked it near the lever handle, just like I'd seen countless cops do on TV shows, and it worked. The door flew inward, banged against the wall, and then bounced back, closing again after I stepped through. Hyacinth stood on the bed with her back against the wall, her cell phone to her ear, no doubt calling them to come and help her.

"Oh, Michael, what have you done? What have you done?" she screamed. "You're wrong; it's not what you think; you're having one of your episodes."

The rest of her words I ignored. I knew what I saw and knew what I knew. I raised the gun and fired once, twice, then three times, aiming each shot to her chest. She spun in the air, losing her footing in the bedclothes, and finished lying sprawled across the duvet.

I fell to my knees, tears streaming from my eyes, my wife's body prone on the bed, bleeding and broken. There was no way back. Now, they would come and take me, but I was too smart for them. I raised the gun, pressed the end of the barrel under my chin, and pulled the trigger.

Epilogue

I awoke with a start, not knowing where I was.

"Welcome back, Michael. You're safe here at Sunnybrook with the three of us. We put you in a tranquilized state to help you remember. We needed you to confront what you did."

Gradually, I regained my senses and recalled that the gun was empty; I had exhausted all the bullets on Caine and Hyacinth and needed to reload to finish the task. Mourning the loss of my wife and disheartened by my failure to end my life, I stood up and went to the gun safe, where I stored the spare box of shells.

I grasped the box and tried to open it, my hands shaking uncontrollably, and I dropped it, spilling its contents all over the floor. I bent down to pick up one measly bullet, which was all I needed to finish the job. Suddenly, the door banged open violently. It hit my forehead, throwing me backward, and my head slammed against the floor. I was vaguely aware of a uniformed cop entering, gun in hand, and then everything went black.

I glanced from one to the other of the three men seated around me, and everything came rushing back. The oldest, with a white beard, was my senior psychiatrist, Dr. Abraham, and to his left sat Dr. Gabriel, an equally qualified psychiatrist. The third man was the young intern I only knew by his first name, Peter.

"Do you remember what you did, Michael?" Doctor Abraham asked gently.

I nodded, unable to speak as the waves of grief and guilt washed over me.

"You've been with us for four months after being in a coma for three weeks. Your condition is called catatonia. You hadn't spoken a word until yesterday, and then acted as if you were innocent. You refused to accept that you murdered your wife and brother, insisting we set you free so you could apologize to Hyacinth. But Michael, you won't be set free for a long time. You can only seek redemption by admitting your guilt and working with us to confront the terrible murders you've committed. Perhaps one day, with care and treatment, you could be set free, but never if you insist you didn't cause their deaths. Do you understand, Michael?"

I understood completely. There was no Village of Last Hope; it was a hallucinogenic drug-induced fantasy.

I had no hope at all.

A word about the author...

I was born in the UK, what seems like an epoch ago, and moved to Australia at age 16. I was a long haired rock guitarist and poet/songwriter, before real life got in the way, and I gave it all up for love.

I've always felt I had tales to tell and won short story competitions and published poetry in my wilder, younger days. More recently, I've written and published twenty novels. While they have mainly been Police procedural thrillers, mainly focusing on Serial killers, they all have a love theme running through them.

I believe love and family are everything. Anything else you gain in life is a bonus.

I live in Perth, Western Australia, and am fiercely patriotic and parochial. My wife is amazing in that she not only tolerates but also encourages me to be a writer. I've been blessed with five children, and I adore them all.

http://stephen-b-king.com

Thank you for purchasing
this publication of The Wild Rose Press, Inc.

For questions or more information
contact us at
info@thewildrosepress.com.

The Wild Rose Press, Inc.
www.thewildrosepress.com